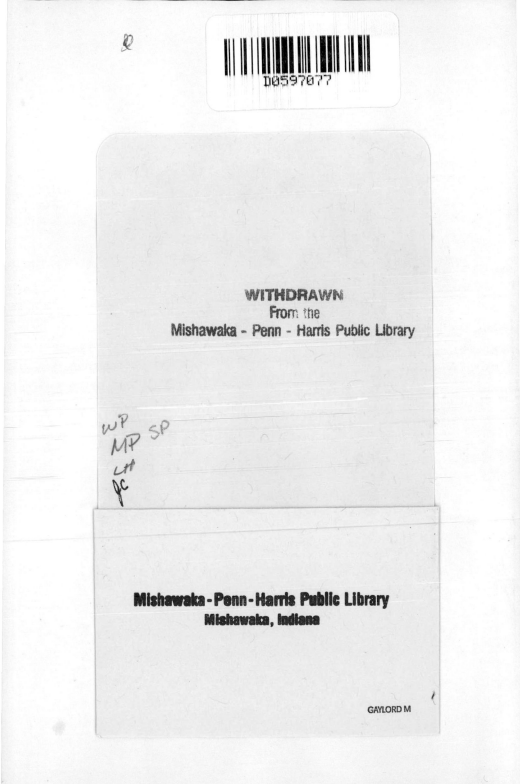

THE FOURTH ORDER

This Large Print Book carries the
Seal of Approval of N.A.V.H.

THE FOURTH ORDER

STEPHEN FREY

THORNDIKE PRESS

An imprint of Thomson Gale, a part of The Thomson Corporation

THOMSON
———✳———™
GALE

Detroit • New York • San Francisco • New Haven, Conn. • Waterville, Maine • London

Thorndike Press® Large Print Core.

The text of this Large Print edition is unabridged.

Other aspects of the book may vary from the original edition.

Set in 16 pt. Plantin.

LIBRARY OF CONGRESS CATALOGING-IN-PUBLICATION DATA

Frey, Stephen W.
   The fourth order / by Stephen Frey.
     p. cm. — (Thorndike Press large print core)
   ISBN-13: 978-0-7862-9740-5 (alk. paper)
   ISBN-10: 0-7862-9740-9 (alk. paper)
   1. Chief financial officers — Fiction. 2. Consolidation and merger of corporations — Fiction. 3. Intelligence service — Fiction. 4. Washington (D.C.) — Fiction. 5. Large type books. I. Title.
PS3556.R4477F68 2007b
813'.54—dc22   2007016758

Published in 2007 by arrangement with The Ballantine Publishing Group, a division of Random House, Inc.

Printed in the United States of America on permanent paper
10 9 8 7 6 5 4 3 2 1

For my wife, Diana,
and,
For my editor, Mark Tavani.

ACKNOWLEDGMENTS

Special thanks to Cynthia Manson, my agent and Gina Centrello, my publisher. Also to Kevin "Big Sky" Erdman, Matt Malone, Andy and Chris Brusman, Jim and Anmarie Galowski, Dr. Teo Forcht Dagi, Stephen Watson, Chris Tesoriero, Gerry Barton, Baron Stewart, Jack Wallace, Gordon Eadon, Marvin Bush, Bart Begley, Barbara Fertig, Bob Wieczorek, Scott Andrews, Paul Taunton, Jeff, Jamie and Catherine Faville, John Piazza, Chris Andrews, Bob Carpenter, Pat and Terry Lynch, and Mike Pocalyko.

PROLOGUE

2002

Michael Rose approached the security checkpoint inside Dulles airport. Six months ago he'd been promoted to chief financial officer of Trafalgar Industries, a publicly traded conglomerate based in northern Virginia, and he was headed to London for a week of meetings with the company's European executive team. It was his second trip to London since being promoted. This time he was bringing Sheila, his wife. She was going to shop and relax, live the good life while he worked.

He sighed. At least the line at the checkpoint wasn't too long.

"This is ridiculous," Sheila muttered, removing her belt and bracelets, placing them in a gray plastic tub beside her purse. "Do I really look like a terrorist?"

"Shoes, too, ma'am."

Sheila glared at the TSA agent behind the

table. *"Shoes?"*

"People can hide things in the soles," Rose explained, slipping off his black loafers. The World Trade Center towers had tumbled down a year ago, but Sheila hadn't been on a plane since then. She hadn't experienced the new security procedures. "Just do it, honey."

"I don't want to do it."

Rose grinned. Without her heels Sheila was barely five feet tall, and he knew she had a complex about her height. That was the real problem here. Sometimes she even wore heels around the house. "Come on."

"You think it's funny that I'm short," she snapped, pulling the heels off and dropping them in the container. "Gives you a big laugh, doesn't it?"

Rose's smile faded. Lately, this was typical. He was hoping the trip would help patch things up, but it wasn't starting off very well.

"Next." The TSA agent on the other side of the metal detector waved Rose ahead once Sheila had passed through. "Let's go."

Rose held up his boarding pass.

"Let me see that," said the agent, snatching it out of his hands.

Rose almost said something, but held back. The guy was probably having a bad day or had a long shift ahead of him. No reason to escalate anything. Just get to the gate, he thought to himself. Always keep your focus on the primary objective. Never let your emotions get in the way.

"Step over there." The agent nodded at an area off to the side where three other TSA people were standing, arms crossed over their chests.

"What's the problem?" Rose asked.

"Just do what I tell you."

Rose stared at the man for a few moments, tempted again. But again he refrained and walked to where the other agents were.

One of the men pointed at a chair against the wall. "Have a seat."

As Rose sat down, he saw Sheila being led off to another inspection area. They hadn't let her pass right through, either. Well, if they weren't out of here soon, she was going to lose it. That was his bet. Patience wasn't part of her personal dictionary. "Sir?" Rose tried to get the attention of one of the TSA people. They were talking about the Redskins football game played over the weekend. "Sir?"

The man who had directed Rose to the chair looked over at him. "What do you want?"

"My flight leaves in a half hour. I really need to —"

"We'll get to you when we're ready."

"Yes, but —"

"That's enough," said the agent sharply. "Next time get here earlier."

Rose leaned back in the chair, doing a slow burn. At least he and Sheila could finally agree on something. This was ridiculous.

Ten minutes passed. The security agents still hadn't given him any explanation about the delay. The three men who'd been talking when he first sat down had moved off, and now a woman was watching him. Rose glanced at Sheila. She was still sitting in a chair as well, talking loudly to the agent that was watching her, waving her arms. This was turning into a nightmare.

Rose stood up. The plane was pulling back from the gate in fifteen minutes. If they didn't get out of here now, they wouldn't make the flight.

"Sit down, sir," the agent who was watching him ordered sternly. "*Right* now."

"I'm going to miss my plane," Rose said calmly. "I'm going to Europe. I've got to be at a meeting in the —"

"I told you to sit down," the agent said loudly, striding toward Rose. "Do it *now*."

"Would you please just tell me what's going on?"

"All right, that's it." The agent waved to several men who were posted by one of the metal detectors. "Turn around and put your hands behind your back."

"*What?* Are you crazy? I haven't done anything wrong."

Seconds later Rose was pushed face-first to the wall by three burly agents. They cuffed his wrists tightly behind his back, then hustled him off toward the ticket counters.

1

Present Day

"My God," Rose murmured. He'd been off in another world, thinking about that day five years ago when he and Sheila had been arrested at Dulles airport. Thinking about how deeply it had affected his life, how it had shaken his faith in his government. How it had taken a year to get to the truth behind what had happened. "Amazing."

David Cortez glanced up, following his boss's line of sight. Cortez had been about to pick up his beer off the smooth, dark-wood bar but stopped with the chilled glass halfway to his lips. "Jesus," he said softly with a hint of a Cuban accent.

Rose tried not to stare, but he couldn't help himself. He'd spent an entire career keeping his nose an inch from the grindstone, doing the right thing, shunning the temptations that were constantly swirling around him as he climbed higher and higher

15

on Trafalgar's corporate ladder. Now, in an instant, this. "She's perfect."

"Yeah, she is," Cortez agreed.

The young woman sat on a tall stool on the other side of the bar, a glass of champagne on the napkin in front of her. She was keeping two young professionals in sharp suits and bright ties occupied without even trying. Both of them were doing everything but juggling to get her attention, but she was playing them off against each other beautifully. Touching their arms lightly, smiling at them demurely with her full, glossy lips. It was an incredible smile. She was an incredible woman.

"I need to meet her."

Cortez turned toward Rose. "Easy, Mike," he warned. They'd worked together since Rose had been promoted to chief financial officer, and they'd gotten close after a lot of late nights at the office. After a lot of Chinese takeout, a lot of black coffee, a lot of good-nights to the kids over the phone. And a lot of guilt. More than anyone else, Cortez knew how vulnerable Rose was right now. "We're almost to the finish line, we've gotta stay focused."

But Rose kept staring. Mid to late twenties, he guessed. Old enough to be worldly, young enough to be impressionable. Not from or with money, either. From where he sat, that engagement diamond on her left hand looked like a microchip — less than a third of a carat, probably closer to a quarter — and her low-cut blouse was straight off a rounder rack at Sears. He watched as the man who he assumed was her husband cut aggressively between the two professionals and kissed her. Watched her react with a kiss of familiarity. A kiss devoid of passion. Watched the two suitors fade into the crowd, disappointment etched into their expressions. Then felt disappointment sink into his own chest. Which was surprising, and frightening, for several reasons.

"Yeah," Rose agreed quietly. He'd heard about this happening, everyone had — the lightning bolt — he'd just never thought it could strike him. Especially now when he was on the lookout for it. "I guess you're right."

Then it happened: They caught each other's gaze, and it momentarily paralyzed him. Her eyes were like lasers cutting through the cigar smoke, low light, and noise. Sparkling beams the color of Caribbean water on a postcard locking onto him and not letting him go, blacking out everything else around them. Rose was the number two executive at Trafalgar Industries, chief financial officer of one of the biggest companies in the world, a corporate superstar at forty-three. But suddenly he felt like an awkward, pimply kid at a high school dance. She was even more attractive than he'd first thought, and not just physically. She had a startling genuineness about her that shone through the potent sexuality. It was a one-two combination he'd never encountered, and he was back on his heels. God, what a risk this would be.

Cortez touched Rose's arm. "Mike."

Rose put his elbows on the bar, covered his face with his hands and rubbed his forehead with his fingertips, wondering where Sheila was. When he'd called home an hour ago, the au pair had told him that his wife had left the house at noon but hadn't been back or called since. He checked his watch: eight o'clock. Maybe it was finally time to hire a private detective.

"Mike."

"Yeah, yeah." Rose glanced across the bar, but the young woman and her husband were gone, presumably headed into the adjoining Morton's Restaurant, one of the best steak houses in northern Virginia. He looked over at Cortez. "You committed to this acquisition, David? You committed to getting CIS?"

Cortez nodded.

"A hundred percent?"

"Absolutely, Mike."

Rose nodded encouragingly, trying to shake the image of the woman from his mind. But that was impossible.

2

"This acquisition *can't* happen."

Bill Granger was the chief executive of Computer Information Systems. CIS was a multibillion-dollar information technology company headquartered in Washington, DC, with offices all over the world. "When we started out six years ago," he said, "you promised me I'd *never* have to worry about a hostile takeover, never have to worry about CIS being a target. What the hell am I going to do about —"

"Enough." Peter Beck glanced out the fifth floor window toward the Capitol in the distance, its bone-white dome starkly illuminated against a cold and starless February night. Beck was executive director of The Fourth Order of Immunity — the I-4 as insiders called it. He had infinitely more to lose in all of this than did Granger, so he had no sympathy for the other man. Hell, he could end up dead just by making this

trip, just by sticking his head out. He was a creature of the underground — literally — and he felt vulnerable in the open. Granger didn't have to worry about it; not yet, anyway. "Suck it up."

"*Suck it up?* Are you kidding me?" Granger's expression twisted violently. "This guy Michael Rose is a pit bull on steroids, Peter. If Trafalgar buys us, the entire operation is at risk. Rose will figure out what we're up to, believe me. And the money trails? They lead straight to you, straight to whatever the hell you do with all that information Spyder gins up. Might take Rose a few months to sniff it out, but he'll get to the bottom of it, you can bank on that. Then all bets are off. At that point, everything blows up, and you and I have to answer to —"

"*I know, I know.*" Beck grimaced, thinking about that nightmare. "Look, I don't know for sure this thing is going down yet. All I've gotten so far from my network is a few whispers about Rose making moves behind the scenes. He still has a lot of hoops to jump through if he and Trafalgar are going to get CIS. He doesn't even have approval from his own directors yet."

"When's the board meeting?" Granger asked. "Next week, right?"

Beck bit his lip. "Tomorrow. They moved it up."

Granger shivered, visibly shaken by the news. "Do we have people who'll help us in that meeting?"

"Oh, yeah," Beck answered confidently, though he wasn't confident at all. "After tomorrow, Michael Rose will be dead in the water. Then we can all take a deep breath and get back to normal."

Granger leaned forward and ran a hand over his bald head. "I hope you're right, Peter, because I'm telling you, Rose is like a freight train without brakes on the downhill side of a mountain. Your people did the psychoanalysis, and I read the report. You can't stop him once he's ID'd a target."

Beck's eyes narrowed. "I can stop anyone."

3

Sheila Rose raced along Georgetown Pike in her silver Mercedes. Raced through the darkness toward the small, upscale town of Great Falls, twenty miles west of downtown Washington, DC. Twisting and turning along the narrow road through the thick woods just south of the Potomac River as fast as she dared. Praying she wouldn't spin out of control on one of the small ice patches left behind by the snowstorm that had passed through the mid-Atlantic the other day. She had to get home before Mike did. He'd worked his fingers to the bone for the last two decades so that they could live in one of the nicest homes in one of the nicest areas of northern Virginia. She ought to care about that, ought to at least appreciate his dedication — but she didn't. All she wanted at this point in her life was excitement. Something Mike didn't seem to care about. At least, not when it came to her.

Which was why she'd started seeing Johnny Sykes. A bartender, for Christ's sake, and only thirty-one at that. Johnny liked to drink, do cocaine, and, when he wasn't tripping, have sex anywhere and everywhere. They'd done it in the backseat of his vintage Mustang in the National Cathedral parking lot, in the basement of the Capitol, in a closet at the bar where he worked in Georgetown. All places they could have easily been caught, which made it infinitely more exciting. She and Mike had never done it anywhere but a bedroom behind a locked door.

Johnny was an animal, she knew. His idea of being responsible was making certain he'd saved enough in tips by Thursday night to buy two eight-balls for the weekend, and he had absolutely no ambition. In fact, he'd told her that he thought ambition was the root of all evil. He lived life only for the moment, on the edge, and she couldn't get enough of it.

Mike was at the opposite end of the responsibility spectrum. Hell, he *was* the other end of it. A straight arrow blinded by ambition arising from some deep-seated insecurity he'd never shared with her. A man who was always thinking about what was at the top of the mountain, not what was on the trail in front of him. He'd have a glass or two of wine with dinner on the weekends, but rarely drank during the week. And it seemed like even when he was relaxing, he was working. Reading those endless corporate reports and charts as they sat by the country club pool or when they went on vacations. But she would have taken a Motel 6 in Ocean City if he could have left his ambition at the office for a week to focus on her. *Just* her.

She smiled as she steered the Mercedes through a sharp turn then over a bridge and a small frozen creek. Johnny. God, he was so hot. That wild, untamed look. That thick, wavy hair that fell to his broad shoulders, those rugged facial features, those muscles everywhere. He looked like the Marlboro Man, all the way up to the Stetson and down to the alligator boots he'd worn this afternoon as they'd strolled arm-in-arm on the mall toward the Washington Monument, doing spoon tips of cocaine from a cellophane bag he had stashed in his overcoat.

Mike was good-looking, too. Very good looking. But in that carefully groomed, buttoned-up military way. Other wives at the country club thought he was dreamy, a prize. She overheard them using those exact words, caught them stealing sidelong glances from behind her sunglasses as she reclined next to him at the pool while he pored over his damn Trafalgar reports. But she was no longer drawn to or impressed by his fighter-pilot-looks and in-charge demeanor the way she had been when she was young. She wanted someone wild, someone who was all into her. She wanted Johnny.

Sheila braked hard entering another tight turn, just as a car was coming the other way. She closed her eyes momentarily and squeezed the steering wheel like she was holding on for dear life as the other car flashed past, very close. The road was so damn narrow.

When the car was gone and the road straightened out, she let out a relieved breath, thinking about what she'd stumbled onto at the house. It was definitely something she should tell Mike about, something suspicious, something that might actually be dangerous. Of course, he might think she was crazy, too. Might think she was being irrational, which he always accused her of. Which aggravated her so much. Besides, it wasn't like she cared about him anymore. She could barely stand being in the same room with him. For all intents and purposes, they'd reached the end of the line. That was it, she thought to herself. She'd finally made the decision. She'd call the lawyer next week.

Sheila spotted the headlights of another oncoming car as the Mercedes crested the top of a long, steep hill. She squinted and held one hand up to her eyes as she headed down and the cars closed in on each other, expecting the other driver to dim his high beams. Instead, the oncoming car suddenly swerved into her lane. She screamed and wrenched the steering wheel to the right to avoid a head-on collision and for several terrifying seconds the Mercedes' right tires hung on the edge of a forty-foot embankment as the other car flew past, inches from her door. Then the back end went out, Sheila lost control and the Mercedes hurtled down the ravine, tumbling over and over through the snow until it slammed into a tree and came to rest upside down.

The other driver skidded to a stop in the middle of the lonely, darkened road, jumped out of the car and sprinted back to the wreck.

4

"Have a drink, Mike." Cortez didn't wait for an answer, just signaled to the bartender, who came right over. "He'll have Shiraz," Cortez said, gesturing at Rose. "Best you got by the glass."

Rose had been drinking club soda since they'd gotten here. "No, no, David, I can't. We've got to get back to the office in a little while to —"

"Don't listen to him," Cortez said to the bartender, flashing an engaging grin. "Just bring it."

Rose chuckled as the bartender turned away. Cortez had become his best friend over the last few years. Not out of choice, out of circumstance — because there wasn't time to have anything other than casual acquaintances outside of work, and he'd lost touch with his college crew years ago. But that was okay, Cortez was a good man, honest as they came. He was the son of a Cuban immigrant who'd been picked up by a Coast Guard cutter forty years ago somewhere south of Key West, bobbing up and down in a leaky wooden rowboat — the only one of seven on the craft still alive. Cortez was short and stocky with mahogany eyes, puffy, dimpled cheeks, and wavy, jet-black hair combed straight back and doused with mousse. He was slightly overweight, ten years younger than Rose at thirty-three, just as driven but not so obsessed with success that he didn't respect his superiors. Rose couldn't have asked for a better right-hand man. Together, they'd made twelve acquisitions over the last five years, taken Trafalgar from obscurity to the *Fortune* 100, wooed Wall Street's best analysts, and made the company's shareholders ecstatic as the stock price climbed and climbed — even during times when the overall market had stumbled.

Cortez raised his beer and touched it to the wineglass after the bartender put it down in front of Rose. "Here's to the board meeting tomorrow, Mike. Here's to getting the go-ahead on CIS."

"We'll get it," said Rose confidently, picking up the glass and swirling the Shiraz around.

Truth be known, Rose enjoyed a good

29

glass of wine. Would have enjoyed several, could have downed a whole bottle himself tonight. Liked beer as well, and loved a good scotch. Had been something of a wild man in college at the University of North Carolina, one of the biggest drinkers in his fraternity. But all that had ended at graduation. He'd flipped on the ambition switch the moment his fingers closed around his diploma that muggy May morning in Chapel Hill.

But he had to admit to himself that it was a struggle every day to maintain focus. Not to take his hands off the wheel every once in a while to have some real fun. He'd been able to keep himself out of bad situations for more than twenty years, but he knew if that certain fuse was lit, everything he'd been working so hard to achieve might go up in flames. Which was why the young woman sitting on the other side of the bar had scared him to the center of his soul. He'd known from the moment he'd laid eyes on her that she could be the spark. And they'd even warned him to watch out for her, or someone like her. Still, he couldn't help but wonder.

"What does Freese say?" Cortez asked. "Has he talked to anybody on the board?"

Colin Freese was Trafalgar's CEO. A Brit

who was more of a figurehead than anything. He was constantly off doing something exotic — climbing Mount Everest, marlin fishing off Costa Rica, hunting red stag in the Argonne Forest. Which was fine with Rose. That disengagement gave him immense freedom.

"He said one of the board members was raising a stink," answered Rose. Two weeks ago, he and Cortez had sent out a presentation to the entire board of directors labeled "Project No-Warning," which detailed the proposed acquisition of CIS. "Said the guy pissed all over what we sent out. Said he was popping off about how we had no business buying an information technology firm. That we needed to stick to our knitting, to manufacturing and energy. That we'd get our asses handed to us buying CIS, buying a company that writes and integrates software."

"Who was it?" Cortez asked.

"Freese wouldn't say. Said it wouldn't be fair to 'out' the guy ahead of time. Said we'd just have to deal with it when he started going off in the meeting." Rose raised one eyebrow. He had a good idea who it was, and he was ready for battle. "But it doesn't matter. We'll roll right over him. There's twelve board members, and all it takes to get the go-ahead on an acquisition is a majority." He smiled. "I've got seven of them in my back pocket, not including Freese."

"I know you do, my man," Cortez said, beaming. He patted Rose's shoulder. "You'll be CEO soon, Mike. Then you won't have to deal with this, with morons who don't know what they're talking about. You can kick whoever the bastard is off the board when you're elected. Cut out the deadwood and be efficient, run this company with a free hand and an iron fist."

Rose chuckled. "And make you CFO, right?" He knew what Cortez's agenda was.

"You got that right," Cortez said firmly, not trying to hide his ambition.

A couple of board members had already approached Rose about the possibility of becoming CEO — soon, in the next year or two — even though Colin Freese was just forty-nine and far from retirement. They'd confided in Rose that they were tired of hearing about Freese's trips around the world on company time, tired of the obnoxious increases in compensation he was demanding every year, tired of the rumors about his rampant infidelity with any young girl he could get his hands on. Rose's eyes narrowed. CEO of Trafalgar at forty-five.

That sounded damn good, and there was no telling how far he could go from there. CEO for a few years, then into politics. He took a deep breath. It wasn't just those board members who'd promised to support him. Someone much more powerful than anybody on the board had also weighed in. Someone who could help him become CEO and help him go a long way in politics, not just locally. This man's influence stretched across the national stage.

"I gotta ask you something, Mike."

Rose looked up from his wine. "Yeah? What?"

"A couple of months ago you mentioned something about an incident at Dulles airport real soon after you were named CFO, real soon after you hired me as treasurer. Seemed like it was a big deal, but you never told me what it was. We were out at dinner and you got a phone call and we never finished the conversation. What was it? What happened?"

Rose bit his lip. He remembered that night. After ending the call, he'd decided not to tell Cortez about the arrest after all. It was too personal.

"Come on, Mike," Cortez pushed. "What happened?"

Rose thought about it for a few moments.

You had to be careful with things like this. Cortez might draw conclusions that were inaccurate, which could end up being a bad scene if he spread those conclusions around. "Yeah, all right." But David wouldn't spread rumors. David was loyal, Rose was sure. "Sheila and I were arrested at security. We were on our way to London."

Cortez's eyes widened. "Arrested? What the hell happened? What did you do?"

"Nothing."

"Oh, come on."

"I'm not kidding. We were arrested and taken to a federal facility in downtown Washington. We had to spend the night there. It took me a year and a lot of legal fees to work through everything."

Cortez banged the bar with his fist. "I remember now. You called and told me one of your kids had gotten sick. You asked me to get in touch with the guys in London and tell them the trip had to be pushed back a week."

Rose nodded. "Yup."

"Well, what happened?"

"I was framed."

"No way. By who?"

Rose took a long swallow of wine. "The guy I replaced as CFO. The guy Freese booted out of Trafalgar to promote me.

34

Turns out the guy's brother was a wheel at the TSA." He shook his head.

"They bugged my house for a few months, even after I found out what happened. The guy and his brother were trying to get something on me any way they could so they could have me fired. I'll tell you something, David, I learned a hell of a lesson from all that."

"What's that?"

"Nobody in this country is safe from the federal government, not if they really want to get you. Especially if you're poor. The reason I was able to fight it was because I had some money, and I could hire people with influence. If I'd been some schmuck making minimum wage, I'd still be in jail."

Cortez shook his head as he finished what was left of his beer, then motioned to the bartender for another. "Be right back, Mike. I gotta take a whiz. I want to hear everything when I get back."

"Yeah, sure."

Rose watched Cortez head for the restrooms, thinking about Sheila. She'd seemed so detached over the past few months, but he couldn't make himself believe that she was really having an affair. She wouldn't do that to him and the kids. He winced. It was so naive to think like that. The worst part about life was that the people you loved and trusted the most were sometimes the ones screwing you the hardest. He shut his eyes tightly. Cortez fit right into that slot, too.

He glanced up — directly into those two tiny Caribbean seas. The young blonde from across the bar was walking straight toward him, about to come within a few feet of where he was sitting. Now he could see her short black skirt and high heels — the long, shapely legs in between, too.

As she passed by, she reached out, touched his arm and squeezed gently. "Hi, handsome."

Then she was gone.

Sheila moaned as she came to, head spinning, barely aware that she was upside down, held in place by the seat belt harness digging into her shoulder. Slowly becoming aware of a throbbing pain in her temple. The warm taste of blood, too.

"My God, are you all right?"

She took a labored breath and turned her head slowly to the left, feeling like she might pass out again. The driver side window had been smashed to bits in the crash and there was a young man peering in at her through the emptiness. His hot breath was misting into the car in the cold, night air. "It hurts so badly," she murmured. "I can't feel my legs."

"I'm sorry," he said, reaching into the car with both hands, gripping her head tightly on both sides and twisting violently. The sharp snap of her neck breaking comforted him, and he smiled thinly. "So sorry."

5

"Tell me about Michael Rose."

Beck struck a match off his heel and lit up a Camel no-filter. He'd never smoked before the I-4. In fact, he'd always hated cigarettes because his mother had a two-pack-a-day habit that had killed her when he was still a young boy. It had seemed counterintuitive when it was first explained to him, but he had learned that disinformation was more effective than no information. Smoking made him harder to track and trace because he changed brands every time he bought a new pack. And being hard to track was vitally important to him as the I-4's executive director. He was a serial nomad, always changing up everything, not just his brand of cigarettes. He constantly hid his moves, tried to avoid routines, tried not to exhibit favorites of anything. He had to be as transparent as possible, couldn't have loyalties. He'd given up everything for the I-4, all ties to family, all bonds with friends. They all thought he'd been killed in a small plane crash in Mexico seven years ago, but the crash had been faked so he could go deep beneath the surface. George Severs had died forever that day — Peter Beck had been born. That was how completely committed he was to the I-4. He smiled to himself grimly. For the first few weeks, it had been difficult answering to a different name. Now it was like he'd always been Peter Beck.

"What's his background?" Beck knew most of it, but he wanted Granger's unedited take on the man.

Granger started to pick up a loose-leaf pad with all of his notes on it, then dropped it back down on the coffee table. There was no need to look at it anymore, he'd studied the pages so many times over the past week. "Rose is chief financial officer of Trafalgar, but for all intents and purposes he runs the show. A guy named Colin Freese is CEO, but he probably couldn't name half the company's subsidiaries if his life depended on it. Rose has done a great job, too. The company's taken off since he's been CFO, so has the stock price. It's up sixteen percent a year for the last five years, not including dividends. Which is way better than —"

"Way better than the Dow or the NAS-DAQ," Beck cut in. "Yeah, I know."

It wasn't that Beck knew about the markets because he micromanaged his own portfolio. Seven years ago he'd been required to put all his holdings into a blind trust and hope his investments would be around when his time leading the I-4 was up. More important, hope *he'd* be around to take them out. He knew why Trafalgar's performance was so good because he was a voracious reader of everything he could get his hands on, including business rags. It made him much better at being the executive director.

"How did Rose get to be CFO?"

Granger started to describe the steps — the positions Rose had climbed through and the people he'd climbed over during the seven years he'd been at Trafalgar prior to being named CFO. Then he realized that wouldn't be answering the question. Beck wanted to understand the man, not the history. He wanted to understand how Rose thought, how driven he was, and, most important, how far he'd ultimately go in a crisis situation. "Rose works twenty-four-seven, and he's ruthless," Granger began. "I don't mean that he's criminal or unethical by any means. In fact, he's got a reputation for being as honest as they come. But he'll use any legal advantage he can find to win." Granger hesitated. "Which he almost always does."

"You're describing every top executive in this country, Bill. What makes Rose any different?"

"His ability to lead," Granger responded right away. "To get people to do exactly what he wants them to do when he wants them to do it. People follow him like he's Jesus Christ or something. He's got this, I don't know, *edge* to him."

"You get all that directly from our insider?"

"Yup."

"Got a picture of him?"

Granger flipped to the back of the pad and pulled out an eight-and-a-half-by-eleven-inch glossy. "Here," he said, holding the photo out over the coffee table.

Beck took it and gazed at the head shot for a few moments. Rose had dark hair cropped close all around, thin dark brows, hazel eyes set slightly close together, a Roman nose, a small scar on a strong chin. But there was more to it than that. Something else emanated from the photograph as clearly as the physical characteristics. It was a quiet confidence expressed in the way Rose raised his left eyebrow slightly higher than the right, the way he set his jaw firmly. There was a sophisticated sense of purpose about him.

"How old is he?" Beck asked.

"Forty-three. Like I said before, they say he doesn't play unless he's ninety-nine percent sure he'll win. Even then he worries."

"He's never played this game before," Beck snapped, dropping the photo on the table and taking a puff off the Camel. "Where'd he go to college?"

"Chapel Hill, the University of North Carolina."

"Is he from North Carolina?"

"No. He lived in San Diego as a kid. Moved away when he was ten."

"Why?"

"When Rose was nine, his father was struck by lightning. The guy was with the electric company out there and got nailed in a storm while he was working on the lines. After he died, Rose's mother started stripping at night to make some extra cash."

Beck's eyes flashed to Granger's. *"Stripping?"* That was interesting.

"Yeah. Apparently, she was a looker. Didn't have any problem getting a gig at one of the clubs in San Diego even though she was in her early thirties."

"Does Rose know?" It was something they could use against him if he didn't, maybe even if he did.

"We're not sure."

Beck pursed his lips. "Keep going. How'd he get to Carolina?"

"His mother met a businessman who fell in love with her."

"While she was stripping?"

"Yup. Met him on the job."

Beck sneered and took another long drag off the cigarette. "That's beautiful. All right, keep going."

"The guy was from Atlanta, but he was in San Diego for a conference. Moved Rose and his mother back to Atlanta into a big house in the suburbs a month after he met her. Married her two weeks later. He was from some hoity-toity southern clan, so they had to keep her past a secret. Made up a story about her being the daughter of a movie exec who'd moved to Europe years ago and died. Something that was tough to check out. Rose turned into the forgotten child after a few years, after the guy and his mom had two kids of their own."

"Was he bitter?"

"We don't know."

"Why the University of North Carolina?"

"That's where the guy who married his mom went," Granger explained. "It was the one string he pulled for Rose."

"Why'd he have to pull it?"

"Rose's high school grades were lousy, wouldn't have gotten him in. The guy paid for everything, too."

"How were Rose's grades in college?"

"Not much better. He was a big partier, barely got his diploma. But he met a woman while he was there and married her the summer after graduation." Granger paused. "Her name was Sheila Adkins."

"As in the *Texas* Adkins?" Beck asked. He'd been putting out his cigarette, but he stopped and looked up.

"You got it."

"But that family hit the skids a few years ago, right?"

Granger nodded. "Yeah, but when Rose married into it, they were hot. He went to work for them right after he married Sheila. Didn't even take her on a honeymoon. Her daddy liked that. Of course, she didn't."

"She saw what was coming," Beck observed. "It's called the ambition train, and she didn't want him to get on. She knew what she was in for."

"Exactly," Granger agreed. "It left the station for Rose right after he graduated, and he never looked back. Went to the University of Texas for his MBA a few years later. Then it was on to Trafalgar when he graduated from B-school, and it's been a rocket ride for him at the company ever since. Spent his first seven years at Trafalgar moving up the chain of command, then was named CFO five years ago. Behind closed doors, some people at the company are saying that Colin Freese better watch out. That if Freese isn't careful, Rose is going to get his job pretty soon." Granger hesitated, anticipating that Beck would find what he was about to say very interesting. "By the way, Peter, Rose paid his stepfather back."

"For college?"

"Yup. Every cent."

So Rose was one of those guys. "How many kids does he have?"

"Two. A girl, sixteen, and a boy, twelve."

"Anything else?"

"Yeah." Granger's eyes narrowed. "His wife is cheating on him."

Beck let out a low whistle. "Nice. Does he know?"

"We don't think so."

"Is it with someone at Trafalgar?"

Granger smiled. "There's actually two of them. One's a bartender in Georgetown, a

45

nobody. And, yeah, the other one works at Trafalgar."

6

"Still no word from my wife?" Morton's Restaurant and the bar were in the basement of a small shopping complex full of high-end boutiques. Rose had gone upstairs to make his calls because there was no cell phone reception in the bar or the restaurant. "She hasn't called?"

"No," the au pair answered in her heavy accent. "I think she said this morning she was going shopping with some friends and then they might go to dinner after that."

The au pair was a plump, twenty-four-year-old Swedish woman named Trudy who was ultimately loyal to Sheila because Sheila gave her extra cash on the side and bought her nice clothes. There was no way to tell if Sheila really had said anything about shopping with friends or going to dinner afterward. The only clue was that Trudy hadn't mentioned that when he'd called before. Seemed like she would have, seemed like it would have been an important thing to let him know then.

"All right, I'll try again later. If you talk to her, please have her call me."

"I will, Mr. Rose."

"Thanks."

Rose slipped the small phone back into his suit jacket. He'd left two messages on Sheila's cell since five this afternoon, but she hadn't returned either of them. Which wasn't like her. They hadn't been getting along lately, but she usually called him right back when he left a message.

It was nine o'clock and his senior contact at Trafalgar's agent bank, Citibank in New York, was supposed to be calling him at the office at ten. Trafalgar borrowed over eight billion dollars from a consortium of banks led by Citi and, as part of the loan agreement, Rose needed approval from the banks to make any major acquisitions — like CIS. His contact was going to confirm that the bank's senior credit committee had approved a big increase in the size of the loan facility to help fund the deal. That the other banks in the consortium had approved it as well. It was more of a formality than anything, but he and Cortez had to go back to the office in case this one guy on the bank's committee had questions. So they had all

the information on the deal right at their
fingertips in case the guy wanted to get into
the details of how the transaction was going
down. The guy always had a few issues with
every deal, made it sound like he was going
to nix everything, then ultimately gave his
okay at the last minute. It was like he got
off on being the one person who kept
everyone else involved in the deal on pins
and needles. It seemed like there was always
one of those guys in every organization.

Rose headed back down the steps and
pulled open the door — just as the young
woman was coming out. Once again, they
locked eyes. Finally he stepped aside and
held the door for her. "Please." He made a
sweeping gesture up the stairs.

"Such a gentleman." She put her hand on
his. "Thank you."

Her fingers were soft and warm, almost
like she had a slight fever. He grinned. "Just
doing my job, ma'am," he said, pretending
to tip his hat. "Just doing my job."

She squinted, like she didn't understand.

"I'm the doorman here at the restaurant."

She tilted her head back slightly and
laughed. "Working for tips, huh?"

God, she really did have a perfect smile.
He checked that engagement ring again:
even smaller than he'd first thought. More

of a friendship ring than an engagement ring. "Gotta make a living somehow, you know?" Her perfume drifted to his nostrils. It was seductive, but not one he recognized.

Her expression turned serious. "Oh, believe me, I know about that."

He was tempted to dig deeper, tempted to try to get to the next level down and see if there was a spark for her or if that smile was just a polite one. If there wasn't any interest — he had to be honest with himself — he'd be disappointed. If there was, he might do something he'd regret. Either way, it was a risk. But he had to know what she was thinking, where she was coming from.

"Do you live around here?" she asked. "Or are you here on business?"

She'd beaten him to the punch, and he loved it. "I live here in northern Virginia. In Great Falls," he added. She was instantly impressed. He could see it in every corner of those sparkling eyes. "How about you?"

"Around here, too."

She was being conspicuously unspecific. She probably lived in a cramped town house in Sterling or Reston and didn't want to tell him, but that was good. That meant she didn't want him to lose interest. Of course, it also meant that she wasn't above conveniently leaving out a detail or two. Which could also mean she wasn't above leaving out something big at a critical moment.

"Well, it's nice meeting you." Rose hesitated, unsure of whether he should say what he was thinking. Which was an unusual feeling for him. He was usually so sure of himself. What the hell? She'd made her comment back in the bar. Why shouldn't he? "See you around, gorgeous." He smiled and started to move by.

But she put her hand on his arm. "Wait, I —"

"You ready to go?" Her husband had appeared behind her out of nowhere.

She glanced over her shoulder at him, then turned away and rolled her eyes.

Rose caught her aggravated expression, then saw her husband's eyes flash to her hand pulling away.

"Is this a friend of yours?"

"He was holding the door for me, Joey," she explained, giving Rose an apologetic look. "He was just being nice."

Joey shrugged. "Coulda fooled me. Looked like you two were having a pretty cozy conversation."

"Please don't do this."

The guy was young. Probably a little older than she was, but not yet thirty. Five-ten — two inches shorter than Rose — with beady

51

eyes, a goatee, a cheap suit, and a jealousy tattoo the size of Rhode Island. The guy had married way out of his league. He'd probably spent a week's salary on dinner tonight just to keep her happy.

Rose nodded to her, then moved past them into the bar. Too bad, she'd definitely wanted to keep talking. But there was no chance of that now.

7

"I don't understand how this could happen."

Beck put another Camel no-filter in his mouth and lighted it. It was his third one since he and Granger had sat down. It wasn't that he liked them — he didn't — or that he was addicted to them — he wasn't. It was his compulsive personality, his need to be constantly multitasking. Even if one of the tasks ended up killing him.

He'd learned about his disorder ten years ago. When he'd first been recruited into the brand new Gray Ops Program while at the Department of Energy enduring two weeks of intense psychological testing. When President Clinton was in office and the top levels of the intelligence infrastructure in Washington were beginning to fear that the nation's enemies were sensing an opportunity. Civilians thought Black Ops were cloaked in secrecy, but they had no idea what "cloaked in secrecy" really meant. No idea that Gray Ops were so much more clandestine, so much deeper in the shadows. For once, the government had kept a lid on something.

So far, anyway, Beck thought, taking the first puff off the cigarette. Which made what they were suddenly facing such a crisis. It could blow that lid sky-high.

"How could Michael Rose get as far as he has with this deal?" Granger continued. "I thought there was too much CIS stock parked with the inside institutions to ever let it get to this point. Rose would never present it to the Trafalgar board if he wasn't sure he could close the deal. Which means he's talked to some of the large institutions and put a price on the table."

"Or his investment bankers have." That would scare the crap out of Granger. It sure had scared the crap out of Beck when he'd heard a few weeks ago. When his contact at the California pension fund had sent him a coded message about CIS "being in play." "And the I-bankers must have gotten enough positive talk back from the institutions to be convinced they could get CIS for Rose."

Granger turned white. "But how? This company was supposed to have been completely out of reach of a hostile buyer."

An unfriendly must have sniffed out the I-4, Beck realized. Or *thought* he had. Somebody with the political muscle to lay traps in the forest and see what they snared. A chilling scenario because it meant Beck would have to shut everything down completely and reorganize somewhere else if the hunter got too close. Which could take years and give the nation's enemies a huge opportunity. Worse, he might not be able to cover all his tracks. If a pit bull like Michael Rose sifted through enough documents and enough bank statements, he might be able to piece the whole thing together. He might find Spyder, too, which would be the ultimate disaster. Might even be able to help the person at the top of the hunting team track down a few I-4 people. Then everything would go up in smoke. Because after you got one person to crack, everyone else was vulnerable. That was always how it went.

The first priority was stonewalling Michael Rose, stopping him dead in his tracks at the board meeting tomorrow so he couldn't buy CIS. Then they could focus on figuring out who Rose was working with, who was ultimately responsible for laying down those traps in the woods. Which was why what Beck faced was so problematic. He had to stop Rose from getting CIS without using all of the assets available to him, without taking the ultimate step as he usually would, like he would with someone they suspected of being a terrorist. He had to keep Rose around so he could find out who was at the top, who was pushing the guy to go after CIS.

Beck took a deep breath. It was strange to suddenly become the hunted. It had been the other way around for so long.

"I don't know how it could happen," Beck finally answered. "But I'm working on it. We'll figure it out." He couldn't be completely honest with Granger, couldn't tell him everything. That might send the guy off the deep end, and there was no way to replace Granger at this point. "Everything will be fine."

"What's the success rate?" Granger asked, switching lanes. "How's it going?"

Beck took a long puff from the cigarette then started coughing, a deep hack. He pounded his chest with his fist, thinking about how the other three members of the I-4's leadership, known as the Directorate, had nicknamed him Frisco a few months ago. Because he was like San Francisco, they said, always on the brink of disaster — a cataclysmic earthquake for the city, a massive heart attack for him. He smoked, he drank, he didn't exercise, he was forty pounds overweight, he had high blood pressure, he had high cholesterol, and his family had a history of coronaries. Unfortunately, there wasn't much he was going to do about it at this point. He was fifty-two, had no time for exercise, and — thanks to the stress of the job — craved his meat, mashed potatoes, and three martinis a night.

"You all right?" Granger asked.

Beck looked up when the coughing spell finally subsided. Granger was ghost white again, probably wondering what he was going to do if Beck keeled over. Granger couldn't call the paramedics or take Beck to a hospital, he'd been coached on that. Calling in people from the outside was out of the question. Beck might say something under anesthesia that would compromise the I-4, so he had to go to a special place if anything ever happened to him. "I'm fine," he croaked. "What did you ask me?"

Granger gazed at Beck uncertainly. "The success rate. Is it getting any better?"

Beck hesitated. "Nope. It's even worse than it was six months ago." That was the last time the two men had met face-to-face.

"It's down to a little over twenty-five percent now."

"What's the total?"

"Almost six hundred worldwide."

Granger shook his head. "So over four hundred innocents since the start of it all."

Beck nodded. The numbers had started to bother him, too. They never had before, not until recently. Specific instances of false identification had always depressed him, but not the gross numbers. The problem was, he was starting to believe that not all of the innocent cases were mistakes, that maybe there were some conscious mistakes. If that were true, it would shake his faith in everything.

"It would make one hell of a story for a reporter."

Beck nodded again. "Oh, yeah," he agreed quietly. "Story of the century."

8

Rose finished his last sip of wine slowly, savoring it as it washed over his palate. Congratulating himself as he swallowed. He'd managed to stay in control once again, managed to keep it to just one glass tonight despite Cortez urging him to have more. Even managed to keep the discussion about what had happened at Dulles that day five years ago to a minimum. He didn't like talking about it, even now.

"Come on, David, we've got to get going," he said, placing the glass down on the bar and standing up. It was after nine thirty. "Got to get back to the office for that call with Citibank."

Cortez finished his beer, standing up, too. "Yup. Let's do it."

Rose dropped two twenties on the bar and turned to go. As he did, he almost ran into the young woman.

"Hi," she said quietly.

He nodded back deliberately. "Hi."

"I just came back to . . . um." She took a nervous breath. "Sorry about my husband. He's such a . . . well, it doesn't matter." She reached for Rose's hand and pressed a piece of paper into it. "Call me," she said, leaning forward so her lips were close to his ear. "Please." Then she headed quickly for the door.

Rose watched her walk away, watched her hips swaying beneath that black miniskirt.

When she was gone, he realized that Cortez was staring at him openmouthed. That almost every man in the place was doing the same thing. Because she was that kind of woman. A showstopper.

He glanced down and opened the small piece of paper. The name above the phone number was Kat. He grinned. Of course it was. It fit her perfectly.

His grin faded. She was either completely innocent, or one hell of an actress. And he had to find out which. His life might depend on it.

9

Rose leaned back in the plush leather desk chair in the den of his house and stared up at the plain white ceiling. It reminded him of the landscape outside, of the four inches of snow that had blanketed northern Virginia earlier in the week. After pulling into the garage tonight, he'd walked back outside to the driveway and gazed around at the peaceful setting, soaking up the solitude of his neighborhood. Thinking about how the board meeting tomorrow was going to be anything but peaceful.

He'd left the office at eleven thirty, more than two hours ago, after he and Cortez had gotten the okay on the CIS transaction from Citibank and the other banks in the consortium. The banks had approved a $3.5 billion increase in Trafalgar's loan facility to support the acquisition, and the guy who was usually a prick on the bank's credit committee hadn't said a word. It was all backslapping and best wishes blaring through the speakerphone this time around.

Of course, Citibank was going to earn two million bucks in fees just for making the facility available for the next ninety days, even if Trafalgar never used it, even if the acquisition didn't go through. So they had good reason to be giddy. It was the first time Rose had offered them so much money up front, but the strategy had paid off — he'd gotten the approval fast. He'd done it that way because he wanted all the ammunition he could get for the board meeting, now only a few hours away. He knew it was going to be a showdown — he'd been told late this evening to expect the worst, that it wasn't just one guy who thought he and Cortez were off the reservation now — and he wanted the biggest gun in the room. Having the financing ready to go would give him a bazooka. He had that other ammunition, too, which he hoped he wouldn't need.

Technically, according to Trafalgar's corporate charter, Rose was supposed to get the CEO's written approval before accepting any offer from a bank that involved paying fees over a million dollars. Unfortunately, Colin Freese was on a private jet heading back from South America after a weeklong safari in the Amazon basin hunting monster anacondas. And he couldn't be disturbed, according to the flight attendant. A flight attendant who sounded like she was serving more than drinks and dinner. He'd heard Freese whispering in the background, telling her to say he was asleep. Freese wouldn't be landing at Dulles for another several hours, when Rose could legitimately demand to talk to him, but he wasn't about to hold off accepting the offer from Citibank now that he had their approval. You never gave bankers a chance to second-guess themselves.

Besides, the board meeting wasn't scheduled to start until noon and wouldn't actually get going until one, so he had plenty of time to get Freese to sign something before then. And it wasn't like he was really worried about it anyway. Freese wasn't going to back the other side in a showdown. Freese loved seeing the company's stock price go up as much as anyone, and an acquisition like CIS could make that price *really* go up. Which would make his big bag of call options even more valuable, and his annual salary increases and bonuses that much bigger. Unless, of course, the board took the extreme and unusual step of replacing him despite how well the company was doing.

Rose relaxed — put his feet up on the big

mahogany desk and his hands behind his head. He loved it in here. Never thought he'd have a place like this back when he was a kid in San Diego. Figured he'd be a blue-collar stiff working on the power lines like his father when he grew up. Never figured he'd have a room in a big house with a big desk, leather furniture, prints of sailing ships and wildlife scenes on the walls, pictures of himself on the bookcases shaking hands with important people, a wood-burning fireplace. It was a beautiful study in a beautiful house. It was a beautiful life.

Except that it was almost two in the morning, and he had no idea where his wife was.

He groaned and brought his feet slowly back to the floor. Sheila was cheating on him, plain and simple. He couldn't ignore it anymore. Well, they'd have it out when she got home, no matter what time it was. They'd come in here, shut the door, and have it out because he wasn't one for letting things like that go unresolved, even for a second. He always felt it was better to hit an issue like this head-on, right away. He wasn't going to let her run around on him anymore, not as hard as he worked to give her and the kids everything they could possibly want. He knew he'd been a ghost lately, but damn it, didn't she understand what it took to make all this real?

He shook his head. It was strange to realize that if she'd just come and talked to him about what was going on, maybe they could have worked something out. Maybe they could have come to an arrangement, like some of the other long-married couples in the neighborhood had. Like Colin Freese and his wife had. It wasn't as if he and Sheila were passionate about each other anymore — far from it. Both of them had lost that feeling for each other years ago, sometime after the birth of their second child, Glenn. After that, Rose had immersed himself in his new job at Trafalgar, intent upon being CFO before he was forty. Working seventy-hour weeks, many nights literally falling into bed when he got home. Sheila had thrown herself into the children's lives, focused on the new big house in Great Falls she had to furnish and accessorize, and become part of the neighborhood fabric — ultimately more for the benefit of the kids than herself, which had to be taking a big psychological toll on her by now, he realized. Eventually, it had gotten to the point that they were barely making love once a month, and then it had stopped altogether. They didn't even have sex on vacation anymore. He couldn't remember the l time they'd shared anything more than a peck on the cheek. Like Kat had given her husband at Morton's. He sighed. If Sheila had just come to him and tried to work it out.

His expression turned grim. There was nothing to work out now. He couldn't stand her lying to him and sneaking around behind his back. It was the deceit that tore at him more than anything. Not so much the thought of her actually being with another man.

Rose pulled the crinkled piece of paper from his shirt pocket and gazed at the name again — Kat. Short for Katherine or Katrina, he figured. It was the third time he'd pulled the paper out to look at it since leaving the bar. He'd already committed her phone number to memory in case he lost it or it got ripped from his hand during an argument. He'd pulled it out again because he liked her handwriting and wanted to see it again. He liked the way she drew a little curly-Q cat tail on the end of the "t" in her name and a smiley face after the number. He put the paper to his nose. He was pretty ure he could smell her perfume on it, too.

He pictured her face again. Pictured those 't features, perfect smile, and turquoise eyes all framed by that shimmering blond hair.

Cortez had given him a hard time about her on the short drive back to Trafalgar's headquarters tonight. Scolded him for accepting the note, then for not throwing it away immediately. David had even tried to grab the note out of his pocket at one point. Rose knew exactly what he was worried about, how self-motivated his actions were. He was terrified that his boss was finally giving in to temptation after all this time and that Trafalgar was going to be a ship without a captain or a rudder at a critical moment. A company with a CEO who was constantly missing in action and a CFO who was chasing a skirt on the brink of the most important hostile takeover they'd ever attempted. Cortez was worried about his own bag of options, salary increases, and bonuses.

Rose had tried to calm David down, tried to assure him that nothing would get in the way of them buying CIS. But it didn't do any good. David kept asking one simple question: Why wouldn't Rose throw away the paper with the woman's number on it? The problem was, Rose didn't have an answer. Maybe he should have thrown it away, but he couldn't bring himself to do it.

There was something about Kat that haunted him, something that told him she was going to be a very important person in his life.

In their entire twenty-year-plus marriage, Rose had never cheated on Sheila. Only once had he ever really even been tempted to. He'd been on a business trip to Europe with Freese right after being promoted to CFO five years ago, and they'd gone to dinner in London with two of Freese's acquaintances. Freese and his friends had shown up with young women on their arms, not their wives, and the other women had brought along a fourth for Rose. A pretty young blonde — not as pretty as Kat, but still very attractive — who'd stapled herself to him right away. He'd expected her to be immature and boring, so he'd been surprised when she turned out to be up on world affairs, even American sports. Surprised to find her fascinating. She'd made it obvious from the get-go that he could have what he wanted that night, but he'd kept to his one glass of wine limit and been able to walk away without any damage.

There was a soft knock on the study door. "Dad?"

Rose's eyes snapped left. That quickly, he felt awful. He'd been fantasizing about what

68

it would be like to be with Kat, what it would have been like to have been with the woman in London. He stuffed the note back in his pocket. Sometimes it was such a pain in the ass being a man. Having to deal with the constant battle against the hormones. He'd always figured that battle would finally be over when he reached forty, but he'd figured wrong. The battle had intensified.

"Yes, honey, come in."

Jamie, his sixteen-year-old daughter, pushed open the door.

Now he felt even worse. Jamie was a young woman herself, probably only seven or eight years younger than Kat. Seeing her in the doorway made the age difference between Kat and himself even more stark, even more dangerous. Cortez had been banging him over the head with that one tonight, too. That Kat was at least fifteen years younger than him, and how was that going to look if he took her to lunch or dinner? *Stupid,* Cortez had answered his own question before Rose even had a chance to respond. And pathetic, Rose thought to himself now.

"Hi, Munchkin."

He'd been calling Jamie that since she was a baby. He'd always been close to her, much closer than he was to his son, Glenn. He and Jamie were both excellent skiers, and that had built a bond between them ever since she was young. Since she was six or seven and he'd marveled at how easily she went racing down the slopes. They'd go off on the steep, wooded trails by themselves while Sheila and Glenn stayed on the easy runs with all the other tourists. It was still that way, had been in Switzerland last winter when they'd all gone to the Alps for Christmas.

"What are you doing up so late?" he asked, beckoning for her to come in. "You've got school tomorrow."

Jamie trotted to the chair — she was wearing baggy pajamas and a big, terry cloth robe — and dropped herself down on his lap. She was small, like her mom, just over five feet tall, brunette and slim. Light as a feather as she made herself comfortable.

"Where's Mom?" she asked, slipping her arms around his shoulders and nuzzling her face into his neck.

Rose could feel warm tears on his skin right away, and he took a quick breath — he hadn't been ready for this. Usually she was more guarded with her emotions, like he was. But he should have known this was going to happen sooner or later. Along with all the normal issues teenage girls dealt with

— boys, cliques, acne, projects for school, getting a driver's license — Jamie was painfully aware of what he and Sheila were going through.

A few weeks ago, they'd been arguing late one night about something petty, a credit card bill or a small ding in the Mercedes door, he couldn't remember, but the spat had erupted into a full-scale war. They'd been down in the finished basement so he'd figured the kids wouldn't hear them. Then Jamie had appeared in the doorway of the computer room, off to one side of the main room, when the yelling had gone ballistic. She'd been in there working on a term paper and there were tears streaming down her cheeks as she sprinted past them toward the stairs. He'd raced after her right away, but her bedroom door was locked when he got to it and she wouldn't open it, wouldn't even answer. Wouldn't talk about it the next morning at breakfast, either. Usually he was gone an hour before anyone else in the house even got up, but he'd stuck around to try to smooth things over with her. She hadn't opened up though. Still hadn't. Maybe that was about to change.

"Mom's out to dinner with some friends, honey," he answered. "They went shopping and —"

71

"It's two o'clock in the morning, Dad," Jamie interrupted, keeping her face buried in his neck. "Trudy tried that one on me, too, but I know all of Mom's friends and they don't stay out until two o'clock on a weeknight. Probably not even on the weekends. Not without their husbands anyway."

"Look, I —"

"Were you guys arguing again?" she asked, finally pulling back and wiping the tears from her face. "Did you get into it this morning?"

He hated the way the corners of her mouth were trembling. "No. Where'd you get that idea? I was gone early, like I usually am."

She sobbed and wiped more tears from her cheeks. "Are you getting a divorce?"

"*No!* Of course not."

"Why? Because you don't want to lose half your money?"

That was out of line. "Easy, Munchkin," he warned, raising his voice just slightly. She would know what that meant.

"I'm worried about you guys." She put her hands to her face. "And scared."

His heart sank. He'd never seen her like this. "You don't need to be scared. Everything's fine."

"Would you ever hurt Mom? Would you

ever do anything to her?"

Rose pulled back, stunned by the question. "*What?* How could you even ask me that? I've never touched your mother, and I never would. I mean, we've never touched you or your brother, have we?" Although maybe Sheila had, and he didn't know about it. Sometimes she snapped. He'd only seen it happen a few times during their marriage, but when it did, it was something to see. "Has Mom done something to you?"

"No."

"Then why would you ask me that?"

"I heard you talking to Mr. Cortez one night on the phone. Your door was open, and I heard you talking to him in here. You said you wished Mom would have an accident or something."

Rose's shoulders slumped, and he looked away. Glanced at the antique globe in the corner beneath the window trying to figure out how he was going to explain this one. He did remember saying that to David during a call last week now that she mentioned it. "Sometimes people say things they don't mean, honey," he said gently, irritated that she would eavesdrop on him like that, but he wasn't going to say anything. "You know that. I'm sure you've done it lots of times. Said something about someone in your class you didn't really mean to someone else in private just because you were frustrated with them at the moment. Well, I do that, too. I say things I wish I could take back. I get frustrated with your mom sometimes, but I love her very much." He searched Jamie's expression for some sort of acknowledgment that his answer was okay. Nothing. "One of the tough things you learn as you get older is that your parents aren't perfect. Kind of bursts the bubble, you know? We say and do things we don't mean just like kids do. I remember when I realized that about my parents. It really threw me for a loop."

Jamie rolled her eyes. "Mom just wants some attention, Dad. She wants you to spend time with her. Not with your reports and your papers, just with her. It isn't that hard to get."

He wanted to explain it all to her. Wanted to tell her how hard it was to make enough money to pay for a six-bedroom house on three acres of some of the priciest real estate on the east coast; to put two kids through private school; to keep up the country club membership; to take the vacations they took. But she wouldn't understand even if he tried, couldn't understand even though she was smart — a straight-A student all through school, unlike Glenn, who barely pulled Bs and Cs. Rose hadn't understood all that when he was young, hadn't understood it until he'd tried to make a real living himself — and he'd even cheated, gotten a head start thanks to the family he'd married into.

"I know," he said hesitantly. "Your mom's told me all that, and I need to get better about it. I need to listen more. I'm sorry, Munchkin."

She stared straight into his eyes. "Daddy?"

"Yes, honey?"

"Can you not call me that anymore?"

He searched her expression again. This time he saw how much she loved him and he choked up for a moment. "Call you what?" he asked, clearing his throat.

"Munchkin."

"I've always called you that."

"I'm sixteen, Daddy. You called me that in front of my friends last weekend when they came to get me here at the house. We were all going to the mall. They still haven't stopped joking me about it."

Rose held up his hands. "Sorry. I won't call you that in front of your friends anymore. I promise."

"No, Daddy, I don't want you to call me that anymore *at all*."

He gazed at her, no sound in the room but the faint tick-tock of the grandfather clock in the corner. She really was a young woman now, and it almost brought tears to his eyes for the second time in only a few minutes. Someday, probably when she had kids of her own, probably at a Thanksgiving dinner or something like that, he'd call her that again out of nowhere. He'd say it without even thinking, and it would be like he'd never stopped calling her that for all those years. They'd share a laugh and a hug, and they'd realize that everything was like it had always been again. But she cared about what her friends thought now, wanted to be accepted like any other teenager did. He couldn't blame her for that, but it still hurt to realize that she was growing up. That she'd be leaving for good soon, because when they left for college, they never really came back.

"Okay," he said quietly. "I won't."

"Thanks, Dad," she murmured. "Don't be disappointed in me."

Rose looked down. She knew it was hurting him, knew he was feeling like he was losing his little girl to the big, bad world. She recognized all that in his tone and his expression. God, she looked so much like her mother had twenty years ago. "I'm not disappointed in you, Munch . . . I mean, *Jamie.*"

The doorbell rang and they glanced up, straight into each other's eyes. He put his tough face on instantly, recognizing that she'd caught fear flash across his face for a split second, just as he'd seen it tear across hers. No one rang the doorbell at two in the morning — unless they had bad news.

"Go to bed, sweetheart."

"Oh, sure, Daddy," she said, racing for the door.

Rose jumped up from his chair and hustled after her. "Jamie!" But she was already to the foyer, already throwing open the door. He felt a burst of freezing February air as he rushed around the corner and saw a Fairfax County policeman standing on the porch, leather jacket zipped up all the way to his chin.

The cop glanced uneasily from Jamie to Rose several times. "Mr. Rose?" he finally asked.

Rose moved in front of Jamie. Suddenly he was shaking and not because of the cold air pouring into the house. "Yes?"

"I need to talk to you, sir. May I come in?"

10

Her name was Vivian Anduhar. She was
Middle Eastern and exotic and it was all
terribly titillating, he had to admit. He'd
never been with an exotic woman before,
never been with a woman who wasn't white.
In fact, he'd never been with a woman who
wasn't white and wasn't from Texas.

Vivian was so different. She was dark. She
was from Amman, Jordan. She'd never told
him that, but he knew all about her.

Dennis Hackett stood behind Vivian,
naked, kissing her neck, pulling her light
blue cotton top up over her beige bra and
over her head as they stood in the middle of
the room at the Marriott Hotel near the
Dallas Airport. They watched each other
intently in the full-length mirror standing in
one corner of the room — they were both
avowed voyeurs. This was the third time
they'd been intimate since starting their affair a month ago. She was an administrative

assistant at a flight school based at a small, general aviation airfield twenty miles west of Dallas. He was a driver for a fuel company that serviced the airfield. She was married with four children. He was single.

Hackett unbuttoned her pants and pulled down the zipper, then slid his hands inside her pants at the hips and pushed them and her panties down to her knees. He quickly unhooked her bra, slid it down her arms, tossed it on the chair, then lightly caressed her shoulders and breasts as he kissed her neck some more. She had full, firm breasts and he felt himself become fully aroused as he squeezed them, then tweaked her huge, dark nipples. She moaned loudly and eased her head back against his shoulder.

"That feels so good," she murmured. "Do it harder."

Her accent turned him on, too. And she liked it rough, which he'd never experienced. It was all new, all terribly exciting.

Suddenly she turned, dropped to her knees, and it was his turn to moan. God, he loved what she did for him, and he desperately wished it didn't have to end so soon.

11

Rose gazed down at Sheila's lifeless brown eyes as she lay on the metal gurney. The sheet was pulled down from over her face to just above her breasts. Her skin was white, almost gray, and there were scratches and bruises on her face, one very bad cut at her hairline, too. They'd tried to hastily clean her up, he could tell, but they'd missed some blood — it was caked inside her nose and at the corners of her eyes. He was aware that the other four men in the room were watching him intently, waiting for the identification, but he didn't nod right away. Maybe because he'd trained himself not to react to anything right away, even when the answer seemed obvious. Maybe because he couldn't actually believe she was lying there in front of him, dead.

Now that he thought about it, no one close to him had ever died. Except for his father, and that had been a long time ago. It wasn't like he'd seen his father's dead body lying on a cold metal table in front of him like this, either. His father had left for work one morning and never returned. It had been that simple, that sanitary. His mother hadn't had a funeral for him, hadn't even buried him so Rose could visit a grave. Just had his father cremated, then tossed his ashes in the ocean off La Jolla, standing knee-deep in the surf while Rose watched from the beach. She'd blown a kiss toward the horizon, then never mentioned him again.

"That's her," Rose finally muttered. God, how was he going to tell Jamie? She pretty much already knew, but she didn't know for sure. There was still doubt, still a sliver of hope, the possibility that the woman who'd run off the lonely ravine on Georgetown Pike wasn't her mother. And he knew she was holding on to that sliver of hope like a life raft in a storm. "That's Sheila." He felt a lump form in his throat and heat at the corners of his eyes. Her lying there was one of the most awful things he'd ever seen.

A white-clad attendant pulled the sheet back up over Sheila's face, and the young Fairfax County deputy with the blond crew cut who'd come to the house an hour ago to ask Rose to accompany him to the morgue tapped him on the shoulder. Motioned for Rose to follow. Led him away from the body toward a conference room they'd passed on the way in.

When they were all inside the small room, the cop dropped his hat in front of the chair at the head of the table and pointed at one of the chairs beside his. "Have a seat," he ordered, pointing at Rose, then at the chair.

The cop's tone seemed brusque, Rose thought to himself as he watched the guy leave the room. Too brusque, almost confrontational. Maybe that was just the way cops were. He didn't have much experience with them. He'd only been arrested once in his entire life, that time at Dulles, and that had all been choreographed.

The other two men sat down on the far side of the table facing Rose. They were dressed in jackets and ties and were gulping down coffee from 7-11 cups. They weren't saying anything, hadn't said anything since they'd appeared out of nowhere and fallen in line behind the deputy and him from out of a darkened doorway as the deputy led him along the scuffed tile corridor to the room where Sheila's body lay. Rose checked his watch. Four ten. Jesus, he wanted to go home.

His cell phone rang, and he pulled it from

his pocket, embarrassed at how loud the ring was. "Home" was flashing on the tiny screen — it was probably Jamie — but he didn't have the heart to talk to her yet. He pushed the "end" button, then put it down on the table.

"Mr. Rose."

Rose glanced up from the wobbly, scratched table. The guy on the left had spoken. He was the older of the two, probably in his early fifties. He reminded Rose of a hound dog with his puffy, creased cheeks, small folds of sagging skin on either side of his chin, and sad, droopy eyes. "Yes?"

"I'm Detective Willis."

The deputy returned to the room with a steaming cup of coffee and put it down on the table beside his hat. Then he removed his leather jacket and sat down. For some reason, the guy was making Rose really uncomfortable. He hadn't on the fifteen-minute ride over here from the house, but he definitely was now. Rose had sensed a change in his attitude in the last few minutes.

"This is Detective Harrison," Willis continued, motioning to his left. Harrison was a young African American man. He had sharp facial features and his coat and tie were much more stylish than Willis's. "He'll be assisting me."

"Assisting you with what?"

"With your wife's case."

That sounded awfully official. Rose was glad they were taking Sheila's death so seriously, but "case" didn't sound like a word he'd heard used a lot when the death was accidental. "Case?"

"Yes, case. The investigation into your wife's death."

"I thought it was an accident." Rose glanced at the deputy. "You told me it was an accident on the way over here."

The cop didn't respond, just gazed straight ahead and sipped his coffee.

"Initially, we assumed it was an accident," Harrison spoke up. "And that may be what we end up determining it was. But there were some things about the scene that made us want to take a closer look."

Rose rubbed his eyes. "Things like what?"

"Your wife had no identification on her at the scene," Willis explained. "No wallet, no purse, no nothing. The glove compartment was empty, too. It was like the car had been cleaned out after she went down the ravine."

"Then how —"

"I ran the plates," the deputy cut in, anticipating Rose's question. "They were still on the car."

"Your wife had a white substance in her nose, too," Harrison said quietly. "It was obvious when they brought her in here. It was all over the inside of both nostrils."

Rose's eyes flashed to Harrison. The young man had said it almost like he didn't want to. Like he understood what a husband who'd just identified his wife's dead body must be going through. Like he also understood that the other two men weren't showing much compassion.

Harrison pursed his lips. "It looked like cocaine. Pretty obvious it was, but we're having the lab work done on it to confirm."

"Cocaine?"

"Did your wife use drugs, Mr. Rose?" Willis asked directly.

"No." He willed himself to take a breath. "Not that I know of anyway. I mean, I've never used them with her. I've never used drugs at all."

"Where was she tonight?" the deputy asked.

Rose shrugged. "Our au pair said she left the house around noon today to go shopping with some friends. And that she was going to dinner with them afterward. That's all I know."

"Did you try to get in touch with her?"

"Yeah. I called her a few times, starting at

about five last night."

"Did you ever reach her?"

"No."

"When was the last time you tried calling her?"

"Around eleven thirty, I think. On my way home from the office."

The cop glanced over. "*Eleven thirty?* You were on your way home from the office at eleven thirty? Where do you work?"

"Trafalgar Industries."

"What do you do there?" the young detective asked.

Rose hesitated. "I'm the chief financial officer." He watched them all exchange a subtle glance. Like it was no wonder he lived where he lived in such a big house. Like now they understood. So the cop had a big mouth. "Look, I'd really like to go home. I need to talk to my kids."

"Right, right," Willis said, like he was talking to his wife while he read the sports page over his morning coffee. "Of course you do." He took a small notepad and a pen out of his suit coat. "We'll get you out of here as fast as we can, but first let me get this straight." He scratched a few notes down quickly before speaking up again. "You started calling your wife around five, the last time you tried her was around eleven

86

thirty, but you didn't try again after that. Is that what you said?"

"Yes."

"Why didn't you try her after eleven thirty?"

"I don't know," Rose answered hesitantly. "I really don't."

"Let me ask you a very difficult question, Mr. Rose. I'm sorry, but I have to do this. Do you think your wife was having an affair?"

God, he wanted to go home. Why were they keeping him here so long? "I have no idea."

"Did it ever cross your mind?"

"Maybe," Rose murmured. "Maybe."

"Where did you go after you left work last night?"

Rose looked up. Willis was staring back at him hard. "Home. Why?"

"You didn't go anywhere else?"

"No."

"You went straight home?"

"Yes."

The room went deathly quiet for a few moments. Finally the deputy spoke up. "Are you having an affair, Mr. Rose?"

12

The Anduhar family had lived in a quiet part of Ralston, Texas — thirty miles from Dallas — for the last eight months. Lived in a blue-collar neighborhood in a three-bedroom ranch house and kept mostly to themselves. Hadn't interacted much at all with their neighbors, hadn't gone out of their way to make friends, had just gone about their business. Jobs for both parents, school for the kids. Had just tried to blend into the landscape.

Which hadn't been easy. The neighbors had started talking among themselves as soon as the Anduhars moved in, before the van had even pulled away from in front of the house. Everyone was wondering what the family was doing there. Most of the people in the neighborhood were white. There were a few black families, a few Hispanic families, but no Middle Easterners. And the Anduhars' presence was quietly causing a commotion in the close-knit community. Especially when people found out that the wife, Vivian, was working at a flight training school at a small airfield ten miles away.

Some of the neighbors tried to be nice to the family. They brought over casseroles, offered to give the kids rides home from the bus stops, some even invited the family over for dinner. The Anduhars politely accepted a few of the gestures, but never invited anyone into their house. And no one could figure out what the husband did. He left early most mornings in an old Honda Accord, but no one knew where he was going or what he did when he got there. Two men in the neighborhood had actually tried to follow him a couple of times, but they'd lost him in traffic. Not because he'd taken any wild, evasive actions, they'd told their wives. He'd just kind of slipped away, as though he was good at it. As though he had a lot of practice.

Now three men dressed all in black stole into the ranch house through the back door; they'd shot the dog the Anduhars kept in the backyard with a single bullet from a gun with a silencer. They were experts at picking locks and made no sounds at all as they entered the home and snuck through the living room and down the narrow hallway toward the bedrooms. Within forty-five seconds, all five occupants had been injected with a fast-acting anesthesia and were unconscious. They would have been out for twelve hours, but it wasn't going to matter. All the men needed was a few minutes.

Two of the men rifled through a small desk in the master bedroom, found the husband's cigarettes, lit one, lit the polyester sheet he was lying on with the cigarette and tossed the cigarette onto the mattress. The third man dropped what he'd gone to get from the truck parked down the lane on the flaming bed beside Mr. Anduhar, then they all headed for the garage.

When they were out of the house they stuck a crude, three-foot-tall cross into the front lawn as the light through the master bedroom window flickered a brighter and brighter orange — and waited. When the house was fully engulfed in flames, they headed to the truck and cruised slowly off into the night.

Three fire engines screeched to a stop in front of the house twenty-two minutes later, but at that point the house was nothing but a ball of flames. By the time the fire was out, the bodies inside the house were burned beyond recognition.

13

Thankfully, Cortez was waiting in his dark blue Lincoln Navigator when Rose emerged from the morgue into the frigid night air. After he climbed into the passenger seat and closed the door, he put his face in his hands and rubbed his eyes hard. It was almost five o'clock in the morning. He was dead tired and the fact that Sheila was gone forever was starting to sink in. As much as they'd been at each other's throats the last few months, she was still his life partner. The woman who'd given him two children he loved more than life itself, the woman who'd supported him while he worked his fingers to the bone. She'd made sure the house was perfectly neat, she'd made sure his meals were hot whenever he finally got home, and she'd taken care of all the annoying details of running a household. She'd definitely been a boost for his career in many ways.

As Cortez pulled away from the curb, some of the wonderful memories started to drift back to Rose. That night he'd first seen Sheila, near the end of his junior year at the University of North Carolina. Being struck the moment he saw her across the room that she could be the one — even before he knew her last name was Adkins and her family was worth millions. Their first date a week later. Their wedding. The births of their two children. Jamie's first word as they were having lunch on the deck of their old house one weekend: Dada.

He reached over and touched Cortez on the shoulder. "Thanks for coming." The thought of riding home with the deputy had been appalling, especially after the grill session he'd been forced to endure. "I really appreciate it."

"No problem," Cortez said, putting his hand on top of Rose's for a moment. "I'm always there for you, Mike. You know that."

Suddenly Rose felt terrible for thinking that Cortez had been selfishly motivated earlier tonight when he'd demanded to know why Rose hadn't thrown away Kat's phone number immediately. Maybe David's motivation had been much purer, maybe the guy just sincerely cared about a family and didn't want to see it blown apart by a young blonde in a short skirt. "I don't know how I'm going to tell Jamie," Rose murmured, dropping his hand back into his lap. Strange, he wasn't as worried about Glenn. Probably because Sheila and the boy had never been that close. Not like Sheila and Jamie were. Like *he* and Jamie were. Glenn was a loner and wanted it that way. He and Sheila had been worried about him for a while, worried about him spending so much time by himself in the computer room in the basement, playing games against unseen foes on the Internet. But the school psychiatrist had counseled them not to worry, that he was just like a lot of boys his age these days.

"You want me to come in with you when we get back to your house?" Cortez asked.

Rose's first reaction was to say no. Telling the kids was something he had to do himself, and Cortez's presence — even if he was in another room — might be unsettling for them. But it sure would be nice to have David around once everything was over. Of course, things might not be over for a few hours. "Thanks, amigo, but you should go home and get some sleep. One of us needs to be thinking clearly at the board meeting."

Cortez looked at Rose like he was crazy.

"You can't seriously be thinking about going to it."

Rose took a deep breath. "I have to. There's no way around it."

"I can handle it myself, Mike."

"Probably, but the board will expect me to be there."

"Your kids are going to need you today. The board will have to understand that."

"I'll go home right after it's over."

"Which might be midnight. Sometimes they go on forever."

"This one won't take that long."

Cortez held up one hand. "This is insane. Your wife just died. You can't be thinking about anything else at this point."

There were always things you couldn't explain, even to your closest friends. "I'll be fine. I can handle it."

"You think you can handle anything, Mike, but even you have your limits."

Rose glanced out the passenger window into the darkness, at the snow piled up on the side of the road. Maybe David was right, maybe it would help to talk to somebody about what had happened back at the morgue. "After I identified Sheila's body, they interviewed me. That's why you had to wait."

Cortez's expression twisted into one of

anger. "*Interviewed you?* What do you mean?"

"They asked a lot of questions about Sheila. And me."

"Like what?"

"Like whether I tried to call Sheila tonight. Like why I didn't try to call her after eleven thirty."

Cortez glanced out the driver window. "Why didn't you try to call her after that?"

"I'd already tried her three or four times at that point, and I had left messages each time." He paused again, longer this time. "I figured she was cheating on me." He glanced over at Cortez.

"Did you call that girl tonight?" Cortez asked. "The one at the bar."

The world turned red in front of Rose. That wasn't fair. "David, how could you ask me that at a time like —"

"I wouldn't blame you if you did," Cortez interrupted.

That had come from left field, from past the fence actually. Rose had figured Cortez was accusing, not capitulating. "What?"

"Sheila *was* cheating on you," Cortez said. "With some bartender in Georgetown. His name was Sykes or something. I can find out for sure if you want me to. I can find out where he works, too."

Rose felt his hands clench involuntarily. "How do you . . . how did you —"

"I had Sheila followed a couple of times," Cortez explained. "I have a buddy who's a private eye, and he did me a favor. Sheila was pulling some crazy stuff, pal."

"My God," Rose whispered. The truth was suddenly harder to handle than he'd anticipated. Now he *was* thinking about her wrapped naked around another man, and it was awful. "Why? Why did you have her followed?"

"It started with that night we went out to dinner a few months ago, when we were first thinking about buying CIS," Cortez began. "In fact, it was the day you first laid the acquisition on me. We went to dinner at The Palm and you kind of let loose a little after we talked about the deal. You told me that Sheila had been acting weird lately."

Rose nodded, remembering. It was the last time he'd let himself have more than one glass of wine at a sitting. He'd had three that night, and let his guard down a little, just as Cortez said.

"That was the first time you told me," Cortez continued. "Then you mentioned it again a few weeks later when we were out to lunch. How she was gone more and more without telling you where she was. How her

96

explanations seemed lame." He patted Rose's knee. "You're a good friend, man. I wanted you to have all the facts if it ever got to a point that you needed them. Sheila was doing you wrong, Mike, very wrong. After all you'd done for her, she was banging some good-for-nothing jerk just for kicks. It makes me wanna puke to think about it. To tell you the truth, I won't shed one damn tear at her funeral."

14

Hackett lay on his back on the bed as Vivian rode him. He was in heaven as she slowly moved up and down.

"Put your hands on my breasts," she ordered.

He did as he was told, sliding his hands from her buttocks up to her breasts.

"Squeeze them hard," she demanded, her eyes rolling back. "Pinch my nipples but stay still. Don't move."

Hackett began thrusting up into her, unable to comply with the last part of the order. It felt too good. She arched her back and bit her lower lip, but didn't tell him to stop.

After a few moments she slumped forward, so her lips were close to his ear. "I want to tie you up."

"Tie me up?"

"Yes," she said in a husky whisper. "It turns me on very much. If you think I'm doing good now, just wait."

How could he say no? "Okay."

Vivian tongued his neck for a few moments as she continued to rise and fall. Then she kissed him deeply before sliding off the bed and slinking toward the bathroom.

She was back moments later with the two thick sashes from the robes hanging in the closet. She climbed onto the bed, straddled his stomach and tightly tied each of his wrists to the bedposts.

He watched her eyes as she secured the knots tightly. The look in them was so intense. Maybe it really did turn her on to do this, maybe she was telling him the truth. Maybe there was no reason to end this yet.

She slipped him back inside her and began moving up and down again, smiling lewdly.

Hackett put his head back and shut his eyes. This was incredible. He'd never experienced anything like it. Maybe there was something to all that talk about exotic women being better in bed.

"Why are you having this affair with me?"

Hackett's eyes opened slowly. "Huh?"

"Why are you having this affair with me?" Vivian repeated, still moving up and down on him. "What are you doing here with me?"

"I like you," he answered simply. "It feels good."

She stopped moving and gripped his chin tightly. "Are you really a truck driver?" she asked squeezing hard. "Or is this about something else?"

Hackett thought he saw a flash of metal in the dim light, thought he'd seen her reach beneath the sheet. *"Red! Red! Red!"* he shouted at the top of his lungs.

The door to the room burst open and three men rushed inside. They had Vivian on her back in seconds, pinned to the floor, towel stuffed down her throat before she could make a sound. One of the men knelt roughly on her shoulders, another on her thighs, putting their full weight on her. Immobilizing her as she screamed in pain into the towel. The third man pulled out a needle filled with clear liquid from a case on his belt, jammed the point of the needle into her hip and injected the fluid. Moments later, her eyelids fluttered shut.

15

Peter Beck hadn't been to bed in three days, but the lack of sleep wasn't bothering him yet. He was still alert thanks to his hourly regimen: four cigarettes, two cups of black coffee, and half of one of those little yellow pills the guy at Base 19 had given him. He knew his limit — another ten hours. At that point, he'd need at least a full twenty-four hours straight of shut-eye.

"We got the woman in Dallas."

Beck looked up from over a fresh cup of steaming java, an ashtray full of extinguished butts on the coffee table in front of him. He was sitting in the mansion's sunroom, which overlooked the Worthington Valley from high up on a hill. It was a beautiful, pristine valley twenty miles north of Baltimore, Maryland, dotted with sprawling thorough-bred horse farms. None of which he could see right now because it was pitch-black outside, first light still half an hour away.

But he remembered the idyllic scene that lay before him from the last time he was here. He'd used this house when he'd come to Washington once before; it was only ninety minutes from the White House. It was extremely nice — and easily secured. The man who owned it was a devout supporter of The Fourth Order. He'd lost a son and a daughter in the World Trade Center attack.

"Where are we taking her again?"

"Base Seventy-seven," Tom Klein answered in his high-pitched voice. Klein was Beck's right-hand man. Had been since the founding of the I-4.

Beck motioned for Klein to sit down in the big easy chair that faced his. He'd grown close to Klein over the last few years and had a great deal of respect for the man. "What about her family?" Beck asked, a slight grin creasing his ruddy cheeks. Klein looked about as intimidating as a kitten.

In his mid-thirties, Klein was short, dumpy, and balding and his high-pitched voice made him seem effeminate. But the soft exterior was a perfect front, a perfect example of how you could never judge a candy bar by its wrapper. Beneath that soft-looking exterior was a man who was absolutely committed to the I-4's mission — and didn't have a compassionate bone in his body. Not for the enemy, anyway. He was obsessed with destroying them, almost too much so. Almost to the point of obsession, of allowing emotion to sway his judgment. Beck winced, suddenly riddled with self-doubt. Maybe it wasn't Klein who had a problem, maybe he was the one with the problem. Beck shook his head. He couldn't think like that.

"Dead," Klein answered, "all of them."

Beck's heart sank. There had been four children. "So they actually burned the house down?" Beck had been against doing that. But by the time he'd gotten word of what was planned, the leader of the unit couldn't be reached. Beck was suspicious that Klein might have held off telling him about what was going down so the unit leader couldn't be reached in time, but he wasn't going to say anything. If he was wrong, Klein would be hurt, and there couldn't be any rift between the two of them if the Fourth Order was going to continue to operate smoothly. "They went ahead with it?"

"Yup. After they shot 'em up with the knockout stuff."

"But what about the woman?" Beck asked, his stomach churning as he thought about the children being consumed by fire. "The cops won't find a sixth body."

"Our guys used a cadaver with roughly the same physical characteristics. They brought the body into the house after they'd put everyone to sleep."

"The CSI people will check dental records."

"There are no dental records," Klein reminded Beck. "The family came to Dallas eight months ago and none of them have been to a doctor or a dentist since they moved in. Which is one of the reasons we were so suspicious. No one in the neighborhood knows where they came from, so the cops won't be able to check records in any other city, either." He chuckled. "The boys stuck a cross on the front lawn after they torched the place. The cops'll figure it was a hate crime. They'll figure it was some drunk redneck in the neighborhood, but they won't be able to tag it on anyone. It's perfect."

"Has the woman told us anything yet?"

"She's still unconscious. The kidnap team had to shoot her up, too, before we could get anything out of her. But her time will come soon enough. If there's anything to get, the boys at Seventy-seven will get it."

Beck knew that was all too true. The interrogators at Base 77 were brutal. He'd been forced to make a trip out there to Idaho himself a few months ago to warn them about their tactics. He'd reassigned a few for good measure after the visit, to make the point very clear. They were getting confessions at a much higher rate at Base 77 than at the other two domestic bases — 12 and 19 — and, over time, they'd realized that a lot of the confessions were false. That the men and women were saying anything they could think of under questioning to avoid the pain. Torture was a touchy business: You had to make sure it was brutal *and* effective. Too brutal and you were wasting your time.

"Probability?" he asked, aware that the toes of Klein's shoes barely reached the floor. The big easy chair looked like it might swallow him up at any moment. At another time, it would have been funny. But he couldn't stop thinking about those four kids. "Remind me again."

"Seventy-five percent. We're very confident on this one."

A 75 percent chance that the woman from Dallas was involved in a terrorist plot. Those were excellent odds, much better than most of the situations they'd been dealing with lately. Well over the Directorate's internal guideline of 25 percent. "I want to be kept up to speed on this one constantly, Tom. I want specifics of each interrogation."

"Yes, sir."

"I want you to contact the guys up there and tell them I'm watching this very carefully. They'll understand what that means."

"Of course."

The spoon in the coffee cup began to clatter as the saucer shook in Beck's hand. He took several quick breaths and put the saucer down on the table beside his chair, careful to put it on a coaster. He'd taken the last little half of a yellow pill ten minutes ago, and it was starting to really kick in. His hands were shaking noticeably, his entire body was starting to buzz. "How many do we have in custody right now?" he asked, gripping the arms of the chair tightly. He could feel perspiration building up in between his fingers.

"Forty-one as of last night's six-o'clock count. Twenty-seven men, fourteen women. Including the people overseas."

"What's that breakdown? Here versus overseas?"

"Twenty-eight at the foreign locations, thirteen here in the States."

Beck appreciated Klein's efficiency, loved how well they knew each other at this point.

How Klein knew exactly what information Beck wanted every hour of the day. Which was why he hadn't made an issue of not being told sooner what the unit commander intended to do to the rest of the Anduhar family. "What about the Trafalgar board meeting today? Is it covered?" He watched Klein squirm. Couldn't tell if it was because of the chair or the question.

"We don't know yet. We're pretty sure we have five members of the board in our camp, but we need six. There are two on the fence. A simple majority and Rose has what he needs."

"What if Rose gets it?"

Klein put a finger to his chin. "Mr. Rose may not make it to the board meeting today."

Beck's eyes flashed to Klein's. He'd caught a tone. "Why not?"

"His wife died last night when her Mercedes ran off the road a few miles from the Roses' house."

This was the problem, the biggest problem Beck faced as the executive director of The Fourth Order of Immunity. He was managing a hundred ultra-Type-A personalities on a day-to-day basis. A hundred men who'd been trained to take charge and achieve their objective at *any* cost — including the loss of their own lives, which had happened to several men of the original corps. They obeyed orders, but they had been given tremendous freedom to interpret those orders, too. Like the leader of the kidnap team in Dallas making the decision to kill the rest of the Anduhar family. It wasn't like the military, where everything was black-and-white. This was Gray Ops. "Did our people do it? Did our people kill Rose's wife?"

Klein looked up, a curious expression on his face. "We're not sure."

"I said from the beginning I didn't want Rose harmed," Beck snapped angrily. He was convinced now that someone was behind Michael Rose, that there was an ultimate enemy lurking in the shadows who was much more powerful than Rose. There were too many coincidences about what was happening to accept the assumption that Rose was simply acting on his own. And it was critical that they find out who it was or this same kind of thing could happen again. They needed Rose alive to find out who that ultimate enemy was. "I made that very clear."

"But you didn't say anything about his family."

Beck held his tongue. This was the only

habit of Klein's he disliked. His willingness to point out Beck's day-to-day failures, or ways Beck could have done things better. "It was understood."

"It wasn't understood two months ago when you told them to —"

"All right," Beck barked, holding up his hand. The pill was really starting to jolt him. "Find out what happened there. Make it a top priority. You got me?"

"Yes, sir."

Beck broke out a new pack of cigarettes, Marlboro Lights this time. No more Camels. "The question still stands," he said, crumpling up the cellophane and cramming it into his pocket, thinking about how he had to make certain that the ashtray was empty and that all the dishes were washed before he left. He had great respect for the man who owned this house, and leaving it in any way other than the way he'd found it would be wrong. "What happens if Rose gets board approval today to go ahead with the CIS deal? What then?"

"He'll launch a hostile tender offer," Klein answered. "Our sources tell us he got a huge commitment from Citibank last night to support the bid. Three and a half billion dollars' worth. And Rose has a shelf registration parked at the SEC that'll let him issue

109

another billion dollars in long-term bonds very quickly. But, if there's any delay on the bond issuance, my mole tells me Citibank will bridge it, that they'll front the billion in bonds. That's why they gave him three and a half. So, even if we call our friend at the SEC, it wouldn't help. A shelf registration's pretty much good to go. Our friend wouldn't be able to hold up the bond issuance for long. And besides, Rose would just draw down the other billion from Citibank."

"Where's CIS trading right now?"

"Forty-three a share. Which makes the whole company worth about a billion and a half."

"Rose will have to pay a lot more than forty-three a share to get control of it, won't he?"

"Sure. We've checked with our people on Wall Street. They tell us he'll probably have to pay nearly ninety a share, which would make the thing worth over three billion." Klein hesitated. "Unfortunately, like I said, Rose's war chest from Citibank is already bigger than that."

"Shit," Beck hissed. "Don't we know someone at Citibank who can help us?"

Klein took in a long, aggravated breath. "Not anymore."

Beck eased back into the chair, trying to

relax, but that was impossible now. He was too hyped up on the pills and coffee. He moved to the edge of the seat, wringing his hands, feeling the perspiration drenching his palms. He could only imagine what his blood pressure was at this point. "How long would it take Rose to get CIS once he announced a tender offer?"

Klein thought for a moment. "I'd have to check the regulations, but I think the tender offer has to be out there for a few weeks to give the shareholders time to decide if they want to sell their shares into it. I believe it's the Williams Act that covers tender offers. Rose has to put a big announcement in the *Wall Street Journal* and the *New York Times* letting everyone know what he's doing. Then he has to mail documents to each and every shareholder giving them specifics of how the whole thing will work. If enough shares are tendered, then Trafalgar controls CIS. My guess is that if it all goes according to plan, Rose will be in full control of CIS within six weeks, maybe sooner."

"Christ." Beck leaned forward and tapped the coffee table with his fingers. "What if another company topped his bid?"

"I think the whole process starts over. What I mean is, the new bidder has to make the same big announcement in the newspa-

111

pers. Then they've got to mail their stuff out to the shareholders as well." Klein leaned forward, too, so his shoes were flat on the floor. "Is that what you're thinking about doing, Peter? Trying to find someone else to buy CIS?"

Beck's left knee was bouncing up and down wildly. "I'm just trying to think of every angle. I absolutely *cannot* let Rose get CIS. The company is so key to our operation. That's how we pay all of our agents, how we fund all of their activities, how we keep the bases in business. Here and abroad."

"We could always park that function somewhere else," Klein pointed out. "It would be a pain in the ass, I'll grant you, but we could do it."

As the executive director of The Fourth Order, Peter Beck knew everything — *all* of the I-4's secrets. Despite how close he and Klein had gotten over the last few years, he hadn't told Klein everything. It was never a good idea to do that, to bring someone below you that far inside the circle. But now he felt like he had to let him in further. They'd never been faced with anything like this before, and he was going to need Klein up to speed on everything about CIS if they were going to make it through this thing unscathed.

"CIS also hides and runs Project Spyder," Beck explained quietly, watching the shock register on Klein's face. Klein knew about Spyder, but he didn't know the details. Not even that it was hidden inside CIS.

Spyder was the code name for a crack team of IT specialists that monitored every financial transaction in the world. And a massive super computer the team used, buried in a remote CIS location, which was armed with the most powerful detection software ever built. Spyder traced deposits, withdrawals, and transfers made at thousands and thousands of bank branches around the world on a daily basis. As everyone in the intelligence community knew, if you followed the money long enough, ultimately you found the criminals. The world knew that the United States government was watching money move — that had been widely reported in the press for some time — but they had no idea the extent to which the Feds were watching. With Spyder, Beck could unearth intimate details of anyone's life because it was too difficult to use cash for everything in today's world, especially if you were a terrorist organization planning worldwide attacks. You couldn't just throw a few thousand dol-

113

lars in a suitcase, hop on a plane, and support the attacks on the World Trade Center towers and the Pentagon. It didn't work that way. You had to move lots of money and you had to move it many times, mostly over bank wires. Truth was, Project Spyder had become the most effective means ever devised of detecting terrorist plots in their early stages.

Did it violate the civil rights of millions of innocent citizens in the United States and abroad? Absolutely. Had it saved many, many lives because it had alerted the agents of The Fourth Order to impending acts of horrific terrorism? Absolutely. Had I-4 agents used information gleaned from Spyder for personal reasons, including vendettas? Absolutely. Was the bigger picture more important than a few minor abuses by insiders? Were the lives of many more important than the lives of a few, even if some of those few were innocent?

Beck blinked, realizing that for the first time since he'd become ED of The Fourth Order, he hadn't been able to answer that question to himself without any hesitation. For the first time since he'd taken over, there was doubt. He gathered himself quickly. He couldn't let Klein see that he'd suddenly lost his conviction, even if it was

114

just a temporary lapse.

"Wow," Klein muttered. "Now I get it."

"What if Rose gets only a small majority in the tender offer?" Beck wanted to know, possibilities zipping through his mind, trying to distract himself from the uncertainty that had crept into his world. "Like fifty-five percent? What then? Does CIS stay independent?"

"Probably not. Again, I'd have to check, but in most states, once you get a majority, even if it's just fifty-one percent, it's a done deal. People who decided not to tender their shares don't have a choice at that point. They get the cash they would have gotten if they'd tendered their shares and that's that."

"Damn it. Well, didn't we build all that poison pill stuff into CIS's by-laws and charter? A staggered board, golden parachutes —"

"We did," Klein interrupted, "but the bottom line is that most of the time all that stuff doesn't really amount to a hill of beans. Besides, Rose knows how to get around it. He and his sidekick David Cortez have made, like, eleven or twelve acquisitions over the past five years. They know the ins and outs of this crap as well as anyone in the game right now. I looked at all the poison pills the companies Rose

115

bought over the last five years had in place before he made the acquisitions, and he's been able to blow them apart in a couple of weeks after taking over. Most times his strategy is a classic bear hug. He makes his first offer one he knows the shareholders will love so that if the board even starts whispering about turning it down, about fighting him off, they get death threats."

Beck felt his heart rate ratchet up a few notches, unable to decide if it was the yellow pills or panic. He hated being outmaneuvered. But, just as Bill Granger had warned, Rose was turning out to be quite an adversary. Too bad he wasn't on their side. Maybe, now that Beck thought about it, they could change that. Maybe they could make him see the error of his ways. Wouldn't that be something?

"I thought we had enough CIS stock parked with friends that this wasn't going to be a problem," Klein spoke up.

Beck didn't feel like rehashing his conversation with Granger. "Names and faces change," he growled. "And, like you said, if the offer's high enough, shareholders fold even if they are supposed to be our friends." He spat. "Money changes everything."

Klein raised an eyebrow. "Seems like we should have hidden Spyder and the bases in a privately held company where we'd never have had to worry about a hostile takeover."

There it was again, Klein's penchant for pointing out failures. "Seems like you ought to —" Beck caught himself in the nick of time. Infighting wouldn't do anyone any good at this point. "There weren't any privately held companies that could handle what we needed, especially with Spyder. They didn't have all the foreign offices. And Bill Granger is as loyal as they come. Which is more important than anything."

"Maybe we should have bought CIS a few years ago, through one of the trusts."

It was all Beck could do not to explode. "Tom, I'm not going to sit here and listen to you second-guess me, damn it."

"Sorry," Klein said quietly.

Klein had finally realized he'd gone too far, Beck could see. But, God, sometimes it took him forever to catch on. "Michael Rose cannot acquire CIS," Beck said, his voice shaking. "Tom, I want you on the phone with our friend as soon as it's light out. I want him in touch with the other board members all morning, telling them that they can't give Rose the okay to move forward. We have to do everything in our power, short of killing him, to make certain Rose doesn't get CIS."

Klein looked up. "Maybe we *should* kill him. Maybe that's the answer."

Beck gazed at Klein for a few moments, then glanced out the window into the darkness. Like an animal, Klein was starting to like the taste of blood.

No good.

16

"Kat."

She was vaguely aware of fingers touching her shoulder.

"Kat."

She moaned, coming to consciousness. She'd been dreaming about having a romantic dinner with an older man who really seemed to care for her.

"Kat!"

"What? Jesus, *what?*" Katherine Hanson sat up in bed and rubbed her eyes. First light was streaming into the room from around the edges of the blinds she'd pulled down before climbing into bed last night — alone for the third time in four nights. She hated the way their bedroom faced southeast, directly at the morning sun this time of year. Hated the fact that Joey wouldn't let her buy curtains to go around the blinds because he was too cheap. "What do you want?" She knew what he wanted. What he always wanted in the morning.

Joey slid into bed behind her, pressing himself against her. "I miss you."

"Then why'd you sleep on the couch again last night?" she asked, yawning.

"I'm sorry. I was watching the Comedy Channel. Dice Clay was on. I haven't seen that one in a long time. He's a funny fucker."

She dropped her head back down on the pillow, moving away from him. "Great."

"Let's make love."

"Please let me sleep," she begged. She'd anticipated this. "I've got to pull a double today." She was a bartender at Clyde's Restaurant in Georgetown — a historic district just west of downtown Washington that was known for its shopping and dining. "Lunch *and* dinner."

"Oh, come on. Please."

"No!" she snapped, pulling away. "Get off me."

He reached out for her shoulder. "Hey, what's your problem?"

"My problem?" She pried his hand off her, jumped out of bed then spun back around so she was facing him, hands on her hips. *"My problem?"* She was fed up with him. "You sleep on the couch all night, then crawl up here at six in the morning because you want sex. Then you go back to sleep until two in the afternoon while I go out and work so we can eat because you can't hold down a job for more than a couple of months." She'd seen that look in Michael Rose's eyes last night at the restaurant when Joey had appeared out of nowhere behind her, and it was haunting her. A look that told her Rose couldn't believe she was married to such a loser. A look she'd seen many times before but had paid no attention to up until now because she really loved Joey. For the first time she understood what everyone had been trying to tell her since even before she'd married the guy last year. He *was* a loser. "The worst part is that you'll sit here all afternoon glued to the computer looking at porn while I'm out there slinging drinks."

"You're right, baby," Joey said softly, patting the mattress. "I'll get another job soon, I promise. There's plenty of real estate agencies I can talk to. I'll have a desk and a phone in a week. Guarantee it. Now, come back to bed."

She shut her eyes tightly and crossed her arms over her breasts. Thank God they didn't have children. That would make it so much harder to leave him. "Go back downstairs, will you?"

"What's wrong with you?" he demanded, his demeanor souring. "Did you go back into Morton's last night and give that guy your number? That guy you were talking to at the door?"

They'd driven separate cars to dinner — she was coming out from the city after working the lunch shift at Clyde's, he was coming into McLean from their townhouse in Manassas, another twenty miles west. That had given her the opportunity to go back into the restaurant without Joey knowing. After she'd kissed him at his car and said she couldn't wait to get home with him, she'd hurried back into the bar, found Rose and given him her number. Then she'd raced home at eighty miles an hour, dodging traffic all the way, managing to make it in the door of their townhouse just a few minutes after Joey had. He'd given her a suspicious look from the couch, but hadn't asked any questions.

"Of course not. I didn't go back in."

"I saw the way you were looking at him."

She'd spotted Rose across the bar at Morton's before he'd spotted her, which was unusual. Usually men spotted her first. It wasn't that she was stuck up about her looks, that was just how it usually happened. She caught men staring at her all the time, and she knew she made herself easier to spot because of the way she dressed — little skirts and tops. But she liked showing off her body, she worked hard to stay in shape. Truth be known, more and more she was enjoying the looks other men were giving her.

A few seconds later she'd seen Rose glance at her out of the corner of her eye while she flirted with the two young professionals. Then she'd given him the stare, and she'd known immediately that he was interested. She'd loved how cool he was later when they'd run into each other in the doorway.

"You're crazy."

"Oh yeah?" Joey climbed out of bed and looked around for a moment, then spotted her purse lying on a chair near the closet. He sprinted to it, rooted through it quickly, and yanked her cell phone out. "Why's it turned off?" he demanded, flipping it on. "And why's your purse up here? You always keep it downstairs."

She caught her breath. Christ, if Rose had called, all hell would break loose. She took a step toward Joey, then held up.

"What's the matter?" He'd seen her subtle move. "Worried I'll find something?"

"No."

The phone beeped several times, indicating that there were new voice mails.

She watched him scroll through her missed calls screen, checking the numbers. "Joey, I —"

"You're lucky this time," he said, teeth clenched, "just your friends." He tossed the phone back down in her purse. "Why'd you turn it off last night? You never turn it off."

"I was tired and Margie's been calling me all the —"

"And you brought your purse up here last night," he said again. "Usually you leave it downstairs. Why'd you do that?"

"I don't know, I just —"

"Why'd you take a step toward me just then? You worried he might have called back?"

"No!" she shouted. "I'm sick of you spying on me all the time. That's all."

"I have to spy on you," he retorted. "You're always flirting with other men."

She groaned. "You're a jerk. Don't be so immature. I never flirt with anyone."

"What about those two guys who were all over you when I got to the bar last night?" he said, moving toward her.

"I was just talking to them."

"Didn't look like just talk to me. The guy in the red tie had his hand on your leg when

124

I got there."

He was directly in front of her now, his face inches from hers. "You're such an ass," she muttered.

"What did you say to me?"

"I said, you're such an *ass!* Leave me alone."

He stared at her hard for several moments, eyes bugging out, then finally stalked out of the room.

As she listened to him pad heavily down the stairs, her shoulders slumped in relief. She'd never seen that kind of rage in his eyes before.

17

When Rose came in the back door through the garage, Jamie and Glenn were sitting close together on the couch in the family room — he'd called to tell Trudy he was only a few minutes away so the kids would be ready. But he hadn't said anything else to her. Jamie was clutching an old teddy bear Rose didn't even know she had anymore, and Glenn was simply staring straight ahead, glasses perched at the end of his nose.

Rose walked to where they sat and knelt down, putting a hand on each of their knees. "Where's Trudy?"

Jamie sniffed. "Upstairs."

Trudy must have heard it in his voice, Rose realized. And she probably felt uncomfortable about being with them when he broke the news, understanding that it was something for the family to deal with alone. She'd only lived with them for a few months.

Rose swallowed hard, then looked up into their faces. Both of them were staring down at him expectantly, eyes wide open, not blinking. "Kids, I've got something bad to tell —"

Jamie leaped up off the couch and raced for the stairs before he could finish.

"Munch— Honey. *Stop!*" He glanced at Glenn. There were already tears rolling down both of the boy's cheeks.

"Go ahead, Dad," Glenn mumbled. "Go after her. She needs you."

Rose took the boy's face in both hands and kissed his forehead. "I'll be back. We'll talk. Okay?"

Glenn nodded.

"You're really growing up, son."

"Uh-huh."

Rose jogged to the stairs, then took them three at a time. Jamie's door was locked when he reached it. "Open up, sweetheart," he said loudly, banging on the door. "Open up!" Trudy's room was just down the hall and Rose saw the door crack open. "Trudy?"

The door opened wider and the young woman stuck her head out. "Yes, Mr. Rose?"

"Will you go downstairs and make sure Glenn's okay?" he asked as she moved toward him. He took a deep breath and shook his head. "Sheila died in a car accident tonight."

Trudy's gaze dropped to the hall carpet and her lips began to tremble.

"I'm sorry to have to tell you like this, but I . . ." His voice faded.

"It's okay," she murmured. "I'm so sorry." She gave him a hug, then headed down the steps.

Rose watched her go. She was a nice kid. He turned and rapped on Jamie's door again. "Jamie. Honey, come on." He could hear her sobbing inside. He grabbed the knob with both hands and twisted hard, but it didn't give. He reached up and ran his fingers along the molding above the door, searching for the wire he'd put up there last time she'd done this. He found it, pulled it down, inserted it in the small hole of the knob, pushed and twisted the knob hard. This time it turned and the door gave way.

Jamie was on her four-poster queen-sized bed, facedown in a sea of pillows. Rose moved to where she lay, sat down beside her and massaged her shoulder gently. "Sweetheart, let me try to help you with what you're —"

"Don't touch me," she cried.

Rose pulled back. "Jamie, I know this is

terrible, but let's deal with it together," he urged softly, rubbing her shoulder again. "Let's deal with it as a family."

"I told you not to touch me," she snapped.

"What's wrong with you?" Rose demanded. "Why are you treating me like this?"

She sat up on the bed, tears streaming down her face. "If you'd just been there for Mom, she'd be alive. It's your fault, Daddy. It's your fault she's dead!"

18

"Michael?"

Rose looked up from behind the desk of his spacious office at Trafalgar. It was a corner office on the twenty-seventh floor — the top floor — of the tallest building in McLean. From it he had a gorgeous, panoramic view of the sun-splashed winter morning, Washington, DC, off in the distance to the east. But he couldn't have cared less right now. He was so tired he could hardly focus on the memo he was trying to read, forget enjoying a view, and so wrung out from what Jamie had said a few hours ago. It seemed like that had hit him even harder than Sheila's death.

"Hi, Tammy," he said quietly to the woman leaning into his office. "Come on in. Close the door, will you?"

Tammy Sable was vice president in charge of corporate communications at Trafalgar. The one responsible for handling all the

details of the tender offer Trafalgar would make for CIS once the board gave its approval to go ahead with the acquisition. She would coordinate with the *Wall Street Journal* and the *New York Times* on the huge announcements that would run in each newspaper. She would demand the complete CIS ownership list from the company's registration agent so Trafalgar could solicit the stockholders. She would field questions from CIS stockholders once the tender offer material had been sent out.

Rose had hired Tammy from a competitor five years ago — two weeks after he'd become CFO — at twice her then-current salary because she had a reputation as being the best in the business at what she did. He knew he was going to be making acquisition after acquisition and he needed an ace in that position. She hadn't disappointed him.

"You all right, Michael?" she asked in a gentle tone as she sat down in the chair in front of his desk. "I hate to say this, but you look, well, awful."

Rose managed a half grin. "And you look as wonderful as ever."

Tammy was corporate all the way. She always wore a suit, the bottom of her skirt never falling above her knees, always wore a blouse buttoned up to her neck, always wore her hair up, and never wore pumps with heels that were more than two inches. She was attractive — tall, blond, and slim — but her facial features had a hard edge to them. As far as Rose was aware, she'd never been married, but that was all he really knew about her personal life. She was a workaholic — always seemed to be here at the office when he was and always had an excuse for why she couldn't make company functions. She never came to the holiday party at the end of the year; never came to the Fourth of July party; always went home at night when Rose held the annual senior executive off-site at a cozy bed-and-breakfast in the mountains west of Washington, even though he reserved a nice room for her at the inn. There were rumors she was a lesbian, but he didn't care if she was or not. As far as he was concerned, what people did on their own time was their own business, as long as they didn't try to push their agendas on him.

"Are you all right?" she asked again.

Rose leaned back and closed his eyes. "Please keep this to yourself." She was going to find out soon enough anyway, and he didn't want her feeling like he didn't confide in her. Other than David Cortez, he was closer to Tammy than anyone else at Trafalgar.

She sat forward in the chair. "Of course. What is it?"

He gazed at her for a few moments before answering, making certain he could say this without breaking down. He didn't want her to see him like that. "My wife died in a car accident last night."

Tammy caught her breath and put her hands to her mouth. "Oh, my God," she exclaimed quietly. "What are you doing here?"

Jamie had asked him the same question an hour ago as he was leaving the house. Not with words, but with her expression. As he'd backed out of the garage, he'd seen her staring down from her bedroom window, a fierce, accusatory glare in her eyes. But maybe it wasn't that he was leaving them a few hours after telling them their mother had died that was the problem, he realized now. Maybe she really did think he was responsible for Sheila's death. Maybe that hadn't been a knee-jerk reaction as he'd hoped, her just striking out at whoever was around because she was so distraught. Maybe she'd actually been glad to see him go this morning.

He'd told Jamie and Glenn to stay home

from school today. Asked Trudy to call both schools and tell them just that there had been a family emergency. Fortunately, the accident had been discovered too late last night for the story to run in any of today's local newspapers. At least the kids wouldn't have to deal with all the phone calls today. They'd have a little bit of time to deal with their grief privately.

"We have a board meeting," Rose spoke up.

"I know, but, I mean —"

"It's a very important board meeting," he interrupted. "I have to be here. As soon as it's over I'm going home."

"Is there anything I can do for you?" she asked. "Anything at all?"

She was wonderful. Tough when it came to business, but a caring person beyond that. "No, but thanks." He pushed the memo to the side of his desk. "I need to tell you what the meeting's about."

"Okay."

"We're going to make another acquisition." After twelve acquisitions together, Rose didn't have to tell her that she needed to keep everything confidential. She knew the drill by now. "It's a company called CIS."

"That big information technology company downtown?"

He saw he'd caught her off guard. Not because he was going to try another hostile takeover. She knew him well enough by now not to be surprised by that. It was something else. "What is it? What's the matter?"

"Um . . . well, it's not really for me to say."

"No, come on, Tammy. We've known each other too long. Spill it."

She shifted uncomfortably in her seat. "It's just that information technology doesn't seem to fit with Trafalgar. Not to me, anyway. We drill for and transport oil and gas in the energy units, we make heavy equipment and chemicals in the manufacturing units. We don't do anything like IT, though." She put her hands up like she thought he was going to be aggravated at her for saying this. "But, look, you're the guy who's taken Trafalgar from nothing to the *Fortune* 100. You're the guy Wall Street loves. It isn't Colin, it's you. It's just that I know we'll get a lot of questions from our investors."

"Which is why I'm telling you now, so you have lots of time to get ready. I know this acquisition doesn't fit with our company. At least, it doesn't seem to on the surface. But David and I have a plan. Which I'll fill you in on after I've got the board's okay."

Tammy grinned. "I'm sure you do have a plan. You and David are always up to something." She smoothed her long skirt. "Are you going for board approval today? Is that what the meeting is about?"

"Yup."

"You'll probably get some flak from them, too."

Rose took a deep breath, reached for his coffee mug and drank the last sip. "Believe me, I know I will."

"Well, let me at least try to help in a small way." She stood up, leaned over the desk, took the mug from him and headed for the door. "You're going to be needing lots of this today," she called over her shoulder. "I'll make sure your cup never gets empty."

He watched her go, thankful that he had such a loyal team around him. He nodded to himself. Loyalty, that was the key. The most important thing you could have from your people. Something he hadn't gotten from his wife. At least, not according to David Cortez.

19

"What's wrong with you?"

"Nothing." Kat moved past Margie into the living room of the small, two-bedroom apartment. "Is Susan here?" she asked, looking around. Susan was Margie's roommate. All three of them worked together at Clyde's in Georgetown.

"No, she stayed with her boyfriend last night." Margie moved quickly to where Kat stood, a searching look in her eye. "Did you have an argument with Joey last night?" she asked, her voice suddenly on edge. "Did you?"

Kat let out a deep sigh. Margie was constantly into everyone else's business. She'd probably be the definition of a busybody if you checked Webster's. She cared that a friend might be hurt or upset, but it was curiosity that drove her. "We had a little tiff. That's all."

Margie's eyes narrowed. "Did he get

physical with you?"

"No, of course not."

Margie gazed at Kat a few moments longer. "He did, I can tell."

"He did *not.*"

"I knew there was something wrong with that guy. I never should have let you marry him. I should have kidnapped you before you walked down that aisle." Margie headed toward the wall phone in the kitchen. "Forget about it, I'm calling the cops."

"You're not calling anyone," Kat said loudly, trotting after Margie and grabbing the phone out of her hand. "I just came over here because I want to use your computer."

Margie looked at Kat curiously. "What's wrong with yours? You guys have one."

"Yeah." She tried to think of a lie off the top of her head but couldn't. She should have figured Margie would ask all kinds of questions and come up with a cover story on the way over, but it was too late now. "Okay, okay. I don't want Joey to see what I'm looking at on the Internet," she admitted. "He's good with all that technology stuff. I know he checks out the sites I've been to on the Web when I'm not home. He's so suspicious of me."

Margie's eyes bugged out. "Ooh, this sounds juicy, girl. Sure, you can use my computer. As long as I get to see where you go."

The world was just one big soap opera, Kat thought to herself. "I can't get any privacy, can I?"

"Nope," Margie agreed with a laugh, leading Kat down a short hallway.

Kat stopped in the doorway of the cramped, cluttered bedroom. There were clothes strewn everywhere and four Coke cans and a half-eaten piece of pizza on a paper plate on the nightstand. "When was the last time you cleaned up in here?" she asked, her upper lip curling at the thought of what might be crawling around beneath this mess.

"A month, probably," Margie answered, pulling out a spindly chair in front of the table the computer was on. She picked up a bra draped over the screen and threw it on the floor near her closet, then patted the seat of the chair. "Have at it."

Kat sat down, put her purse on the table and clicked to the Internet. When the search engine was ready, she typed in Trafalgar Industries, clicked "go," and waited for the company's home page to appear.

"Trafalgar Industries?" Margie stuck a piece of bubble gum in her mouth and started smacking her lips. "What are you doing? I

thought maybe you were going to some on-line dating site."

"You'll see."

When Trafalgar's home page came up, Kat clicked on the "People" section of the site, then went to the "Senior Executive" subsection. Michael Rose was the second executive listed, just below a man named Colin Freese who was the CEO. She clicked on his name and his picture came right up.

Margie leaned over Kat's shoulder to get a better look. "Mmm, interesting. I like what I see." She patted Kat's shoulder. "Details, girl, details. What's going on here? Am I looking at why you and Joey got into it last night?"

"Stop it." Kat quickly scanned Rose's bio. "Don't give me a hard time."

"Come on," Margie pushed, annoyed that she wasn't getting answers. "Tell me what happened."

"Nothing."

"This is silly. You know I'll get the story out of you sooner or later. I'll get you drunk tonight after work and then you know you'll tell me. So you might as well tell me now."

Kat rose from the chair and moved to the window, dodging piles of clothes as she went. She peered through the slats of the dusty blinds, half expecting to see Joey's truck out there in the snowy parking lot. "I'm tired of Joey's crap. I'm tired of the way he treats me." She groaned. "He slept on the couch last night, then he woke me up at six this morning looking for sex. He can't keep a job, and he looks at porn all day. I mean, *really.*"

Margie waved disgustedly. "He's such a loser," she agreed, twirling her hair with her finger. She had short, dark curly locks. "He couldn't make money even if he worked at a mint. You should have run away from him as fast as you could at the beginning. I told you that when you first met him. Everyone did." She gestured at the screen. "What's the deal with Mr. Corporate?"

"I met him last night at Morton's. He was at the bar. I was waiting for Joey to show up for dinner."

"Joey took you to *Morton's* last night?" Margie asked, surprised. "That's kind of expensive for him, isn't it?"

"I paid."

"Of course." Margie sat down in front of the computer. "So, this Michael Rose here," she said, scrolling through the information, "he's good-looking, but is he nice? He looks kind of intense."

Everyone seemed nice when you first met them, Kat thought to herself. It wasn't until after you'd known them awhile that you got a better idea of what they were really all about. After they'd gotten tired of putting up that false front. Sometimes even then you never really knew for sure. People always had bad things hiding behind secret doors of their personalities. "Seems like it. He's very charming."

Margie grinned. "Charming? I don't think I've ever heard you use that word to describe a man before."

"He's smooth." It wasn't like she'd had that much time with Rose. But she could still tell he was a cool customer. A man who probably didn't mind using people. Which was something she needed to be careful of.

Margie leaned back in the chair and folded her arms. "Says here he's married. Got a couple of kids, too."

"Really?"

"He's older. Forty-three. Jesus, since when did you turn into a home-wrecker?"

Kat glanced away from the window. "Why am I a home-wrecker all of a sudden? Nothing happened, we just talked."

"Did you get his number?"

"No."

Margie stared for a few moments. "Oh, no," she said loudly, "you gave him *your number*."

Kat stared at Margie for a few moments, then winced. "Yeah, I did," she admitted.

"Has he called you yet?"

"No."

Margie rose from the chair and moved to where Kat was standing. "There's no future with this guy, honey. He'll never leave his family. It would be too expensive. His wife and her attorney with the take-no-prisoners attitude would rake him over the coals. This guy has spent his career getting to where he is. No offense, but he isn't going to blow it all on you. Even if you are the prettiest girl in town." She hesitated. "Which you are."

"Thanks, Margie. That's nice of you to say." Kat clenched her fists at her sides. "I know what you're saying, too, about him not leaving his family. I mean, it's not like I'm even thinking that way. I don't even know him. But there's something about him, Margie. I felt this real strong attraction to him right away. We stared at each other over the bar for a few —"

"No, no, no," Margie said loudly, throwing her hands in the air and waving them. "I don't want to hear it. Yech, you're gonna make me sick." She rolled her eyes. "He's trouble, nothing but trouble, Kat. If he calls, don't call him back. Let him go. You hear me? Let him go. He'll use you, and that'll be it."

Trouble sounded right, Kat realized. But it also sounded a lot better than what she had now. "You're right," she agreed quietly. "I should do that, I should just let him go." There was no chance in hell of that happening. If Michael Rose didn't call her in the next twenty-four hours, she'd go looking for him. She shrugged. "What was I thinking?"

20

The atmosphere in the Trafalgar boardroom was electric. Rose sensed it the moment he walked through the darkly stained, oak double doors. You could have heard a pin drop on the long shiny table, and the ten men and two women had their game faces on — lips set in grim, straight lines, eyes narrow and focused, none of them reclining in the big, comfortable leather chairs that surrounded the table. Even Colin Freese, who, in addition to being the CEO of Trafalgar was also its chairman, seemed pre-occupied as he sat at the far end of the table. Usually, he was Mr. Personality before he called the meeting to order, regaling the board members close to him with stories of his latest adventure while he smoked his favorite pipe. Not today. He was smoking his pipe, but he wasn't talking about his anaconda hunt in South America.

Rose sat at the opposite end of the table

from Freese, as he always did, with Cortez directly to his right. Rose and Cortez weren't technically board members, but they attended every meeting, even when the agenda didn't include an acquisition. The board members always had questions about Trafalgar's financial performance and how Wall Street was rating the company's progress. So Freese had Rose and Cortez attend these meetings to answer the tough questions because he couldn't.

Freese rapped on the table with his pipe to start the meeting, the way he always did. "Let's get going," he announced loudly. "We've got a lot of ground to cover today. Does everyone have a copy of the minutes from the last meeting? I want to get them approved before we —"

"Colin, let's not waste time with all that administrative bullshit."

Rose glanced up from his copy of the minutes. The man who'd interrupted Freese was Grant Boyd, a senior partner at Watson Thatcher, a large, prominent law firm in Washington, DC. He was a white-haired, red-faced, tough-talking son of a bitch who had no problem whatsoever asking the hard questions. In fact, he seemed to enjoy it — the only board member who came across that way, who was rude more often than he was polite. Boyd and Rose had gotten into it several times at these meetings over the past five years, and now Rose knew exactly who had "pissed all over" his presentation, as Freese had put it.

"I'm a busy man," Boyd continued in his heavy Georgia drawl. "Just like everyone around this table is," he said, nodding at several board members, trying to reach out to them in his backhanded style. "Let's cut to the chase, let's get right to it." He pointed at Rose and Cortez. "The Lone Ranger and Tonto down there at the other end of the table want to buy Computer Information Systems. A company that doesn't have anything to do with what Trafalgar does now, with the markets that our company has been successful in up to this point."

Out of the corner of his eye Rose saw Cortez bristle, saw David's fists clench in rage, his jaw tighten. Boyd's attitude aggravated Rose as much as it did Cortez, but he kept his expression impassive. He'd learned over the years to control his outward shows of emotion during these meetings. Learned that showing emotion was the quickest way to lose the board's support on a deal. He'd been turned down on the first two acquisitions he'd proposed, and it had hurt. But he'd figured out what he was doing wrong the second time. They didn't want passion out of him. Didn't want table slamming wrath-of-God, we're-going-to-take-over-the-world kind of stuff. They wanted stone-cold objective analysis.

"This board has done an excellent job guiding the management team over the past five years," Boyd went on. "We've been strong when we've needed to be strong. Put our collective feet down and reined in the younger people who might have led us places we would have ultimately been very sorry to have gone." He hesitated, for effect, making sure he caught a few more eyes before continuing. "This is one of those times. We cannot let Mr. Rose take us down the path he is suggesting. Even if we won CIS in a takeover battle, and it turned out to be a good move financially, we'd still be sorry." Boyd held up his hand. A signal to the others that he was changing directions for a moment. "Any way you look at this thing, it would get ugly. And we'd make a lot of enemies in this town we don't want to make. If there's one town we don't want enemies in, it's this one. But putting all of that aside," he said, raising his voice to make his point, "we must send our cowboy and Indian a message. And that message is this: We need to stick to our knitting. We can't go buying companies that operate in industries we don't know anything about." Boyd leaned forward, stuck his chin out, and glared down the table at Rose and Cortez. "Ladies and gentlemen, I am dead set against this acquisition for a lot of reasons, and I'm sure everyone else in here agrees with me. I suggest we put this matter to a vote immediately so we can all get on with our day, to things that really matter." He turned toward Freese. "What say you, Mr. Chairman?"

Beck glanced at his watch. It was one-fifteen and he could feel his strength ebbing. Another few hours and he'd be down for the count, snoring loudly in an upstairs bedroom of the big house no matter what emergency was unfolding. He just hoped he could stay awake until they'd gotten definitive word out of northern Virginia. He glanced out the window. The view below him was beautiful — two big horse farms covered with several inches of pristine snow. He shook his head. It would be nice to be able to truly stop and smell the flowers, or whatever normal people did. At least for a while. Maybe forever.

He wasn't just tired because he'd been awake for three straight days. He was getting tired of the fight, too. Of constantly living in the shadows, of making life-and-death decisions every day, of killing innocent people in addition to the ones who wanted to wreak terror around the world. The consolation was that the I-4's efforts had made a difference, a big difference. He was convinced that the cutthroat, license-to-kill tactics were working. Terrorist organizations around the world were finding it harder and harder to carry out the kinds of massive attacks they wanted to, proven by the fact that there hadn't been many lately and that I-4 agents were assassinating more and more of the top terrorist leaders on a regular basis — as soon as they filled vacant spots almost. Which also proved that the only way to fight the bastards was on their own disgusting level. With brutality. With murder. For a good man, that took a heavy toll. Because inevitably you killed innocent people, too.

Beck turned away from the window when Klein walked back into the room. "Any word, Tom?"

Klein shook his head.

"When was the last time you spoke to Mr. Boyd?"

"Thirty minutes ago. We still only had five board members in our camp for sure, but Boyd had two more people to talk to." Klein grinned. "Including the one with the tax problem."

Beck chuckled. He was just glad he was in control of Spyder. Those people and their computers seemed to be able to find anything. It would be awful to be on the other side. "Yup. Thanks to Spyder, Mr. Rose is about to be ambushed by the man he least expects it from."

"I think it would be premature to put the CIS matter to a vote just yet," Freese answered deliberately. "I think we should hear what Mike and David have to say first." He looked around. "Does anyone else have any comments before I ask them to begin their presentation?"

The rest of the board members shook their heads.

"Good." Freese glanced at Boyd with a raised eyebrow, then pointed down the table at Rose. "Go ahead, Lone Ranger, it's your corral. Just watch out for Marshall Earp over here."

Rose watched Boyd's face turn a bright red. "Thank you, Mr. Chairman, I appreciate the chance to present this very attractive opportunity to you and the rest of the board." He always spoke formally in this setting, as did everyone. "Please turn to

151

page three in the presentation deck. We'll get started."

21

Sherman LeClair was a bitter, bitter man.

He was also a calculating man. He'd lived his entire life dedicated to a single mantra, to one lovely little cliché: Don't get mad, get even. At least, don't show your enemy that you're mad, his father had always counseled. Then he'll be alert, and you always want the element of surprise on your side if you're going to inflict the most devastating payback.

So, when LeClair had been abandoned by his best friend after being the man's loyal servant and toiling in the background doing the dirty work for almost thirty years, he'd faded quietly into the darkness without shouting or screaming. But even as he was sitting on the couch in the Oval Office, being fired and degraded, he'd been planning his revenge. Even as he'd been staring at his old friend, the president of the United States, listening to how badly he was going to get screwed but how he still needed to be a team player and take it like a man. For the good of the country. Translated — for the good of the administration.

LeClair had needed an outlet for his bitterness and rage. A way to distract his mind from the awful things he wanted to do to his new ex–best friend. From the terrible and inaccurate accusations that had been written and reported about him in the national press and on nightly talk shows for months afterward. He'd always heard that physical activity was an effective way to distract the brain, great therapy for the mind. That fly-fishing and hitting golf balls on the range were especially good for people over forty-five. To do either effectively, he'd been told, you had to concentrate, you couldn't think of anything else. He'd tried golf when he was younger and remembered being more frustrated at the end of his lesson than at the beginning. So he'd chosen fly-fishing. Over the last two years, since the debacle, he'd become very good at it.

He smiled as he drew the forty feet of fluorescent green fly line and ten feet of clear monofilament leader back over his right shoulder one more time, hesitated a few moments as he let the line load in the air behind him, then gently but firmly pushed the nine-foot graphite Winston rod to the ten o'clock position in front of his body. The line shot forward and to the right of the drift boat, then settled on the surface of the picturesque Blackfoot River, thirty miles northeast of Missoula, Montana. The large streamer pattern at the end of the leader, tied to resemble a small rainbow trout, plopped down on the riffled water, then disappeared beneath the surface. Immediately, LeClair mended the floating line to the left, downstream. Put a big arc in the line by flipping the tip of his rod in a circular motion. Put the arc in the line so the water would pick up the line and the leader and therefore the streamer more quickly and whip it downstream. Which was entirely opposite of the normal method of mending — putting the arc in the line up into the current so it *wouldn't* have an effect on the line quickly and the lure would be left to drift more naturally for a few seconds. It went against everything he'd been taught up until now, but he'd learned to trust the young guide who was steering the boat.

"Nice cast," the guide muttered under his breath. He'd taught LeClair a lot over the last two years and was clearly enjoying how much the older man had picked up. "We ought to get something here."

When LeClair noticed a split-second hesitation of the strike indicator — a small piece of bright pink material affixed to the leader that floated on the surface — he lifted the rod high in the air.

"Got him!" the guide shouted as the tip of the rod bowed over almost 180 degrees. "That's a bull trout. No doubt. Good man!"

LeClair felt a rush of exhilaration as the huge fish started peeling off line and the reel whined. There were rainbows, browns, cutthroats, and brookies in this river as well, but none of them grew to the size of a big bull trout. LeClair had been stalking a trophy bull for a long time — caught a few smaller ones in the twenty-five-inch range — but hadn't hooked a giant yet. This one felt like a shark at the end of his line, he thought as the guide rowed the boat toward shallow water. So LeClair could get out and fight the fish from land. So he could run back upriver if the fish suddenly decided to take off that way.

Ten minutes later the fight was over and LeClair was kneeling in six inches of water near the shore holding a heaving forty-two-inch green-backed bull trout out in front of him with both hands so the guide could snap a couple of photos before they put the fish back into the cold, gin-clear water of the Blackfoot. When the camera work was done, LeClair carefully released the fish, making certain to hold its nose into the current so water would wash through its mouth and over its gills until it finally swam slowly away.

"Nice job," the guide said as he leaned on his long net, watching the trout disappear into the depths of the river. "Beautiful fish."

"Thanks, Roger." LeClair blew on his fingertips. He was wearing gloves, but the fingertips were cut out so he had more dexterity. They were wet and freezing. "That's the most fun I've had in a long time."

"Biggest fish I've ever seen in Montana." The young man held the camera up. "Can't wait to show the guys back at the fly shop. They wouldn't believe me without these."

LeClair's cell phone rang.

The guide groaned and rolled his eyes, looking up into the snow-covered mountains rising from the sides of the river like he was looking to the heavens for divine intervention. "Jesus, Sherman, didn't I tell you to leave that damn thing back in the truck? It ruins the experience for you, me, and —"

"Roger," LeClair said quietly as he removed the small phone from his fishing vest, "why don't you make us some coffee while

157

I'm gone?" He never raised his voice, even when he was so mad he could barely see straight. He'd learned how to do that from his father, too. "Got me?"

The young man nodded respectfully. In the two years they'd known each other, he'd never heard LeClair use that tone. But he recognized it instantly and all that it communicated: Young man, shut up and do your job. I'm paying you and I'm paying you well, and if my cell phone rings again, ask me if you can answer it like my secretary. "Yes, sir."

"Good lad." LeClair trudged off through the snow toward a grove of pine trees. "Hello."

"Buck?"

"Yes, this is Big Buck." Everything on this call would be in code.

"Big Buck, this is Eagle."

LeClair glanced back over his shoulder. The guide was busy doing as he'd been instructed — making coffee. "Hello, Eagle." He glanced at his watch. Eleven thirty mountain time, one thirty in northern Virginia. "What do you have?"

"Just confirmation that our friend the Oil Can is leading the fight against us at the meeting."

The Oil Can was code for Grant Boyd —

a reference to Oil Can Boyd, a Boston Red Sox pitcher from years ago. "Does he have the firepower?"

"Word is he has four other people in his corner, and there are two on the fence. If they get six, they can stop us."

"Did you give our man the weapon?"

"I did. Pete has the package."

Pete was code for Michael Rose, a reference to Pete Rose. LeClair loved baseball, always had. Now that his wife was gone, fly-fishing and baseball were his favorite things in the world. "Good. You'll call me when it's done."

"Yes, sir."

"Thank you."

LeClair flipped the cell phone closed and slipped it back into a side pocket of his fishing vest. It was absolutely imperative that Michael Rose and Trafalgar get CIS. Getting CIS was only the beginning — there would be a lot of hurdles to leap after that if they were going to slice the pig open for the world to see and let the whole thing run its course back to the White House — but CIS was where it had to start. The next few hours were going to be crucial, his chance to ultimately exorcise the bitterness that controlled him. His one chance at revenge. But there was nothing he could do right now except sit tight, and he hated not being in control. Hopefully, there was another big bull trout waiting for him in the depths of the Blackfoot that would take his mind off the payback he craved.

LeClair gazed up into the snowy mountains, covered by an unbroken coat of sweet-smelling pine trees. It was beautiful out here. Pristine and remote — they hadn't seen anyone since they'd left Missoula early this morning. This was some of the last untouched wilderness in the lower forty-eight. Maybe someday he'd actually be able to enjoy it.

22

"Ladies and gentlemen of the board, thank you for your attention."

Rose closed his copy of the presentation book. He'd been at it for an hour and a half, and he was drained, but exhilarated, too. He and Cortez had done a solid job of making the case for the CIS acquisition. He could see it in the eyes of most of the board members, in the way they were nodding along with what he was saying. Not in Grant Boyd's eyes, but Boyd was never going to be convinced that this was a good move.

"In summary," Rose continued, "David Cortez and I believe that the combination of Trafalgar and CIS will generate tremendous long-term benefits for our shareholders. On its own, CIS is a wonderful company, worth a great deal more than where the stock market values it today. That's the meat in this deal, what we can bank on right out of the box. That, by itself, CIS is a great investment." Rose hesitated for a moment, remembering for the first time since he'd started the presentation that Sheila was dead and that Jamie blamed him for it. He cleared his throat, hoping no one had noticed his momentary distraction. "The sizzle in the deal is all the benefits CIS brings to our other existing business units," he continued. "Their advanced IT products will make Trafalgar's energy and manufacturing divisions much more efficient and competitive, as well as enable us to access an entirely new *huge* customer, the federal government. CIS is deeply entrenched inside many of the large government agencies that could be big buyers of our products in both the energy and manufacturing units. Their connections in the agencies would be invaluable to us." He looked around. "Questions?"

"Have you contacted CIS yet?" one of the women wanted to know. "Have you had any preliminary discussions with them?"

Rose shook his head. "We wanted to wait until after this meeting. No point in getting Bill Granger all riled up for nothing." He saw that some of the people around the table didn't understand who Granger was. Mostly the out-of-towners. They hadn't mentioned his name in the presentation.

"Granger is the CEO of CIS."

"Would it be hostile?" Freese asked, striking a match and relighting his pipe. "Would they fight it?"

"Depends on the price."

"Bill Granger will fight this acquisition no matter what price Trafalgar offers," Boyd spoke up firmly.

"How do you know?"

"Granger and I have a mutual friend. The guy told me Granger is dead set against any acquisition. Especially any offer to buy CIS that comes from a company that isn't already in the information technology industry."

"That's so irresponsible," Cortez blurted out. "That flies in the face of his duty of loyalty to the CIS shareholders. He should always be looking out for their best interests, not his."

"Easy," Rose murmured, putting a hand on David's arm.

"CIS is currently trading around forty-three dollars a share, correct?" another board member asked. "Isn't that the number you guys had in the presentation?"

"Forty-four dollars and thirty cents as we speak," Cortez answered after pressing a few buttons on his PCS device and accessing the Internet. "It's gone up more than a buck a share since we've been in this meeting, and it's gone up on very heavy trading volume." He glanced around the table. "Looks like the rumors have already started."

Rose watched several of the board members carefully, trying to gauge their reactions to the news of the price run-up. They had all been sending out e-mails on their Black-Berries during the meeting, which wasn't unusual. It was rude, but it was standard operating procedure for these people. They were impatient individuals by nature, with many other responsibilities. You'd have to shackle them to keep their hands off their personal communications devices. The real problem was, you never knew what messages they were sending or to whom they were sending them. It always amazed Rose that people who were already wealthy would risk jail by breaking the law for a few dollars more. Like it was their God-given right to trade on inside information. Like they were entitled to whatever they could get because they thought of themselves as so important. Seemed stupid to him — he'd never do it — but he knew that kind of insider trading went on all the time.

"We've got to keep this thing very quiet," Rose urged.

"No, we don't," Boyd retorted. "Because there isn't going to be anything to keep quiet."

"What price are you thinking about offering?" the other woman on the board asked, paying no attention to Boyd.

"I want the authority from the board to go up to ninety dollars a share."

There was a collective gasp from around the table.

"That's ridiculous," Boyd said loudly, banging the table. "At that price we'd be paying over $3 billion for CIS. How could you possibly propose we pay that much?"

Rose smiled. Boyd had stepped right in front of the train. "Last night Citibank's credit committee approved $3.5 billion of loan facilities for us to buy CIS. A $2.5 billion seven-year-term loan and a $1 billion six-month revolver to bridge the long-term bonds we're planning to issue. They seem to think the price isn't out of line." He could see that the possibility of paying a one hundred percent control premium — paying twice what the market currently valued the company for in order to get a majority of the shares — had stunned people around the table. How quickly they forgot, he thought to himself. He'd proposed the same control premium range for each of the last

165

seven acquisitions, and they'd all paid off handsomely. "I'm not proposing that we start off at ninety dollars a share," Rose made clear. "We'll start at eighty. It's a price that'll get CIS's attention, and their shareholders' attention. But it isn't our final offer. Who knows? Maybe we can get this thing for close to eighty. If we can, it's a slam dunk."

"I think we should take a bio-break," Boyd suggested, turning toward Freese. "We've been in here for almost two hours. What do you say, Mr. Chairman?"

Freese thought about it for a few moments. "All right, fifteen minutes. Then we'll start up again. Then we'll come back in here and give Mike the okay to move forward."

Boyd stared at Freese fiercely for a few moments, then rose out of his chair and stalked from the room.

Rose glanced over at Cortez and winked. Boyd was a pain in the ass, but he wasn't getting much support from around the table. Everything was going exactly as planned.

23

Southern Idaho was a long way from Dallas, especially because they weren't driving on interstates and they were making certain they didn't break the speed limit on the back roads they were using. But they were already well into New Mexico because they were only stopping to refuel. The utility van was custom-built so they could quickly shove Vivian Anduhar into a shallow well hidden beneath the floor in the back, in case they were pulled over by local cops. And, on the off chance that an overzealous officer inspected the inside of the van and pulled up the trapdoor to the well, they had license to kill him. They had license to kill anyone. The ultimate objective was more important than any individual.

"So, was she good?"

Dennis Hackett and another agent sat on the floor in the back of the van watching Vivian. She lay between them on her left side, wrapped in a sheet from the Dallas Marriott. Her wrists and ankles were secured tightly behind her back, and she was still unconscious. The van didn't have windows in the back, so no one could see in.

"Yeah," Hackett answered, thinking about how she'd been writhing on top of him a few hours ago, wishing his imagination hadn't run away with him. They'd torn the bed apart but hadn't found a knife. He could have kicked his own ass. He'd had permission to go as far as he wanted to in order to get information from her. He could have kept her in bed all night. "She was."

As they crested the top of a steep hill and began heading down the other side, Vivian moaned and her eyelids slowly opened. She was still feeling the effects of the drug they'd pumped into her in the hotel room.

"She's coming to," the other agent called to the two men upfront. "What do you want me to do?"

"See if you can get anything out of her," the team leader called from the passenger seat. "Sometimes they can be real vulnerable when they're just coming out of it." He turned in the seat and pointed at Hackett. "Go on, Dennis."

Hackett crawled close to where Vivian lay

and gazed down into her bloodshot eyes. "Talk to me," he said authoritatively. "We'll be a lot easier on you than the guys we're taking you to."

She swallowed several times, trying to find saliva in her mouth. "Water," she gasped. "Please."

"Tell me what's going on in Jordan," Hackett demanded. "Tell me what your people are planning. Then maybe I'll get you some." He picked up a bottled water and waved it back and forth in front of her face. "See?"

"Please."

"Nope, not until you start talking."

She whispered something he couldn't hear.

He leaned down so his ear was right by her mouth. *"What?"*

"My family," she whispered. "Are they all right?"

"They're fine, Vivian. Now tell me about Jordan. What's going on there? Why were you working at that flight training school?"

She gazed up at him, a distant look in her eyes. "I don't know what you're talking about. I swear. I just liked you. I just wanted to have some fun. Why have you done this to me?"

Hackett rose up. "We're not going to get

anything out of her."

The leader chuckled harshly from the front. "The boys at Seventy-seven will. But maybe we'll try one more time before we get there."

"How's it going in there, Michael?" Tammy called from her office. She'd spotted Rose moving quickly past her door in the hallway.

He leaned back into her doorway. "It's going fine. We're taking a fifteen-minute break. Like you predicted, we're getting some pushback. But I think by the end of the meeting we'll get the nod."

"Who's giving you the pushback?" She hoped she wasn't being too nosy, but it seemed like a natural question to ask.

Rose checked up and down the hallway, then stepped inside her office. "It's Grant Boyd. He's being his usual prick self."

"Anybody else jumping on his bandwagon?"

Rose cocked his head to the side. "You're awfully interested this afternoon."

Tammy rose quickly from her chair, moved to where Rose stood and plucked the empty coffee cup out of his hand. "Give me that," she said with a smile. "Go back to your office. I deliver."

"Thanks."

She made the coffee just the way she knew he liked it, then, as promised, delivered it to him. He was on the phone when she came into his office, so she put it down on a coaster and left without saying a word.

Back at her office, she closed the door, sat down and pulled her cell phone from her purse. Started to push the buttons several times — then stopped. Michael had been so good to her. Given her great year-end bonuses and healthy raises, never asked her a single question about her personal life. Even chastised one of the other senior executives who'd started spreading rumors about her being gay. She started to put the phone back into her purse, then took a deep breath.

Finally, she groaned softly and dialed the number. Hated herself for doing it.

Jamie headed quietly through the house toward her father's den, still dressed in her baggy pajamas and robe. Trudy and Glenn were down in the basement. Trudy was watching her favorite show — a rerun of *Queer Eye for the Straight Guy* — and Glenn was playing computer games against some unseen enemy on the Internet. She took one more look over her shoulder, then cautiously opened the den's door and moved inside.

She always used to love it in here, because being in here meant she was alone with her dad, and he was her idol. *Had been,* anyway.

She moved to the desk and reached for the top middle drawer. The drawer her dad kept all his odds and ends in — pens, paper clips, change. She'd spied that note in his shirt pocket last night as she'd been sitting on his lap, just before the cop had rung the doorbell. Thought she'd seen a phone number on it in a woman's handwriting but she wasn't sure. She'd checked his dirty shirt bag this morning after he'd gone to the office and found the blue pinstripe he'd been wearing last night, but the note wasn't in the pocket. Maybe it was in here, she figured, pulling the drawer back. It wasn't like he had to worry about her mom snooping around his desk anymore.

She peered inside and pulled out what looked like the paper she'd seen in his pocket last night and gazed at it. After a few moments the paper began to shake in her hands and the numbers blurred before her eyes. The note was from someone named Kat.

24

Colin Freese zipped up his pants and headed for the sink in the personal bathroom connected to his office. Grant Boyd was such a pain in the ass, Freese thought, turning on the hot water. He was going to call their corporate counsel in New York and see what he could do about having Boyd kicked off the board. Freese had no idea how the process worked, but there had to be some way to say good-bye to the horse's ass. Boyd had been on the board for twenty years, since well before Freese had taken over as CEO, since before he had turned Trafalgar into what it was today — with a little help from Mike Rose, of course. He had no loyalty to Boyd whatsoever.

Freese finished washing his hands and reached for the towels stacked neatly beneath the soap dispenser as the lone stall door swung slowly open behind him in the mirror. "Jesus Christ." Shock turned into

173

anger when Grant Boyd appeared. Freese leaned back against the wall in relief, chest heaving. "What the hell are you doing in here?"

"Sorry," Boyd said insincerely, moving to the sink and turning the water on. "Your assistant said it would be all right if I used your bathroom. Hope you don't mind." He smiled as he washed his hands. "I'd say I scared the piss out of you, but you probably don't have any left at this point, huh?"

Freese was still breathing hard. "Damn it, Grant, don't do that to me again."

Boyd reached for a towel. "Listen, Colin, I don't like how it's going in there," he said as he dried his hands. "I don't want Rose getting the go-ahead for this acquisition."

Freese couldn't believe it. Boyd wanted some alone time with the chairman so he could privately register his complaint. "Well, Grant, fortunately there are eleven other board members in that room who feel differently about the acquisition. Including me," Freese said firmly. "Mike Rose has a lot of credibility with them, and with me." He dropped the towel into a hole in the marble countertop. "Michael's been a big help to me as far as taking this company from nothing ten years ago to where I've brought it today. So I'm going to take his advice. You'll have your chance to vote in a few minutes. You'll be disappointed, but you'll have your chance."

"You haven't done anything to build this company," Boyd countered, leaning forward so he was in Freese's face. "You've been off joyriding on company dollars for the past five years while Rose has done all the work. I know about you. You barely made it back from South America this morning to make this meeting."

Freese smiled serenely. "Yes, but I did make it, Grant. I made it, and I'm ready to give Michael permission to go to a hundred dollars a share to buy CIS if he wants it. So he can make me look even better."

Boyd tapped Freese on the chest. "Spent last night on the company G-Five banging a cute little brunette over Central America, didn't you, Colin?"

Freese shook his head. "I've had enough of this and enough of you." He made a move for the bathroom door.

But Boyd stuck out a thick arm and stopped him. "Wouldn't bother your wife if I told her all about your adventure at thirty thousand feet last night, would it?" He sneered. "I can't influence you that way because my people tell me you two have an arrangement. You and your wife seem to think it's okay to be married and screw around with other people."

Freese edged slowly back, until he was against the wall again, a bad feeling overtaking him. Boyd was driving at something. It scared him that Boyd knew about the brunette, but not because Boyd might call his wife. Boyd was exactly right. He and his wife did have an arrangement, and his wife wouldn't care so long as he kept her in diamonds and Mercedes and let her screw all the pool boys she wanted to. What frightened Freese to the tips of his fingers and toes was that Boyd knew about the flight attendant at all. What the hell else did he know about? And how had he found out?

"My wife and I have been married for forty years," Boyd volunteered, "and we've never been unfaithful to each other."

"That's nice, Grant," Freese said quietly.

"It *is* nice. *Damn* nice. My wife and I believe in old-fashioned values, Colin. We believe in what this country was founded on, those kind of solid values, and we're not going to let people like you destroy them. Not going to let people like you be soft on the element that would try to bring down the morality of this country."

"Of course," Freese agreed haltingly. He didn't know what to say, didn't really have any idea what Boyd was talking about. He wanted to get out of here as fast as he could, but he realized that Boyd was about to drive the dagger home, about to tell him what awful thing he had on him. It had always been one of Freese's talents — knowing what the other person was about to say. He was almost telepathic in that way. He just hoped what Boyd had found wasn't —

"You've got a tax problem, good buddy," Boyd said, breaking into a huge smile as he broke the news. "A couple of tax problems, actually. The options the board gave you four years ago were taxable at the time we gave them to you, but you didn't declare them on your U.S. return that year. You got a hundred thousand calls at a penny a share when Trafalgar's stock was at twenty-four dollars. That's two point four million dollars of income you didn't declare. With interest and penalties, that's going to be quite a bill. Not to mention the fact that you'll probably go to jail if I phone a few friends of mine at the Justice Department to let them know what happened. That you mentioned to me you had no intention of ever declaring that income so they can prove you knew what you were doing the whole time." His smile grew wider. "Right after I get off the phone with my deer hunting pal,

177

the assistant commissioner of the Internal Revenue Service. Who by the way has lots of friends across the pond over in London who are very senior people at the Inland Revenue, your taxing authority. You've still got your British citizenship, and you've got some real issues with not declaring income over there, too."

Freese's knees buckled and his shoulders sank down the wall a few inches. Everything Boyd had said was true. "What do you want?" he said.

"Your vote, you idiot. I don't want Rose getting the board's approval to move forward on the CIS acquisition. How many times do I have to say it?"

"Fine," Freese agreed meekly, "you've got it." He turned, put both hands on the marble countertop and hung his head. "But it won't matter. Michael's got ten other votes in there. All he needs is seven."

"Wrong," Boyd snapped. "Without you all he has is six. And according to Trafalgar's by-laws, Rose needs a majority to carry a motion. A tie, he loses."

"How did you —"

"Don't worry about it."

Boyd must have found something awful on each of whoever the other four were, too, Freese assumed. Everyone had skeletons in their closet and somehow Boyd had figured out where to look in his. "Why are you so dead set against the CIS acquisition?"

Boyd leaned in close again. "Like I said, Colin, don't worry about that. Just vote like I told you to and don't ask any questions. As far as you're concerned this conversation never happened. I find out you tell anyone what we just talked about, and you better hightail it somewhere very far away because the tax boys will be on your heels. Right behind them will be the Justice Department. You understand?" Without waiting for an answer, Boyd turned and headed out of the bathroom.

Freese sank to his knees when Boyd was gone, chest pounding, palms sweating. He'd always thought of Grant Boyd as nothing but a windbag. Watson Thatcher was a top law firm in Washington, but Boyd seemed like he was more of a figurehead there than anything. At least, that's what Freese had always thought. Suddenly his opinion had changed.

The young couple headed out of customs at New York's Kennedy Airport arm-in-arm, kissing as they walked. They were just getting back from a two-week honeymoon in New Zealand. They'd spent a week on both islands, taking in the incredible landscape the small nation had to offer. The Southern Alps, mammoth waterfalls, turquoise water even inland, prehistoric-like forests with ferns the size of a small house, glaciers, beaches, Scottish highlands — they'd enjoyed an incredible time.

Frank Davis was a teacher in the Connecticut public school system. His wife, Ellen, was a low-level engineer at the Groton nuclear submarine facility on the coast.

"Excuse me." A tall, brawny man approached them as they came to the end of a long corridor, holding his hands up to indicate that he wanted them to stop. He was dressed in a pair of blue slacks and a white button-down shirt with a "TSA" emblem on one arm. "Would you two follow me?"

Davis glanced down. The man was wearing white Nike tennis shoes. Something about that caught his eye, made him wonder. Didn't they usually wear dark shoes? Maybe he was just imagining things. "What's the problem?" he asked cordially.

"We just want to ask you a few questions."

"What's going on, Frank?"

Davis glanced over at his wife. She scared easily, always had. "I don't know."

"It's just routine," the man assured them,

pointing toward an open door off the corridor.

"This is not routine," Davis retorted, backing up a step and pulling Ellen away from the man. "I'm not going in there and neither is —"

Davis swallowed his words as two other men rushed up from behind, grabbed him by the collar and arms and hustled him into the small room. Two other men grabbed Ellen and forced her inside the room, too. He tried to shout, but before he could, both of them had been gagged.

Thirty minutes later Davis was headed for Base 12. Ellen was on her way to 19.

25

When the board was reseated and Colin Freese had officially called the meeting back to order, he opened the floor for questions. There were a few, but in the middle of a discussion on the specific synergies CIS would bring to Trafalgar's other divisions, Grant Boyd cut in.

"Let's get to the vote," he suggested gruffly. "We've heard enough."

"Wait a minute," Cortez said loudly from the end of the table. "This is ridiculous. We've got questions from the board, and we're going to answer them all before we —"

"It's all right, David," Rose said calmly. "We're ready for a vote." He glanced up at Freese. "Mr. Boyd has a point. We've gone on for a long time in here." Strange, Colin wasn't smoking his pipe anymore. It was the first time Rose could ever remember seeing him without it in a board meeting.

"What do you think, Mr. Chairman?"

"Yes, I . . . um . . . I think that's a good idea."

Cortez leaned over toward Rose. "Colin seems like he's out in right field," he whispered. "Something's wrong."

Rose had noticed it, too. It was as if Colin was off in another world. As if he suddenly had no interest in what was going on in the boardroom at all. "I know."

"I've got a bad feeling about this."

"Don't worry, it'll be fine."

"Someone want to make a motion?" Freese spoke up, looking around expectantly.

One of the women leaned forward over the table and raised her hand. "I will."

"Thank you, madam board member. Please go ahead."

"I move that we give Mr. Rose authority to proceed with the CIS acquisition up to a reservation price of ninety dollars a share," she said in a strong voice so everyone could hear.

"So moved," Freese agreed. "All in favor?"

Six board members raised their hands.

"All opposed?"

The other six board members, including Freese and Boyd, raised their hands.

"Unfortunately," Freese muttered, his

voice barely audible, "the motion is tabled."

"What?" Cortez leapt from his seat. "You've got to be kidding me, Colin."

Rose shot up out of his chair, too. That had come from nowhere, something he hadn't been told to anticipate. "I want to see you right away," he said loudly, pointing down the table at Bert Alderson, one of the board members who had voted against the acquisition. "In a private caucus."

It was Boyd's turn to stand up quickly. "No way," he said, jabbing his finger at Rose. "It's over. No private caucuses." He turned toward Freese. "End the meeting now, Colin."

Freese nodded.

Like a beaten puppy, Rose thought.

"Is there any other business anyone wants to discuss?" Freese asked in a low voice.

There never was at this point. It was just a standard procedural question. Rose flashed a quick look down the table at the woman who had made the original motion. They'd always gotten along well, and she'd always been complimentary about the outstanding job she thought he was doing as CFO.

"Yes," she spoke up loudly, nodding back at Rose subtly. "This is ridiculous. No one voiced any objections the whole time about the CIS acquisition except Mr. Boyd. It was obvious where he stood, but not where any of the rest of you were. None of you people who voted against made a peep about this thing the entire time. I want to give Mr. Rose a chance to have his private caucus with Mr. Alderson."

"You can't do that," Boyd blurted out. "It's not allowed in the —"

"It's definitely allowed in the bylaws," the woman snapped back, anticipating what Boyd was about to say. "Remember, I'm a lawyer, too, Grant. I know what I'm talking about."

"Close the meeting," Boyd ordered Freese. "Now."

"You do," the woman spoke up, her gaze flashing to Freese, "and I'll call our corporate counsel in New York. We'll see what he has to say about that."

Freese glanced at Boyd and shrugged. His hands were tied. "There's nothing I can do, Grant," he muttered.

Boyd gritted his teeth, watching Rose lead Alderson out of the room.

"It's been too long," Beck fretted, barely able to keep his eyes open at this point. Checking his watch for the third time in the last five minutes. "Something's gone wrong."

"Why don't you go upstairs and get some sleep?" Klein suggested. "I'll wake you up as soon as I hear of any developments."

"Because the developments ought to have already *developed.* I don't want to shut my eyes for two minutes and have you wake me up again. Besides, do you really think I'd be able to get any sleep right now anyway? Christ, Tom, use your brain."

"Sorry, sir."

Beck waved and shook his head immediately, feeling bad. "No, no, I'm sorry. I'm just beat. I'm just worried that somehow Rose is going to get the go-ahead from the Trafalgar board to move forward. The guy scares me," he admitted, thinking about what Bill Granger had said. About how you couldn't stop Rose once he was locked onto a target. "He's damn good."

"But Grant Boyd sent us that message. Colin Freese collapsed when he hit the guy with the tax problems. He said he'd vote with us. That gave us six board members against. It's done," Klein said firmly.

"I'm glad you're so confident."

They sat in silence for a few moments.

Finally, Klein spoke up. "By the way, sir, we detained that couple coming back from

New Zealand. Got them at Kennedy Airport. They're taking him to Base Twelve and her to Nineteen."

"They're newlyweds, right?" Beck asked, looking out over the valley, remembering the memo Klein had put together for the Directorate.

"Yes."

Beck's expression turned grim. "How old are they?"

Klein picked up a pad to check his notes. "He's twenty-seven and she's twenty-six."

"What do they do again?"

"He's a third-grade teacher in the Connecticut public school system, she's an engineer at the Groton nuclear submarine facility."

Beck stroked his chin. He hadn't shaved in two days and his whiskers were at that rough, prickly stage. "Tom, what do you think the odds are that this couple is really involved in some kind of terrorist plot?" He'd asked the other three members of the Directorate the same question last week when they'd voted on whether to detain the couple, but it hadn't done any good. The other three had voted in favor of taking them into custody as soon as they were back on American soil.

Klein shrugged. "The information seemed

credible."

"But a third-grade teacher?"

"Well," Klein said quickly, "I don't think anyone really believes he's involved, not directly anyway. The focus is on her."

"She's twenty-six, for crying out loud. We checked out her job at Groton." Beck snorted angrily. The report he'd read on them was coming back to him now. "She has no high-level responsibilities. She just joined the facility a year ago," he said, staring at Klein. "She's a grunt, a nobody."

Klein stared back for a few seconds, then looked down at the floor.

Beck shut his eyes tightly. God, he hoped this whole thing wasn't spinning out of control.

Fifteen minutes after Rose had led Bert Alderson out of the boardroom, he led him back in. Alderson was the CEO of a large coal mining company based in Wyoming. A big buyer of some of the heavy equipment Trafalgar manufactured in its Denver plant. "I call for a revote," said Rose quietly when everyone was seated again.

"You can't call for a revote," Boyd snapped angrily. "You can't call for anything. You're not a board member. Besides, the vote's already been taken and logged.

We can't vote on it again." He sat back in his chair. "But nice try."

Rose glanced at Cortez. That was a wrinkle he hadn't thought of.

"Technically, Mr. Boyd is correct," Freese spoke up. "Once a vote is taken on a motion, we have to wait at least thirty days to vote again."

"Then I'd like to make a new one," declared the woman who'd made the initial motion. "I move that we give Mr. Rose the authority to proceed with the CIS acquisition up to a reservation price of ninety-*five* dollars a share."

Rose saw Boyd's jaw drop.

"Given the change in the reservation price," the woman continued, "this is a vote on a different motion." She glanced up the table at Freese. "Mr. Chairman?"

Rose watched Freese swallow hard. Obviously, Boyd had gotten to him at the break, but it wasn't going to matter now.

"Um . . . I uh . . ." Freese glanced at Boyd, then quickly away. "So moved," he uttered. "All in favor?"

The same six members who had voted for the motion raised their hands right away. Then, slowly, Bert Alderson raised his hand, too.

■ ■ ■

Sherman LeClair had switched from the streamer, the baby rainbow trout imitation, to a dry fly. Which was a tiny speck of feathers, wool, and thread tied to resemble a small caddis fly that had just hatched on the surface of the water. It was February, but it had warmed up to almost forty degrees on the Big Blackfoot today. It almost felt warm and, surprisingly, there were bugs swarming around.

"Right in there," the guide said quietly, pointing at a small pocket of water behind a large rock jutting out of the Blackfoot downstream and to the left of the drift boat. He turned the craft so LeClair would have an easier cast. "Regular mend, this time."

"Got it."

LeClair started his false casting routine, shooting the heavy line behind him first, then in front, never allowing the line or the fly to touch the water. Stripping out more line from the reel with each back-cast. Finally, on the sixth forward motion, he let the tiny insect imitation flutter to the surface just behind the big rock. Instantly a huge green head appeared out of nowhere and slammed the fly. Just as fast its tail disappeared in a boil of water.

"Rainbow!" the guide shouted. "Big one, too. Not as big as that bull trout you caught, but it's a football. Damn nice cast, Sherman."

LeClair didn't answer. He was too focused on the task at hand, making sure the line stayed taut as the twenty-five-inch fish came sailing three feet out of the water, beautiful dark red stripe down its side — from its cheek to its tail — flashing in the rays of the Montana afternoon before the fish disappeared into the depths again. Then, suddenly, the line went slack. LeClair wanted to curse, but he kept his composure and slowly began reeling in the line. It would have hurt more if he hadn't caught that bull trout earlier. Sometimes you had to look at the positive side, too.

"Damn it!" the guide shouted, banging one of the oars against the side of the boat loudly. "Too bad. Nothing you could have done about it, though. The pig must have wrapped the leader around a log on the bottom and broken you off. These fish know their home pools so well."

LeClair had a hard time believing that the fish, though beautiful, was smart enough to intentionally wrap a leader around a submerged log to break itself free. He'd noticed over the last two years that sometimes Roger gave fish more credit than they deserved.

His cell phone rang. He pulled it from his fishing vest and checked the number. This was it. "Roger, I need to go to shore."

"Yes, sir."

"Hello."

"Big Buck?"

"Yeah, hold on a second."

"Okay."

LeClair waited for the guide to get him to the riverbank. When he was out of the drift boat and into the woods, he spoke up again. "This is Big Buck."

"Big Buck, it's Eagle."

"Go ahead, Eagle."

"Pete knocked in the winning run. The score was seven-to-five, and it was the bottom of the ninth when he finally pushed the winning run across. But he got it done."

LeClair wanted to shout out and pump his fist in elation, and, if the guide hadn't been within earshot, he might have. "Good news," he said calmly. "I'll be back in range tomorrow. We'll talk then. And you'll be coming to see me on Monday."

"Yes, sir."

LeClair closed the phone and slipped it back into his fishing vest. Then he brought a finger beneath one eye and brushed away

a single tear. It was the best news he'd gotten in two years. Maybe ever.

26

Rose moved quickly into the garage adjoining the Trafalgar building and headed in the general direction of where he thought he'd parked his car a few hours ago. He knew it was somewhere in the back of the cavernous space because he'd come in so late this morning and the only spots available were miles from the elevators. He'd never realized how packed the lot was during the day because he was always in early and out late, when most of the spots were empty.

For a few moments he couldn't find the Buick sedan, and he stood there looking around a sea of sheet metal and glass. It always frustrated him when he couldn't remember something as simple as this. True, it was because he'd been so tired and distracted, laser-focused on what he wanted to say in the board meeting. But still. And he wanted to get home to the kids as fast as possible. He'd only been gone a few hours, but, at this point, he felt bad for having left at all. Now that he had his board approval to go ahead with CIS, he had to get back to the family.

He was always looking ahead, he knew. He was never just happy in the moment. Sheila had always given him such a hard time about that, but it was a curse, not something he could control. She called it always looking toward the top of the mountain, he called it always looking around the bend. But they meant the same thing. He grimaced as he looked around, searching for the car. Maybe it was simply that he'd never met the person who could distract him enough from trying to look around the bend.

Suddenly Rose got the idea to pull out his keys, hold them high in the air above his head, point them at where he thought the car was and push the button. When he did, he heard a beep. He pushed the button again and got a lock on the location, thanks to catching a flash of orange parking lights this time.

When he reached the Buick, he tossed his briefcase in the back and eased in behind the wheel. The sedan was conservative, consciously so. He didn't want flash, at least not at the office. He had a Porsche at home that he drove on weekends, but he always drove the Buick to work and didn't have a reserved parking space right by the elevators the way Freese did. Rose had a different attitude about that. He was sensitive about what others in the office thought. He knew how sticking your wealth in others' faces could grate on them, make them despise you. He didn't like to flaunt the fact that he was the second-highest-paid person in the company — even though anyone could find out by going to the Internet and pulling up Trafalgar's required Securities and Exchange filings. Rose had overheard others talking about the "big boat" Freese drove and how the CEO pulled his yacht right up to the dock while everyone else had to hoof it in from the satellite lot. Fortunately, Freese wasn't around that much, so people didn't see the Mercedes all the time. But even on days when he knew Colin wasn't coming in, Rose wouldn't park in the reserved spot. He let Freese's secretary have it, and he was constantly amazed at how one small act could generate so much goodwill.

As he pulled out of the garage and headed for home, Rose took out his cell phone and turned it on — he'd shut it off for the board meeting. After it came to life, it started beeping loudly. When the din was over, he glanced at the tiny screen — there were nine new messages — but he didn't feel like checking them right now. He wanted to do something else: Call Kat. Her note was at home in his top middle desk drawer, but he knew the number by heart. It had been running through his mind like one of those songs you couldn't get out of your head, except that he didn't want to forget this tune. He held the phone up and began to dial her number. But after he'd pressed a few buttons, he stopped, then pressed the "end" button as the sedan rolled up to a red light. He wasn't ready yet.

When the light turned green and he was moving again, he thought of the look on Bert Alderson's face when they'd gone into their private caucus. Poor guy. Rose had no idea what Grant Boyd had used to get Alderson's vote on the CIS motion — hadn't asked Alderson while they were alone — but it hadn't taken long to change Bert's mind. Alderson's mining company was having terrible financial problems. Nothing that had hit the press yet, but the company was months behind on payments to Trafalgar for millions of dollars of equipment, as they were to lots of their vendors. A minor issue for the multibillion-dollar Trafalgar, but a nuclear holocaust for Alderson's company because it would set bankruptcy proceedings in motion if Rose pressed for payment. Rose had been giving Alderson time to finish up negotiations on a new bank deal that would give the mining company the flexibility to come current on its trade debt, including what it owed Trafalgar, and it would only be another week or two before the deal would be done. But in their private caucus, Rose had made it clear to Alderson that if he didn't change his vote, Trafalgar would demand payment for the equipment *immediately* — as in, as soon as they left the small conference room they were using, Rose would head to his office and call the lawyers. Not even back to the boardroom first. He'd said it quietly, almost apologetically, but he'd been very clear.

Rose had been watching Grant Boyd as Alderson raised his hand after the new motion, swinging the vote in favor of going after CIS. The guy's face had turned ten shades of red, finally settling into a bright crimson. It had been satisfying to see, he had made things so personal in the meeting. In fact, Boyd had done him a huge favor. Now Rose could go to ninety-five dollars a share for CIS. He'd been thinking the board would only give him ninety. It had been a big win and Cortez had actually shouted out loud and done a little dance when they'd gotten back to Rose's office after the meeting was over.

The vote that had shocked Rose was Freese's. Obviously, Boyd had gotten to him during the break somehow, too. Threatened him with telling the world about something awful he'd done. No way of knowing what it was and Rose hadn't had time to confront Colin after the meeting about it, he'd been so focused on getting home.

Rose glanced at his cell phone, thinking about how Sheila had enjoyed hearing about days like today at Trafalgar during the early years of their marriage. But how at some point her interest had faded, an indifference had crept into their conversations when he talked about work. She'd start humming as he was talking, sometimes even leave the room when he was in the middle of a story. Finally he stopped talking about Trafalgar, didn't even mention to her that he'd been promoted to chief financial officer when it happened. She hadn't appreciated how hard he worked for the family, and she'd cheated on him. She'd been coming back from seeing her lover when she'd run off the road, for Christ's sake, undoubtedly still coked up. The detectives hadn't called yet to

199

confirm that the white powder in her nose was cocaine, but he had no doubt it was. Cortez had given him a little more color on what his private eye friend had seen, and it was clear from the accounts Cortez related that Sheila had gone off the deep end. He felt the anger building inside him. Supposedly she'd even had sex in a car in the National Cathedral parking lot. The whole thing disgusted him.

Still, it struck him as strange that Cortez would take it on himself to have Sheila followed. Strange that Cortez would do that without saying something first, he thought as he turned off Route 7 and headed north toward Great Falls. But maybe it was for the best. It was always better to know the real story, he believed. Better to have the facts no matter how you got them or how much it hurt. You could never bury your head in the sand. That just set you up for something even worse later on.

Rose brought the cell phone up in front of his face again. Kat's number kept playing over and over in his mind. He started breathing a little faster, felt his heart rate tick up a notch. He swallowed hard, then started pressing the buttons. He felt like that awkward kid at the high school dance again — but now he enjoyed the feeling.

■ ■ ■

"Sir."

Beck heard something, but he was still half in his dream. He was in a courtroom, the judge at a trial with hundreds of defendants. He'd sentenced them all to death by hanging — men, women, children. There'd been a gallows in the courtroom, and he'd witnessed the first execution. A five-year-old girl hanged by the noose.

"Sir."

"What?" He sat up on the couch and rubbed his eyes, trying to remember where he was. Tom Klein was peering down at him.

"Bad dream?"

The world came into focus, but Beck's heart was still pumping hard. "I'm fine," he said, pulling the glove off his left hand. He never would get used to that. Another reason to get the hell out of this thing. "What is it?"

"I've got some bad news," Klein said grimly. "The Trafalgar board gave Michael Rose the go-ahead for the CIS acquisition."

Beck's head fell slowly into his hands. "But that's imp—" He interrupted himself. Obviously it wasn't impossible. "Get me a phone, Tom." He had no choice, he had to deal with this emergency now, even though he could barely keep his eyes open, barely form coherent sentences. "I've got to talk to Bill Granger."

Thank God she'd kept the phone on vibrate. It was so noisy in the bar she never would have heard it. Kat dug it out of her pocket and gazed at the incoming number, even as Margie was yelling a drink order at her from the other side of the bar. It was just three o'clock, but it was Friday and the bar was packed. It hadn't slowed down since noon.

"Vodka martini with a twist!" Margie shouted again, headed toward the kitchen to pick up a food order.

But Kat didn't acknowledge her. She was too focused on the phone number flashing on the screen. It wasn't one she recognized, but it was the right area code: 703. She raced out from behind the bar and through the front door of the restaurant onto the sidewalk beside M Street in Georgetown, the main drag. "Hello," she said, trying to stay calm. "Hello."

"Kat?"

Her heart skipped a beat. She recognized the voice. "Yes?"

"Kat, this is Michael Rose. We met last night at Morton's. We talked a little at the door when you were leaving, then you came back in and gave me your number."

"Hi, Michael." She liked that he sounded a little nervous. Not quite as cool a customer as she'd run into in the doorway leaving the place. And she liked that he called himself Michael, not Mike. Michael seemed more romantic. She made a mental note to call him that when they got together — if they did. "How are you?"

"All right. I, um . . ." His voice drifted off.

"Thanks for calling," she spoke up quickly, putting her hand over her ear as a horn blew loudly on the street close to where she was standing. Not wanting the conversation to drag. "I just want you to know I don't usually do that kind of thing. Give my number to someone I don't know, I mean. I'm not that kind of girl."

"No, of course not."

"It's just that, well . . ." God, this was so difficult. Best to be direct, she figured. "I . . . I was attracted to you. I don't know how else to explain it."

"Thank you. I'm flattered." Rose hesitated. "So, what did you have in mind?"

Her heart sank. She hoped he wasn't trying to get her right into bed, hoped he wasn't going to suggest they meet at a hotel and jump in the sack. That would be such a turnoff. "I was thinking, I mean I —"

"How about lunch sometime?" he interrupted. "Be a nice way to get to know each other a little. What do you think?"

She smiled. Perfect. A gentleman, just like she'd been praying for. "Sounds great. How about next week?"

27

Bad luck. The van had blown a tire on a lonely stretch of desert road in southern Utah and now they were rummaging around the vehicle looking for the wrench that would get the spare off the back door. It wasn't where they thought it would be and the longer they sat out here the more vulnerable they were.

"Get her out of here while we change the damn tire, Jones," the leader barked from the front seat angrily. He pointed at Monty Jones, the agent who'd been sitting across from Hackett. Then at Vivian Anduhar, who was still lying on the floor bound and gagged, her terrified eyes wide open. "I don't want some local yokel County Mountie coming by, getting curious, and us having to do something drastic. No reason to look for trouble," he groused.

They hadn't put her in the well since they'd last filled up with gas two hundred miles ago. It was scorching hot in there, and the leader was afraid she wouldn't make it to Base 77 if they forced her to stay down there for more than a few minutes. Then he'd take a bagload of crap because the top people were all over this one. They were convinced there was a very good chance she was involved in a big attack they'd heard whispers about from their overseas sources.

The leader jabbed out his window toward a large rock formation fifty yards away. "Take her out there and keep her there until somebody comes for you."

"Yes, sir." Jones quickly undid the ropes binding the woman's ankles. He was short, stocky, and red-haired. He'd been a CIA agent in Paris before being recruited into the I-4. He looked young and innocent. He was anything but. "Come on, honey," he ordered, dragging her toward the sliding side door. A hundred miles ago they'd dressed her in a gray T-shirt, green GI khakis, and black PFC boots. Right after they'd finally stopped in a lonely spot in northern New Mexico and allowed her to urinate by the side of the van. "All clear?"

The leader checked. Nothing but a straight, endless black ribbon stretching out beneath a clear blue sky in both directions as far as the eye could see. "All clear."

"Come on," Jones ordered, pulling the woman outside. She fell down beside the vehicle and ripped the khaki pants on a rock, skinning one of her knees badly. He jerked her back to her feet right away. "Let's go. None of that oh-I'm-so-weak bullshit with me," he said. "You understand?"

"See if you can get something out of her while you're out there," the leader yelled after Jones as he jumped from the van to help change the tire. "See if you have better luck than our man Hackett did. I'm tired of the guys where we're going getting all the credit. Let's break this one before we get there this time. Let's get some of the glory for once."

Jones grinned over his shoulder as he hustled her along through the scraggly underbrush. "Yes, sir." This was going to be fun. License to kill was one thing, license to torture was another. It was much more fun, and given what he'd just heard, he was going to assume that's what he had. "Come on, honey. Double-time it."

He led her behind the rocks, a series of huge boulders forty to sixty feet tall, and into a crevice where there was a cave extending fifteen feet back beneath two of the boulders. "Get in there," he snarled, giving her a hard shove.

She fell on the rocky floor of the cave and cried out as pain shot through her wounded knee and her shoulder. Jones paid no attention, grabbing her by her dark hair and forcing her against the wall in a sitting position, hands at the base of her back. He yanked the gag from her mouth. He liked the way she was looking at him with those big brown eyes, scared out of her mind. It turned him on. He'd never interrogated a woman before. This was going to be fun.

"Please may I have some water?" she begged, glancing at the metal canteen hanging from his belt. "I'm so thirsty."

"Yeah, sure, right away. How about a steak, medium rare with potatoes au gratin and a nice Cabernet while we're at it?" He grinned and knelt down in front of her, running the backs of his fingers along her soft cheek. "No way, sweetheart. Unless of course we make a deal."

"What kind of deal?" she gasped, barely able to speak, her throat was so dry.

"You heard the captain. Give me some information. For starters, why don't you tell me what you and your husband were doing in Dallas?"

Her head fell slowly back against the cave wall. She was exhausted. "What do you mean? We were just living there. I swear to God."

"Whose God you talking about? Mine or yours? Don't confuse the real one with your fake idol."

She didn't answer.

"Where were you before you were in Dallas?" Jones demanded. "And you better tell me the truth, sister," he added quickly. "Because we'll check out every detail of your story." He leaned forward so his face was just inches from hers. So she could smell the pre-made pastrami sandwich he'd bought and devoured in six bites when they'd last filled up the van at that convenience store. "If you lie about even one little thing," he warned, holding his thumb and forefinger barely apart, "you won't make it to where we're headed. Not alive, anyway."

"Boston," she answered. "We moved to Dallas from Boston eight months ago."

"Why'd you move?"

"My husband got a better job."

Jones chuckled. "Your husband's a baggage handler at the Dallas Airport for crying out loud." He made it sound like her husband was still alive. He figured if she knew her family was dead, she'd clam up forever. "How much better can that be than what he was doing in Boston?"

209

"He was working the graveyard shift at a Seven-Eleven. He almost got killed one night by two guys who held up the store. The other man he was working with did get shot and died a few days later in the hospital. Our children hated their schools, and the weather was awful. We wanted a better way. At least with the job in Dallas he's getting medical benefits."

"None of you ever went to the doctor or the dentist the whole time you were in Dallas," Jones pointed out, pulling the canteen off his belt and unscrewing the black cap. He caught her gazing at the canteen longingly. "Doesn't sound like you care that much about having benefits."

"My husband has to be on the job nine months before he's eligible for them," she explained, running her tongue over her chapped lower lip. "He's almost there. We have the kids' appointments lined up. You can check that out."

"What are the doctors' names?"

She hesitated. "I don't remember. The names are on the refrigerator door."

Not anymore, Jones knew. The house was a pile of ash and soot. "Tell me about your job at that flight training school." Jones put the canteen to his lips and took several long gulps, making certain to let the clear cold water run out over both corners of his mouth and down his chin so she could see it. He wiped his mouth off with the back of his hand. "We found out that you let several people into the program without getting all the proper identification. Two of them were A-rabs, like you. Shady fuckers, too."

"The owner told me to do it like that. Lots of people got into the program without all the right papers. The owner told me himself not to be too tough on people who applied. He said he had to make money. He said the new government regulations were putting him out of business."

"That's not what he told us."

"What *would* he tell you?" She tried to swallow. "Did you check his records? Did you see all the missing paperwork with the people I didn't process? The ones other people processed."

"Everyone else's paperwork was perfect." Wasn't true. Far from it, in fact. Like she said, the owner ran a shoddy operation. The thing was, *none* of the people she'd processed had given the school all the required information and the two Arabs hadn't given her any information except their names — probably fake — and their address. And they hadn't come back to take the remaining lessons they'd already prepaid for after

211

the I-4 had made its first visit to the flight training school three weeks ago. They'd quit their jobs, too — and left their apartment in a big hurry. At least, that's what it looked like when Jones and another agent had shown up at the address they'd given on the application — guns drawn — and broken in. The place looked like a tornado had hit it. "You've been talking to someone in Amman, Jordan. Who?"

"My family. That's where my husband and I are from."

Jones held the canteen to Vivian's lips for a moment, then pulled it away as she closed her eyes and opened her mouth. "No. Someone else, too. I told you not to lie to me."

She gazed back at him for a few moments. "Please can I have a sip? Just one sip?"

He ran his fingers through her hair. "You're prettier than your pictures. Kind of sexy in those fatigues, too. Now I can see why Hackett was so into this assignment." He grinned. "He said you were very . . . passionate."

"I cared about him." Her eyes dropped. "Until this morning."

"Must not have cared much about your husband."

Vivian shut her eyes tightly. "It was wrong.

It's just that my husband and I have been together so long. Sometimes it's hard when you know each other that well."

"I thought you Arab girls didn't mess around on your men like that. Thought they cut your hands off if you did."

"Like I said," she whispered, "it was wrong. I got what I deserved."

"Maybe you'd like to be passionate with me, honey," Jones suggested, reaching for the bottom of her gray T-shirt and pulling it up a few inches. "What do you say?" He held the canteen close to her lips. "Mmm? I like that brown belly of yours."

"Please don't do this," she pleaded.

"Don't want any water, huh?"

She shook her head.

He pulled the T-shirt up over her breasts suddenly. "First let me get a look."

But she twisted away from him violently before he could.

He screwed the cap back on the canteen quickly and replaced it on his belt, then grabbed her chin and pulled the T-shirt up again. Those long nipples were so brown. He could feel himself becoming aroused. God, it had been a long time. "Come on, honey. Hackett says you're a dirty girl. Says you love being bad." He pushed her onto her back roughly and straddled her, pulling the T-shirt up to her neck, exposing her breasts once more.

"Stop it!" she shrieked.

His strong, stubby fingers closed around her neck. "You're going to give me what I want. I don't care how we do it, but you're going to give me what I want."

"Please," she begged. "Please don't do this to me."

"Then give me some information, something important. Tell me who you're really talking to in Jordan."

She tried to roll away, but he was too heavy.

"You're very stupid," he muttered, unbuttoning his pants. "I'll go a lot easier on you than they will at Seventy-seven." His eyes raced to hers, realizing his mistake instantly — giving away the name of the base. And her eyes were right there waiting for his. He could tell by her expression that she recognized he'd said something wrong, something he shouldn't have. "Don't you tell anyone what I just said," he hissed, standing up, re-buttoning his pants, then touching the handle of the long knife with the six-inch serrated blade that hung beside the canteen. His heart was racing. It had been an awful slip of the tongue. "If you tell anyone what you just heard, they'll kill you."

She nodded slowly.

They would, too. He wasn't lying about that. Still, she might try to use it, he realized. Might be stupid enough to blurt it out in the middle of a torture session thinking it might buy her some time. Or, if she was really smart and she knew the game, she'd tell them that he'd said that — and more. Completely made-up things but she'd have credibility at that point. She'd say he'd told her a few other things in return for sexual favors and that she wanted to negotiate. She might even try telling them he was a double agent and she wanted to give them enough to really hang him. At the very least, his career would be over. At worst, they'd throw him in jail. The I-4 was a paranoid organization from the top down — for good reason.

Jones wrapped his fingers around the knife's thick handle. He had to kill her, he realized. There was no other way. The leader of the group would be pissed off, but Jones would explain it away as too aggressive a torture technique. A mistake, but he was protected against that kind of mistake.

He pulled the long knife slowly from its sheath and held it up. You could go to jail if they thought you were a spy, but not if you killed someone.

She screamed when she saw the shiny silver blade, rolled onto her stomach and began wriggling pitifully toward the back of the cave using her toes to push herself forward, hands still secured behind her.

He pounced on her, jerked her head up with his left hand to expose her soft neck, and lunged forward with the knife.

Rose was almost to his house in Great Falls when his cell phone rang. He picked it up off the passenger seat and smiled when he saw the number. It was Kat. It had only been ten minutes since he'd called her, but now she was calling back. He liked that. She was the romantic type. Of course, if Cortez heard about this, he'd say the girl was the psycho stalker type and now Rose was dealing with someone who "wouldn't be ignored," as Cortez liked to quote Glenn Close from *Fatal Attraction.* But Kat didn't seem like that type.

"Hello?" No answer. *"Hello?"*

"Oh, God, did I — Michael?"

"Yeah, it's me." Suddenly he was disappointed because he realized what must have happened. She must have accidentally hit the redial button. "Kat?"

"I'm sorry, I must have pushed redial. You must think I'm such a dope."

He pulled into his driveway and stopped in front of the garage but didn't press the button to raise the door yet. "Actually I was thinking maybe you wanted to say hi. I was hoping you did anyway."

"Really?" she asked breathlessly after a few seconds.

He looked up at Jamie's window. She wasn't there. "Yeah," he admitted, "really."

"Aw, that's so nice. Well, I can't wait for next week. Tuesday, right?"

"Tuesday at noon," he confirmed. "At that place out in Leesburg."

"The Station?"

"Yup, that's it." There was an uncomfortable pause. He wanted to keep talking to her, wanted to suggest that they get together on the spur of the moment tonight at some out-of-the-way bar in northern Virginia after the kids had gone to sleep. It was hitting him suddenly. How lonely he was, how lonely he'd been for years. But meeting her tonight was out of the question, even if she could get away from her husband. He had to be home for the kids tonight. "I'll talk to you later. Maybe I'll try you on Monday."

"I'd like that. Bye, Michael."

"Bye." He glanced up at Jamie's window. She was there this time, staring down at him with that glare in her eye. The same one

217

she'd given him this morning when he was leaving.

Someone grabbed Jones's wrist, then body-blocked him off her from behind. *"What the —"* he shouted as whoever it was tumbled onto the cave floor beside him. He scrambled to his knees, waving the knife out in front of him — at Dennis Hackett, it turned out. Jones lunged toward Hackett out of reflex.

But Hackett was faster, and a martial arts expert. He slammed Jones's jaw with the heel of his boot, rotating on both palms while they were flat on the cave floor and scissor-kicking. Jones tumbled backward against the far wall with a loud groan. The knife went flying and Hackett retrieved it quickly, tossing it out of the cave just as Jones came at him again. But it was a feeble attack. Seconds later Hackett had Jones facedown, one wrist all the way up at the back of his neck, completely immobilized.

"What were you doing?" Hackett demanded.

Jones spat sand and pebbles from his mouth. He was breathing hard. "Doing what I was told. Trying to get some information out of her before we get to . . . before we get to where we're going. You heard the captain tell me to do it."

"Yeah, but he didn't tell you to —"

"He was going to kill me," Vivian sobbed, tears streaming down her cheeks. "I wouldn't give him what he wanted, and he was going to kill me."

"You fucking animal," Hackett yelled, forcing Jones's wrist higher, almost to the top of his head.

Jones yelped as bolts of pain shot through his shoulder. "She's lying! I would never do that."

"Bullshit!"

Hackett gritted his teeth and shook his head hard. It was happening, he could feel it. What they'd warned him could happen — sympathizing with the detainees, showing them compassion. But he couldn't help it. And it wasn't because he'd been intimate with her, that had nothing to do with it. It was the house outside of Dallas bursting into an orange fireball while he watched from the street that had gotten to him after six years in the I-4. Even if she and her husband were deeply involved in some sinister plot designed to kill thousands of people, it didn't matter. There were four children in that house, four young lives snuffed out as they lay unconscious from the dope he'd injected into them. They weren't involved in any terrorist plot, they were just living life. It was the first time he'd known from the start that he was killing innocent people, the first time he'd killed children.

And this was their mother lying on the floor of a cave in southern Utah.

"You're a genius," Kat said, laughing and shaking her head after she ended the call with Michael Rose. She and Margie were in a back room of Clyde's. She'd gotten one of the waiters to cover for her at the bar for a few minutes. "An absolute genius. A devil, too," she added with a sly grin.

Margie shrugged. "I'm the mother of manipulation. Now Mr. Corporate will be thinking about you even more all weekend. He won't be able to *stop* thinking about you. As a matter of fact, he probably thought about asking you out tonight while you were on the phone with him."

"No way."

"Oh yeah. See, at first, when he saw your number come up on his screen, he thought you were really calling him, and it made him feel great. Probably made him feel like he had the early advantage in the relationship, too. Like you cared more about seeing it go someplace than he did. But when he assumed you weren't really calling him, it made him feel vulnerable, made him understand how much he wants to see you again."

Margie was right. Kat had heard the disappointment in Rose's voice as soon as she'd acted like she'd accidentally hit the redial button. It was so obvious in his tone. "I should hire you as my personal relationship consultant."

A worried look crossed Margie's face. "Yeah, well you've got another relationship to worry about," she said, dodging a box full of liquor lying on the floor as she headed out of the little room. "And I don't think you're going to need a consultant for that one. I think you're going to need a bodyguard."

Jamie was standing just inside the door when Rose came into the house from the garage, arms crossed tightly over her chest. "Hi, honey," he said, noticing her unfriendly posture. "You look beautiful." She'd showered, done her hair and put on a pretty dress and a blue sweater. She looked so much older. More like her mother than ever.

"I need to talk to you," she said.

He put his briefcase down on a table by the door, beside a picture of Sheila and him at a New Year's Eve party two years ago.

The photograph was inside a shiny sterling silver frame, and it was obvious now that he looked at it for the first time in a while that they weren't having a good time. Not with each other, anyway. Sheila had probably put that picture on the table to try to tell him something, hoping he'd see it as soon as he walked in the house every night. But he hadn't noticed it until now. "Okay, sure." He glanced around. "Where's everyone?"

"Glenn's downstairs playing guess-what games against some other shut-in loser, and Trudy's upstairs taking a nap." She put her hands on her hips. "Can we go to your den?" she asked.

"Let me just say hi to Glenn. I'll be —"

"Daddy. It's *very* important."

"Okay, Munchkin." He winced. "I mean, *Jamie.* Sorry, honey," he apologized, heading through the house. "I'm still getting used to this name thing. It's hard to break old habits."

"I'll bet," she said, following him into the den and sitting on the leather couch that was against one wall.

Rose had been about to collapse into his desk chair — he was suddenly exhausted after holding himself together with coffee and adrenaline for the board meeting — but he stopped. He'd heard a nasty tone in her voice, like she was accusing him of something. "What's going on?" he demanded, sinking slowly into the chair. "Why am I getting this from you? We're supposed to be helping each other right now." He saw her eyes mist over and suddenly he felt awful. He had to be the rock no matter how hard it was right now. "I'm sorry, honey. Come here and sit on my lap."

"I don't want to."

"Why not?"

Jamie brought one hand to her eyes, hiding them. "I just don't."

Rose saw tears falling from beneath her hand onto her sweater. He hurried to the couch and sat down beside her. "Honey, I'm sorry. I shouldn't have snapped at you like that. It's just that I'm kind of at the end of my rope, too." He slipped his arm around her slender shoulder and gently tried to pull her close, but she resisted even as the tears started pouring down in torrents. "What is it, Jamie? Why won't you let me in? We've always been so close."

She sobbed softly. "Who were you talking to when you pulled up in the driveway just now?"

Rose felt as though he'd been electrocuted. "My office. We had a big meeting today and I was talking to one of the folks who works for me about it."

"Mr. Cortez?"

"Uh, no. Another man."

"Who?"

He put his hand on her knee. "What's this all about? Why the inquisition?"

"Can I look on your phone? Can I look at the number?"

Rose laughed uncomfortably. "Why would you want to do that?"

"Can I?"

"Well," he stammered, trying to think of some way to head this off, "my phone's out in the car."

"I'll go get it," she said, starting to stand up.

He caught her by the wrist and forced her back down as tenderly as he could. "I wasn't talking to anyone at my office," he said.

"Who were you talking to?"

He hesitated, trying to find the words. "A friend."

"A friend named *Kat*?"

He felt like he'd been shocked again, this time twice as hard. "How do you know about —"

Jamie pulled the piece of paper with Kat's number on it from a pocket of her dress and held it up. "I did a bad thing, Daddy," she said, her voice hoarse. "I went in your desk, and I found this." She dropped the piece of paper on his lap. The side with writing on it landed up. "I'm sorry."

Rose clenched his jaw, gazing down at the note. He wanted to yell at Jamie, wanted to ground her for a year and take away her driving privileges. Wanted to teach her a lesson for invading his privacy. But he couldn't, it wouldn't be right. Now wasn't the time. She'd just lost her mother, she was just trying to deal with one of the most awful things a child could face. Plus, she had him nailed dead to rights.

He took a deep breath, he didn't know what to say. He wanted to explain to Jamie that he'd never once cheated on her mom in all their years of marriage, that he'd always been faithful to Sheila. But he knew that wouldn't mean much to a daughter because that was what a father was supposed to do — be faithful. Sixteen-year-old daughters didn't understand that most husbands and wives did cheat on each other at some point. That being together for what seemed like an eternity made them tired of each other and made them need to seek out someone else just because they were different. That didn't matter to daughters. Mothers and fathers were supposed to be together for eternity.

He wanted to tell Jamie that Sheila had actually been coming back from cheating on him when she'd run off the road and died. That Sheila had been in bed with another man last night, wrapped around the guy, doing drugs with him. But that wasn't going to happen, either. First of all, Jamie wouldn't believe it. Second, she'd blame him for it if she did come to believe it. Third, it would destroy her to think that about her mom once it sank in. He couldn't tell Jamie that. Full stop.

He thought about telling her how lonely he was. How he wanted somebody he could talk to about his day at the office like Jamie always wanted to tell him everything that had happened to her that day at school. That he wanted to be able to tell somebody about his dreams and his frustrations. But dads weren't supposed to get frustrated, he knew. They were supposed to be able to handle anything, they were supposed to be the last line of defense for little girls. The ones who were always there to protect their daughters against all the terrible things in life. They weren't supposed to be vulnerable, ever. Just tough — always.

He wanted to tell her all those things and why he was really talking to the woman. Why he *had* to talk to her. How important it was. But of course, he couldn't.

Rose slipped his finger beneath Jamie's wet chin and tugged on it gently, so she was looking up at him. He gazed into her young eyes for several moments. "I'm sorry, honey. I'll try to be a better father."

28

Kat slipped the key into the town house lock as quietly as she could and turned, wincing when the door creaked slightly as she pushed it open. It was three in the morning. Hopefully Joey was asleep, or out with his friends. She hadn't looked in their one-bay garage to see if his car was in there, just pulled hers in front of the closed door. When they'd last spoken around ten, she'd told Joey it was going to be a late night, that Clyde's was packed. He'd mentioned that he was thinking about going out to a local bar in Manassas with some friends. She'd quickly told him to stay out as late as he wanted. He hadn't seemed to like that very much.

She slipped her shoes off by the front door and padded down the hall carpeting to the kitchen. She made sure to turn her cell phone off, then stowed her phone back in her purse and her purse in the big drawer beside the dishwasher where she usually kept it. She glanced over the counter into the small living room. Joey was in there asleep on the couch with the TV tuned to some boxing match from decades ago that was being shown in a grainy black and white. He loved boxing, always watched *Sports Century* on ESPN to catch the old fights.

Well, good. She didn't want to sleep with him tonight anyway. Hopefully he'd gotten the message about coming up at six in the morning looking for sex, too. He wasn't going to get it if he tried *this* morning, that was for sure.

She climbed the steep stairs to the second floor, peeled off her clothes — she hated the way they smelled when she got home but that was just a given when you worked in a restaurant — threw them in the hamper, dove into a Washington Redskins T-shirt, brushed her teeth, and slipped into bed. She pulled the covers up around her chin, loving the way her body warmed up quickly beneath the thick, down comforter her mother had given her for a wedding present. Joey always kept it so darn cold in the house to save money on the heating bill. She inhaled deeply, thinking about Tuesday as she started to drift off. She was looking forward to lunch with Michael Rose so much.

"What is this number on your cell phone?"

Kat bolted up in bed. Joey was standing in the doorway holding a cell phone — presumably hers. She could see the outline of his body and the phone in the light from the hallway. "What are you talking about? I thought you were asleep."

"Whose number is this?" he demanded, stalking toward her, sticking the phone's lighted screen in her face. "Tell me, damn it! It's not one of your friends. I know all their numbers. This person dialed you, then you dialed them back. *What's going on!*"

She could see Joey's face twisted in rage, like she'd never seen. Suddenly she was scared. "It's nobody!" she shouted back, scrambling out of bed, trying to make it past him.

But he caught her, curled his fingers tightly around her upper arm.

"What is your problem?" she yelled, glancing down at his fingers curled around her. "Have you lost your mind?"

"I want to know whose number this is," he demanded, his voice shaking with anger. "I want to know who this bastard is."

"It doesn't concern you."

"Some guy messing with my wife and it

doesn't concern me? The hell it doesn't. I'll call this guy right now if you don't tell me what's going on," he warned, holding the phone up as if he was about to start pressing buttons. "I swear to God."

"You're blowing this way out of proportion," she said, cringing as she shook herself loose from his grip.

Joey's shoulders sagged. "Look, I'm sorry, honey. It's just that I don't like the thought of some guy going after you." He reached for her. "Are you all —"

As he leaned in, she grabbed the phone, taking him by surprise. She hurled it against the dresser beside the armoire before he could react, and it smashed into several pieces, scattering tiny electronic shards all over the bedroom. Now he couldn't get the number.

"You think that's going to stop me?" he yelled. "The phone's listed in my name, you idiot. I can get the number in the morning from customer service." He started at her with his fist raised.

She backed up quickly against the wall and held her arms out. "You touch me and I'll call my friends. I swear to God."

He sneered, but dropped his hand to his side. "You talk big and bad about these 'friends' of yours. I'm so scared. A couple of busboys from Clyde's probably. Well, go ahead," he urged, heading toward the bedroom door. "Call them. I'll be ready."

29

Base 12 was located on Long Island, near a town called Upton and very close to the Energy Department's Streamhaven Lab facility. It was fifty miles east of Kennedy Airport on an old vineyard the government had purchased for almost nothing from an elderly Greek shipping tycoon. The Coast Guard had discovered a substantial cache of cocaine during a raid on one of the old tycoon's ships that was steaming toward the port of Wilmington, North Carolina from Colombia. The government gave the old man a stark choice: Sell the land at a bargain basement price or face prosecution. The sixty-seven acres were worth tens of millions, but the old man had sold it for fifty grand and an agreement not to allow his ships to make port in the United States ever again.

He'd signed the deed to the land over to a blind trust domiciled in Switzerland by way of Antigua. No one would ever be able to identify the true purchaser of the property. In short order, the transaction was further masked when the land was turned over to the I-4 without any official documents drafted.

Having Base 12, or the "Vineyard," as it was known to the insiders, was extremely convenient for The Fourth Order of Immunity. There were two major airports on Long Island, Kennedy and La Guardia, and the I-4 detained more travelers at these two facilities than at the next ten airports combined. The only routes off Long Island by vehicle were via toll bridges and tunnels or through Manhattan, which posed serious risks to the I-4. Other federal, state, and local law enforcement agencies were extremely active at these spots, and there had been two incidents early on in the I-4's existence during which detainees had almost been discovered in the wells of vans. Having a base on a relatively small island presented other problems, but the Vineyard was located a mile from the island's north shore and there was always a boat waiting to whisk detainees away to a pontoon plane if things suddenly got hot.

The white van pulled to a sharp stop at a small gate and the driver and a lone sentry exchanged passwords. Then the vehicle moved down a dirt road toward an old gray barn in the middle of the property. Unlike Bases 77 and 19, which were heavily guarded, the key to this facility was transparency. The I-4 simply wanted to blend into the background at Base 12, which wasn't to say that the facility lacked security. The Vineyard still produced wine every year, but the people working the grapes were all new now that the government owned it — and they all carried automatic weapons.

Two men quickly slammed the barn's heavy wooden sliding door shut after the white van cruised inside, then hustled to the vehicle and helped two other men pull a shackled and harried-looking Frank Davis out of the back. They led him to a small side door and a specially installed elevator, then forced him inside when the door opened. The two agents who had shut the barn door accompanied Davis into the elevator.

"Where's my wife?" Davis asked softly. They'd removed his gag as they were waiting for the elevator door to open. He hadn't seen Ellen since just moments after they'd been forced inside the small room at Kennedy Airport where they'd been gagged, shackled, and blindfolded. He'd watched them assault her, unable to help because the three men holding him down in the room were too strong. Watched until they'd slipped the blindfold over his eyes and everything had gone dark. "What have you done with her?"

"Shut up."

When the elevator stopped, one of the agents bent down and unlocked the shackles on his ankles and tossed them to the side of a tunnel the elevator had opened up onto, which reminded him of a mine shaft. It was damp and smelled of mildew down here. They grabbed his elbows and hurried him forward to the third door on the left. Inside the dimly lit room were two chairs and a table.

"Sit in the chair facing the door," the man who'd undone the shackles ordered in a tough voice.

"Yes, sir," Davis agreed, his head bowed forward as he shuffled into the room as though he was still wearing the shackles.

The two agents remained at the door, stepping aside only when their superior emerged from another door farther down the tunnel.

He nodded at them as he brushed past wordlessly and entered the room. They would stay just outside in case there was any trouble. When the door was closed, he nodded to them again through the small Plexiglas window that was two inches thick. Then they locked the door from the outside.

"What were you doing in New Zealand?" the interrogator demanded, sitting on the edge of the table in front of Davis.

"What the hell's going on here?" Davis asked, trying to fight tough with tough. He was a tall, slim man with thinning curly brown hair and a scruffy beard. "I have rights."

The interrogator laughed. "Yeah, that's what everyone thinks." His expression turned sour again. "You have rights when I say you have rights. Now, tell me what you were doing in New Zealand."

"I was on my honeymoon."

"How does a third-grade public school-teacher from Connecticut afford a two-week honeymoon in New Zealand? Neither of your families has any money. Your father's a brakeman for the Burlington Northern Railroad out of Eugene, Oregon. Your father-in-law drives a bakery truck."

"We both work," Davis explained, frightened by how much this man knew about his family. "My wife makes good money. She's an engineer."

"At the Groton nuclear sub facility," the

interrogator added quickly. He jabbed Davis so hard in the shoulder he almost fell off the chair. "Yeah, I know that. *Now tell me what you were doing in New Zealand!*" he thundered. "Who did you meet there?"

"No one," Davis protested. "I mean, we met some people, other tourists. We were just there for fun. That was all."

"Were you with your wife the whole time?"

"Well, I um . . . let me think."

"Did she ever go off on her own, ever go *shopping* one day by herself?" asked the interrogator. "Huh? Huh?"

"Maybe once or twice. I, I can't remember exactly." Davis was sweating profusely. "It's hot down here."

"It's seventy-two degrees, it's very comfortable. What's your problem?"

"I don't have a problem. Except that you're a maniac and —"

The interrogator reached behind his back and pulled a .38 caliber revolver from his belt. He leveled it directly at Davis, who quickly brought his shaking cuffed hands to his face and turned his head. "Now," the guy said, his teeth gritted, "what were you doing in New Zealand?"

"Nothing, damn it. I keep trying to tell you. It was our *freaking* honeymoon. That's all."

"Liar!" The interrogator grabbed Davis by the back of his collar, pulled him out of the chair and slammed him against the plywood wall of the room. Then held him by the throat with one hand, shoved the barrel of the gun into his mouth with the other and started pulling the trigger. "Five empty chambers, one bullet!" the interrogator yelled. "Better give me something while you've still got a chance!"

30

Joey's eyes opened slowly. He glanced at the cable box on top of the television, checking to see what time it was. Five-thirty in the morning. As he came to full consciousness, he realized he needed to take a piss. As he'd hit his late twenties, he'd been waking up more and more often in the middle of the night to go, especially nights that he'd been drinking. He'd polished off a twelve-pack waiting for Kat to get home last night from Clyde's. Waiting for the chance to check her new cell phone for any new numbers on her dialed and received calls lists.

He pushed the blanket down, swung his feet to the living room floor, rose up from the couch, and stretched with a loud yawn. After forcing Kat to have sex with him, he'd come back down here to sleep on the couch. She wasn't going to call anybody, including the cops. She'd never do that. She knew if she did, once he posted bail he'd make her pay. He smiled to himself as he headed toward the small bathroom by the front door. She always talked a big game about what she was going to do to him, what she was going to have her "friends" do to him, but it was all bullshit. There was nothing to it.

When he was done in the bathroom, he flipped off the light and started heading back toward the couch, but hesitated at the foot of the stairs. He wanted sex, and damn it, she was his wife. It was her obligation to give it to him.

He started up the stairs, then stopped when he heard a clicking sound coming from the kitchen. He turned his head and listened intently. There it was again, a tick-tick-tick. "Sounds like the oven," he muttered to himself, turning around and heading past the counter to the stove. Sure enough, the oven was on, turned all the way up to 550 degrees, as high as it could go. He could feel the heat pouring out of it even through the door. It was uncomfortable just to stand in front of it. He stepped back a little, then bent down and looked through the window, trying to see what Kat was cooking at such an early hour of the morning. But there was nothing inside, just the smell of the pot pie she'd made a few nights ago wafting to his nostrils. "What is she doing?"

"She's not doing anything."

Joey rose up quickly and spun around, terror surging through his body. There were two huge men standing a few feet away, towering over him. He could just make out their hulking forms in the darkness. "What do you want?" he asked feebly, choking on the words, barely able to get them out. He had nowhere to run. They were blocking his escape route to the hall.

He backed up as they came at him, a flash of heat hitting him when his ass touched the red-hot stove. "Get off me!" he shouted as they grabbed him by the arms and spun him around so he was facing the stove. One of the men pulled down the oven door and an inferno hit him. Now he knew why the oven was turned on. *"No, no, please!"* he screamed, putting both feet up on the top of the stove, doing anything to keep himself out of there. The skin on his soles felt like it was going to melt off, but he kept his feet up there, fighting the men furiously. *"Kat, help, help! Call the cops! Jesus Christ, help me!"*

"She isn't going to help you," one of the men hissed as they forced Joey's feet off the stove and pushed him onto his knees. "She's the one that called us. She's been telling us about you for a while. About what an asshole you are. She couldn't take it anymore, tonight was the last straw, and now it's time to pay. So, in you go you little shit."

"Yeeeeaaaah!" he screamed as they forced his head toward the open oven. The heat seared his cheeks, and he could feel his eyebrows and eyelashes singeing. He tried to fight the men, but they were way too strong for him. "Please don't do this!" he begged as they forced his head forward inch by inch.

Suddenly they let him go, and a wave of cool air hit him when he fell backward onto the floor. He opened his eyes, looking up at the men from the linoleum, gasping for breath. His cheeks still felt like they were burning off.

One of the men knelt down next to him and grabbed him by the throat. "I'm gonna give you some advice, boy," he snarled. "Advice that might save your life one day. *Might,*" he repeated to make his point. "Keep away from your wife from now on. She calls me and tells me you even accidentally brush up against her in the closet getting dressed in the morning, and you'll regret it. You'll end up in that oven next time with the door locked shut. From now on your wife comes and goes as she pleases, and you don't say a word, not even if she stays out all night. And you don't even ask her for sex, you just be glad you're alive." He started to relax his grip, then tightened it again. "Oh yeah, and as far as going in her purse, checking her phone, going through *any* of her things. She tells me you've been doing that, and it's the same deal." He smiled with two big rows of teeth. "You'll be like the turkey at Thanksgiving dinner. Roasted to a golden brown." His smile faded. "Do we understand each other?" he asked, sliding his hand away from Joey's neck.

Joey nodded. "Yes," he whispered.

"You say 'sir' to me, boy."

"Yes, sir," he murmured, suddenly aware that Kat was standing beside the counter watching. "Yes, sir."

31

Rose sat in his den at home staring down at the piece of paper Kat had written her number on. Staring at it in the dim light of the lamp on the table. It was six in the morning. He hadn't slept in two days, but strangely he wasn't tired. He'd gone to bed at midnight, but tossed and turned, then flipped on the TV and watched two movies — *Braveheart* and *Patton*. He'd been thinking about Sheila, wondering what the detectives had found at the crash site that had piqued their interest enough to consider her death suspicious, not accept it as just another accident. They hadn't told him anything other than the fact that she had no identification on her, the glove compartment was cleaned out and that it appeared she was snorting cocaine. They'd indicated they would be contacting him, but they hadn't. He didn't know how to take that, didn't know if it meant they'd decided there was really nothing to investigate, or they'd found more and didn't want to tip him off as to how deeply they were digging. You didn't have to be a rocket scientist to figure out that they were suspicious of him knowing more than he was saying about what had happened to Sheila.

Tuesday, he thought, gazing at the note. That was when he was supposed to have lunch with Kat. He couldn't deny that he was looking forward to it, couldn't deny that basically he couldn't stop thinking about it. About her. That even when he tried to focus on what he had to do at Trafalgar, especially cranking up the hostile bid for CIS, she kept creeping back into his thoughts. Jamie would be so disappointed in him if she ever found out that he'd gone to lunch with a young woman.

He closed his eyes and put his head back, picturing Kat again. The sweet face, the blond hair, those glistening eyes. How she'd gazed back at him from across the bar at Morton's, mesmerizing him, paralyzing him. Which had never happened to him before. He could still remember the feeling he'd experienced the first time he'd seen Sheila in college, but that was nowhere near as intense as this. He literally couldn't wait to see Kat again. The weekend was going to go by like a turtle race.

"Dad."

He almost fell out of his chair at the sound of Jamie's voice but managed to slip the piece of paper with Kat's number on it into his pocket quickly. "Honey, you scared me to death." She was standing in the den's doorway. "Come on in."

She didn't, she stayed by the door. "Can't sleep, huh?" she asked.

"No, I can't."

"You must be exhausted, Daddy. Why don't you try to get some sleep?"

He shook his head, glancing at the grand-father clock. "I can't. It's almost time to go up and take a shower."

"Are you going into the office?" she asked glumly.

"I have to."

"But, Daddy, it's Saturday. Can't you wait until Mon—"

"I'm meeting Mr. Cortez for a few hours, honey. There's some really important stuff we *have* to go over. But I'll be home by noon, I promise." His face brightened. "How about this? You, Glenn, Trudy, and I go out to dinner tonight. You pick the place. At dinner we'll talk about a ski vacation in the next couple of weeks, somewhere out west for a few days. There's still time in the

247

season. We'll plan it all out tonight, what do you say?"

"You're going to kill yourself," Jamie said quietly. "You're going to have a heart attack or a stroke or something."

"I'm young, and I think I'm in pretty decent shape," he said, smiling and patting his stomach with both hands.

Jamie pursed her lips. "Do you remember when my friend Lynn Johnson's father had a heart attack last fall? He was only forty-nine. He was a businessman like you."

"He weighed two hundred and forty pounds, and he wasn't that much taller than you," Rose pointed out, rising from the chair. "Come on now."

"I just don't want to see you, I don't want you to . . ." Her voice faded away as she buried her face in her hands.

Rose moved to her and hugged her tightly. "It'll be all right, honey. It'll be fine."

"Why do you have to work so hard, Daddy? What's the point? Glenn and I already have everything we could ever want. Why can't you slow down a little? I can't lose you, too."

"It's not that simple."

"Explain it to me, then."

"It's just . . . there's a lot to . . . it would take too long."

"What you mean is that I'm still too young. That I wouldn't understand. Right?"

"No, no." That was exactly what he was saying. She was getting too sophisticated. She really was a young woman now. "What I mean is, there isn't time because I have to go to the office," he said softly. "If you want to talk about it when I get home today, we will." Maybe it would be good for her to hear about all that was involved in this lifestyle. Maybe he'd been wrong. Maybe she was old enough now to understand.

Jamie looked up at him through her tears. "Daddy, did you ever have an affair while you were married to Mom?"

He gazed down at her and shook his head. "No, I did not," he said firmly. "I don't care what your mother told you about me, I never cheated on her the whole time we were married."

"She said you never did." Jamie paused, her lower lip quivering. "She said you were the best man there ever was. She said I'd be lucky to find someone like you someday."

He smiled down at her sadly. "When did she say that to you?" It couldn't have been lately, he thought — not in the last six months, anyway. They'd been at each other's throat constantly.

"She said it the other morning before I

went to school. The day she died."

"Really?" he whispered.

"Yeah." Her dark eyebrows furrowed together. "Do you think Mom ever cheated on you?"

Rose stared at Jamie for a long time. "No, honey, she didn't. I'm sure she didn't."

32

The Fourth Order of Immunity derived its name from the fact that this was the fourth time in United States' history that the executive branch of the federal government had covertly given a tiny cell of undercover agents the license to kill with no risk of prosecution. The fourth time an administration had given its permission to take the ultimate step in order to achieve its objective. To kill anytime the agents deemed it necessary and not be held accountable, even if they murdered a completely innocent person — whether that victim was American or foreign, whether that victim was killed in the United States or abroad.

An agent could be expelled if the Order's four-member leadership, the Directorate, determined that the agent had been guilty of gross negligence or recklessness in carrying out his duties, but that had happened only twice. Those two men had been expelled during the Third Immunity, during the mid 1950s when McCarthyism was the creed. When the then acting Directorate had determined that communism had become too great a threat to the American way of life and that U.S. agents needed the ability to take the ultimate step without fear of reprisal from their own country and stamp out the Red Tide. Both men had died of natural causes in the '90s after living out their lives comfortably in Europe, thanks to generous pensions clandestinely paid to numbered accounts every month from an anonymous trust.

The money paid to the ex-agents had ultimately come from the Atomic Energy Commission in the early years, then later the Energy Department. But first it had passed through something known as the Catrelle Foundation. And that had sanitized it.

As a group, the Directorate had only three specific duties. First, to determine in their sole discretion when an Order of Immunity began. Second, to determine when an Order of Immunity ended. Third, to agree on which individuals the agents would detain for interrogation. The second and third duties required a simple majority for approval, but the first, the decision to initiate an Immunity, required a unanimous vote by the Directorate. Other than those items, the executive director — Peter Beck at this point — was responsible for managing everything. And for keeping it absolutely secret.

The Directorate had always been composed of four individuals: the executive director, the president's personal emissary, a high-ranking military officer, and a senior corporate executive. They were members of the Directorate for as long as they wanted to be — or until they died or were incapacitated — even if they were no longer active in the military or corporate America. No one outside the Directorate, other than the president, knew who all four members were, and only a few other people, including any retired, former members of the Directorate knew that the I-4 even existed as an organized entity. Even the agents didn't understand that there was an independent, covert organization supporting them that had been in existence for almost a hundred and fifty years and had nothing to do with the CIA, the DIA, the NSA, or any of the other secret government organizations. They were told only that their superiors had determined that the country faced a crisis, and that they were being given special powers until otherwise advised. They were told that they were no longer officially members of their original agencies — usually the CIA, DIA, or the FBI — but would return to them when the crisis had ended. They had no idea how the three domestic interrogation bases were funded and maintained, in addition to the five the I-4 operated internationally, or what Project Spyder was or how it helped them. Likewise, the people inside Spyder had no idea who was using the financial information they gleaned to interrupt terrorist attacks. They assumed it was the CIA and the FBI. They had no clue as to the existence of the I-4, either. Everything was neatly compartmentalized to preserve the entity's secrecy.

The First Order of Immunity had lasted only a few weeks, after the assassination of President Lincoln in 1865. The Second Order had lasted three years — the final three years of the Manhattan Project in the 1940s when there was intense suspicion of a high-level leak within the team engineering the atomic bomb. The Third — a result of the country's intense paranoia regarding communism — four years. And the Fourth Order was ongoing, already the longest of all the Immunities, having been declared on September 12, 2001.

The original Order of Immunity was initiated by two of Lincoln's cabinet members who approached a senior military officer hours after the assassination at Ford's Theatre, panic-stricken that the South would be reenergized and rise out of the ashes after hearing what had happened to the North's leader. Initially, the plan was only to implement a curfew in Washington, but it had expanded quickly from there. By early in the morning after the assassination, the general had secretly recruited fifteen men of unquestionable character from one of his divisions and given them independent powers to pursue anyone suspected of being involved in the conspiracy to kill the president. One of those powers was immunity from prosecution were they to kill anyone during their pursuit, even if that person turned out to be innocent of any crime. The rumor was that the unit had shot three men, one of whom was innocent. The Order of Immunity was born.

Interestingly, no Orders were initiated after the assassinations of Presidents Garfield, McKinley, and Kennedy. Garfield and McKinley because it was quickly determined that the men who had shot these presidents were acting independently and that there was no national crisis. Kennedy because he had tried to disband the organization as soon as he'd learned of it.

33

Beck and Klein sat in a comfortable room of the spacious bunker inexplicably nicknamed the "House" by the executive director of The Third Order of Immunity over half a century ago. But it was a nickname that had stuck. The ten-thousand-square-foot cavern, excavated a hundred yards below ground level, had served as Beck's base of operations for the last seven years, since the fiery private plane crash near Puerto Vallarta in which he was supposed to have perished. Several articles had run in the *Washington Post* and the *New York Times* mourning and praising the former senior Energy Department official's great contributions to the agency during his twenty years of service. But there had been no funeral, just a memorial service, as his family had been told his body had been burned too badly to even remove what was left of it from the plane.

Beck had convalesced here at the bunker for several weeks after the crash, recovering not from any injuries — he'd never even been to Mexico in his life — but from hours of plastic surgery. The surgery was intended to alter his facial features enough to fool family, friends, and acquaintances in case there was ever a chance meeting. Even more important, to fool the enemies of the United States. Then he'd taken up permanent residence in the bunker when the other three members of the Directorate had confirmed him as the new ED — after making certain he had fully recovered from the operation.

When the doctor had finally removed the bandages and Beck was able to gaze into a mirror at himself for the first time since the surgery, he'd been shocked at how much they'd been able to change his physical appearance. For the better, he'd mused as he'd stared at himself approvingly in the glass. He seemed tougher looking, and he liked it. His jaw and chin were more pronounced, sharper and stronger, and his puffy cheeks had been sliced away. Problem was, they hadn't done anything to the rest of his body, which remained paunchy thanks to his bad diet, drinking, and lack of exercise. He'd promised himself as he'd stared into the mirror that morning that he was going to make amends and retrofit the rest of his body to augment his new face — there was a full gym in the back of the bunker and plenty of time to work out — but it hadn't happened. The stress of being the I-4's ED had taken care of that. In fact, he weighed fifteen pounds more now than when he'd taken over.

The bunker was also where the Directorate met as a group once every three months, when there was an active Order, to stay up to speed on everything that had occurred in the last ninety days. Otherwise, they met here once a year, as they had from the late '50s until September 2001. Weekly meetings regarding who was to be detained by the agents were held by conference call in code on secure phone lines arranged by the Secret Service on the president's orders alone. However, no other business was discussed just in case someone was listening who wasn't supposed to be.

The bunker lay beneath the grounds of the Argosse National Laboratory in Dupage County, twenty-five miles southwest of Chicago. The Argosse campus was one of nineteen research facilities — in fact, one of the largest of the nineteen — across the country operated by the Department of

Energy. Scientists at the campus were supposed to be focused on general energy-related research and environmental management, but there was also a significant amount of resources dedicated to national security at Argosse: pipeline protection, advanced storage and transportation techniques for emergency fuel supplies, and the headquarters of the I-4.

A good deal of the campus's fifteen hundred acres was heavily wooded, so it was a perfect place to base the operation. Close to the biggest city in the Midwest, making travel to and from easier, but also veiled inside a heavily protected government facility. The entrance to the elevator leading down to the bunker almost three hundred feet below the surface was hidden in a thick grove of pine trees in the middle of a rock outcropping. Access to the hidden door required fingerprint and pupil identification, though it wasn't as if intruders would discover anything sensitive if somehow they managed to penetrate the bunker. Beck kept nothing of any importance in the bunker, other than in his brain, and if intruders captured him they would get nothing out of him.

During Beck's plastic surgery, the doctors had also implanted a special switch on the left side of his left palm — a quarter of an inch below the skin — which could only be activated by Beck holding his left little finger against the spot on his palm above the switch for ten consecutive seconds. When the switch in his palm was activated, it immediately detonated a capsule of cyanide that had also been surgically implanted in his body in the lining of his stomach. So even if Beck was handcuffed, he could still commit suicide, thereby denying his captors any chance to torture him. Beck had to be careful about sleeping because he could accidentally activate the switch and detonate the cyanide capsule if he lay the wrong way. So, he always wore a glove on his left hand when he slept, which effectively prevented activation of the switch and therefore detonation of the capsule.

Construction of the bunker had begun in 1947 as part of a larger project to protect President Truman. High-ranking government officials assumed after the bombings of Hiroshima and Nagasaki that the United States would not be the only country with the atomic bomb for long, given their suspicion of a leak at the Manhattan Project. It proved a fortuitous assumption when the Soviet Union conducted its first successful atomic test in 1949, followed by the United

Kingdom in 1952, France in 1960, and China in 1964.

The Atomic Energy Commission had built fifty presidential bunkers at strategic locations around the country by the end of 1949. The Secret Service could theoretically get the president into one of them and protection from an atomic attack in no less than two hours from wherever he was. The bunkers had been active until the mid '90s when it was determined that they were no longer necessary. The other forty-nine had been mothballed, but the one at Argosse had remained active as it had doubled as the headquarters of The Third Order, then remained the Order's central command.

"Chin up, Peter," Klein said, yawning.

Beck glanced over. Klein was lounging on a sofa on the other side of the coffee table watching CNN and munching on a doughnut. Beck grunted a reply even he didn't understand, then rose from his chair and padded toward the kitchen. They'd driven across the country from Baltimore yesterday, Sunday, because he didn't fly if he didn't have to. It was better for security if he didn't, and, more to the point, he was afraid to. He hated planes, always had, which was why it was eerie that they'd chosen to fake his death with a plane crash.

He'd always had an awful premonition that it was how he would really go someday.

Beck had spent most of Saturday asleep in an upstairs bedroom of the estate outside Baltimore, trying to regain his energy and licking his wounds after being outmaneuvered in the Trafalgar board meeting by Michael Rose. He hadn't eaten all day Saturday or on the drive to Chicago from the east coast yesterday, feeling bad about his weight — he was up to two twenty-five. Feeling especially guilty about wanting to horse down a Big Mac or a Whopper the way Klein had several times during the trip. The little bastard could eat anything, but never gained weight.

They'd gotten here at ten thirty last night, eleven thirty eastern, and gone straight to bed, he in his back bedroom, Klein in one of the four guest bedrooms. Now he was famished. He quickly fixed a ham and cheese sandwich — mayo, no mustard — then headed back into the living room. He often ate lunch for breakfast and breakfast for dinner. He loved an omelet filled with melted cheese and bacon for dinner.

"Now what?" Klein asked.

Beck put the plate on the table in front of his chair, sat, picked up the sandwich, and took a huge bite. God, that was good. Too good, he thought to himself. Ham, cheese, mayonnaise, tomato, and bread all blending together in his mouth to form one fantastic momentary distraction from all his responsibilities. He'd probably have a second sandwich, this time with some barbecue chips. Maybe even a third after that. That was the problem with starving himself for a couple of days. Afterward he binged and ended up ultimately gaining more weight than if he'd just eaten normally during that time. So be it. He loved to eat. Maybe he should just let it all go and eat whatever he wanted whenever he wanted to. Let the food kill him and be done with all this pressure.

"We wait," Beck answered. Thankfully, Klein hadn't brought up the CIS situation during the drive back to Chicago, obviously sensing that his boss needed a break from focusing on it. "We let Michael Rose start his attack and see how the market reacts. Maybe we won't have to do anything at all."

"Well, you know that's a pipe dream because —"

"And I'm going to talk to some of our friends this week," Beck interrupted. "See if I can get another bidder ginned up. Hell, this could end up being a real positive for us," he said, trying to make himself feel better about what was going on. Trying to see some silver lining to it. "If we could get one of our friends to buy CIS, somebody who runs one of the big conglomerates in this country, maybe we could bury CIS as a subsidiary inside it. Insulate it for good."

"Got anybody in mind?"

Beck nodded. "Yeah, but I don't want to talk about him yet. I need to make a couple of calls this afternoon. Then we can talk. Obviously, I'll need your help on that." He took another bite of the sandwich, almost finishing it. He'd eat at least one more. If he could just put off that urge for a third one, then he'd feel better. "Did we get that woman to Seventy-seven? That woman from Dallas?"

"Yes," Klein answered quietly.

"What's wrong?" He could tell by Klein's tone and expression that there was some kind of issue. It seemed like there always was. At least, a lot more often now than at the beginning of all this. Nothing was ever easy.

"There was a problem in Utah. Fortunately it was in the middle of nowhere."

Beck pushed both thumbs into the soft bread, making deep indentations, then dropped what was left of the sandwich on the plate. "What kind of problem?" he demanded, aggravated even before hearing

265

the details.

"The leader of the team gave one of his men the go-ahead to start the interrogation phase early."

"*What?* That isn't their job. They know that."

Klein's face turned grim. "They had a flat tire, and they had to get her out of the van for a while. Apparently the captain gave one of his men permission to rough Ms. Anduhar up while she was out of the van. My guess is the captain wanted some glory, wanted to be the one who broke her. They knew we considered her a code Alpha."

Alpha meant there was an extremely high probability the detainee was involved in an imminent, major terrorist plot. There had only been a few such cases since the beginning of The Fourth Order.

"The guy who was in charge of her for that fifteen minutes went too far, confirmed by another guy in the team who stumbled onto what was going on in the nick of time. The guy was about to kill her. She's made all kinds of claims about him trying to rape her during the interrogation, too."

"Who was it?"

"Sir? What do you mean?"

"*The captain.*" Klein knew exactly what he meant. He was protecting the guy. "Remind

266

me of his name."

"It was Captain Turner."

Beck gritted his teeth. "Right, Turner." The guy was a cowboy. Tremendously effective, but quick to push his orders over the limit.

Beck eased back in the chair, closed his eyes and ran his fingers through his hair. Vivian Anduhar was making accusations of rape and she had no idea how bad it really was, that her family was gone. Of course, she never would. Now that Captain Turner had chosen to take that huge step back in Dallas — torching the entire house and killing the other five members of her family — Anduhar would never be released from custody. She'd be shipped around the world until she died of old age or had an accident of some kind.

God, he hated this part of the job. He'd almost considered bringing Turner up on recklessness charges with the Directorate when he'd first heard about the fire and the death of her family, but that was a huge step to take. Ultimately, a lot of agents would hear about the charges, even though Beck tried to keep them compartmentalized into small teams. Even if the Directorate didn't vote to expel Captain Turner from the I-4, it would send a shiver throughout the organization and you didn't want your agents losing confidence in their ability to go as far as they needed to go. Or losing confidence in their leaders. Of course, you couldn't have the I-4 turn into some kind of Inquisition, either.

He groaned. They were almost positive Vivian Anduhar and her husband were involved in something sinister, something on the level of the World Trade Center attacks, and that whatever it turned out to be was going to go down in the next thirty days. But they weren't *absolutely* certain, not yet. The reality was she might be innocent. It had only happened like that once before, where they'd called a code Alpha and been completely wrong. He'd barely been able to keep going after that, barely been able to get out of bed in the morning for a week. Two small children and the detainee's wife had been killed in a car accident that hadn't really been an accident, and the detainee had turned out to be absolutely innocent. Just a hardworking man who'd been in the wrong place at the wrong time. At this point he was at the international base in Japan. The poor guy would never see the light of day again.

"The good thing is," Klein continued, "our people in the Middle East picked up some coded chatter over the weekend about a major terrorist group over there losing contact with one of their primary connections here in the States. Some crap about fire and brimstone, too. We think it might have something to do with the house burning down."

Beck's shoulders slumped. At least that was something to hang his hat on.

"And the Davis woman is now at Base Nineteen in Tennessee, the woman we detained at Kennedy Airport coming back from New Zealand with her husband."

"I don't want those people harmed," Beck snapped. "It was a mistake to detain them." It was the first time he'd ever admitted to Klein that he thought the other three members of the Directorate had made a mistake overruling him on a vote. Voting to detain the schoolteacher and his engineer wife. "You understand?"

"I made it clear to our people at both locations." Klein hesitated. "Unfortunately, Peter, before I could make contact, they used some pretty rough tactics on Frank Davis, the husband, at Base Twelve, at the Vineyard. But it's all right now."

"What did they do to him?" Beck asked apprehensively.

"Russian roulette."

"Shit." Beck banged the table. Maybe this thing really had gone on too long. The agents were getting harsher and harsher on the detainees, crueler and crueler.

Early on, several psychologists had warned Beck about the possibility of this syndrome developing, agents getting drunk on power. People taking greater and greater liberties with an immense amount of power as time wore on and potentially losing control of themselves and their actions. He'd gathered as much information on it as he dared — only one of the psychologists had pushed him on why he was asking, and he'd never called her again. Maybe it was actually starting to happen, he realized, and there were only two alternatives if the agents were falling victim to the syndrome as a group. First, you could expel the agents who were the most abusive, particularly the ones at the top. The problem with doing that was that then you had a significant number of men out there who were bitter and knew too much. So the secrecy of the I-4 could easily be compromised. The second alternative was to simply end the I-4, which could potentially have an infinitely greater negative impact on the world than expelling a few bad apples.

"Davis didn't tell them anything, either,"

Klein said, as though he found that fact curious. "Not even after the interrogator pulled the trigger the fourth time. Not even when it was up to a fifty-fifty chance that Davis would get his head blown off the next time the guy pulled the trigger."

"Of course, he didn't," Beck said angrily. "Because he didn't have anything he *could* tell them. Davis doesn't know anything. He's a damn third-grade schoolteacher."

Klein scratched his head. "Yeah, but usually the detainees make up something at that point because they're so scared. They'll say anything to get the guy to take the gun out of their mouths."

Beck suddenly realized how the news of the fire at the Anduhar house in Dallas and the deaths of the other five members of Vivian's family hadn't hit him nearly as hard as the deaths of the two innocent children and their mother had last year. Maybe he was falling victim to the syndrome himself. The psychologists had warned him that he wouldn't see it coming.

He shook his head. He couldn't think on it now. "Do you have the list for tonight?" Generally, the Directorate met by phone on Monday nights to cull through the list of potential detainee targets. "I want to go through it before the meeting."

"No, but I'll —"

"I want it in an hour," Beck said sharply, taking the last bite of his sandwich as he stood up and headed back to the kitchen with the empty plate. He didn't want the second sandwich anymore, he wanted a martini. A strong one. It wasn't even eight o'clock in the morning. "Make it thirty minutes," he called loudly over his shoulder.

34

Sherman LeClair opened one of the three general e-mail accounts he maintained from his laptop computer as he sat in front of a dancing fire in the living room of his cabin in chilly northern Vermont — and almost smiled. Late last night, after he'd gone to bed, his Montana fishing guide had sent a message with several attachments. LeClair clicked on the first one. A moment later he was staring at himself struggling to hold that huge bull trout as he knelt in the shallows of the Blackfoot River. He gazed at the powerful-looking fish for a long while, admiring the breathtaking beauty nature could create.

Then he glanced at himself, which was much more difficult. He'd always hated looking at himself in pictures or the mirror. He'd never liked his face, even as a kid. He'd always found it plain with features that didn't seem to fit — big ears that stuck out too far, thin lips, eyes spread wide apart, large nostrils. At least he'd been blessed with a powerful build as a younger man. In his football days at Ohio State he'd weighed a strapping two hundred and forty pounds as a standout tight end, and he'd managed to stay in decent shape even into his late fifties, despite the stress of being the president's chief of staff for three years. But now his build was gone, and he was just an old man who wasn't much to look at. Down to a meager one eighty-five hanging on his gangly six-foot-five-inch frame. His face was particularly gaunt.

He winced and closed out the picture, then the e-mail, not bothering to look at the other five pictures Roger had attached. It was too painful, too much of a reminder of what he'd been through. The awful dejection of being kicked out of the administration as the public fall guy by his oldest friend the commander in chief, and the ensuing obsession with revenge. Both of which had taken away his desire to eat, almost taken away his desire to live. He used to eat at least two helpings at dinner, now he barely finished one. Of course, he used to eat his wife's good cooking, but now she was gone, too. Most nights he ate peanut butter and jelly sandwiches or spaghetti out of a can.

LeClair swallowed hard, remembering the day the president had asked him into the Oval Office out of the blue, alone, without his staff. Remembering it like it was yesterday. It had been the worst day of his life. Even worse than the day they'd gotten the news four years ago that Judy, his wife, had an inoperable malignant brain tumor — if he was being brutally honest with himself. His entire world — professional and personal — had disintegrated as he sat on the couch listening to the words coming from his old friend's mouth. One second he'd been at the pinnacle of power, the next just another Washington has-been. Booted out of the administration supposedly for being the one responsible for hiring an ineffective and terribly unpopular secretary of defense. And continuing to bang the table in support of the man, a friend of both LeClair's and the president's, even when it became obvious to everyone else on the president's staff that the man had to go. Which had all been lies, a spin concocted for the press so the president could put distance between himself and the deposed and severely disliked secretary of defense in front of the upcoming election.

LeClair had never been the one to suggest

that the man should be secretary of defense in the first place, and certainly hadn't banged any table in support of him staying on when others, including the president, had suggested it was time for him to go. In fact, the situation had been completely reversed. LeClair had been the first one of the president's closest advisors to bring up the possibility of firing the secretary, well before the shouting by the press for his resignation had risen to deafening decibel levels. But somehow memories inside the administration had turned selective, a conspiracy had formed behind his back, and suddenly LeClair was out on his ass, the victim of dirty politics.

Adam Pierce coughed politely as he stirred his espresso.

LeClair glanced at Pierce, who was sitting across the room, then picked up the laptop off his knees and set it down on the antique wooden table beside his chair. He stared at Pierce for a few moments thoughtfully, then gazed out the sliding glass doors that overlooked a stream running down off the mountain behind his house and through his heavily wooded backyard. Later this morning, after Pierce was gone, he'd trudge out there through the snow and wet a line. Even in winter you could pull a few brook trout

out of the deeper pools if you used the right lure. The brookies in his stream were tiny compared to that bull he'd caught in Montana, but they were infinitely prettier. The prettiest trout of all.

Pierce coughed again, a little louder this time.

"Yes, Adam," LeClair said softly but firmly, "I know you want to get going. I know about the storm headed this way." It was just starting to turn overcast. High wispy clouds were moving in.

"Oh, no, sir. Don't worry about that. It's just that I —"

"Enough," LeClair interrupted, holding up one hand.

Adam Pierce was a southern California guy. All the way from his surfer blond hair to his permanent tan to his Gucci loafers to his laid-back attitude. Pierce was in his early forties, but seemed much younger. Maybe because he had a boyish charm, which appealed to LeClair because he'd never been able to act that way himself. It seemed to LeClair like he'd been acting older than he was ever since graduating from college, seemed like he'd never been able to let go and really enjoy himself. Or maybe Pierce seemed young because he'd never been married, and his list of Washington conquests was impressive, to say the least, from newswomen to politicians, single and married.

Pierce had started at the Energy Department because it was far from California, not because he needed a job. He was from a wealthy Orange County family, and his father had sent him to Washington after graduating from the University of Southern California because it was a respectable position, albeit poorly paying, and to get him three thousand miles away from his surfer buddies, who his father felt were bad news. The job was only supposed to last a few years, but Pierce had never left. And, almost despite himself, he'd risen to a fairly senior position within the department. Then he'd been abruptly fired — the result of a sexual harassment charge brought by an administrative assistant who had never proven a thing — at the same time LeClair had been ambushed by the administration.

LeClair had taken advantage of the fact that Pierce was bitter, and jumped on the fact that his relationship irons inside the Energy Department were still hot. Pierce had loved the scenario LeClair had laid out at their first meeting at a bar in Union Station, fascinated to hear about the Energy Department's secret — hiding The Order of

Immunity. Fascinated to hear how the department he'd worked in for twenty years was so involved in the government's clandestine operations, yet he'd never had a clue. He'd been enthusiastic about getting back at his bosses, to some extent because he wanted revenge, but mostly because he had nothing better to do and it sounded exciting.

Pierce lived in a beautifully decorated Georgetown town house and drove a Ferrari — which had always irritated his bosses at the Energy Department, LeClair had learned. Helped them believe the administrative assistant's sexual harassment story very quickly. They could barely afford suburban four-bedroom boxes and American cars on their government salaries, and they didn't appreciate Pierce flaunting his silver spoon status in their faces. Pierce loved that Ferrari more than anything, LeClair had also learned. More than any of his conquests. Pierce had figured out how to drive in light Washington snowstorms — albeit like a grandmother with both hands clinging to the wheel in the ten and two positions and his foot never leaving the brake — but always called in sick if the prediction was for more than three inches. He couldn't stand snow. That part of his

California upbringing had never left him.

The storm heading east was supposed to start late this afternoon and dump almost a foot of snow on Vermont. Pierce was itching to get into his rented sedan and hightail it south toward the airport in Montpelier, LeClair could tell. Itching to get out of the state before he was stuck in it for a few days. At least the young man had shown the gumption to come up here in the face of the storm.

"What do you hear?" LeClair asked.

"There's definitely a disturbance in the force," Pierce answered with a smirk. He had a deep throat inside the Energy Department, which was how he was getting his information on the whereabouts of Peter Beck. "But, remember, my guy doesn't know what we know. He's just the Gray Ops interface between the department and Catrelle Management. He has no idea what Beck's really in charge of. He just knows that he's supposed to pay Catrelle Management when Beck tells him to. That's all he knows and that's all he does. Even the people at Catrelle don't really know what's going on, just bits and pieces."

LeClair nodded. That was true, the guy wouldn't know much. Which was how they kept everyone in the dark, he assumed. By going to great lengths to compartmentalize as much as they could. "Why do you say there's a disturbance?"

"Beck went to Washington this past weekend. Usually he stays in Chicago according to my guy, almost never travels away from his home base. And," Pierce continued, before LeClair could ask another question, "my guy said Beck sounded pretty stressed out on the phone. Usually, he's a real cool cat, but he sounded like he was upset about something this time."

"He went to see Bill Granger," LeClair said quietly. "I'd bet my life on it. He's figured out that there's a problem, he just doesn't know who's coming at him." He set his jaw. "Well, let it begin."

"Who's Bill Granger?"

LeClair hesitated. He and Pierce had been working together for six months, but he hadn't told the younger man everything. Far from it. Maybe it was time to let loose a little, time to allow the younger man further inside the circle so he felt more a part of what was going on. He had sensed that Pierce was losing interest over the last couple of weeks: a subtle tinge of boredom in the tone, a need to repeat things a couple of times when they were speaking. He couldn't lose the man — and he wouldn't.

He was too good at manipulating people.

"Bill Granger is the chief executive officer of Computer Information Systems."

"Of CIS?"

LeClair suppressed a smile. Pierce was right back in line. He could see it in the younger man's eyes. "Yes."

"That computer company Catrelle Management pays under contract?"

LeClair nodded.

"After Catrelle gets the money from the Energy Department, right?"

"Right."

The Energy Department was extremely accommodating about funding secret operations, according to Pierce's inside contact. Though, of course, the man inside had no idea what the operation was called or what it did. But people at the Energy Department were accustomed to working with the State Department and the CIA on these kinds of things, LeClair knew, so it made sense that they wouldn't ask questions. It made sense that they would send extra money to Catrelle Management LLC when they were told to. They probably appropriated the cash from the department's general expense budget, and those incremental proceeds for Catrelle were never missed or mentioned by the General Accounting Office. The Energy Department's budget was too large for the government accountants to question such a relatively small deviation, even if they had found it. Twenty-five million a year was nothing to the Energy Department or the GAO.

A curious expression came to Pierce's face. "What is the deal with Catrelle? Is it part of the government or part of the private sector?"

"It's a hybrid," LeClair answered.

"What do you mean?"

"Catrelle Management LLC is the operating entity of the Catrelle Foundation," LeClair said. "The Catrelle Foundation is a trust that was established by a man named Ethan Catrelle back in 1898 to fund a variety of general medical and scientific research in partnership with the University of Chicago. They got to use the university's facilities as a result." LeClair had done a lot of digging in order to piece all this together. "Ethan Catrelle was from Pittsburgh. He made millions in the oil industry, but somehow he got crossways with John D. Rockefeller, who was basically responsible for founding the University of Chicago. Catrelle wanted his daughter, Ann, to go to the university, but Rockefeller got in the way of her admission thanks to the feud. So

Catrelle established the foundation and bought his daughter's way into the school when Rockefeller wasn't looking."

"I still don't get what that —"

"Patience, Adam," LeClair interrupted, holding up his hands. "In the early twenties, the federal government approached the trustees of the Catrelle Foundation about establishing a partnership." LeClair had called on some old friends at the CIA to get to the bottom of this, and it had taken all his political acumen not to arouse their suspicions with his questions. Old friends who'd be livid when they found out why he'd asked — if he was successful getting his revenge. But the hell with them. They hadn't rushed to his corner in his hour of need. "The people working at the foundation had come up with some major breakthroughs, particularly in certain scientific fields. The government told the trustees they wanted to ramp up the research and development even further with federal money, make it a fifty-fifty thing with Catrelle. See, the people at Catrelle were working on a fixed budget, basically whatever interest income the endowment generated every year. The feds said they'd increase that so the research could go faster, so the foundation could get even more credit for bigger technology breakthroughs. Sounds good, right?" LeClair asked. "If you were a trustee, you would have agreed to it, wouldn't you?"

Pierce thought about it for a few moments, then nodded. "Sure. Why not?"

"Exactly. The thing was, the government had another agenda. Even back then they wanted the ability to hide money flows. They wanted the ability to mask who they were really paying. The money that went into the Catrelle Foundation was actually from the Department of War. It didn't look like it to the trustees, but it was."

"The Department of War," Pierce repeated. "That's pretty wild. Isn't that what the Defense Department used to be called?"

"Uh-huh."

"When did they change the name?"

"In 1947. The Department of War actually became the National Military Establishment for two years, then, in 1949, they finally changed the name to the Department of Defense." It was interesting how people thought political correctness was a recent phenomenon, but it wasn't. The government had realized after World War II that Department of War sounded too aggressive, as though the United States was a nation bent on combat, on domination. They realized that "defense" sounded much better to a civilized world. "And that name, the DOD, stuck."

"But the trustees didn't understand what was really going on?"

"Didn't have a clue. And, over time, the feds moved their people into the Catrelle treasury staff so they could make certain of where their money was going. So they could take a more active role in the trust and use it for bigger and better things. At first, it was just to secretly pay an agent here or there. Then it got bigger and bigger. The government people at Catrelle appear to be employees of the trust, but, if you look at their résumés, you'll see that they were all with the government at some point." Le-Clair cleared his throat. He could feel a twinge when he swallowed, like he was coming down with a cold. He'd still go fishing. He was addicted to it now. "The key to it all is that the trust operates behind a veil, really a wall. It's a tax-exempt organization so the IRS doesn't see anything, and it isn't technically a government organization so the General Accounting Office doesn't see anything. It's hidden from everyone, which is exactly what the Gray Ops guys want." He hesitated. "It's interesting. Catrelle Management also directs operations at four of the Energy Department's national laboratories, including one outside Chicago, one in Idaho, one in Tennessee, and one on Long Island."

Pierce glanced up. "You mean . . ."

"Yes, I do. I think the Order also has operations at those places."

"But I thought this was a Defense Department thing."

"It was, originally. My guess is they pushed it out of there when the Energy Department was created back in 1977. Didn't want something so secret in a department that's always under a lot of scrutiny from the GAO and the press. Nobody really thinks about the Energy Department as being involved in anything secret so it's a great place to hide covert activities." LeClair paused. "The thing is, CIS is doing a lot of bona fide work for the Energy Department, too. Funneling money to the agents is a rounding error on their general ledger. There's a big contract in place with the Energy Department covering a lot of software implementation and integration at all of the national labs that Catrelle manages. So, if somebody ever decided, for whatever reason, to give Catrelle an enema audit, they wouldn't find anything. Just payments under a contract with an escalator to a company with a strong reputation of doing excellent work for the Energy Department and other areas of the federal government. Even if they dug into the CIS books, they'd have to know exactly what they were looking for even to begin to find anything. And by the time some low-level GAO accountant started really digging into the CIS books, you better believe someone would have him pulled off the project — or killed."

"So, let me get this straight," Pierce said. "The Energy Department pays Catrelle Management to operate these four national labs. Then Catrelle pays CIS under a legitimate contract to do software and integration work at the labs. Then CIS funnels money to the Order's agents. That's the trail."

LeClair nodded. "I'm pretty sure that's how it goes."

Pierce smiled thinly. "How did you ever find all of this out?"

LeClair's eyes narrowed. It was the first time he'd ever admitted this to anyone. "I bugged the president," he said with a grin.

"What?"

"It's not hard if you know what you're doing, and I had easy access. It wasn't like the Secret Service was searching me every morning when I came to work, and I never used any devices with metal in them to bug him so I never set off any of the detectors."

"But why would you do it? You were the chief of staff, for crying out loud."

"Near the end I got paranoid," LeClair confessed. "I thought something was up when I was shut out of a few meetings, or I was told about them after the fact. So I paid closer attention to his schedule, and I bugged some of the meetings I wasn't invited to, plain and simple. Put the mikes down right before the meetings were held and took them away right after the meetings were over." LeClair cleared his throat again. "One day the president met with a guy I'd only seen a few times, and whom I'd never been allowed to meet with. Supposedly, he was an old friend of the president's, but that sounded kind of thin to me. His name was Wes Barry." He took a deep breath. "When I replayed the recording and heard what they'd been talking about, I couldn't believe it." LeClair grimaced. "But that recording would never stand up to scrutiny. I need hard evidence if I'm going to take down the administration," he said, his voice turning emotional.

"But you must still have friends in Washington or New York who would start an investigation of the Energy Department or Catrelle Management."

"What would they find? Nothing," LeClair answered his own question before Pierce could. "No, the key is CIS. That's where everything has to start."

"What about calling someone at the SEC? Don't you know someone there? Or someone who knows someone? I mean, CIS is a public company. They fall under the SEC's purview. They could do an audit."

"I tried. But what do I tell them to look for? Secret accounts? Secret payments? Secret files? Bill Granger is tight with the administration. Nobody at the SEC wants to piss off Granger and ultimately the administration because they've heard some bullshit rumor about secret payments."

Pierce nodded. "Which is why you need Michael Rose. To go through the CIS books with a microscope and find the smoking gun."

"Yes," LeClair murmured. "That's *exactly* why I need Michael Rose."

35

When he first saw Sheila's Mercedes, Rose couldn't believe his eyes. It was horrifying. Nothing but a gnarled, twisted mass of steel, wires, and rubber. As far from the sleek, silver machine he'd bought last year as he could imagine. It was easy to understand how she'd been killed now that he saw what was left.

The Fairfax County deputy who'd come to the house early Friday morning when he and Jamie were in the den had called him yesterday afternoon — Sunday — to tell him he could have access to the car this morning. Not that there was much to see, the cop had warned sternly, almost as if he was urging Rose not to go. But if Rose wanted to take pictures for the insurance company, to prove it was a total loss, he could. The lab people were finished with it, and they were trucking it to a salvage yard south of Washington off Interstate 95.

The deputy had also informed Rose on the same call that Detectives Willis and Harrison would be coming to see him at the house tonight around eight. That he *needed* to be home, that the au pair needed to be home, too. He hadn't said any more than that, and Rose hadn't asked. There was no point. The cop obviously wasn't going to preempt the detectives, and asking questions would only make him seem guilty of something.

Rose walked slowly around the car, his shoes crunching on the frozen top layer of snow. He shook his head when he bent down and saw a pool of dried blood on the ceiling — the cop had told him at the morgue that the car had been upside down when they'd gotten to her. He shivered and pulled his long coat tightly around his body when he straightened up. It was a raw, gray morning and it was strange to be out here in the middle of all these automobile carcasses, not in his comfortable office at Trafalgar. He glanced over his shoulder, but the crusty old guy in overalls who'd opened the gate and then led him to the Mercedes had already limped back to his small cigar-smelling office. A red Jetta across the muddy, rutted road bisecting the salvage yard caught Rose's eye. It was in even worse shape than Sheila's Mercedes. Someone must have died in that crash, too. He shook his head. God, this was a strange place.

Rose leaned into the Mercedes through the smashed driver side window. He hadn't come out here to take pictures of the car for the insurance company. His agent had read the news account of Sheila's death in the *Washington Post* on Saturday and called yesterday to give his condolences. There wasn't going to be any issue about being covered. He'd come here to pay his last respects to Sheila, strange as that sounded. To try to understand what she'd endured in those last few terrifying seconds of her life. The funeral was going to be the day after tomorrow, but that would be a very public affair. There would be several hundred mourners at the church and he'd be busy thanking them for coming at the reception. It wasn't like he'd be alone with his thoughts — or with her. This seemed more like the place to do that.

He reached up and touched the large brown stain on the ceiling fabric — apparently she had bled profusely from her head wounds. He swallowed hard, thinking about what she must have gone through. This was where her life had ended, screaming piti-fully as the Mercedes hurtled down the embankment. It was awful to think about. He hadn't gone to the crash scene yet, but he was going to do that today as well, on his way home from the office. Maybe visiting these two places would give him some kind of closure.

Rose reached for the leather console between the two front seats. Sheila had always kept pictures of Jamie and Glenn in a compartment at the back of it and he tried to open the main flap, wondering if the cops had taken the photos. But the flap was jammed shut from the force of the crash. He pushed harder and it popped off its hinges suddenly and flew into what was left of the passenger seat, startling him, making him pull back out of the car quickly.

"Jesus," he muttered to himself, looking around. It was starting to snow. Small grainy flakes.

As he leaned back into the car, Rose noticed that he'd cut his finger on a shard of what little remained of the driver side window. One of the pieces of glass was jutting out of the bottom of the window frame like a shark's tooth. He put his finger in his mouth and sucked on the cut for a moment, tasting blood and then a tiny sliver of glass which he spit into the snow.

He took a deep breath and leaned back

inside the car again, feeling through the change and candy wrappers for the small latch of the compartment at the back of the console. He finally found it, pushed it to the left with his thumb and the small door sprang open. The photos of Jamie and Glenn fell out, followed by a small piece of paper. He picked up the paper, smearing it with blood from the cut on his finger, then held it up, sucking on the cut again as he read the words. Biting down on his finger hard when he realized what he was holding: a love note.

A graphic letter to Sheila from someone named Johnny.

36

"Please don't hurt me!" Ellen Davis shrieked as one of three huge men standing outside the tiny cell pulled back its sliding door. She grabbed one of the bars at the back of the cage and wrapped her arms and fingers tightly around the cold steel as two of them lumbered inside the cell. "Please," she begged softly, looking up at them with terrified eyes, tears rolling down her cheeks. "Please."

After she and Frank had been forced into that room off the corridor coming out of customs at Kennedy Airport, Ellen had been bound, gagged, and blindfolded, then carried roughly down a flight of stairs over a man's shoulder to a vehicle — a van, she assumed — where she was dropped on the floor on her side. After what she guessed was a thirty-minute ride, the people who had kidnapped her put her in a small plane for what seemed an hour flight. Then it was back into another van for what had seemed like forever until they'd gotten here, wherever here was.

Rural Tennessee. Elm Ridge, specifically. The grounds of another of the Energy Department's national laboratories. And Base 19.

"Why are you doing this to me?" she sobbed as they tore her fingers, then her arms from the bar and hoisted her to her feet. She was small — just five-five and thin — so she was no match for them. "What's going on? What did I do? What do you want from me?"

But they said nothing as they dragged her down a short hallway. At one point she tried to break free, tried to run, but it was no use. They laughed at her as they held her arms even tighter and pulled her along.

They took her to a sterile, windowless ten-by-ten room with cinder block walls. There was a large hook hanging from the ceiling and a tub of water two feet deep positioned directly beneath the hook. Once inside the room, two of the men forced her to lie facedown on the cold cement floor, tied her thin wrists together behind her back, then her pale ankles together, too. The third man pulled the hook down from the ceiling while the other two secured her, and, when she

297

was tightly bound, he slipped the hook between her ankles and the rope binding her ankles together over the hook. Then he went to the wall and began to crank a winch, slowly pulling the hook up. Lifting Ellen's ankles, then knees, then waist off the floor as the other two men made certain that her head didn't hit the tub as her body rose off the floor.

Finally the hook, and Ellen's ankles, were almost to the ceiling. Her body swung slightly from side to side above the tub of water as her head hung a foot above the water's surface. Then the man by the wall reversed the direction of the winch — and Ellen started to scream. Click by slow click her head descended toward the water. Her screams intensified as she came closer and closer to the surface. She began to struggle violently, pulling herself up at the waist as her dangling shoulder length brown hair reached the water. The man by the wall stopped her descent, allowing her to wear herself out. After forty-five seconds her stomach muscles failed, she could no longer struggle and her body hung straight down. When the top of her head was an inch from the water's surface, the man by the wall stopped her descent again and flipped a small piece of metal into the cog of the winch so the hook, and her body, would stay where it was.

He moved away from the wall and knelt down next to the tub of water. "We want to know why you were in New Zealand, Ms. Davis. We want to know what you and your husband were doing there."

"We were on our honeymoon," she sobbed.

"That's the same thing your husband said," the man hissed, "but we know there's more to it than that. You were meeting your contact, or he was."

"I don't know what you're talking about!" she shouted. She was terrified of drowning, always had been. "I swear."

He stood up, walked to the winch, un-latched the metal stop and slowly let her body down toward the tub of water.

"Stop! Please, God, make him stop!" she screamed.

But the man didn't stop — and God didn't help. The man let her head dip into the water.

With the little strength she had left, she pulled herself up again at the waist. Pulled her head out of the water, coughing and sputtering as her wet hair hung straight down, dripping. Pulled herself up until the lactic acid buildup in her abdomen was too much to take and her head fell back into the water with a splash. She screamed beneath the surface, desperately trying to lift her head up out of the water again. She was barely able to get her mouth above the surface for a split second, just long enough to gasp one breath.

The man nodded to the other two men who pulled her up, holding her so that her forehead was still submerged.

"Tell me," he demanded. "Tell me who you met in New Zealand."

"It wasn't me!" she shouted. "I didn't meet anyone." She hesitated. "It was my husband. He made the contact. He's the one talking to them. Not me."

The three men exchanged glances, then the man by the wall moved beside the other two, staring down at her as she gasped for breath, water dripping back into the tub from her face and hair. "What does your husband hate the most, Ms. Davis?"

"I . . . I don't understand. What do you mean?"

"What gives him nightmares? What makes him wake up at night screaming? What's his worst fear?" The man chuckled. "Tell me now or it's back down in the water you go. And this time we don't pull you out."

37

The traffic heading north toward Washington on Interstate 95 was awful, creeping along at a snail's pace. It had taken Rose nearly an hour to get from the salvage yard to Trafalgar's headquarters — a distance of only twenty miles. But he'd hardly noticed. He kept reading the love letter over and over. Kept reading one paragraph in particular in which the guy reminded Sheila of them having sex in the closet of the bar where he worked. Of how turned on she'd been, how obvious it was to him that she was in ecstasy. Rose had almost run into the car ahead of him in the stop-and-go traffic at least a dozen times. Finally, when the snow had begun to really come down, he'd put the note in his coat pocket and promised himself he wouldn't look at it again. He'd turned on the radio to his favorite talk show. Thirty seconds later he was staring at Johnny's chicken scratch, more furious than before.

Rose swung the Buick into a parking spot in the back of the garage and screeched to a halt — it was almost ten o'clock and the lot was packed. He grabbed his briefcase off the passenger seat and pulled himself out of the car, slamming the door and heading toward the elevator bank that seemed like it was miles away. Sheila had been carrying on a torrid affair with a bartender, for God's sake. While he was working his fingers to the bone to make sure she had everything she could want. That was even more shocking to him because her daddy's oil company had hit the skids a few years ago, so she couldn't count on the dividend checks anymore. She hadn't cared how hard he worked, or, apparently, that her deceit might be discovered. Cortez's revelation that he had Sheila followed and that she was having an affair was one thing. Actually reading her lover's note was another. It had made the affair seem much more vivid, much more deceitful. He hadn't been this angry in a long time. Not since finding out his senior year that Sheila had gone out with one of his fraternity brothers behind his back.

As Rose neared the elevators, he saw

Colin Freese's big car swing into his personal spot. Rose changed directions, cut through two rows of cars, and reached the space just as Freese was climbing out of the driver's seat.

Freese waved when he saw Rose. "Hello, Mike." His voice echoed in the cavernous garage.

"Hello, Colin."

They stood a few feet apart, by the trunk of Freese's car, facing each other. They hadn't spoken since the board meeting.

"Sorry about Sheila," Freese finally said, his voice subdued. "I read about it over the weekend. Tragic, just tragic."

"Thanks for your concern." Rose could hear the strain in his own voice.

"Something wrong?"

Rose didn't answer. He was thinking about how Freese had tried to torpedo the CIS acquisition, remembering how Freese had slowly raised his hand as a vote against the motion to buy CIS at the board meeting. More disloyalty heaped on top of what he'd already discovered this morning at the salvage yard. What the hell was wrong with people?

"Let's go inside," Freese suggested. "It's cold out here."

Rose stuck his arm out. "Not yet."

Freese stared down at Rose's arm stretched across his chest, then slowly raised his eyes to meet Rose's. "What's this all about?"

"I want to know what happened at the board meeting. Why did you vote against the motion to buy CIS?"

Freese glanced away. "What difference does it make? You got your approval."

"It makes a big difference, Colin. The CEO and CFO of a company should always be on the same page, at least in front of the board. It's terrible for them to see you not supporting me."

"I don't want to talk about it." Again Freese tried to move past Rose.

Again Rose stopped him with a hand to the chest. "I want an answer, Colin. What did Grant Boyd say to you at the break? What does he have on you?"

"Get your hand off me," Freese snapped.

"Not until you answer me."

Freese sidestepped Rose quickly.

But Rose caught him by the back of the collar and spun him around. Then grabbed his tie just below the knot and wrapped it around his hand. Freese was a small man and Rose easily controlled him. "Answer me, damn it!" he yelled, backing Freese up against the side of the next car over.

"Have you lost your mind?"

Rose could feel himself reaching that point of no return. All the stress and anguish he'd been dealing with for the past few days was coming together at once, and suddenly he wasn't sure he could maintain control. He wanted to smash Freese's face into a bloody pulp. "Tell me what Boyd has on you, Colin."

"Take your hands off me or I'll call the police."

"Tell me!" Rose demanded.

"I'll have you fired."

"Try it," Rose dared. "I wish you would, Colin. I really wish you would, because according to the bylaws you'd have to take it to the board. You can't fire me on your own. We both know who would win that battle." A surge of satisfaction raced through him when Freese grimaced. "Now," he said in a low voice, teeth gritted. "Did Grant Boyd force you to vote his way on the motion to buy CIS?"

Freese stared back at Rose for several moments, a blank look on his face. Finally, ever so subtly, he nodded.

38

Vivian Anduhar stood on the precipice of a rocky cliff as a raw Idaho wind whipped through her dark hair, a drop of over five hundred feet just a step away. Her wrists were secured tightly at the small of her back. Two men stood behind her, making certain she didn't fall off — for now. But she didn't really care any longer. In fact, she half hoped they would push her off the cliff so it could be over with, so she wouldn't have to endure this anymore. A few seconds of anguish, then it would be done.

They'd been torturing her since four o'clock this morning at Base 77. Given her a few days to recover from the long drive out of Dallas, tried to give her a false sense of security, like things weren't going to be as bad here as the men in the van had told her. Then they'd lowered the boom.

The grueling session had started with the same technique Ellen Davis had endured at

Base 19. Vivian had been suspended upside down above a tub of water, then lowered slowly into it. She'd done exactly as Ellen had. Struggled wildly to keep her head above water. She'd been able to do it for longer than Ellen had because she was in better shape, but ultimately her stomach muscles had failed, too, and her head had splashed beneath the surface. They'd pulled her up forty-five seconds after she'd gone under, choking and sputtering, but she'd told them nothing.

At first light, they'd marched her outside into the bone-chilling twenty degree cold, stripped her naked, tied her to a post, then sprayed her with icy water. Again, she hadn't cracked even though icicles had formed all over her body and her hair had frozen solid.

Finally, they'd allowed her to dress, hoisted her into the back of a jeep and driven her up a dirt road to the top of a mesa. Then dragged her out and forced her to the edge of the cliff.

"This is it, Vivian," the man in charge said gruffly as he stood behind her. Beside another man who was holding her. The man in charge was short but extremely strong with a crew cut and a scruffy beard. "This is the end of the line. You tell me something or I push you off." He glanced at the man holding her, then leaned around her body so she could see him. "You understand?"

"I understand," she whispered, barely able to speak. She'd gone hoarse from screaming while they were lowering her head into the tub, and her teeth were chattering because she was still so cold from being drenched with water in the freezing cold. Her core body temperature was down to ninety-four degrees.

"Then talk," the man demanded. "Tell me who you are in contact with in Jordan. Tell me about the plot."

Her chin dropped slowly to her chest. "I keep telling you, I don't know anything. I just want to go home."

"You tell me, damn it!" the man shouted, grabbing a fist full of her hair and yanking her head back out of frustration. He'd never had anyone who'd gone this long without at least making something up. "I want an answer, and I want it now."

"I don't have any answers," she gasped.

He grabbed her away from the other man, pulled her away from the edge of the cliff and smashed her left cheek with a heavy right hand. She tumbled to the icy ground but made no sound. She couldn't, she had no strength left. And it wasn't as if the punch had really hurt. She was too numb to feel it.

She was vaguely aware of hands grabbing her and pulling her up. Of her toes being dragged across the frozen ground as they forced her back to the edge of the cliff. Of wavering unsteadily at the edge. Then, slowly, as if in a nightmare, falling forward.

Then everything went black.

39

Rose dropped his briefcase on the floor beside his desk, eased into his chair, and swiveled around so he could take in the view of northern Virginia below him. So he could take in the dark, foreboding skies and the vulnerable landscape beneath it. The system was only supposed to drop a few inches on Virginia with most of the heavy stuff going north of Washington into New England. But even a few inches could throw this area into chaos. And there was another, more powerful low pressure behind this one that forecasters were saying could dump as much as a foot and a half on northern Virginia next weekend. It was turning out to be a tough winter. Typically, they didn't get more than a few inches all season.

After a few moments Rose groaned, put his head back and shut his eyes. He'd almost beaten the hell out of Colin Freese in the parking garage. Not just because

Freese had been a traitor in the boardroom last week — he should have expected that with everything else going on. Down deep, Freese was a weak and egocentric man. Translation: He probably had tons of skeletons hanging in his closet and would buckle in a heartbeat under the threat of them being revealed. In fact, he had buckled to Grant Boyd. No, he'd wanted to slam Freese's face because suddenly everything had come to a head and Freese happened to be the unfortunate one standing in front of him at the exact moment his defenses had collapsed under the pressure and the stress he'd endured in the last few days. Sheila's death; the CIS acquisition; how tired he suddenly was; finding the letter from Sheila's lover in the console of her smashed Mercedes; the meeting with Sherman LeClair slated for later this week; Jamie blaming him for Sheila's death; the cops coming to the house tonight to grill him. Suddenly it had all been too much, and he'd come as close to snapping as he ever had in his life. It was actually the fear of death he'd seen in Colin's eyes as he'd jacked the smaller man up against the car that had brought him hurtling back to reality. Thank God, too. Assault charges were the last thing he needed right now. Detectives Willis and

Harrison would probably salivate if they heard about that.

Rose rubbed his eyes. He hadn't thought about Sheila going out with his fraternity brother behind his back in such a long time. It was strange how that whole incident had flashed back to him in his moment of rage in the parking garage as he'd pinned Freese up against the car.

The guy's name was Scott Wilson. He'd been a sophomore, two years younger than Rose. Rose wasn't particularly close to Wilson — there were sixty guys in the fraternity and you couldn't be good friends with everyone — but he hadn't done anything wrong to Wilson, either. Rose had gone to pick up Sheila one night at her apartment in Chapel Hill where she lived with three other girls, they were going to a movie, and he'd noticed a familiar sweater draped over a chair in Sheila's room. An unusual white knit sweater with two blue stripes across the front. Wilson's sweater. He'd recognized it right away because the guy wore it all the time in the winter. Rose had grilled Sheila about it later when they were alone. She'd finally admitted to seeing Wilson a few times, but sworn up and down they hadn't done anything, that they were just friends.

A few days later Rose had overheard a

couple of Wilson's friends chuckling snidely about how Wilson had been banging some sorority girl. Rose hadn't heard them say the name of the girl, but he had a damn good idea who they were talking about. And after that it always seemed like Wilson was smirking at him when they saw each other. It could have been just his imagination — maybe Wilson's friends were talking about another girl, or it was Sheila they were talking about and she had lied about how far he'd gotten with her. Either way, Rose had always been suspicious of what had really happened between them.

He shook his head as he gazed out at the menacing clouds scuttling across the sky. It was amazing how you remembered things like that years later, when you hadn't thought about them in so long. How you never really got over them, either. How they lodged deep in the recesses of your brain waiting to spring out of nowhere at you when you were least expecting them to. He'd asked Sheila about the incident with Wilson a few years later, after they were married, when he was thinking about going to a fraternity reunion. She'd just rolled her eyes and groaned. But she hadn't denied it, either. They hadn't gone to the reunion.

"Mike."

He swiveled in the chair to face the door. Tammy Sable and David Cortez were standing there.

"Come in," he said, waving.

"How are you?" Tammy asked in a concerned voice, a compassionate expression on her face as she moved into the office, notebook pressed to her chest. "I was thinking about you all weekend. It's just so terrible about Sheila."

"It is, and thank you for those kind words." He motioned at the two chairs in front of the desk, then for Tammy and Cortez to sit in them. "Look," he said, holding up one hand and interrupting Tammy as she was about to say more. "The funeral is Wednesday at All Saints out in Great Falls. Two o'clock. I want you both there. I *need* you both there. No excuses. Okay?"

They both nodded.

"Other than that," Rose said, his voice dropping, "please don't talk about it again. I really appreciate you two being so concerned, but it would help me more if you just wouldn't mention it anymore. All right?"

They nodded again.

"Good." Rose drew himself up in his chair, then leaned forward and put his elbows on the desk. "Let's get to work.

We've got a lot to do and not much time to do it in." He always said that when they were at the front end of a hostile takeover. It always made him feel good to say it, but this time it made him feel especially good. It comforted him. The game was on and he knew he'd be distracted by it today, distracted from all the bad stuff swirling around him. Which was good. He needed to give his mind a rest from all that. "Give me the updates. Tammy, you first."

She glanced down at the open notebook in her lap. "I've drafted the Offer to Purchase notice which will go in the *Times* and the *Journal.* Just used the boilerplate from the last deal and changed the names and the numbers." The notice was an announcement of the transaction that took up an entire half page of each newspaper, most of it written in print you needed a microscope to read. "Do you want to review it?"

"No." After so many deals together, Rose trusted her completely. It was all legal crap anyway. "Send them over to Howard as soon as we break from here." Howard Fogel was Trafalgar's corporate attorney at Wachtel Lipton in New York City. Rose pointed at Tammy. "Eighty-one a share, right?" Eighty-one dollars a share was the opening offer price he and Cortez had decided on

315

Saturday morning. They would go up from there if necessary, but it was a healthy premium to start off with. Seventy-four percent above CIS's closing price Friday on the New York Stock Exchange. A classic bear-hug bid. "That's what you put in the draft for Howard, right?"

"Yes. Eighty-one a share." She looked up. "When do you want the notice to run?"

Rose thought for a moment. "Let's put it in the papers on Thursday. We should have everything else ready by then. At least close enough that we can let the rest of the world officially know what we're up to."

"Got it," Tammy said, scribbling in her notebook.

"Officially," Cortez said. "That's the polite word, isn't it? Did you see all those people sending e-mails out during the board meeting? I'll bet half of them were sending instructions to their brokers to buy as many CIS shares as they could get their sweaty hands on. In code, of course."

Rose's expression turned grim. Cortez was probably right. "Let's hope not." He turned his attention back on Tammy. "What about the list of —"

"I've already ordered the list of CIS shareholders from the company," Tammy interrupted, anticipating Rose's question.

"That was one of the first things I did after the board meeting on Friday. I was hoping it would be in my e-mail by the time I got in this morning, but no luck. If we don't have it by noon, I'll e-mail Howard and ask him to make one of those rattle-the-saber calls he likes to make so much."

Sometimes companies under attack dragged their feet in providing the list of their shareholders to a hostile acquirer. They did it to make it harder for the acquirer to contact the target's shareholders directly — and to buy themselves more time to come up with a defense. Completely ignoring the demand was illegal, but a lot of targets didn't hurry to comply, either.

"And," Tammy continued, "I've notified our printing company downtown that we'll probably need at least ten thousand packages of the Offer to Purchase and proxy forms. I've also given three of my assistants CIS's latest annual report and TenQ so they can start boning up for the blizzard of calls I know we'll get."

Rose smiled. She was a tiger, so together. He turned toward Cortez. "How about you, David?"

"I've got two of my analysts drafting the actual Offer to Purchase."

The Offer to Purchase was much longer

than the notice that ran in the newspapers. It was an extensive booklet mailed directly to the target's stockholders that described both companies and the transaction in depth. It also gave the stockholders instructions on how to tender their shares.

"We should have that document ready for Howard by end of business today."

"What about the Citibank loan agreement?" Rose asked. He hadn't had time to make a checklist, but he really didn't need to at this point. All of this was second nature. "I liked the call we got from those guys the other night, but you know me. I don't assume anything is done until I've got a signature on the bottom line. Sometimes even then you don't know for sure."

"Citibank's lawyer e-mailed a first draft of the agreement to me over the weekend. I went through it at home yesterday. There were a few glitches."

"There always are."

"Of course," Cortez agreed. "Well, let me go through it with the guy at Citi today. I've got a call scheduled with him in thirty minutes," he explained, glancing at his watch. "Hopefully we'll have a second draft by first thing tomorrow morning. You should wait and look at that one. Let me see what I can get first."

"What about the press?" Tammy asked. "How do we respond?"

"Anybody from the press calls today and the answer is a polite 'no comment,' " Rose instructed. "I don't care who it is, even if it's a friend, somebody who's given us good pub in the past. I want to reach out to Bill Granger first."

"You want me to call him?" Cortez volunteered. "Want me to set up the meeting? Give him a little perspective on what you're thinking ahead of time?"

Rose managed a grin. "As long as you can keep yourself under control." Which was like the pot calling the kettle black, he thought to himself ruefully.

A hurt expression spread across Cortez's face.

"I'm kidding," Rose said. "Sort of. I thought you were going to strangle Grant Boyd at one point during the meeting on Friday."

"You really blame me? *He called me Tonto.* What a prick."

Out of the corner of his eye, Rose noticed Tammy look down and bring a hand to her mouth, trying to hide a smile. "That was totally uncalled for," Rose agreed. "But don't worry, I've got something in store for him."

Cortez brightened. "Oh, yeah? Good."

"Yeah, go ahead and call Granger," Rose said. "I can meet with him anytime except Wednesday afternoon. And give him a few sound bites ahead of time. I want to hear how he reacts."

"He might not take my call," Cortez pointed out.

"If he doesn't, make sure to tell his secretary that I'll be disappointed." Granger would understand what that meant: If he didn't cooperate, he might not have a job when the transaction was over. Of course, if Sherman LeClair was really on the level, Granger might not *want* a job afterward. In fact, he might disappear afterward, and not necessarily of his own volition. That was how dire the implications of this thing were, according to LeClair. "Got it?"

"Got it."

"Good." Rose clapped once. "Let's get to it then. We've got a lot of ground to cover. I need to check in with a few people in Europe while they're still in the office."

Tammy and Cortez stood up and headed out, understanding that the meeting was over.

"David," Rose called when Cortez had almost reached the doorway. "Come back a minute, will you?" He gestured after Tammy.

"Close the door."

Cortez closed the door and retraced his steps to his seat. "What's up?"

Rose pursed his lips. This was difficult. "I want to talk to that guy you had follow Sheila," he said quietly. "That private eye buddy of yours."

"Why?"

"I want to know about this man she was fooling around with," Rose admitted. "I want to know his name, I want to know where he works." Rose could tell right away that Cortez didn't like the idea.

"I know you told Tammy and me not to mention this again," Cortez began hesitantly, "but Sheila's gone, Mike. I mean, what's the point of talking to my buddy now?"

"Don't worry about it." Rose wasn't going to tell Cortez about the love letter. "Just get me your guy's number."

Cortez shifted uncomfortably in the chair. "Mike, please don't take this wrong, but I *really* don't think you should —"

"Are you going to put me in touch with him or not?" Rose asked, his voice calm but forceful. He couldn't remember the last time they'd had words, the last time he'd felt even the least bit irritated at Cortez. But David had decided to have Sheila followed on his own, which was pretty gutsy, even though Rose understood why he'd done it — to protect a friend. Which was okay, as long as that was his true motivation behind it. But Cortez had volunteered to make the private eye available, and Rose was going to take him up on that. "Tell me."

Cortez held his arms out. "Or what?"

Rose leaned back in his chair and folded his arms across his chest, allowing silence to be his friend, to work like water building behind a dam. He'd learned a long time ago that your silence made people of lesser rank very nervous, whether it was on the phone or in person. They felt like they had to fill the dead air with conversation or they'd melt, and more often than not, they'd tell you something they shouldn't — or what you wanted to hear — because they'd run out of anything else to say. He could already see Cortez starting to sweat.

"I just don't want there to be any trouble, Michael."

Another sign that Cortez was nervous. He never called him Michael. "Why would there be any trouble?"

"Leave the asshole alone, man. You don't have anything to prove. He's a nobody, a freaking nobody. Okay?"

"If the board really does name me CEO

soon, I want to make you CFO immediately. I really do. But I have to know that you're with me one hundred percent in everything I do." Rose leaned forward. "Do you understand?"

40

Frank Davis was lying on the bunk of the cell with his hands behind his head when they came for him.

Since the Russian roulette incident, which had happened as soon as they'd brought him here from Kennedy Airport a few days ago, they hadn't bothered him. Just fed him three squares a day and left him alone. It had been boring as hell to stare at the ceiling hour after hour, and he was worried to death about Ellen. To the point that it was impossible to sleep without having nightmares about what they were doing to her. But he hadn't been forced to endure any more torture sessions. He even wondered if the Russian roulette had been real. If there'd really been a bullet in one of the chambers.

It had been strange to use the tiny stainless steel toilet in the corner of the cell with that camera mounted on the wall just below the ceiling staring at him from across the hallway. But, other than that, the boredom, and how worried he was about Ellen, things hadn't been too bad. The food had actually tasted good. Maybe because he usually ate frozen dinners at home or stopped at the local strip mall for takeout. Ellen almost always got home after he did and she rarely cooked. She worked late a lot, until eight or nine o'clock many nights. At least, that was what she said she was doing.

He sat up on the bunk and swung his bare feet to the cement floor, actually glad to see them, to have human contact despite what they had done to him. "Hi, guys," he said cheerily to the two men who entered the cell after pulling the heavy sliding door back. They were the same two men who had escorted him down the elevator the first night he'd been here, then brought him back to the cell when the Russian roulette thing was done. "How you doing?"

"Fine, Frank," one of them said in a friendly voice. "Just fine."

"What's going on?"

"We want to ask you some more questions."

"Oh, okay," said Davis politely. "I want to cooperate, I want to help you any way I can."

"Not here, Frank."

"Sorry." Davis stood up, turned around and crossed his hands behind his back. Assuming the guy with the handcuffs hanging from his belt was going to use them.

"That's all right, Frank. There's no need for that. Just come with us. We just want to have a nice chat with you."

Davis fell in behind the man who'd been talking and the other one fell in behind him so he was in the middle. They were being too polite, he thought as they moved along the mildew-smelling corridor. But maybe they'd come to the conclusion that they'd made a colossal mistake and were about to let him go. Maybe they just needed to tell him if he ever mentioned any part of this to anyone, he'd pay. After all, wouldn't they have kept torturing him if they thought he was involved in some sort of terrorist plot?

As he turned a corner and followed the man through a doorway into a large room, he instantly realized that they weren't about to let him go. Far from it. He wheeled around and tried to dash out, but the doorway was blocked by three huge men who grabbed him and twisted his arms painfully behind his back.

"My God, please don't do this to me," Davis moaned, searing pain knifing through both shoulders as the men forced his arms even farther back behind him. "I can't take it, I can't. I'll have a heart attack."

Suddenly he realized that Ellen was still alive, or at the very least that these people hadn't murdered her right after they'd been thrown into that room coming from customs. It was the only way they could have known this. And as fast as he'd been elated at knowing she might still be alive, he came crashing down because he knew she'd turned on him to save herself. Which maybe was understandable because everyone had a breaking point. Still, he'd never thought she could do anything to hurt him.

His lip curled as they forced his face up against the thick clear plastic wall of the enclosure. Inside it was a massive king cobra — sixteen shiny black feet long with a body as thick as a football in the middle. It had been slithering around the base of the enclosure, but stopped when they shoved him up against the wall and moved to where he was. It hesitated for a few moments on the floor, bringing its body into several large coils, then slowly rose up the side of the cage until its eyes were level with his, only inches away on the other side of the clear wall. Davis watched its long forked tongue flick in and out for a few moments as it tasted the air, then shut his eyes tightly, unable to look anymore. His heart was pounding so hard he could hear it, and he was already sweating profusely from every single pore in his body.

"That's right, Mr. Davis. It's a king cobra. It hasn't been fed in a week and my men have been agitating it for the last two hours with electric shocks and pitchforks."

Davis recognized the voice right away. It was the same man who'd stuck the gun in his mouth the other night.

"Your lovely little wife, Ellen, told us all about your phobia of snakes. She told us about that day you both went to the Bronx Zoo last year and you couldn't go in the reptile house. How you couldn't even watch a show about king cobras on the Nature Channel with her one night. She was very helpful with all of that."

Davis tried to swallow but he didn't have any spit. His mouth had gone completely dry. "Please don't do this," he whispered, imagining the terror of them forcing him through the small door he'd spotted and into the enclosure. The terror of seeing that huge snake strike at him.

"Your wife also informed us that you weren't in New Zealand just for your honeymoon like you've been telling us. Like you've been *lying* to us."

"She was just telling you what you wanted to hear," Davis muttered. He could imagine the awful, disgusting things they must have done to her, suddenly wondering if she was close or far away and if they were forcing her to watch what was going down right now on a monitor somewhere. She didn't handle pain well, and, if any of her torture sessions had involved water, she might have told them anything. When they went to the beach on the Sound in the summers she wouldn't go into the ocean any farther than up to her ankles. "She doesn't know anything."

"I don't doubt that," the man said coldly, "but *you* do."

"I don't, *I swear*. I've been trying to tell you that."

He smiled. "Well, let's find out."

"Oh, *God!*" Davis shouted as the men forced him toward the small Plexiglas door with brass hinges. Unlike the Russian roulette, there was no uncertainty involved here. There was always the possibility that the next chamber wasn't loaded when the gun was in your mouth, but this cage was *definitely* loaded. *"No, no, no!"* He struggled violently, catching sight of the snake slithering effortlessly along the base of the enclosure as he tried to yank himself free, adrenaline coursing through him. But it was no use. He wasn't going anywhere, not until they wanted him to.

Davis watched as two of the men crawled through the door armed with shields and ten foot long tongs to grab the snake. He felt himself getting sick to his stomach when he saw the massive snake rise up quickly into its strike position, and he stopped struggling. He let his eyelids close and he went limp, hoping they'd think he'd passed out. But someone grabbed his scrotum through his pants. His eyes flashed open and he groaned loudly at the explosion of pain. It was the man who had been speaking to him.

"Don't try to fool me, Mr. Davis," the man snarled, finally letting go. "It won't work." He nodded at the two men holding Davis. "In you go."

Despite the lingering pain, Davis grabbed the door with both hands as they forced him through the opening. *"All right! Jesus Christ all right!"* he shouted, catching a glimpse of the snake lashing out at one of the men holding the tongs. "I'll tell you everything," he said, breaking down and starting to sob. "Everything."

41

Rose looked up as the door swung open. Only one person in the entire company would barge into his office without bothering to knock. "Hello, Colin," he said calmly as Freese appeared in the doorway.

Freese closed the door and stalked to the front of Rose's desk.

"Have a seat," Rose offered, forcing himself to be polite despite the anger that flashed inside of him just at the sight of the man. Freese was weak, and Rose hated weakness in anyone or anything. He'd always known it about Colin, just never seen it like he had on Friday. He'd never been affected by it so directly, either. The more he thought about it, the more it aggravated him, the more he couldn't just get past it. Maybe he should start thinking seriously about running Trafalgar, about running Freese out of here, too. "Please."

"No need," Freese replied curtly. "This

won't take long."

Rose eased back in his chair.

"I've called another board meeting," Freese said. "I'm going to request their permission to terminate your employment with Trafalgar Industries. Unfortunately, like you said, under our corporate bylaws I can't fire you on my own. I have to have the board's consent. So I'm going to get it. Then I'll fire you."

"Fire *me?*" Rose stood up slowly. "On what grounds?"

"Fraud."

"Are you crazy? You're the one who uses company assets like they're tools in your garage and everyone knows it. I'm clean. That's a fact."

"Grant Boyd doesn't think so," Freese retorted. "And he says he has the evidence."

Rose snorted. "Grant Boyd doesn't have anything. Just a weak CEO who's willing to say and do anything to save his job." He watched Freese's mouth twitch. "A CEO who can be manipulated very easily thanks to all the baggage he carries around." Freese hadn't come clean out in the parking lot this morning with exactly which suitcase Boyd had used to sway Freese's vote, just that he'd been intimidated into changing it. "You're pathetic."

"You'll be out on your ass within a week," Freese snapped. He gazed at Rose for several moments, then managed to calm himself, managed to relax his expression into his normal in-charge smirk. "Have a nice day, Michael."

Rose watched Freese walk out. It was just as Sherman LeClair had warned. The stakes had suddenly shot into the stratosphere.

Beck sat down in his favorite chair of the bunker living room, the recliner. Klein was already sitting on the sofa on the other side of the table. The deputy director had arrived ten minutes ago, but Beck had made him wait while he finished a call with another member of the Directorate in his personal office, which was connected to his bedroom. He'd let the call go on longer than it needed to. He'd spoken loudly so Klein could hear that it was going on longer than it needed to. Maybe it was to get Klein back for being willing to question his actions. Beck *really* hated that about Klein. He had no idea how hard it was to lead this thing.

"What is it?" Beck asked, starting a crossword. He had to be doing more than one thing at a time, even more so these days. He couldn't help himself. It really was a sickness. It was just a good thing that Klein was accustomed to the idiosyncrasy so he didn't complain about not getting his boss's full attention. "What's so important?"

"Two hours ago," Klein began, "our people at Base Twelve broke the guy we detained at Kennedy Airport coming back from New Zealand with his wife. That guy Frank Davis."

"The third-grade teacher?"

"Yes."

Beck put the crossword down on his lap. "What did Davis say?"

"He confirmed that our operatives in the Middle East were right on the money," explained Klein. "A certain terrorist cell in Jordan is in the final stages of pulling off another major attack on the United States using commercial airliners. This time the target is Chicago. Specifically, the Sears Tower and the Hancock Building. It's imminent, too."

"Jesus," Beck whispered.

"Turns out Davis's brother-in-law works for one of the food-service companies that delivers meals to jets at the Philadelphia airport," Klein continued. "The people in the Jordanian cell approached Davis about six months ago and offered him money — a lot of it, you wouldn't believe how much —

to convince his brother-in-law to help them. Obviously they made it very worthwhile for Davis's brother-in-law, too. Through Davis. Seems the terrorists didn't want to go directly to the guy because those food-service people are monitored very closely these days. The terrorists figured we'd be a lot less likely to watch a third-grade school-teacher. Anyway, Davis's brother-in-law took the bait."

Beck felt his body tingling. It was times like these that made up for what they'd done to the innocent people over the last six years, that had once made him believe in the Order.

"Hi, son," Rose called, moving into the computer room of the basement. "How was school today?"

"Wait, Dad," Glenn said loudly. "I've almost got this guy."

Rose watched Glenn move the mouse with one hand and bang on the keyboard with the other, amazed at the boy's hand-eye coordination. Glenn never looked at his fingers as they moved quickly and skillfully about, just kept his eyes locked on the screen. Now that's my son, Rose thought to himself proudly. Here was something they had in common, something that had been passed down through the genes: The ability to locate a target and stay laser-focused on it to the exclusion of all else.

Rose moved closer to get a better view. A 3-D image of a U.S. Ranger clad in desert fatigues and armed with a machine gun was chasing another 3-D figure dressed all in black — also armed with a machine gun — through a medieval castle. Monsters of all shapes and sizes were popping out from behind corners, breathing fire, spitting venom, and hurling spikes at both men as they raced down darkened hallways, into candlelit rooms and up stone staircases. Finally Glenn made a daring move, had the Ranger leap across a moat of boiling oil in a courtyard, and cut off the terrorist's escape. A quick burst from the machine gun and the terrorist was down and the screen exploded into a rainbow of colors.

"Got him!" Glenn shouted, banging the desk with his small fist. "Got him!"

Rose whistled, suddenly fascinated — and distracted, he realized. He'd been mesmerized for the few seconds he'd been watching. He had forgotten all the bad stuff. Maybe that was why kids loved these games so much. "Nice job."

Glenn turned in his chair. "Thanks, Dad."

"Was that against the computer?"

"No, another person."

"One of your friends?"

Glenn shrugged. "Nope, never met him. In fact, it might be a girl. I just know the computer name. Bad Ass 9999."

Rose shook his head, worried that he didn't know more about what Glenn was doing down here. He'd always counted on Sheila to watch things like this. He pointed at the screen. "Glenn, I don't like you playing against people you don't —"

"Don't worry, Dad. I'm not stupid. I'd never IM or e-mail anyone I don't know."

"Can they find out where you live or who you are somehow when you play against them?"

"No way. It's completely —"

"Dad."

Rose glanced back at the doorway. Jamie was standing there. "Yes, honey?"

"Two men are here to see you. They said they were with the police department."

Rose cursed under his breath. Willis and Harrison. They were forty-five minutes early. As a very nice favor, Tammy Sable had agreed to take the kids out to dinner tonight. He hadn't wanted Jamie or Glenn to be here when the detectives arrived. But now that plan had gone up in smoke.

"Thanks, Jamie," he said, patting her head

gently as he moved past.

"Dad," she called after him.

He turned. "Yes?"

"What do they want?"

"Now that we know what's going on with Frank Davis and his brother-in-law, what do you want me to do?" Klein asked, watching Beck scribble an answer on the crossword.

"Did we get specific timing on the attack?" asked Beck after a few moments.

"A few days," Klein answered, irritated that Beck was still working on the puzzle. "That's all." He understood that the guy had a problem, that it wasn't all Beck's fault, but his inability to focus seemed to have become worse in the last few weeks. "We don't have much time. And I've already got people at the Philadelphia airport watching Davis's brother-in-law."

"Good. Did Davis tell our people at Base Twelve what the terrorists want his brother-in-law to do? Is it to hide weapons on the planes?"

"Exactly." Klein had to give Beck credit. The guy still hadn't taken his eyes off the puzzle, but he seemed fairly engaged in the conversation. But he needed to be more engaged, *a lot* more engaged. "And to take care of the cockpit door locks."

"Got it. What else did we get out of Davis? Did he give away who his contacts are? How he gets in touch with them?"

"They were still interrogating him when I left to come over here. Apparently what they threatened him with worked very effectively. He caved right away as soon as he understood what was going to happen to him. So I'm thinking they'll get all that stuff out of him, too. And, of course, we have feet on the ground in Jordan. We can make the raid ourselves."

Beck looked up from the puzzle. "What did they do to Davis to get him to spill his guts?"

Maybe Beck had been doing this for too long, Klein thought. Maybe that was the problem, the reason he needed to have constant distractions to make it through the day. The pressure must be unbelievable and Beck had been doing this longer than any other Executive Director ever had, at least during an active immunity. Klein knew that Beck took things like the deaths of Vivian Anduhar's children very hard, to the point that he could barely force himself out of bed in the morning for a while afterward. But then why would he be so curious about how they tortured Davis? Why would that make him look up from the crossword? Seemed like that would be something he *wouldn't* want to know about.

"They brought in a king cobra and started forcing Davis into a small enclosure with it," Klein answered.

"A *king cobra?*"

"Yeah. Apparently Davis has a terrible phobia of snakes, can't stand them. Especially king cobras. He broke right away when he saw the thing slithering around the cage."

"How did we find out about his phobia?"

"His wife."

"She told us in order to save herself?"

Klein nodded.

"Christ," Beck muttered, "what a wonderful world we've built for ourselves here in the Order. We keep an innocent man confined for the rest of his life. We kill children. We turn a wife against her husband, get her to tell us his biggest fear so she doesn't get tortured anymore. Beautiful. I can only imagine what the guys in Tennessee did to get her to talk, to tell us about the snake phobia." He held up his hand and pointed at Klein. "Tell me they didn't rape her, Tom. Please tell me they didn't do that."

"They have their orders, sir. They are strictly forbidden from engaging in any kind of sexual abuse as a means of gaining information during interrogations." Like half-drowning Ellen Davis was all right, Klein thought. Then keeping her confined for the rest of her life or killing her when they were finished with her. How did that make any sense? But maybe that was how Beck rationalized what he was doing, how he kept his sanity. By trying to make certain the women weren't sexually abused. Maybe he was finally getting close to the breaking point. Then what? "As far as I know, that hasn't happened once since The Fourth Order was declared."

"How would you know?"

Klein hesitated. "Frank Davis was taking money from terrorists, sir," he reminded Beck, trying to get him back on point as well as to divert his attention. Klein had his suspicions that there had been sexual abuse going on, particularly out in Idaho, at Base 77. "He knew what he was doing. He knew what the people who contacted him were doing. How he was helping them try to kill thousands of people in one day, how the people he's working with want to scare everyone in this country so badly that they can't live normal lives. Frank Davis deserves everything he gets."

"Yeah, but we're talking about his wife."

341

"She knew what he was doing. That's what the guys in Tennessee said. She knew he was meeting his contacts in New Zealand."

Beck clenched his teeth, muttered something unintelligible and started on the crossword again. Feverishly this time.

"Should we detain Davis's brother-in-law, sir?" Klein asked. "You have the power to do that on your own under these circumstances."

"No," Beck answered. "I want to talk to the others on the Directorate first."

Klein nodded. "How about Michael Rose?"

Beck looked up again. "What about him?"

"I spoke to Grant Boyd this morning. Rose is already getting ready to announce the takeover of CIS."

Beck allowed his head to fall back on the chair, let the crossword fall to his lap again.

He looked exhausted to Klein. "I think it's time to do something there," Klein suggested.

"Like what?"

"Kill him."

Beck groaned. "Killing isn't the answer to everything, Tom."

"Maybe not, but I think it's what we have to do in this case. I know you want to try to find out who's pushing Rose to do all of this, but I really think we need to just be done with the guy and take our chances. We can't let him find Spyder, that would be a disaster. If he takes over CIS, he will."

"We *have* to find out who he's working with. We *have* to find out who our real enemy is. We can cut Spyder out of CIS if we need to."

"Then let's detain Rose," Klein pleaded, uncertain of how you could cut Spyder away from CIS so quickly. Worried that Beck didn't understand the complexities of doing that. "Come on. We'll take him in. We'll find out who he's working with or he'll be sorry."

"Torture isn't the answer to everything, either," Beck said disgustedly. "Jesus Christ, pretty soon we'll be no better than the terrorists. In fact, we'll be worse. At least they're attacking an enemy. We'll be declaring war on our own people."

"You're exaggerating, sir."

"Am I? *Am I really?* What stops it from coming to that, Tom?"

"You need some sleep, sir. You're just tired."

"And you need a dose of reality."

Klein managed to keep his expression passive despite the turmoil boiling inside him. Peter Beck had gone soft and he had to do something about it.

"Hello, detectives." Rose shook hands with both men. First with Willis — the older one who looked like a hound dog out of the Mississippi backwoods, then with Harrison — the younger, sharp-dressing African American. "Let's go back to my den," he suggested. Out of the corner of his eye he saw Jamie watching from down the hallway. "Would you like anything to drink?"

"Nah," Willis said gruffly. "Is the nanny here?"

"Yes," Rose answered, leading them toward his den. "Do you want me to get her now?"

"Not yet," Willis said as he and Harrison settled onto the couch. "We'd like to talk to you first."

"Fine." Rose closed the door to the den, then sat in his desk chair.

The detectives exchanged a glance, then Harrison began. "Mr. Rose, your wife died of a broken neck. That's what the autopsy revealed."

Rose grimaced and shook his head. "That's awful." He thought he saw a shadow moving outside the den, through the small crack between the bottom of the door and the hardwood floor. It had to be Jamie trying to overhear the conversation. "You said the car was upside down when your guys found it, right? That's a pretty steep embankment at that spot on Georgetown Pike. She must have really gotten tossed around inside the car," he said softly. "It's hard for me to think about."

"I'm sure it is," Harrison said comfortingly. "The thing is, she was still in her seatbelt harness when the guys got to her at the bottom of the hill. She was upside down, and she had some bruises and cuts on her head, but nothing that would cause enough trauma to kill her, not enough to break her neck. At least, that's the coroner's opinion."

"What are you saying?" Rose asked quietly.

"We're saying," Willis answered slowly, "that she may have been killed after the accident. That she may have been murdered."

"Murdered?" Rose whispered. "You can't be serious."

"I'm very serious."

"The substance in her nose was definitely cocaine," Harrison spoke up. "She'd done a lot of it that afternoon."

Rose brought a hand to his head. "My God."

"I know this is difficult to talk about,"

Harrison said, "but we have to ask."

Rose nodded. He knew what was coming.

"We're pretty sure your wife was having an affair, but we're not sure who it was with yet." Harrison hesitated. "Do you have any idea who it could have been?"

Rose thought about the note hidden in the console of the smashed Mercedes, about how seeing it had made him feel. "No, I don't."

42

Rose was fifteen minutes late for his lunch with Kat because he didn't want her to think he was too excited about it. It seemed juvenile, but he couldn't help it. He didn't want to come across as desperate.

So he'd made a point of driving more slowly than normal on his way out to the quaint town of Leesburg, Virginia, west of Great Falls by fifteen miles and just to the east of the Blue Ridge foothills. Driving the speed limit, not his usual nine-miles-an-hour over. He'd been tempted to take the Porsche, to heighten the experience, and to impress Kat if they walked out of lunch together to the parking lot. But he hadn't, fearing Jamie might find out and ask why he hadn't driven the Buick today. She knew why he had a Buick for work, they'd talked about it because he was always trying to teach her. He felt guilty about seeing Kat and not telling Jamie, but that hadn't stopped him from coming. He had to know what was going on with the young woman, had to understand the real motivation behind the note she'd pressed into his hand so firmly at Morton's last week.

Of course, the being-late charade was probably stupid. She must have heard the edge in his voice when he'd called her last week and understood immediately that he was looking forward to lunch at least as much as she was.

The Station was a nice place. Cozy but not too cozy. Not inappropriate for a first lunch. In the late eighteen hundreds, it had been a railroad station for the Virginia & Western, fallen into disuse after World War II, then been restored twenty years ago and turned into a restaurant. The food was excellent, especially the seafood, and, most important, he'd never been here with Sheila. Somehow that made him feel better.

He moved to the maître d' stand warily, wanting to spot Kat before she spotted him — he'd always hated being taken by surprise, ever since he was a child.

"The name is Mike Rose."

The maître d' glanced down at his reservation book. "Yes, sir," the man said politely, gesturing for Rose to follow him. "Right this way."

There were only a few other tables taken, and he spotted Kat as he and the maître d' came around a column. She was sitting at a table in a far corner, gazing out a window, chin on her fingers. She looked so pretty he almost laughed out loud at the thought that she was here to meet him. She was wearing a low-cut dress — maybe too low-cut but so what — and had her long blond hair pulled to one side so it fell down her left shoulder over her breast. As he was almost to the table, she saw him and smiled.

"Hi, there."

Out of the corner of his eye, Rose spotted a table of middle-aged women sitting at another table give them a second look. Then a third. It was exactly as Cortez had predicted. Rose had caught the maître d' raising an eyebrow, too.

"Hi."

The table was a square four-top. He'd expected to sit across from her during lunch, but she pulled out the chair to the right of hers so they could sit next to each other. He took the menu from the maître d' and put it down on the table without looking at it, showing her he was in no hurry. Which he wasn't. Cortez and Tammy had everything humming as far as the CIS acquisition went. Everything was on track to announce the takeover on Thursday.

"How are you?" he asked.

"Fine." She slid her fingers to the back of his hand for a second.

They were so warm. "Sorry I'm late." God, he could hardly think straight with her skin on his. How pathetic was this? "I got caught in a meeting."

"I was getting a little worried," she said, tapping her watch. "I thought maybe you were standing me up."

He hesitated until the waiter had walked away, thinking about how he would have fought through a blizzard to make it to this lunch. "I doubt very much you've ever been stood up in your life."

"Maybe once," she said softly. "But thank you. That's nice of you to say."

He picked up the folded linen napkin on the plate in front of him and spread it out in his lap. Saw Kat quickly reach for her napkin, too. Definitely not from money. Not that he would have known you were always supposed to put a napkin in your lap as soon as you sat down at a table if his mother hadn't married that second time. He swallowed hard. He hadn't thought about his father in a while. He sure would have sacrificed that etiquette lesson — and all the other perks the businessman from

Atlanta had provided — to have his dad back. It had always been the only source of emptiness in his life, until he and Sheila had grown apart.

"You all right?" he asked.

"What do you mean?"

"Your hand, it's so warm."

"That's just me. I always run a little warm." She hesitated. "I've been looking forward to today . . . a lot."

Those eyes of hers were even more incredible than he remembered. There were gold flecks floating in the aqua, like planets swirling around a dark sun. "Me, too," he admitted, glancing away. He almost felt like he'd say something he shouldn't if he gazed at her for too long.

She smiled. "Sure you weren't followed here, Michael?"

His eyes flashed to hers. Instantly he wished his reaction hadn't been so fast and furious.

"Jeez, I was kidding," she said with an easygoing laugh. "Sort of. I mean, if I was your wife, I wouldn't let you out of my sight. I'd keep you under lock and key at all times so the other women in the world, like me, wouldn't have the slightest shot at you."

He grinned self-consciously, trying not to pay attention to her, but it was tough.

Several tables of young professional men had just walked in, and they couldn't take their eyes off her. He was feeling like the alpha stallion in the paddock for the first time in years. Maybe in forever. Another juvenile sentiment, but, hey, it felt good. He couldn't deny it.

She leaned forward and put her elbows on the table. "You're a very attractive man."

"Do you always say exactly what you're thinking?" In his world, people often didn't. "It's amazing."

"You're the chief financial officer of Trafalgar Industries, one of the biggest companies in this country. I thought you'd appreciate directness. The fact that I'm being efficient, not beating around the bush."

His eyes narrowed. "How do you know where I —"

"Sorry to interrupt. Welcome to The Station."

Rose glanced up at their waiter.

"Can I start you all off with something to drink?"

"I'd like a Captain and Coke," Kat said quickly. She put her hand on Rose's arm before he could order. "Don't be boring, Michael. Have fun."

He gazed back at her, thinking about how hard he'd worked for the last twenty years.

How even though he wasn't technically doing anything wrong by having lunch with her, he knew she could prove to be that fuse that would light the explosion and destroy everything.

Then again, maybe she was the answer. She was so beautiful, and even though he barely knew her, it was like they'd been together before. Like there wouldn't be that uncomfortable period to get through. Maybe it was her relaxed manner, maybe it was the way she kept touching him tenderly with those warm fingers. Whatever, he could feel himself opening the door just a crack to catch a glimpse of the temptation.

Of course, maybe he didn't have to worry about Kat lighting the fuse because maybe someone else had already beaten her to it. Colin Freese had followed through on his threat and called a board meeting, looking for their approval to fire Rose, promising to present evidence that would convince the board to act. Tammy Sable had snuck Rose a hard copy of the e-mail this morning right before he'd left to come out here, and it was unnerving to read the words. He hadn't done anything wrong, but, big as the stakes were, people might be willing to go to any length to frame him. The board meeting was scheduled for two weeks from yesterday.

Just in time to derail the CIS deal.

"Come on," Kat urged quietly. "Please."

This could end up being such a mistake. He'd promised himself he wouldn't give in. Damn it. "Do you have Sierra Nevada on draft?"

"Sure," the waiter said.

"I'll take one of those." Rose watched Kat break into a huge smile. A smile of satisfaction. Like she was happy he was having a beer, but even happier that she'd convinced him to do it. "Do you guys frost your mugs?"

"Absolutely."

It was chilly outside today but warm in the restaurant. One cold beer would taste good, and he would absolutely keep it to just one. No more than that no matter how hard she pushed. Then it wouldn't be such a mistake. By the time he made it back to the office, he wouldn't feel anything. "I want it really cold."

"You got it. Be right back."

"Now," Rose said when the waiter was gone, "how did you find out who I was?"

"One of the bartenders at Morton's told me."

Of course. He and Cortez were in Morton's at least once a week. They knew all the bartenders — and the bartenders knew them.

"Then I went on the Internet, to Trafalgar's website, and read all about you," she continued. "Pretty impressive, but I didn't think senior corporate executives were so good looking. Not as young as you, either. I always thought men like you were shriveled up, gray and hunched. Not dashing."

"Enough of the ego stroke," he said, chuckling, a depressing thought striking him. "What, are you looking for a job?" The corners of her mouth turned down and he could tell that he'd hurt her right away. "I'm sorry." He put his hand on hers. "It's just that I'm not used to this."

"I'm not trying to snow you," she said quietly. "I told you on the phone on Friday. I was attracted to you as soon as I saw you. And I actually saw you first. I noticed you as soon as you walked in the bar. Usually it's the other way around."

"I'm sure it is," Rose agreed, still discounting her compliments. "What about your husband?" He tapped her small engagement diamond. "Given what I saw Thursday night, I doubt he'd be very happy about this lunch."

"No, he wouldn't," she admitted. "But I don't care." The tone of her voice strengthened. "*Because* of what you saw Thursday night. He's such a jerk. Everyone tried to tell me that before I married him, but I didn't listen."

"You're stubborn, aren't you?"

She looked up.

Like a daughter would look up at a father. Like Jamie had looked up to him. "The more people tell you to do it one way, the harder you try to do it another. Right?"

She smiled wanly as the waiter put their drinks down on the table. "Maybe." When he was gone, she touched his wedding band. "What about you? Would your wife care about us having lunch?"

He glanced down at the thick, plain gold band. He'd debated on the drive out here about whether to wear it or not. About whether to tell Kat what had happened to Sheila. "Of course."

"How long have you been married?" she asked, picking up her drink and holding it toward him.

Rose picked up his mug, gently tapped her glass, then took a sip. It seemed so odd to be drinking in the middle of the day. He hadn't done this since college. "Twenty-one years." God that beer tasted good. His eyes flickered down to the top of her dress cutting across her breasts, revealing so much.

He was irritated with himself instantly. He hadn't meant to do that, it had just sort of happened. Usually he was much more in control. She was going to think he was so rude. "How about you?"

"Almost two years."

"How old are you?" he asked.

"Twenty-seven."

"What do you do?"

"For a living?"

He grinned. "Yes, for a living."

"I'm a bartender in Georgetown."

His jaw clenched involuntarily. So was Johnny Sykes. Cortez had finally given Rose the name and number of his private eye buddy — after the not-so-subtle warning about staying loyal — and the guy had told him everything. Even where Sykes worked in Georgetown. Rose was going down there this evening to have a little chat with Sykes, right after he met with Grant Boyd.

"Where? Come on," he pushed when she hesitated. "You know where I work."

"Clyde's."

Good. That wasn't where Sykes worked. That would have been too much of a coincidence, something he would have gone right to Sherman LeClair about. Not waited to tell him during their meeting on Thursday.

"What's your real given name?" he asked, taking another long swig of beer. She had almost finished her drink, already, and it felt strange to be lagging behind a woman. That would never have happened at Carolina. "You don't have to tell me your last."

"Katherine, and my last name is Hanson." She waved to the waiter and held up her glass, then finished the last sip. "I don't mind telling you." She pointed at his mug. "Kinda slow, aren't you?" She patted his arm again when he went right for the mug. "I'm just teasing. I know you're not a big drinker. I watched you the other night. You drank Coke most of the time. Then you nursed a glass of red wine like it was two hundred proof or something."

"I was going back to the office."

"*Sure* you were. At nine o'clock at night?"

"Absolutely." Suddenly it was important to him for her to know he wasn't some kind of weak sister when it came to drinking. "We had a call with our lead bank in Manhattan."

Her eyes widened. "Do you go to New York City a lot?"

"Every now and then." He went up at least once a month on the Metroliner to meet with Citibank and the equity analysts at the big investment banks. "It's fun."

She moaned. "God, I'd love to go to New York."

"Never been?"

"No," she said quietly, as though she didn't want to admit it. "I've never been out of the state of Virginia. Can you believe that? I grew up in Norfolk, down near the beach. Then I moved up here a few years ago with a friend from high school because I heard the money was good." She rolled her eyes as the waiter put down her second drink. "The problem is, it's so expensive to live around here. Yeah, you make more money, but, net-net, you don't live any better being a bartender here than you do in Norfolk or Virginia Beach. But I met Joey, so I stayed." She grabbed the waiter's arm before he could walk away. "Could you bring him another beer when you have a chance?" she asked sweetly, pointing at Rose.

Rose put his hands up. "Oh, no, I can't."

"You can and you will."

"But I've only half finished this one," he said, laughing. He could feel the alcohol starting to affect him.

"He'll be ready by the time you get back." She grinned at the waiter and shooed him away. "I'm a bad influence, Michael, but you knew that. It's why you came today."

He took a long swallow from the mug. "What do you mean?"

"Well, I have this picture of your life."

"Oh?"

"Yeah. Tell me how close I am." She guzzled half the second Captain and Coke before getting started. "You've got this beautiful, gargantuan colonial house on a couple of acres somewhere off Georgetown Pike. It's filled with expensive furniture, two or three All-American kids who probably get straight A's at some private school that's basically an automated feeding system for Princeton and Harvard, and a burly golden retriever who camps out at your feet in your study at night while you finish your fifteen-hour day going over late e-mails and reports you need to soak up for early meetings the next day." She paused to take another swallow of rum and Coke. "Then there's your wife. She's pretty. Not as pretty as she was when you met her twenty-two years ago or whatever, but she's still the best-looking mom in the neighborhood. And she's got classic beauty. She's tall and slim with long lines and never wears anything the least bit revealing even at the country club pool. And you and she haven't cut loose in years. You can't remember the last time you got drunk or smoked dope together, and you probably only have sex a couple of times a month, if that. You're tired of asking her for it, and she's just plain tired. Her life's all about the kids and your life is all about your career and those two things don't seem to meet very often." She smiled and raised one eyebrow. "How am I doing?"

Rose closed his mouth, just now realizing that it had fallen open as she'd been talking. "You're wrong," he said. "She's barely five feet tall. And the dog is a black Lab."

She smiled. "Still pretty good, huh?"

He exhaled heavily. "Yeah, pretty good."

"Which is why you're here."

As the waiter placed another iced mug full of Sierra Nevada down in front of him, he gave her a curious look. "How's that?"

"Any outsider would say your life is perfect, what anyone would want. I don't know how much you make, but I bet with all the bonuses and stock options and whatever else you get from your company, it's like more than half a million dollars."

Now she was giving away her age, and maybe a little about her background, too. She had no idea what a *Fortune* 100 executive made. She thought five hundred thousand was a lot of money. With everything, he'd made more than five times that last year, but he wasn't going to tell her that.

He was tempted to impress her, and maybe if this had come up four or five beers down the road, he would have. But he managed to stay in control. And he wasn't going to have four or five beers. This second one would definitely be the last. There was no way she was going to convince him to have another.

"Right?" she asked. "Over half a million?"

"Right."

"Jesus." She shook her head.

Impressed with just that number now that she had gotten him to admit it, he saw.

"Unbelievable. What do you do with all of that cash?" she asked.

"Pay a lot of taxes."

"Poor baby," she said sarcastically, patting his shoulder. "I feel so bad for you."

"If my life's so perfect, then why *am* I here?"

"Because you can't stand your wife anymore."

He stared at her for a few moments. "Oh, really?"

"Yup. Look, I talk to guys like you all the time at Clyde's. They get drunk and they try to pick me up. They tell me how they can't stand to even look at their wives anymore, how their wives never want to have sex. They tell me they'll do anything for me, buy me whatever I want, if I'll just go out with them. I know the deal."

"And you've never gone out with any of them?" he asked. "Never been tempted to see what it would be like. Never given your number to one of them?"

She gazed at Rose for a few moments, swirling her drink, then took another swallow of it. "No."

She was lying, he could tell. She hadn't glanced away, but the intensity in the turquoise eyes had faded — the golden flecks had gone to yellow for a moment — like she was disappointed in herself for something, still beating herself up for it. It was the same look she'd given him when he'd made that crack about her never having been stood up, and she'd answered that maybe there'd been one time.

And as silly as it seemed, the fact that she'd cheated on her husband once made Rose jealous. It was as if she should have known she was going to meet him. As if he was really going to do anything with her. As if he had any right whatsoever to feel jealous.

He picked up his mug and glanced down because the glass seemed so light, surprised to find that it was nearly empty. He'd almost finished two beers in less than ten minutes, and she was ordering them a third round. But he didn't try to stop her this time. "Why me?" he asked after the waiter had acknowledged her wave from across the restaurant. He gazed at her intently, trying to decode her expression, trying to figure out if she'd been sent by the other side or if this lunch and what could follow was all outside of that — just a young woman looking for true love, or a sugar daddy. "Why now?"

"I told you," she answered quietly, "I was attracted to you the moment I saw you. Very attracted."

His eyes flickered down to her chest again involuntarily and, as they came back up, he knew she'd seen his look. But the dress was cut so low. It had to be just barely covering her nipples. It was almost impossible *not* to look. "I'm sorry, it's just that I —"

"It's okay," she interrupted. "Why do you think I wore this? I wanted you to look. I like dressing sexy, I like the stares, I like the attention. I won't deny it. It's fun, and it sure helps with tips at work."

"I bet," he muttered, really starting to feel the beer now.

"You like it, too," she said, caressing the back of his hand lightly. "You don't want to admit it, but you do. You like being with a sexy woman, not somebody who covers up like an Eskimo even when it's ninety degrees in August." She nodded past him. "You like that the guys over there who've been drooling over me since they walked in have been looking at you, too, like you're the man. You like that I drink, that I like to have a good time." She ran her fingertips through his hair. "You like that I'm different. I'm what you want, Michael."

"Why are you coming on to me so strong, Katherine?" He'd surprised himself a little that he'd used her full given name, but surprised her in a *big* way. It was obvious in her expression, obvious that she liked it, too.

"I've already told you. I felt something as soon as I saw you. That's so unusual for me."

"You could have anyone you want."

She rolled her eyes. "Oh, sure I could. Maybe for a night, but then they'd drop me like a bad habit. I'm a nobody, a nothing. I know that, Michael. Maybe I'm fun to look at, but my family's from the wrong side of the tracks so I'm not something anyone who's anyone is interested in for long. I'm not like your wife. I'm not from a society family. I bet *she* doesn't need to be reminded to put her napkin in her lap as soon as she sits down."

"How do you know about my wife?" he asked suspiciously.

She looked at him like he was crazy. "I don't, I'm guessing."

"Right, right."

"But I saw something different in you," she continued, "something that told me you wouldn't hold the fact that I'm a nobody against me."

Rose winced. He'd always wondered why he'd married Sheila. He'd been attracted to her right away, but when he was being completely honest with himself, he knew he'd been more attracted to her after finding out who she was and how much money her daddy had. Marrying her had made the first few years after college much easier, which he knew it would.

"You're different," she said softly. "Different from any other man I've ever met."

"You don't even know me."

She gazed deeply into his eyes. "Oh, yes I do."

What was so compelling was that it seemed like she really meant and believed what she was saying. She couldn't be acting, couldn't have been sent from the other side. She wasn't being emotive, wasn't drooling with bitterness and resentment, she was just being matter-of-fact. She'd crossed her knees and her arms over her chest tightly without even noticing, which was a good sign to Rose because it meant she was being sincere. He'd taken all those body language translation courses years ago, and, according to the PhDs, she was being genuine. But then of course, how could she know him so well?

"I assume you aren't working tonight," he said, pointing at her glass.

She put her head back and laughed. "See, that's the difference between you and me. I drink before work, you drink after it." She leaned over and wrapped one of his hands in both of hers. "Why don't you come down to Clyde's tonight? I'll save you a seat at the bar. Then we can go out afterward. I should be able to get off by ten."

"Jamie. *Jamie!*"

Jamie stopped and turned around. She'd been heading to her bus, the fourth one in a line of twelve, several textbooks pressed to her chest. She winced when she saw who was calling out to her. It was Carol Chesney, a girl in her class she didn't get along with at all. Mostly because Carol's boyfriend had asked Jamie out early in the school year behind Carol's back. Jamie had turned him down flat, but Carol had found out and

367

blamed Jamie, not her boyfriend. Told everyone that Jamie had been the one to ask her boyfriend out, not the other way around. And, of course, he'd told everyone the same thing. It had been a rough couple of weeks.

"What's up, Carol?"

Carol put her hand on Jamie's arm, and her expression turned sad. "I was so sorry to hear about your mom. It's terrible."

Jamie gazed at Carol for a few moments. She hadn't been expecting this. "That's nice of you to say."

Carol shrugged. "I know we're not, like, best friends, but I'm not that bad a person. I know how I'd feel if I lost my mom, and I would never wish that on anyone."

"Thanks."

"And I'm glad your father's getting over your mom so fast."

Jamie's eyes shot to Carol's. She'd suddenly heard a familiar tone in Carol's voice. "What are you talking about?"

"I just talked to my dad," Carol explained, holding up her cell phone. "He was out in Leesburg today having lunch. He told me he saw your father with a woman, said they were having a really good time together, drinking and laughing. Heck, my dad made it sound like they were going to be heading right to a motel after they left the restaurant." She smiled. "Well, gotta go. See you tomorrow."

The world blurred in front of Jamie's eyes as Carol turned and headed for her bus. A moment later the tears came.

43

"I'm glad we could have this time to get together to chat like two old friends, not like two blood enemies." Grant Boyd walked with Rose toward a corner of the spacious office that looked more like a mansion's living room than the place where Boyd managed an elite Washington law firm. There was a comfortable three-seat sofa, two big wingback chairs, a coffee table, even a small bar against the wall behind one of the chairs. "Sit down, Michael," he said in his thick southern accent.

Boyd had been guiding Rose toward the sofa, but Rose changed course at the last second and went for one of the chairs instead. The chairs were higher off the floor than the sofa, and he didn't want to be looking up at Boyd while they spoke. He wanted every advantage he could get right now. He could see Boyd's irritation at the maneuver by the creases that appeared suddenly around the corners of the older man's mouth and the way his face turned a brighter red so quickly.

Normally, he wouldn't have been so bold, given that they were on Boyd's turf, but he was still feeling the effects of the six beers he'd had at lunch with Kat. They'd had an incredibly good time, he had to admit. Better even than he'd anticipated. He was actually thinking of stopping by Clyde's over in Georgetown — where Kat bartended — before heading home. It wasn't too far from here. That might be a dangerous move, might really ignite the fuse, but he couldn't stop thinking about her.

The only negative about the lunch was that Rose had spotted the father of a girl in Jamie's class eating lunch at The Station, too. A guy named Dave Chesney, a successful commercial real estate agent in northern Virginia. But Chesney had been sitting way on the other side of the restaurant, near where the doors used to open to the railroad tracks, so, Rose hoped, he hadn't seen them. On the off chance he had, he wouldn't tell his daughter about it. No one would be that inconsiderate. Or was that naive, too? Was it just like trying to convince himself that Sheila wasn't having an affair when he'd known damn well she was?

"Can I get you anything, Mike?" Boyd asked.

Rose popped another breath mint as he sat. He'd driven from Leesburg directly to downtown Washington and, during the fifty-minute ride, he'd sucked on mint after mint. The last thing he wanted was Boyd to smell the beer on his breath.

"No thanks. I'm fine, Grant."

Boyd sat at the far end of the sofa and crossed one leg over the other at the knee, reclining into a relaxed pose.

But Rose could tell it was forced, that Boyd wasn't really feeling relaxed at all. That this was all choreographed, but Boyd hadn't practiced it enough.

"I'm glad you could come in today, Mike."

"I'm glad you called." Boyd had phoned this morning at eight thirty. Rose had never heard him so friendly. "Sorry I couldn't make it down here until now." It was after four o'clock. "I got caught up in a few things."

"Well, I don't want to be nosy. So I won't ask what those things were."

Rose glanced up. Boyd was smiling like the cat who'd swallowed the canary. Maybe paranoia was starting to set in because of everything else that was going on, but at this point was it *that* crazy to think he was being followed? After all, Sherman LeClair wanted him to be so careful about coming to their meeting on Thursday. Which was why all the extra arrangements had been made with Adam Pierce.

"First of all, let me say how deeply saddened I am by your loss," Boyd continued, "by the death of your wife. Colin Freese passed the sad news along to me yesterday afternoon when we spoke on the telephone. I remember meeting Sheila a year or so ago at that function on Capitol Hill when my wife and I ran into you both. She seemed like a lovely woman."

"Thank you." Freese had probably passed along the sad news about Sheila while he and Boyd had been plotting to kick Rose out of the company. He gritted his teeth, imagining that conversation. "Yes, she was a lovely woman."

Boyd hesitated a moment, nodding slightly, as if he was paying his respects to the dead. "Well, let's get to the point," he finally said, "why I asked you to come. By the way," he said, interrupting his train of thought, "I do appreciate you hoofing it all the way down here. I know it's a long way from McLean, from your office at Trafalgar. I hope you had some other reason to fight the traffic," he said, smiling again.

"No, I don't have any other reason to be down here," Rose answered. "But that's all right. I thought us having a face-to-face was important, too. Just like you said this morning on the phone. And I always want to do whatever I can to accommodate one of our board members. You all have been very helpful to us over the past few years, very supportive."

Boyd's smile tightened. "Well, maybe you can find something fun to do for a while after we finish because the traffic will be hell until at least seven. Bumper-to-bumper all the way out the Toll Road. Call a friend and go over to Georgetown for a drink or something. It's right around the corner from here. But I'm sure you already know that. Point is," he said, his voice rising before Rose could speak up, "I wanted to talk to you about last week's board meeting. I felt bad about the way I acted. You know, I'd had a rough night." He patted his stomach. "Ate something that didn't agree with me at all — oysters I think it was — and I was in a pretty nasty mood. I'd been up hugging the porcelain princess all night." He chuckled insincerely. "No excuses, but I was looking for a fight." He hesitated. "And by God, I found it, didn't I? You and Cortez had your six-shooters on, too."

"Grant, when you called David and me Tonto and the Lone Ranger at the start of a meeting, it didn't make us feel very good. Especially David. You know?"

Boyd held up his hand and furrowed his heavy salt and pepper brows. "I understand, believe me I do. That was very bad form. Like I said, I was taking my oyster frustration out on you guys."

Bullshit, Rose thought. This show of contrition was clearly Boyd trying to play good cop, which he didn't do very well. Just as Freese wasn't very convincing playing the bad cop. But he'd go along with the charade for a while, to see what was what. Maybe he could pick something out of this he could relate to LeClair on Thursday.

"Why do you want CIS so badly?" Boyd asked directly. "What is it about the company that makes it so exciting to you? For the life of me, I still don't get it."

Rose took a deep breath. This would be a complete waste of words, but he'd go through the motions anyway.

He explained the synergies he and Cortez believed CIS would bring to Trafalgar. Improving the company's information technology systems and the new customers they would have access to as a result of the CIS acquisition. The same way he and Cortez had explained them last Friday, but in a more condensed version.

When Rose was done, Boyd shook his head and grinned. "Well, it all sounds fascinating, even the second time, but a little farfetched, too. I say that with all due respect and with no ill will intended."

Boyd was being so damn polite, but the specter of the board meeting two weeks from now hung over the room like a dark cloud. Neither of them had mentioned it yet, but they both knew that was the real reason they were sitting down. Boyd wanted to turn up the pressure on Rose, and Rose wanted to show Boyd that he felt no pressure at all. That he knew the rest of the board would believe he was innocent of whatever Boyd and Freese would try to trump up.

"None taken."

"I wonder if you aren't stretching on this one a little, Michael," Boyd said.

"Stretching? What do you mean?"

"The acquisition sounds great when you're talking about it because you're a very good speaker. But when I really think about things, I don't see it. I wonder if you don't have another motive in all of this."

"Oh?" Rose hadn't been sure if Boyd was actually involved with the people on the other side or just sincerely concerned that CIS wasn't a good target for Trafalgar — until now. The mention of "another motive" convinced Rose that Boyd was involved. Involved with the people who were using CIS to conduct secret and criminal government activities, according to LeClair. "And what do you think that other motive is?"

Boyd put his hands behind his head. "How'd you get the idea to go after CIS?"

"I've been thinking about it for a long time," Rose answered. "I've known about CIS for a while obviously, because it's headquartered in Washington. But I'd have to say I started getting serious about the idea maybe six months ago. When we had some bad information technology issues at our heavy equipment division out west."

"Uh-huh," Boyd said, unconvinced. "You sure somebody else didn't put the whole idea into your head out of the blue?"

"What do you mean?"

Boyd chuckled again. "You sure someone didn't approach you and put the bug in your ear to go after CIS for a different reason? Not because of all these supposed synergies the combination of Trafalgar and CIS will have?"

Rose hesitated. "I'm *very* sure."

"Because I'd want to know about it if

someone did."

"I'm sure you would." Rose could tell that Boyd was getting frustrated.

"Michael, we've all heard that old saying about how things aren't always as they appear. Well, that's what we have here. I can't be too specific with you, but there's more going on beneath the surface at CIS than you know, than you could possibly imagine. Much more. I've already told you more than I should, but it's something you should think about."

"Oh?" Rose tried to sound surprised. "Like what?"

"As I said, I can't be specific." Boyd leaned forward and pointed at Rose, his expression turning grave. "But it would be a very good idea for you to back off this thing. To find something wrong with CIS, something that makes the company not a good acquisition candidate for Trafalgar. The problem can be real or imagined, I really don't give a damn. But if you cooperate with me and come up with something that the board buys as a good reason to back away from CIS, I give you my word that I'll support you on anything else you and David Cortez come up with. No matter how far out in left field it is. And, maybe more important, I'll take care of that board meeting Colin Freese has scheduled in two weeks. In fact, I'll turn the tables on him in front of everyone. He thinks I'm going to frame you for fraud, which I know you know, but I'll actually disclose to the board some things Freese has done. Things that will cause the board to fire Colin instead of you. I know for a fact Freese will walk out, he'll have to. Then I'll nominate you to be CEO. What do you think about that?" Boyd leaned back, letting everything he'd said sink in.

Well, Rose thought, no more drinking during the day for me. His head was spinning. He hadn't expected this at all. He'd expected to be threatened, then have to stick out his chin and tell Boyd to pound salt. Not to have Boyd tell him he was going to do a one-eighty on Freese and ambush him. But how much could he really trust Grant Boyd?

"But make no mistake," Boyd growled, "if you decide not to play ball, if you decide not to back off the CIS acquisition, you will pay."

That was more like it. That was what he'd expected.

"Your career at Trafalgar will be over," Boyd kept going. "That might be the least of your problems. In fact, there might be another funeral or two in your family real soon."

Rose clenched his teeth and shot up out of his chair. "If anything happens to my kids," he said, his voice shaking, "I'll hold you responsible, Grant. Personally. So, if you do anything to them, you better make sure you do it to me, too. Otherwise, you'll be very, very sorry."

Glenn stood in the doorway of the computer room in the basement, watching Trudy tap out an e-mail. He'd gotten home a little early from school today, and he was psyched to go to battle against an enemy who'd gotten very lucky last night. They'd agreed to wage another war this afternoon, and he wanted to warm up beforehand. He'd thought about it during the day, about how he wasn't going to lose today, how he shouldn't have lost last night.

He was going to ask Trudy to let him on, but he hesitated, watching the au pair's fingers dance across the keyboard. He'd never seen Trudy on the computer before, figured she didn't even know how to turn it on much less how to use e-mail. It had always sounded a little silly to him when she'd claimed she was completely computer illiterate, but he hadn't thought much about it. Now he was thinking a lot about it.

He turned and headed quietly toward the stairs.

44

Georgetown lay just to the west of downtown Washington, overlooking the Potomac River from high up on a bluff rising from the northern shore. It was a high-end enclave of mostly expensive boutiques, restaurants, bars, and pricey town houses — much like Rodeo Drive in Los Angeles except that it was done mostly in neocolonial as opposed to chic. It was also home to Georgetown University. The dark spire of the university's gothic cathedral was a readily recognizable landmark for powerboaters during the summer when they anchored just north of the Key Bridge, which connected Washington to Virginia, on this wide, calm section of the river.

Rose sat on a stool at the Hog's Breath, a small bar at the eastern fringe of Georgetown. Unlike the more upscale establishments closer to the center of the area, the Hog's Breath catered to a younger, less affluent set — mostly Georgetown students who were at least twenty-one as well as younger ones who could pass for of-age or who knew one of the bartenders. The place was dark, plain, and smelled of stale beer and peanuts. A dive compared to most of the other places around — or Morton's in McLean — but Rose liked it. It reminded him of a place he and his fraternity brothers had frequented in college. Another dive on a lonely road in the countryside outside Chapel Hill near a tobacco farm. The owner of the place was so desperate for business he hadn't worried about serving under-age kids — until a guy from another fraternity had flipped his car on the way home one night drunk out of his mind and killed himself and the owner had been hauled off to jail. The place had been shut down, and they'd been forced to drink at the fraternity house, which was illegal, too, but neither the police nor the administration had ever tried to enforce the law.

Rose picked up a glass of cold beer — his third in twenty minutes — and took several swallows. He was sitting at the sticky, dark wood bar, watching Johnny Sykes flirt with a pretty young woman wearing a tight top and a leather miniskirt. She couldn't have been more than twenty, but Johnny wasn't having a problem serving her. Other than the three of them, there were only a few other people in the bar.

He hated how good-looking Sykes was. Hated how easy it was to imagine Sheila leaning over a mirror lying on a nicked-up coffee table in front of this bastard's ratty couch in his disheveled apartment doing a line of cocaine, then raising up and kissing him passionately as she made sure none of the powder spilled out of her nose while she clutched the straw or rolled up bill she'd used to snort it with. How easy it was to picture her wrapped around him naked in some broken down four-poster bed he hadn't made in weeks. Rose turned the glass upside down and finished what was left of the Budweiser. No Sierra Nevada here, just the basics.

"Want another one?" Sykes called, glancing over at him after giving the young woman a smile that told her he'd be right back.

Rose nodded. "Yeah." He was still thinking about the shocker Grant Boyd had laid on him thirty minutes ago in his living room of an office. The offer to ambush Colin Freese at the board meeting two weeks from now. To reveal whatever terrible secrets Boyd had on Freese, then throw his support behind Rose as the new CEO after Freese left the room, disgraced. Rose didn't doubt that Boyd had the goods on Freese — Freese would never have voted against the CIS acquisition if Boyd didn't. But you never switched horses in the middle of a race. He'd learned that lesson a long time ago, the hard way. Because you couldn't trust people who would switch anything in the middle of anything. You had to be loyal to the people who'd gotten you where you were.

"Here you go." Sykes put a fresh beer down in front of Rose and grabbed the empty glass. "Enjoy, friend."

"I'm not your friend," Rose said tersely.

Sykes stopped halfway back to the woman. "What was that?" He put the empty glass down on a stainless steel refrigerator unit beneath the bar and ambled back to where Rose sat. "I don't think I heard you right."

Rose took a sip of the fresh beer, then glanced up and stared evenly into Sykes's irritated eyes. "I said, I'm not your friend."

Sykes ran a hand through his long brown hair. "What's your problem, pal?"

"You."

"*Me?* What the hell did I ever do to you? I've never even seen you before."

"You screwed my wife," Rose answered calmly.

"Oh, Jesus." Sykes extended his arms outward from his sides, palms up, fingers spread and gave Rose an embarrassed grin. "Hey, I'm sorry, man, but I never ask if they're married, you know? They just want to have fun, and so do I. Besides, anybody who makes the mistake of getting married is asking for it in my book." He winced, trying to hide a mischievous smile. "What a shitty thing to say. Sorry again." He pointed down at the glass in front of Rose. "That one's on the house, okay?"

"Sorry and a beer doesn't cut it. Not in my book."

"Well, there's not much else I can do," said Sykes, starting to turn away, rolling his eyes at the woman sitting on the stool.

"Sure there is. You can talk to the cops. The two detectives who are out there looking for you."

"What?" Once again Sykes moved back to where Rose was sitting. "What are you talking about?"

Rose stood up. "My wife's name was Sheila. Maybe she used a different name with you, but that doesn't matter. What matters is, she's dead. And the cops think you killed her." Even though Willis and Harrison had never made any such accusation, it made him feel good to watch Sykes's eyes widen.

Sykes swallowed hard. "Are you . . . are you Michael Rose?"

"Yeah," he answered, dropping a twenty on the bar beside the beer glass. The beers were only two bucks apiece, but all he had was twenties and he wasn't going to wait around for change. "I just wanted to see what you looked like before I called the cops." They had asked him several times if he had any idea who Sheila might have been seeing. "To tell them who you are and where you work." With that, Rose turned and headed for the door.

"Hey, wait. *Hey!*"

But Rose didn't wait. He kept walking, right out the door and into the cold, dark night, the soles of his shoes crunching on patches of crusty snow covering the brick sidewalk.

He'd only made it a few paces away from the entrance to the bar when he heard footsteps behind him, then felt a heavy hand on his shoulder. He whipped around. Johnny Sykes stood in front of him. Rose hadn't realized how tall the guy was with the bar separating them. He was at least six-four, and he seemed broader now that they were both standing. Yup, he could see Sheila going for Sykes. Hell, he could see any woman going for Sykes.

"I didn't kill your wife," Sykes whispered, breath misting up in the air in front of him. "She was fine when she left here the other day, and you can tell the cops that. You can tell them that they're welcome to come and talk to me anytime they want. I don't have anything to hide." He pointed at Rose. "In fact, I'd really like it if they would. Because I'll tell them all about how much she hated you, how she asked you for a divorce a few weeks ago and how you told her it'd be a cold day in hell before you gave it to her. How you told her you'd kill her before you'd let her walk away with half your net worth and a monthly alimony payment that would choke a horse. How you'd break her neck if she even called a divorce attorney." He tapped Rose on the chest hard. "And I'll tell them all about how you've got a girlfriend yourself. Some jailbait blonde with legs up to her neck." He broke into a wide, dimpled smile. "Yeah, your wife was fine when she left here the other day. After I banged the hell out of her in a dressing room at that clothes shop over there," he said, pointing at a store across the street. "I love that little mole on her left ass cheek, just love it. How do you like that, Mr. Fucking Corporate? Huh?" This time he shoved Rose hard with both hands. *"Huh?"*

Rose cocked his right arm and slammed Sykes's jutting chin. He'd been in a couple of fights in college, and one thing he'd learned was to always take the big shot first, never hesitate. Sykes had asked for it with the shove, and that was because Sykes had severely underestimated his enemy. Rose had always packed one hell of a punch. All those fights in college had ended in ten seconds or less. Just like this one.

Sykes crumpled to the icy sidewalk in a fetal position, clutching his face and moaning as Rose headed off.

45

"What's the deal?" Tom Klein demanded, teeth chattering. He was talking on an outside pay phone in downtown Chicago, near the Bulls' basketball arena, and it was frigid. Five degrees with the wind chill. Beck was back at the bunker, with no clue about what Klein was doing. Klein had decided to take matters into his own hands because Beck seemed to be letting up just when he ought to be bearing down. "What did the guy say?" They wouldn't use names on the call.

"Basically nothing," Boyd answered. Boyd was on a pay phone as well. A few blocks from his office in downtown Washington near Union Station. It was cold where he was, too, but not like Chicago. "I asked him to tell me who put him up to the acquisition, and he told me nobody had. He told me it was all his own idea. But he was lying, I could tell. I've been reading faces for forty years, and that guy was lying to me. But he wouldn't say who he was working with."

"Did you tell him about ambushing the asshole who runs the show now?"

"Yeah, I told him. I also told him that if he didn't cooperate, there might be a few more funerals in his family this month."

"Why did you say that?" Klein demanded. Suddenly understanding what Beck meant when he whined about trying to keep a hundred Type-A personalities in line. He hadn't told Boyd to say any of that to Michael Rose. That might be the final outcome because it might become clear that Rose couldn't be stopped any other way, but now the guy was going to be on the lookout for it, which might make it a lot harder to execute. Especially if there was someone backing him, someone who could put bodyguards around him. Now they might have to act fast. "Jesus Christ."

"You tempt people with a carrot," Boyd lectured, "then you wave the stick in their faces. You show them the good *and* the bad, both ends of the spectrum. What they can have, what they can avoid. It works every time. Give the guy a few days to let everything sink in. He'll be back to us. I guarantee it."

Klein turned away as a sudden blast of icy wind hit him directly in the face. God, it was awful here in the wintertime. Why in the world did people make it their home? "Yeah, well, we'll give it a couple of days, then we'll go to plan B." Klein wasn't so sure Rose would give in. But he had the benefit of seeing the psychological profile. "Let's talk again on Friday, as agreed." They already had times and places worked out for the next five calls, thanks to the fact that they'd been going back and forth last week about the Trafalgar board meeting and what Boyd could use to influence Colin Freese. "Talk to you later."

"Hey!"

Klein had been about to hang up. "What?"

"What are you guys running through the target? What kind of operations and what kind of funds? I want to understand."

"I can't tell you. You know that."

"How did you dig up all that stuff on the CEO?"

"How many times do I have to say it?" Klein asked, teeth gritted. "I can't tell you."

"Look," Boyd snapped. "I've been a loyal soldier for a long time. I've done exactly what you and your boss asked me to do. Now I want to know the deal."

"I told you, I —"

"Does your boss know about this call?"

Klein hesitated.

"I knew it," Boyd said loudly. "You're on your own with this one, aren't you? Out at the end of a thin branch."

"I have to be," Klein admitted. "I told you, he's gone soft. Right at the wrong time."

"Be that as it may, my young friend," Boyd said nastily, "I'm sure he'd appreciate a heads-up call from me telling him that his deputy director is running around behind his back undermining what he's trying to do. Don't you think he'd appreciate that call?"

The answer was an obvious yes. Klein shivered as another gust of five-degree wind knifed through his coat. Maybe this wasn't going to be as straightforward as he'd figured.

46

"I know this is a crazy thing to say, but I missed you." Kat glanced up at the ceiling of the intimate restaurant and shrugged. "I mean, it's only been a few hours. What's wrong with me, Michael?"

He liked the way she always called him by his full given name. Sheila had never done that. She'd always called him Mike, or something far less pleasant when they were arguing. He liked the way Michael sounded, and it sounded even better when Kat said it. He was going to always introduce himself that way from now on.

"But I really couldn't wait to see you again," she continued. "I couldn't stop thinking about you."

He was starting to like how she said exactly what was on her mind all the time. Or what he hoped was really on her mind. He hadn't gotten over that last tiny seed of doubt that she could be working with the other side. Maybe he never would get over it. At least, not until all of this was over.

Listening to Boyd this afternoon, he'd realized that he really could be risking his life going after CIS. Sherman LeClair had warned him he might be right up front. He couldn't blame LeClair for sugarcoating anything. The older man had been straight up about it all. Even seemed a little relieved when Rose told him he had a gun at the house. LeClair had shaken his head and warned Rose he might have to use it at some point because the people they were dealing with would stop at nothing to keep the secret. Rose shivered, replaying that grim conversation in his mind.

"We had such a good time at lunch, didn't we?"

He gazed at Kat. She was absolutely gorgeous, even more stunning and sexy now that she'd changed from her green Clyde's barkeep shirt into a little black dress and high heels, and let her hair down. Of course, even with that unflattering bartender outfit on, she'd been prettier than any other woman in Clyde's, now that he thought about it. He glanced around. Every man in here kept trying to steal glances at her — as so many men at Clyde's had tried to get her attention, too — without their girlfriends or wives noticing. Rose had already overheard one woman two tables away warn the man she was with not to let his eyes wander again or he'd be sitting in here by himself.

Kat reached across the small wooden table, pushed the candle to one side, and took one of his hands in both of hers. "I don't know how long it's been since I've enjoyed a lunch so much," she said softly, "and now here we are again. It's already been the best day I've had in a long, long time and it's not over yet. I love it."

After leaving Johnny Sykes lying in a heap on the icy sidewalk in front of the Hog's Breath, Rose had headed to Clyde's. It was just after six o'clock when he'd gotten there, and the place was packed and noisy. Clyde's was a popular attraction for locals and tourists because it was connected to the big, three-story shopping mall in the center of Georgetown. But, as promised, Kat had saved him a seat at the bar so the crowd hadn't been a problem. Much to the irritation of five men who were crowding around the empty stool when he arrived. Five men who looked a lot like the guys at Morton's who'd tried to engage her.

She'd bought him glass after glass of the best Shiraz the bar stocked, as well as dinner, and snuck shots the whole time so she'd be ready to go when they left. Ducking out of the bar area for thirty seconds every fifteen minutes or so, then reappearing, her expression turning glassier and glassier upon her return from each trip. Still, she and another woman skillfully kept up with the blizzard of orders from the servers and patrons. She never missed a beat despite how much she drank.

Finally, thirty minutes ago, a third woman had shown up and Kat had been able to leave. She'd changed in the ladies' room, then they'd left and walked to this quiet restaurant near the university. He'd enjoyed the ten-minute stroll immensely. The night air was crisp and clear, tinged with a hint of wood smoke from the town house fireplaces farther up the hill, and she'd slipped her arm in his as soon as they were out the door. It had been very romantic. Just like Kat had said at lunch, he couldn't remember the last time he and Sheila had done anything like that. He kept asking himself why. Why had they let it slip away? Let it get to the point where they really didn't like each other anymore?

Now he and Kat were sitting across from each other at a little corner table of this intimate place, drinking champagne. She'd told him champagne was her favorite drink at night.

"Tell me about yourself, Michael," Kat said. "You made me talk about myself all during lunch. Now I want to hear about you."

"There's not much to say."

"Come on," she pleaded. "That's ridiculous."

"What do you want to know?"

She hesitated for a few seconds. "Okay, are you a republican or a democrat?"

Good question, he thought. She was starting from the top and working down. "What do you think?"

She squeezed his hand and smiled. "You are *the* most difficult person to get to know, or you're the most modest person I've ever met. I can't decide which."

"No, seriously, which one do you think I am?"

She took a sip of champagne. "Republican, obviously. You have to be. Big business, the establishment, the whole nine yards."

"If you were so sure, why'd you ask?"

She shrugged. "I don't know. I don't like republicans, because I'm working class all the way. Just like my parents, and they're democrats. Maybe I wanted to see if we'd have our first argument. I know you're never supposed to ask about religion or politics, but I like getting things out on the table."

"Well, I'm a democrat."

"Really?"

He could see her surprise — and her happiness. Once again, it seemed sincere, not an act. "Yeah, I always have been. I'm a big believer in personal privacy, in keeping the government out of our lives. If it weren't for that one issue, I probably would be a republican. I don't believe in handouts. I believe that you get out of something what you put into it." He shook his head. "But I can't get over how much the government is trying to rule our lives, even spy on us. And it's getting worse."

Kat leaned forward, a mischievous grin spreading across her face. "Why are you so worried about it? Do you do bad things behind closed doors?"

"No more than anyone else," he answered with a grin, rubbing his right hand. It was sore from smashing Sykes's chin. "How about you? Do you do bad things?"

"I'd love to, but I can't stand my husband."

"Speaking of your husband, what did you tell him about tonight?"

"He thinks I'm working late. What did you tell your wife?"

"Same thing."

"Won't she call your office to check on you?"

"No. She stopped doing that a *long* time ago."

"That's too bad."

"Yeah," he agreed softly, gazing at the candle. "But now I've met you." It amazed him to say that. She was already beginning to rub off on him.

She squeezed his hand again and smiled. "Yes, you have. And I know it's just the opening act, but it's a nice one. I hope it's not a short show."

He nodded. "Me, too."

She pulled her hands away and stood up. "I need to go to the little girl's room." She leaned down and kissed him on the cheek. "I'll be right back."

As she moved off, Rose noticed several other men in the place watching her. Like hawks watched mice in the field from high up on their perch. It was incredible how she caught men's eyes so fast. Nature at its best, the natural selection process in high gear. The thing was, she was genuine, too. It was hard for him to believe a woman as beautiful as her could be so nice, but it seemed she was. What in the world was she doing with that character he'd met at Morton's?

He noticed her purse hanging on the

outside of the chair. No good, he thought. An easy target for the pickpockets who worked Georgetown hard. He reached over the table, grabbed the straps and was about to put the purse down on the table beside the wall when he saw a ripped piece of newspaper poking out of the top. He glanced toward the restrooms, then pulled the newspaper out, careful not to rip it. Interested in what interested her.

When he saw what it was, he swallowed hard. It was the *Washington Post* article about Sheila's death.

It had seemed strange to Glenn that Trudy would claim to be computer illiterate, then sit there banging away on the keyboard faster than he could. But then, a lot of things had seemed strange about Trudy over the past few months.

When she volunteered to go to the grocery store to pick up a couple of items for dinner, she'd always be gone for an hour and a half, but the store was only fifteen minutes away. She'd never tried to make friends in the area the whole time she'd been with them. She kept a lockbox hidden in her closet — he'd found it one day when he was snooping around in her room after she'd gone shopping with Jamie, but he couldn't find the key anywhere. And she never talked about her family or where she was from. She was supposed to be from Sweden, but that was all she ever said. She never went into detail about where in Sweden she was from or told them anything about her family. They'd always assumed she was just shy. Glenn had never mentioned anything to his parents, but maybe it was time to say something to Dad.

He tried one more password, but it didn't work. He'd found her username on Yahoo! easily — he'd just pressed the forward button once. But the password block had been empty. He sat back in the chair thinking, trying to figure out what she'd use. But it was hopeless.

"What are you doing?"

He spun around in the chair, heart instantly racing, wondering how he was going to explain this. Then he sank back, as quickly relieved as he had been shocked. It was just Jamie.

47

It was almost midnight when Rose and Kat reached her car. It was parked in an all-night underground garage a block away from Clyde's.

While they were walking, he couldn't stop thinking about that newspaper article tucked in her purse, and how Johnny Sykes had accused him of having a hot blond girlfriend who was young enough to be his daughter. Maybe things were even more choreographed than he'd figured. Maybe Sykes had said something about a hot blonde not because Sheila had relayed anything to him — Sheila *couldn't* have known about Kat, which was why Rose had discounted it as nothing but a wild guess by Sykes outside the bar — but because Kat was in touch with Sykes. Or they had somebody in between relaying things to them.

"Nice car, huh?" Kat asked sarcastically,

pointing her keys at a red Ford Focus with a couple of dings in it. The car chirped when she pressed the unlock button. "What do you drive, Michael?"

"A Buick."

"No, I mean on the weekends when you don't have to worry what your coworkers think."

Could she really be that intuitive? "Something else."

She tilted her head back and shook her hair, then moved in front of him and put her arms around his neck. "Why are you such a mystery? Why won't you let me in?"

He gazed into her eyes. He wanted so badly to believe that she wasn't part of anything, wanted to let her in. "I've learned to be careful. It comes with age."

"Do you like me?"

He looked away and grinned in spite of himself. She had that knack about her. That knack of being able to make him smile even when he didn't want to. Sheila had never been able to do that to him. "I like you very much," he admitted, smelling that same perfume he'd inhaled when he'd run into her coming out of Morton's. The same perfume he was sure he could still smell a trace of on the note she'd pressed into his palm. "I think you know that."

"Then you don't need to be careful."

Her full lips — the focal point of that gorgeous smile — were just inches from his. "That's exactly *why* I have to be careful." Because I don't want to get hurt, he thought.

"I'm an open book."

"I don't have a clue who you really are. I've only known you for a few hours."

"You know me," she said firmly. "We've got some details to go through, some gaps to fill in here and there. But you know what kind of person I am." She pressed herself against him. "I know what kind of person you are. We're so right for each other, Michael," she whispered. "I knew it the second I saw you."

She was pushing so hard. Which made him feel good. And vulnerable. And suspicious. He ought to be writing off everything she was saying. But he was finding that harder and harder to do despite the article in her purse. "So, what? So I just divorce my wife and turn my back on my kids?"

She looked away. "I'm not saying that. Not yet anyway. Down deep I'm a hopeless romantic, I'll grant you that. But I'm no fool, either. Let's see where it leads, see what happens. I don't think you would have met me for lunch, then come to see me tonight if you weren't curious. And, unless I'm crazy, we just had a pretty good time."

They'd had a wonderful time — had two bottles of champagne, laughed and joked with each other, touched a lot. Even though he'd seen that article in her purse, he couldn't help but let himself get right back into it when she got back to the table. She was full of life and enamored of him. Which he hadn't experienced in a long time — someone being so into him. And it hadn't been as intense with Sheila even when he was infatuated with her at the beginning. He was human, and tipsy, and Katherine Hanson was hard to resist. Nearly impossible, in fact.

But there was still that doubt. Kat knew Sheila was dead, and she was acting like she didn't. Why?

"I did have a good time," he admitted quietly. "A very good time." He started to ask her the question, then stopped.

"What is it, Michael? Go ahead," she urged. "Ask."

He shook his head and looked around.

"Come on," she pleaded. "You've been wanting to ask whatever question it is since I came back to the table that first time. I can tell. Now what is it?"

Be corporate, he told himself. Be like you

would be if you were leading a Trafalgar acquisition. In that situation there wasn't a question he wouldn't ask, a stone he wouldn't turn over. When he and Cortez were trying to find out where the corporate bodies were buried or if the books at the target were cooked. He was a tough son of a bitch when it came to that. Be that way now, he kept telling himself. But it was hard. This was different.

"Katherine —"

"I just love it when you say my name like that."

"Please, Katherine."

"Sorry, sorry," she apologized, giggling and letting her forehead fall to his shoulder.

She was drunk. How could she not be after all the shots she'd slammed at Clyde's in the back while he was sitting at the bar, then drinking an entire bottle of champagne herself? "Why are you acting like you don't know my wife is dead?"

She raised her head slowly off his shoulder and gazed up at him. "What?"

"Why are you acting like you don't know my wife just died in a car wreck?" he repeated, her perfume wafting to his nostrils again. He was ready for her to start yelling at him for going in her purse. Or go completely cold and tell him she never wanted to see him again. But she didn't do either. Once again, she surprised him.

"I'm sorry," she said, her voice low. "I should have told you I knew as soon as I found out."

There was simply no predicting this woman.

"I didn't know how to bring it up," she continued. She exhaled heavily, obviously having a hard time with this. "See, I have this friend named Margie who works with me at Clyde's. She's the only one who knows that I gave you the note at Morton's. I went to her apartment the next morning to look you up on the Internet, on the Trafalgar home page after the bartender told me who you were. I went to her place because I didn't want my husband looking at the sites I'd gone to on our computer. I didn't want him following me to your bio page, and figuring out what was going on. He could have done that, right?"

Rose nodded. "Unless you'd erased your tracks after you were done." He didn't know that much about computers, but he knew that people who did could trace where you'd gone unless you covered it up.

"Well, I don't know how to do that."

"Then he would have been able to see exactly where you'd gone," Rose said, relieved that she'd been smart enough to use another computer. There was no telling what her husband would have done if he'd figured this out. That night at Morton's he'd struck Rose as extremely jealous, and unstable. "He could have followed your clicks right to my bio."

"That wouldn't have been good. Let me tell you."

"Was this friend of yours, Margie, at Clyde's tonight?" Rose asked.

"She left before you got there," Kat explained. "She worked the lunch shift, but she waited around for me because she wanted to give me the newspaper article she'd seen. The one I assume you found in my purse."

It sounded so bad when she said it, like he'd been rooting around in her purse indiscriminately. Not seen the newspaper sticking out of her purse and done nothing more than pull it out. "Look, I was moving your purse off the chair so it wouldn't get —"

"It's all right," Kat cut in. "I'm glad you found the article. Like I said, I didn't know how to bring it up. Anyway, I guess it was in the newspaper over the weekend, the thing about your wife's death, I mean. But Margie didn't read it until yesterday afternoon. She does that, reads the weekend newspapers on Monday 'cause she usually pulls double shifts on weekends since the money's better. So she doesn't have time to read them those days. But I give her credit. I don't even read the papers during the week." She hesitated. "That's when I found out, when Margie gave me the article. It was only a little while before you showed up tonight, and I couldn't really say anything at Clyde's with all the noise. Then we were having such a good time at the other place. I didn't know about it at lunch, I swear."

It sounded plausible. Not wanting to say anything because they were having such a good time and she figured bringing it up would ruin the mood. Suddenly he had that sinking feeling in the pit of his stomach, like he'd been way too tough on someone who didn't deserve it. "I'm surprised you saved me that seat at the bar after you found out what happened."

She raised an eyebrow. "To be honest, I was a little weirded out. My first reaction was, wow, this is the first time I've ever *really* wanted someone and the person who could get in my way of having him ends up dead the same night. I figured I had a connection with the devil I never knew about."

"And your second reaction," Rose spoke up, "was how could this guy have had lunch with me today and be coming to see me tonight a few days after his wife was killed in a car accident. Right?"

"Well . . ." She paused. "The thought crossed my mind," she admitted. "But, I still wanted to see you. And now I'm glad I didn't let it get in the way."

"Did you read the whole article?"

She nodded. "Yeah. It said your wife was killed when her car ran off Georgetown Pike a few miles from Great Falls. It rolled down an embankment or something real late that same night we met. I know that road. It's tight and curvy. Real bad at night."

"Do you know where she was coming from?"

Kat shrugged. "Sorry. Maybe I'm the devil's child, but I don't have ESP."

"Seeing her lover," Rose answered. "A man she was having an affair with."

Kat stepped back and put her hands to her mouth. "You're kidding."

"He's a bartender down here in Georgetown."

"Oh, God." Her shoulders shook, like a chill had just raced up her spine. "That's crazy."

He liked the fact that she didn't ask what

the guy's name was or where he worked. Of course, maybe she already knew. "It is crazy. She'd been seeing the guy for a few months. He'd gotten her into drugs. All while I was trying to make a living."

Kat slipped her arms around his neck again. "It's fate, Michael. You and me. You know it is. That's what's really crazy."

He'd never believed in fate — but that didn't mean he couldn't start now. "*You're* crazy."

And then she kissed him. He'd never felt lips so soft in his life.

48

They were standing on the Mall in the midnight darkness a few hundred yards from the Washington Monument. Standing just outside the glow emanating from the monument, which seemed to be reaching for the stars. Grant Boyd was bundled up tightly in a long overcoat, a scarf, and a ski hat, but Tom Klein's overcoat was unbuttoned and he wasn't wearing a scarf or a hat. It was twenty-nine degrees, but the wind was barely moving the leafless branches of the nearby trees. It felt like springtime to Klein, who was used to the bone-chilling temperatures and gale force winds he'd left behind in Chicago.

Klein had made a snap decision while he was on the pay phone freezing his ass off outside the Bulls' basketball arena. He needed an ally and Grant Boyd was going to be it. There was a distinct possibility that if he didn't bring Boyd further inside the circle, Boyd might actually call Peter Beck and let him know what was going on. Which would have dire consequences no matter how you looked at it.

So, after hanging up with Boyd, Klein had flagged down a taxi and headed right to O'Hare without even packing a suitcase. He was going to hop the last flight out to Washington because he couldn't bring Boyd into the circle over the phone, and he needed to make certain the guy was back on the reservation immediately. Talking about the I-4's secrets over the phone was out of the question. Someone who shouldn't could easily pick up their conversation. What he was going to tell Boyd had to be conveyed in person.

"What's the deal, Tom?" Boyd asked directly, pulling his green plaid scarf up over the tip of his nose. "Why did I tell Colin Freese he had tax evasion issues, and how the hell did you find that out in the first place?" Now his voice was muffled. "Why have I been fighting the CIS acquisition so hard?"

"Because CIS is a cutout."

Cutouts were companies and individuals engaged in legitimate businesses, but also involved with the covert activities of the United States government. They secretly supported the government by putting agents on the payroll who didn't spend ten minutes working on the company's legitimate businesses. They secretly supplied hardware to black operations. They executed covert operations at target locations while they were conducting legitimate business — like bugging a foreign embassy while they were installing a phone system. Historically, cutouts had been used mostly in the international theater. But more and more, they were being used to conduct domestic operations as well. To spy on American citizens.

"A very important cutout."

"I figured that," Boyd said with a wave of his hand, as though it was obvious. "I hope you didn't come all the way from Chicago on the spur of the moment tonight just to tell me that."

Boyd wasn't going to accept the forty-thousand-foot explanation, Klein realized. He wasn't going to be satisfied with the basics, he was going to demand details. "You've got to swear to keep this completely confidential, you can't tell anyone."

"Don't play games with me, son," Boyd snapped. "Somebody thought I was worthy enough to use, so I figure I'm worthy enough to know what's going on. And don't worry, I'm not going to tell a damn soul."

"Who called you originally?" Klein asked curiously. "Who was the first person to make contact?"

Boyd hesitated. "A man named Wes Barry. He used to be CEO of one of the big defense companies. He's a close friend of the president's. I'd met him a couple of times at party functions, and we'd talked about how they were good friends. That's why I listened to him right away. I didn't question his credibility."

That made so much sense, Klein thought. A defense industry CEO who was close to the president. As he thought more about it, Klein realized that Barry was probably the president's personal emissary on the Directorate. Beck had never told him who the other three members of the Directorate were, despite the fact that Klein asked many times — twice on the recent trip back from Washington to Chicago. But Beck had remained mum about their identities. Klein could understand the silence during the first few years. But he'd proven himself an honest and loyal member of the I-4, and Beck should have been willing to bring him closer to the center by now.

"When did Barry first call you?" Klein asked.

"About four months ago."

"What did he tell you?"

"He told me I would be doing the president a personal favor if I'd help keep CIS independent," Boyd explained, his tone terse. "He told me not to ask why, just to do it. That if I did it, good fortune would come to me. It was kind of like one of those damn chain letters, except that this time I actually did receive good fortune."

"How?"

"A big patent infringement case that one of my partners was working on for a corporate client of ours suddenly went our way. Out of the blue the judge in the case found in our favor, and our client was able keep selling their rip-off personal communications devices to the public at half the price the guys who'd invented it were. Understandably, they were ecstatic. They thought they were going to be in that lawsuit for years, even thought they might go bankrupt because that was really the only product they had. Three months later the guys who invented the device crash and burn, our client is swimming in cash, and we get a ten-million-dollar fee. They think we walk on water, but I know the truth."

"You think the administration got involved?"

"I know they did. No one actually called

to tell me, but I've never seen a case like that reverse directions so fast. I know that judge, and he's a tough son of a bitch on rip-off artists. Which our clients basically are."

"Anybody else ask you to do them any favors?"

Boyd's expression twisted in aggravation, and he pointed at his own chest. "Now look, Klein, I'm the one who's supposed to be asking the questions."

Klein glanced at the Washington Monument. "Okay, okay."

So he started at the beginning, with the history of the Order, how this was the fourth one since 1865, and what its objective was.

"But I don't know everything," Klein said when he was finished. "Beck's kept a lot to himself, kept me in the dark."

"I can understand that," Boyd agreed grudgingly.

"Hell, he just told me the other day about Spyder."

"Spyder?"

Klein noticed Boyd perk up instantly. "Yeah. I mean, I've known that it existed for a while, but I didn't know where it was hidden. All it could do."

"What is it?"

"It's how we watch basically every money transaction in the world and ID the ones that matter. There's billions of wires, right? So just because we can track them doesn't mean we find the ones that can tell us anything about terrorists. But some very talented software architects at CIS wrote a program that scans almost every single transaction worldwide and picks out the ones that matter. The ones that are kicked out have to be reviewed by human eyes, but —"

"But Spyder's already done ninety-nine point nine percent of the work," Boyd interrupted, grasping the power of the project immediately. His eyes narrowed. "Got to be some very high-powered hardware supporting the software and the people."

"No doubt," Klein agreed.

Which was why Klein doubted that Spyder could be moved as fast as Beck kept saying. And they wouldn't have much time once Rose took over. There'd have to be a record of all of CIS's properties, payroll records of the team supporting it, something that would lead Rose right to the supercomputer before it could be disassembled and moved if Beck waited too long to give the order to get it out. Rose might even already know where Spyder was — thanks to whom he was working with — and be able to send people in as soon as Trafalgar won the takeover battle. Beck had admitted that Spyder had been used to spy on innocent Americans, too. The courts would shut it down immediately. Their most effective technique of identifying terrorist activity would be destroyed — along with the Order.

"But how is it possible?" Boyd asked. "How can Spyder have access to all those transactions?"

"The government already had access to most of the transactions through SWIFT, European BankWire, and a couple of other institutional funds transfer networks. And CIS was able to gain access to even more data through its international offices. CIS has been working with many foreign banks for a long time, so when they were at a job site doing legitimate work, they did some things the banks didn't know about, too." Klein could see that Boyd was fascinated. "Besides, if a terrorist is going to do something in the United States, more than likely he's got to move money into this country. Which is exactly how we just identified an imminent major attack."

"Are you serious?" Boyd asked breathlessly.

"Absolutely."

"Planes again?"

"Yes."

"My God."

"Yeah, and thank God for Spyder. It identified a wire coming into an account at a bank in Connecticut that we were aware had been used before by people who were under suspicion. The account had been dormant for a while, but Spyder keyed in on it instantly the second the new money came in, the second it went active again. We tailed the guy who withdrew most of the funds, and watched him meet with a woman who worked at the submarine facility in Groton, Connecticut. Watched her and her husband meet with some other people we were suspicious of while they were on their honeymoon in New Zealand. We detained them on their way back into the country, worked a little magic, and got them to admit what they'd done and who they were working with."

"Worked a little magic," Boyd repeated. "You mean you tortured them."

"You have a problem with that?" Klein snapped.

Boyd stared at Klein for several moments, then shook his head slowly. "No, I do not. No problem whatsoever."

"Good."

421

They were silent for a few moments, then Boyd spoke up. "That attack you mentioned, you say it's imminent?"

"It would be if we hadn't identified it," Klein said proudly. "If Spyder hadn't worked so well. Like I said, we've got the middleman in custody. We'll know when he gets the word on the specific planes from the terrorists. And we're already watching the people who would actually stash the weapons on board the planes. We'll know as soon as anything happens."

"Yeah? Well, I've got an idea for you."

Rose squinted against the blinding high beams of an oncoming car, white-knuckling the steering wheel as the car zipped past, wishing he was sitting in his Porsche instead. Georgetown Pike zigged and zagged and the lanes seemed like they were a measly five feet wide at some points. The Porsche would have taken the road like a TGV on special rails, but the Buick was a different story. Instead of being in total control, he felt like he was on the edge the whole time. Fortunately, since it was late on a weeknight, there weren't many other cars out here.

A wave of sadness hit him as he guided the car over a tight bridge and a frozen creek, then up an incline. The spot where

Sheila had died was very close, on the other side of the hill halfway down the long slope on the right. He'd meant to come out here yesterday, but he'd gotten caught up with Tammy and Cortez on CIS matters. A meeting with Tammy and her assistants, then a long conference call with David and Citibank. They were almost ready to make the announcement. So he'd come this way tonight, drawn to it but not really knowing why. He hadn't planned to stop, but maybe he would if he could find a place to pull over.

Rose eased off the accelerator as he crested the hill, but the car maintained its speed as it began to descend. He spotted another pair of headlights at the bottom of the hill climbing quickly toward him. He could tell by the way the car was darting through turns as it climbed — a quick move to the left, then to the right. "Turn your high beams down, damn it."

A hundred yards between them now and the guy still had his high beams on. Rose raised a hand to his eyes.

As he did, the other driver seemed to dive into his lane. *"Jesus!"* There was hardly any room on the right to maneuver, just the steep fall-off Sheila had tumbled down less than a week ago. He swung the Buick as close to the right shoulder as possible. Pebbles and sticks kicked up into the wheel wells, creating a deafening din and for several terrifying seconds the Buick hung on the edge — then the other car swerved back into its lane. As they flashed past each other, Rose realized that the other car hadn't actually moved into his lane at all, that the other driver had just been following the curve of the road. His shoulders slumped and he let out a long sigh of relief as he steadied himself. With everything that was going on he was feeling vulnerable, and paranoid. But maybe, at this point, that was healthy.

The last fourteen hours had been exhausting: the meeting with Boyd and the confrontation with Sykes, bookended by his times with Kat. He smiled faintly, thinking about how he'd told himself after each cold beer at The Station that the next one would be his last. How she'd barreled right through his objections like a freight train through a tunnel and convinced him to have another, then another, sometimes not even bothering to ask him, simply ordering before he could say no. How he liked that. How he'd wanted to have one more at the end — a seventh for crying out loud — but it was Kat who had put an end to lunch because she had to go home and get ready for work. He'd urged her to stay, but she wouldn't, and he'd been disappointed. Then she'd leaned over, given him a gentle kiss on the cheek and whispered that she couldn't wait for him to get to Clyde's later, and he'd melted like butter on a hot plate.

Then there'd been tonight. She'd felt so good in his arms as they'd said good night in the parking garage, pressing her slender body to his. But that wasn't the overpowering memory, that wasn't what was giving him that soft-glow feeling in his chest, wasn't what was making him look forward to their next date so much he could hardly contain himself. It was that beautiful smile. How it captured everything about her so perfectly, how it was her essence. How good it made him feel.

He wanted it for his own, wanted everything about her to be his own. Inconceivably, she'd already captured him, already pierced the armor he'd worn for twenty years. A week ago he hadn't known she existed, now he was obsessed with her. He kept telling himself over and over to pull back, that the newspaper article in her purse might not have been so easily explained away if he hadn't let her explain it away. That she was the spark he'd been fearing for so long. That at least he needed to go slower. But he couldn't.

The headlights in the Buick's rearview mirror reeled him instantly back to reality. They were incredibly bright, blinding him momentarily when he glanced back. Then, for an instant, they disappeared. Only because the car behind him was so close to his bumper the beams were obscured by the Buick's trunk.

"Damn it." Rose punched the accelerator, aware that he'd been going too slowly even for this road as his thoughts had drifted back to Kat. "I'm going, I'm going. *Sorry.*"

For a few moments he pulled ahead, then the car behind him accelerated, too, catching up in a heartbeat. They raced around a tight turn like two stock cars at the Daytona 500, the one behind drafting off the one in the lead. Rose could feel the Buick's suspension straining, tires screeching on blacktop as he tore ahead. But he sensed that he couldn't slam on the brakes, couldn't stop, because whoever this was wanted him to do exactly that.

The car behind him darted to the left, into the oncoming lane, at the head of a straightaway. Then he lost the lights as it pulled alongside. He jammed the accelerator to the floor twice, kicking the Buick into a higher gear, pulling ahead again. Now it was a drag race, and, once again, the other car gained ground, pulling alongside, then nosed ahead.

Rose glanced left and thought he saw long hair tumbling down from beneath a ski hat, then his eyes flashed ahead again as another pair of headlights gleamed into view. The car beside him banged into him, forcing the Buick to the right. Rose shouted out of fright and anger and almost lost control, almost slammed into a utility pole planted a few inches from the roadway. He jerked the steering wheel to the left and clipped the other car with the Buick's fender, forcing it back to the left. He had to stay ahead, he kept telling himself. He couldn't let whoever this was get ahead of him.

As the oncoming car closed in, whoever was chasing him tried to force him off the road one more time, but Rose punched the accelerator again and inched ahead just enough, so there was no way the guy was going to make it ahead of him before the head-on crash. Suddenly the driver beside him slammed on his brakes, then the car spun wildly as the driver tried to pull back in behind Rose. Rose could see his pursuer's headlights wavering crazily in his rearview mirror as the oncoming car raced by, horn blaring, then he couldn't see the car behind him anymore.

When Rose made it home, he didn't bother looking at the damage to the Buick. He just closed the garage door, raced inside, armed the alarm, and sprinted up the steps to his bedroom closet and a strongbox containing a Berretta 9mm. He pulled it out, grabbed one of the clips, shoved it into the handle of the gun, then chambered the first round. If Johnny Sykes showed up here in a few minutes, he was going to be sorry he had.

49

"Jamie." Rose stood beside the black limousine as his daughter walked away, head down. "What are you doing?"

"What does it look like I'm doing?" she muttered.

He shivered. It was a cold, gray afternoon in northern Virginia. The weather forecasters still weren't sure if the Alberta Clipper barreling down out of Canada into the Midwest was going to drop a significant amount of snow on the area or head up into New England like the last one had. But the temperatures ahead of the system were dropping fast. It was barely twenty degrees outside. Tonight it was supposed to get down into the single digits. "Jamie!"

"What?" she snapped, finally stopping to turn and face him. "What do you want?"

Rose did his best to ignore several people who had cast curious looks at them. The steady line of mourners filing out of All

Saints Church had to walk directly past them to get to the parking lot. He moved hurriedly to where she was standing. "What's wrong, honey?"

"Nothing."

He'd sensed her mood growing even darker this morning as they were eating breakfast — blueberry pancakes, her favorite, which he'd fixed himself like he used to when she was little. It hadn't helped. He'd realized over the weekend that Jamie and Sheila had been closer than he'd thought. He'd started to realize a lot of things he'd missed over the years because he'd worked so much.

"You're coming with Glenn, Trudy, and me in the limousine behind the hearse." He motioned back over his shoulder. "I told you that."

She wiped her eyes. "I'm going with one of my friends," she said, starting to sob. "I don't want to go with you. I'm going with one of my friends."

He pulled a white handkerchief from his coat pocket and held it out for her. "Why not?"

She took the handkerchief and pressed it to the corners of her eyes, then gazed up at him. "Isn't it enough that you killed her?" she asked.

"Jamie."

"Did you have to disrespect her so fast?"

Rose could feel the eyes of the mourners boring into him, sensed that people coming out of the church had stopped to stare — and listen. "What are you talking about? I loved your mother."

"Then why did you go to lunch yesterday out in Leesburg with that blond hottie who looked like —"

"Stop it!" he hissed. Christ, Chesney had called his daughter the minute he'd seen what was going on. Couldn't anyone keep their mouths shut? "You have no idea what I'm going through."

"And you have no idea what *I'm* going through!" She took a step toward him, so they were very close. "No idea what it's like to have one of my classmates come up to me right as I'm getting on my bus and tell me how her father saw you getting drunk with some girl who's young enough to be my sister the day before my mother's funeral. How you had your hands all over each other at the table. How it looked like you were in love." She was sobbing hard now. "I hate you, Daddy. *God, I hate you!*"

"Where did you go last night?" Beck asked.

Klein looked at Beck like he was crazy.

431

"What are you talking about?"

"I couldn't get you. The only time I can't get you is when you're on a plane. Last night your phone went straight to voice mail three times, and I didn't hear back from you until late this morning. Usually, you get back to me a lot faster than that."

Klein shrugged. "I don't know what happened. I was up in Chicago the whole time, in my apartment. Right where I'm supposed to be."

Beck's eyes narrowed. Maybe he should finally start using Spyder to help himself. Everyone else had, for Christ's sake.

It was after four o'clock when the hearse pulled to a stop in front of the funeral home garage in Vienna, a town close to McLean and Great Falls. The driver waited for the double-wide door to rise all the way up, then moved ahead carefully into the garage beside a stretch limousine. When the door was down again, the driver opened the rear hatch of the hearse.

When Rose heard the hatch go up, he pulled back the blanket and crawled out, stamping his shoes on the cement floor a couple of times to get the mud off from his walk through the woods. Then he moved quickly to the limousine and eased onto the seat beside Adam Pierce. The driver of the hearse shut the door after him.

"Hello, Michael."

Rose had met with LeClair several times over the past few months, but only once with Pierce, the last time he'd met LeClair. That had been three weeks ago. "Hello, Adam."

"I assume everything went all right. No problems?" Pierce nodded toward the door. "The driver called to tell me he was pretty sure no one was following him."

"Yeah, everything went fine."

As the burial ceremony was ending, Rose had slipped between two huge boxwood bushes to one side of the cemetery — near Sheila's fresh grave — then moved into the thick pine forest rising from the other side of a low stone fence. A short trek through the snowy woods and he made it to a back road used by the cemetery's maintenance workers. The hearse was just coming into view around a curve as he broke from the tree line, and it had stopped only long enough for him to crawl into the casket bay and cover himself with the wool blanket.

It seemed like a lot to go through, but Le-Clair was being very careful at this point. Probably for good reason, Rose thought, given what had happened last night on

Georgetown Pike. Thankfully, neither Johnny Sykes nor anyone else had shown up at the house. Rose had stayed awake until three o'clock watching the lane in front of the house from a guest room window, but everything had stayed quiet. He'd fallen asleep on the floor in front of the window, loaded pistol on his chest.

"Good." Pierce nodded at the door again. "We're going to wait here for a few minutes to see if we spot anything suspicious, then we'll get going."

Rose scratched his cheek. The wool from the blanket had irritated his skin. "Fine."

"How's everything going with CIS?"

Rose gave Pierce a rundown on what was happening with the deal. By the time he was done, they were swinging out of the garage.

"The glass on this thing's tinted pretty dark," Rose observed.

"Bulletproof, too."

Rose raised an eyebrow. He didn't know if that was good or bad. Obviously, it was good if someone tried to take a shot at them. But maybe it was bad that LeClair thought it was necessary in the first place.

He took a deep breath, thinking about last night, about whoever had tried to run him off the road. He'd only gotten a glimpse of the driver, but it sure looked like Johnny

Sykes. Maybe Sykes hadn't wanted to talk to the detectives after all. Because maybe he had something to hide.

There was no problem getting into the house. The alarm wasn't engaged because the au pair had disengaged it after Rose thought he had secured the house. From behind a grove of trees, the man had watched her climb into the limousine that had picked everyone up at the house to go to the funeral, then climb back out, holding one finger up like she'd forgotten something. An Academy Award performance.

He moved through the back door and smiled. It was there on the island counter of the kitchen, exactly where it was supposed to be. This girl was good, he thought, popping the lock and reaching inside. Too bad she wasn't going to make it more than another week.

Klein's heart was pounding as he entered the Hotel Amalfi in downtown Chicago. For all he knew, he wouldn't make it out of this meeting, might be murdered in the room. He glanced at the young woman sitting behind the office desk in the intimate lobby. It was a contemporary, European-style hotel. No traditional high counter, just three

435

office desks. He tried to smile at her as he headed toward the elevators, but it was impossible. His lips seemed frozen. He just hoped he'd see her again on the way out.

Inside the elevator Klein pressed the button for the fourth floor, finger shaking crazily, breathing hard. The trip was over much too fast, suddenly he'd wanted it to last for hours. He hesitated inside the car for a few moments when the doors opened, then swallowed and headed toward room 438. He hesitated again at the room door, hands sweating. Finally, he rapped twice, as he'd been told to. The door swung open instantly, so fast it startled him and he stepped quickly back until he hit the far wall hard.

The man at the door waved him in. "Come on," he ordered gruffly.

Blood was pounding in Klein's brain as he stepped through the doorway, heard the door close behind him. No way out now. There were two big men behind him. These could be the last few moments of his life — or the greatest.

Wes Barry sat in a chair in front of the window smoking a cigarette, mauve drapes drawn tightly behind him. Even though Barry was sitting, Klein could tell he was short, which made Klein feel better; at least they had that in common. But Barry was thinner, like a rail, with a full head of neatly combed silver hair parted by a razor sharp line on the left side, and he had dark, piercing eyes. He was small but intimidating. Until a few years ago he'd been the CEO of Bender Aerospace, the biggest supplier — by a four factor — of military aircraft, missiles, and tanks to the defense department. He might be retired from Bender, but Klein knew he hadn't retired from the business of running the country. He was one of the president's most trusted advisors.

Klein stopped a few feet away. He didn't try to shake hands and Barry didn't encourage the greeting by holding out his hand.

"What do you want?" Barry asked.

"I want to talk to you about Peter Beck."

Barry spread his arms. "Why did you come to me? Why would you think I even know who Peter Beck is?"

Klein summoned all his courage. Barry would either love this or hate it. This would be the seminal moment of the meeting. "There's no reason to bullshit, Mr. Barry. We both know why I came to you."

Barry stared at Klein for a few moments, then nodded ever so subtly. "All right, tell me everything."

50

LeClair was waiting for them inside a small, redbrick house located on the Maryland side of the Potomac River a few miles outside the Capital Beltway. In a house that seemed like it ought to be owned by an old lady and her spinster sister. It had a white picket fence around the yard, an ancient Chevy in the driveway, frilly curtains in the windows, two cats lolling on the kitchen floor and two long aprons hanging from the pantry door. LeClair was sitting in the living room on a paisley upholstered couch reading a fly-fishing magazine. The curtains in the room were drawn, obscuring what little light of the day remained. The only light came from a dim floor lamp standing beside the couch.

Rose was surprised — and impressed — by the number of bodyguards: two inside the front door, two in the kitchen, two in the living room. He'd assumed from the start of all this that LeClair was acting somewhat on his own. Able to access people of influence, of course, given that he'd been the president's chief of staff, and he had Pierce. But not that he was supported by a crew of men who looked like they could beat the pulp out of an entire forty-five-player professional football team all at once, just the six of them. Rose eyed the sports jackets of the two men standing by the living room door. They had to be packing some pretty impressive heat, too, because one jacket lapel was bulging out much further than the other on both men.

LeClair put the magazine down on the table in front of the sofa, then nodded to the bodyguards who headed out of the room. "No problems?" He gestured at two chairs across from the table. "Sit."

Rose shook his head as he took the chair to LeClair's left. "No."

"Sorry to make you do all that from your wife's funeral, but it seemed like the best way to keep our relationship invisible. Particularly as we close in on our first objective. I doubt our enemies expected you to slip away from All Saints Church in the hearse."

"It's all right." It had been strange to do it that way, he had to admit, especially leaving

Jamie and Glenn with Trudy without telling them what was going on. But, of course, he couldn't tell them. It would probably make Jamie hate him even more, if that were possible. "Are you really that worried about me being followed?"

"I'm concerned that our enemies wonder why you seem so determined to bag CIS. They must assume you're working with someone because, as we discussed, CIS doesn't really fit with Trafalgar's other businesses. They'll figure there must be an ulterior motive here, that someone's pushing you, if they haven't already. Translated: Yes, I'm worried that you're being watched. Very worried. If not all the time, sometimes. And, as we get closer to acquiring CIS, I think the surveillance will increase." LeClair's expression softened. "I'm truly sorry about your wife. It's awful."

"Me too," added Pierce quickly.

Rose discounted Pierce's condolences. He hadn't said a word about Sheila on the way over here, even though he knew Rose was coming directly from the funeral. But LeClair's words seemed sincere. Beneath that tough exterior, there seemed to be a caring man. One weighed down by enough resentment to sink an aircraft carrier, but still. "Thanks, Sherman." Rose nodded at Pierce quickly. "By the way, there are detectives working on my wife's case."

LeClair's eyes snapped to Rose's. "Case?"

"That's what I said. Case."

"What's going on?"

"The coroner and the detectives think my wife was killed *after* she ran off the road and went down the embankment," Rose explained. "They think she was alive after the crash. They think someone killed her in the car, snapped her neck while she was still strapped into the seat upside down."

"Do they have any suspects?"

Rose shook his head. "If they do, they haven't told me." It almost seemed like LeClair was sizing him up with that gaze, wondering whether a husband had killed a wife.

"If you need any help with this, if things get uncomfortable, you let me know," LeClair urged. "Right away." He glanced at Pierce. "Call Adam."

"Help? What do you mean?"

For a few moments, LeClair raked his bottom lip with his prominent top two front teeth. "Sometimes local detectives make rash judgments. They want to solve things so bad and they want to do it fast."

"Sure, but what do you mean?"

"You know what I mean. We can help lead

them in another direction, away from you."

"I didn't kill my wife."

"I didn't say you did, but, statistically, I bet husbands are a good place to start for these guys. We can't let anything get in the way of the ultimate objective, especially at such a critical time." LeClair pointed at Rose. "If there are problems on this front, you will call Adam right away. Am I clear on this?"

Amazing, Rose thought. LeClair didn't care one way or the other about Sheila. Didn't care how she'd died, if she'd been murdered, and, if she had, who was guilty. Didn't care if *he* actually had killed her. Not one bit. It was all just distant background noise. All he cared about was bagging CIS. Christ, his bitterness could sink the entire Pacific fleet. Which meant he was obsessed with revenge. Anytime anyone was obsessed with anything you had to be even more careful because their judgments could so easily be clouded.

"Very clear."

"Good." LeClair leaned forward. "When will you announce the acquisition?"

"Tomorrow."

LeClair nodded, flashing a slim smile that faded as quickly as it had appeared.

But Rose had seen it. It was the first time

he'd ever seen LeClair even close to showing that kind of emotion. "The announcement will be in the *Journal* and the *Times*.
It'll make one hell of a splash."

"Yes, it will," LeClair agreed. "In lots of
different corners." His expression turned
grave. "And it will increase the pressure on
us. By nature, humans are visual. They rely
on sight much more than any other sense.
Our enemies have heard rumors about the
acquisition, but seeing the notice in the
newspapers will make it much more real for
them. Suddenly they'll realize that we really
are moving on them. They'll be more likely
to take drastic action. You must be very, very
careful."

Rose help up his hand, thinking about that
incident on Georgetown Pike last night.
Maybe it hadn't been Johnny Sykes after
all. "There is one small problem."

LeClair and Pierce glanced up in unison.
"What?" LeClair asked.

"I might not be chief financial officer
much longer, so announcing the deal might
be as far as we get."

"Why would you be out?" Pierce wanted
to know.

"They're framing you with something,"
LeClair said. "Right?"

"Yes," Rose answered. LeClair had sized

443

up the situation immediately. Should have figured he would. Hell, he'd been victim of the ultimate in dirty politics so, of course, he'd recognize the fix right away. "They're drumming up fraud or something. There's nothing to it. But with these guys, given what you've told me you think they have . . . well, who knows what'll happen?"

LeClair raked his lower lip again. "Is there?"

"Is there *what?*"

"Is there really nothing to it?"

"Nothing," Rose said forcefully. "Nothing at all."

"How did you find out what they were planning to do?" LeClair asked. "Overhear someone?"

"No, they were very up-front with me." Rose laughed, recalling Freese's breathless threat. "Colin Freese actually came right out and told me."

"He's an idiot," Pierce said. "Just a corporate joyrider from what we understand. He doesn't have the brains to frame you."

"Grant Boyd is involved, too."

"It isn't Boyd, either," LeClair said confidently. "Or Bill Granger, the CEO of CIS. It's the people in the background, our real enemies. The people who control the purse strings and the politics, the people at the

444

top who are directing the mission. They're the ones who can manufacture something for Freese and Boyd to hang you with. They're the ones with the most to lose if this thing is blown wide open."

"Like I said," Rose murmured, "I haven't done anything."

"Like you *also* said, we're dealing here with people who can rewrite history. Do you really think it would be a problem for them to create fake bank records and destroy the old, real ones?"

"No," Rose agreed quietly, experiencing an eerie flashback. To the nightmare at Dulles Airport four and a half years ago. How it had taken a year and three hundred thousand dollars in legal fees to finally clear himself. "I don't."

In their first few meetings, LeClair had explained to Rose that U.S. citizens were being spied on, their privacies invaded, that there were terrible abuses going on. That it was all being carried out in the name of counterterrorism, but that it had gone too far. That it had gotten out of control. That the people in charge were also targeting citizens they knew were innocent just to settle personal vendettas, just to push self-ish agendas. That's what LeClair had said, but he'd never provided any real hard evidence, either. Of course, he'd promised to support Rose in his drive to be CEO of Trafalgar. Maybe that had colored things, too.

"Tell me everything, Sherman," Rose murmured. "Everything you know. What's really going on here?"

LeClair's eyes flickered to Rose's.

LeClair didn't really want to say anything, Rose could tell. But he realized that this was a critical juncture, that he had to put some meat on the bones at this point if he was going to get complete commitment.

"I believe there are secret prisons in this country," LeClair began, "and that American citizens are being tortured at these prisons in the name of getting information about terrorist activities. But that many of the people being tortured aren't guilty of anything except being on the wrong side of the people in charge."

Rose's eyes opened wide. "Tortured?" he whispered.

"Yes."

"But that's . . . that's insane." Rose glanced at Pierce who seemed riveted, too. "That could never happen in this country."

"Don't be naive, son."

Rose winced. Of course it was naive. Hell, look what had happened to him. Someone with a grudge had screwed his life for a year because the guy had a brother who could do something about it. A brother in a position of power who couldn't be touched. Rose's legal team had finally pieced together what had happened, but in the end, nobody's head had rolled because they couldn't prove a connection between Rose taking the guy's job at Trafalgar and the arrest at Dulles. They couldn't find the smoking gun, probably because there wasn't one. Just discussions between the two brothers that could never be proven.

"What's your evidence?" Rose asked.

LeClair smiled and pulled a small recorder from his jacket pocket, placing it in the middle of the table. "I thought you might ask that." He pushed a button and what sounded like computer-generated voices began to speak. The voices were discussing who to detain and take to the "bases"; how many people were currently being held; how many of them were innocent; people they were going to detain even though they knew the targets had no knowledge of any pending terrorist acts; and the performance of someone they kept referring to as the "ED."

Rose's mouth fell slowly open. "Who's talking?"

"A man named Wes Barry" — LeClair

hesitated — "and the president."

"Of the United States?"

"Oh, you've heard of him then?" LeClair huffed impatiently. "Of course, the president of the United States. He was using voice camouflages to mask their identities, but the second voice is your president. The camouflage thing is a common technique at the White House when the president is talking about highly sensitive subjects in a private meeting. Goes back to Watergate," LeClair explained.

"They were talking about innocent people," Rose said, voice hushed. "Like they didn't give a damn." LeClair's recording wouldn't stand a chance in court, and the possibility that he'd manufactured it was obvious. But there sure were a lot of people trying very hard to keep Trafalgar from acquiring CIS. That single fact made Rose believe that the recording could be real. "And they were talking about people they knew had nothing to do with terrorism, but they were going to screw them anyway just because they could."

"It's like Sherman said," Pierce spoke up. "They don't care, they think they're above the law. Listen, I worked in the Department of Energy for a long time. I know. It isn't about reality. It's about those who are in power staying in power, and keeping those who are out of power out. It's very simple."

"But torture?"

LeClair laughed harshly. "What makes you think the U.S. is so different from Russia or China or any other country? Maybe we're a little more open, maybe the press gets a bit more access. But, in the end, when it really comes down to it, men in power want to stay in power."

Rose shook his head, awful memories of that day at Dulles rushing back to him. How helpless he'd felt when they cuffed him and hustled him off to a car waiting in front of the airport as hundreds of travelers watched. How the cuffs had cut into the skin of his wrists as he'd sat in the back of the car waiting for what seemed like forever to be driven off; how the cops enjoyed harassing him because he was white collar; how the prosecutor downtown kept asking him who he was working with. Christ, maybe if it had been a few years later, he would have been whisked off to one of the bases these men on the recording had mentioned. He shivered. It all seemed so crazy, but the thing he kept coming back to was how hard Boyd was trying to keep CIS independent. How Boyd had physically threatened the kids if Rose didn't back off.

"How did you get this?" Rose asked, nodding at the device.

"I bugged the meetings. When I started getting frozen out of them, I realized I was in trouble. I bugged them to find out what they were doing to me and why, but this was what I got."

"Where are these bases the guys on the recording are talking about?"

LeClair shook his head. "I don't know."

"We think they might be at some of the facilities the Energy Department runs," Pierce spoke up, eager to be a part of the conversation. "Some of the geographically remote national labs."

Rose could tell LeClair wasn't happy about Pierce volunteering information, and it surprised him that they hadn't choreographed this meeting more precisely. Of course, maybe it was meant to look like a miscommunication for some reason. He was beginning to realize more and more that LeClair was a master manipulator. Which made it all the more surprising that he'd been kicked out of the White House. "Why do you think that?"

This time Pierce hesitated, glancing at LeClair uncertainly.

"Okay," LeClair nodded. "Here's the deal." He gestured at Pierce. "Adam was at the Energy Department for a long time, up until a few months ago. Thanks to a friend, he's very aware that there are secret payments routinely made by Energy to CIA and FBI clandestine operations. The ones that interest me are the payments made to something called the Catrelle Management group. Catrelle then sends the money from the Energy Department to CIS. Catrelle also manages five of the national labs Adam just mentioned. It's too much of a coincidence."

"But the money Catrelle sends to CIS could be on the up and up," Rose argued. "The government contracts private companies all the time to do work like that, information technology stuff."

"Agreed," LeClair said. "But payments like that would be made on a regular basis, once a month or something. The payments to Catrelle seem to be made randomly, and it's always the same guy who calls looking for the money."

"Does this guy have a name?" Rose asked.

"His name's Peter Beck," LeClair replied, "but you won't find him anywhere, at least not the man we're talking about. We've been at it for three months, but every Peter Beck we've tracked down hasn't been our man."

"It's an alias."

451

"Maybe." LeClair pointed at the recording device. "In another one of the recordings I made, the president and Wes Barry mention his name. Beck's the ED of whatever organization they keep referring to on the one you just heard. So, he's real to them." LeClair held up his hands. "Besides, the payments we're *really* interested in are the ones we think CIS makes. The ones to the agent network and the bases, wherever they are. Which, of course, is the whole reason I asked you to use Trafalgar to acquire CIS. So we can dig in and find the payments, find out who CIS has been paying so we can find the bases and the agents. So we can prove that this thing goes all the way to the White House."

Rose was still trying to accept that there was even a remote chance of what LeClair and Pierce were saying could be true, that there were domestic torture prisons. Christ, the more he thought about it the more he wondered if he might have escaped going to one of the bases himself just by the razor's edge. He took a deep breath. Suddenly he was more resolved than ever that he was doing the right thing teaming with LeClair, even if there was a selfish agenda, too. If the man was so far off center, why would Boyd care so much about the CIS acquisition? At the very least, they had to see if CIS was making suspicious payments and who they were going to. He smiled thinly. If anyone could find those payments, he and Cortez could. It would be almost impossible for CIS to hide them at this point, even if they did try to re-create history.

"One more thing, Michael."

Rose snapped out of it. "Yes, Sherman."

"Be on the lookout for anyone new coming into your life, even if the way they've appeared seems random and completely normal."

Rose felt his face — his whole body — tense up for a moment. "What do you mean? Why?"

"I'm worried that our enemies would use this person to try to get as close to you as possible. So they could follow your every move, know what you're thinking." LeClair rubbed his chin. "Has anyone like that come into your life in the past few weeks?"

Rose chewed on it for a moment. "No."

Beck picked up the phone in his study three hundred feet below the snowy Illinois landscape and dialed the number he'd dialed so many times before — but never in this way. Never for his own purposes. He gritted his teeth. It was so easy to fall into this trap, he could see. To use the tremendous power Spyder provided for your own purposes. To spy on an enemy. Or a friend. He hated understanding what those who ruled him felt, but this was the problem with it, with the entire premise of the Order. Everything was too accessible. It was too easy to abuse it, and then it became like a drug. You couldn't *stop* using it.

He heard the familiar voice on the other end of the phone. "Hello?"

After seven years of this, Beck felt like he knew the man in Idaho, even though they'd never broken the vow of formality. It was as if they could communicate with the slightest changes in tone. The words almost didn't matter. "This is PB," he said quietly. This was how the conversation with Spyder always began.

"Proceed PB."

Just that simple dialogue was part of the code. A procedural code. Involving words, requiring words, but also requiring the procedure — the dialogue itself. "I'm on run number 7652."

There was a short silence at the other end of the line while Spyder checked the run number — code for ID. Which changed every day per a preset rolling schedule that made it nearly impossible for the outside world to penetrate.

"Go ahead, PB. Run number 7652 is normal. I concur."

"Thank you. PB 7652 requests an ATM data search for a Thomas H. Klein during the last seven days." Beck then gave Klein's social security number to Spyder. "This is a Q request." Meaning that he wanted it within fifteen minutes. That it was of the highest priority. If Klein had made a large cash withdrawal late the other night, it would be a pretty good indicator that he'd made a quick trip somewhere. Especially if that withdrawal had been made at O'Hare or Midway. An even better indicator if the withdrawal had been made at an ATM in the destination city.

"Roger that, hold please."

Beck gazed at the picture of the president hanging on the wall over his desk. He'd always thought the process was pure, thought the names the Directorate brought up for detainee consideration were all credible and that the "innocents" were sincere missteps. But not all of them were, he now knew. Most of them were, but not all. The powers above him were using the Order for other purposes, too. For personal purposes. Detaining individuals who had no connection to terrorism, who they knew had no knowledge of or involvement with terrorist plots. They were detaining people under that guise, but for other, selfish reasons.

Like Vivian Anduhar. Early this afternoon Beck had stumbled onto the truth about all of that. That Vivian Anduhar had been a call girl for the president's brother when she lived in Boston. That the president's brother, who was governor of Massachusetts, liked Arab women. That his handlers had paid her a thousand dollars a night for her services three to four times a month. But when he'd stopped using her because he'd found a younger woman he preferred, she'd threatened to expose him, to tell her story, unless they kept paying her. So they'd kidnapped her and killed her family under the guise of her being involved in a terrorist plot — perfect cover because she was Arab, talking to someone in Amman constantly, and her new job in Dallas was at a flight training school. It had made Beck sick to his stomach when he found out the real story and now he wondered how many people his agents had detained because the other members of the Directorate had agendas.

"Hello."

"Yes."

"Sorry, PB, but we can't execute your

ATM data search on the subject."

The picture of the president blurred before Beck's eyes. "What are you talking about? Why not?"

"Um . . . I don't know. I've never seen this before."

Beck heard a tone in the man's voice he never had. "Talk to me. What's going on?"

"I can't," the voice said hesitantly. "You're on your own. That's all I can tell you."

First, Rose had promised himself that he wouldn't return Kat's three calls until tomorrow. LeClair's warning about someone new showing up in his life out of nowhere had jolted him — she had shown up out of nowhere and she seemed over the top about him already. Then, when he'd picked up his cell phone as he was almost back to the house in Great Falls and realized that he couldn't resist calling her, he'd told himself he wouldn't meet her as she'd suggested on her messages. Then, when he'd agreed to get together at a bar in Reston halfway between their homes, he'd sworn he wouldn't have a drink, that he'd keep it to soda. Now, as he lifted the glass of Shiraz to his lips and gazed into her glistening eyes, he realized he had a bad problem.

"I'm glad you came," she said as they sat at the crowded bar, their stools close. "I've been sitting here for two hours drinking Captain and Coke because I couldn't go home. Joey thinks I'm working." She giggled. "Drinking and thinking, about you. Margie thinks I'm crazy, but I don't care."

There was a tiny haze around the gold flecks near her pupils, he could see. Evidence that she was telling the truth, that she had been sitting here for two hours drinking. He glanced around, aware that many of the men in the place were giving him the stink eye. Kat was easily the most beautiful woman in the place. On top of that, it was a blue-collar joint, so he stuck out like a sore thumb dressed in the dark suit and tie he'd worn to the funeral.

"I thought you weren't going to call," she said over the loud music. "I was worried, Michael. I called you three times. I just thought after last night . . . well, you know."

"It was a long day," he answered, feeling the red wine warming his body. It was cold as hell outside and he hated the cold.

Kat looked down sadly, as if she felt bad for what she'd just said. "I'm sorry. Are you okay?"

"Yeah." He'd told her that the funeral was this afternoon. Obviously she'd forgotten.

"It's just that I missed you," she said slipping her hand onto his, then leaning over and kissing him on the cheek. "I miss you more and more all the time."

Rose caught the scent of her perfume as she leaned back. She was wearing something different tonight, and it was great on her. As was the little top she was sporting. He caught a look from one of the three men who'd been talking to her when he'd walked in. If looks could kill, the guy's eyes would have been high-powered rifles. She'd jumped off the stool when she'd seen him and waved and the men had rolled their eyes at one another and faded into the crowd, especially when she'd given him a long hug.

"I missed you, too," he admitted quietly, checking out the television screens over the bar.

"Do you like pro basketball?" she asked, following his gaze.

He checked the screen again. "Actually, I thought it was college."

"No, it's the Wizards and the Knicks. They're playing at the Garden in New York."

He grinned. Beautiful, sweet, and up on sports. "How do you know that?"

"I'm a bartender, Michael," she said in a voice implying that he ought to know why.

"Helps with tips if I can talk sports." She smiled. "Besides, I actually do like sports. Football more than basketball, but I'd watch anything in Madison Square Garden. It's such a cool place."

"It is. Maybe someday you'll get there."

"Oh, I've been," she said, taking another sip of rum and Coke. "Saw the Rolling Stones there last year. As old as he is, Mick Jagger's still amazing."

Rose felt like he'd been kicked in the stomach. Yesterday she'd sworn she'd never been to New York. Maybe there was more of a story behind that article being in her purse than she was admitting.

From his car he watched them come out of the bar, hand in hand. Watched their shadows head to her car and embrace for several minutes despite the bone-chilling cold. She seemed so damn taken with him, not acting at all. He'd been waiting for almost three hours, motor running the entire time to keep the heat, and the fuel gauge needle was almost on empty. But now he was glad he'd waited. He'd wanted to see her with him, just to make sure.

He pressed his arm to his side, feeling the pistol in his jacket. It was comforting to feel it there. An old friend willing to help in any way required. No questions asked.

"Take me somewhere, Michael. Please. I want to make love."

He'd had four glasses of red wine in an hour and he was feeling it. He knew he needed to put the tough question to her, figure out her real agenda, but it seemed like he was powerless in her presence, desperate for her affection. He shook his head. No. He had to find his discipline, had to listen to that voice shouting at him from the back of his head. "Katherine, I —"

She interrupted him, pulling his lips to hers and kissing him deeply.

And that voice in the back of his head faded away like an echo into the hills.

51

"Are you worried about Rose being kicked out as CFO?" Pierce asked when LeClair finally reappeared. He was pissed, but he managed to keep his temper in check. The older man had said he wouldn't be gone long, but Pierce had been cooling his heels down here for hours watching the Wizards play the Knicks while LeClair was upstairs doing who knew what. He'd been about ready to walk out, figuring LeClair had fallen asleep. "Sounds pretty serious, Sherman. It could screw up everything."

"I'm not worried about it at all," LeClair said calmly, easing down on the couch. He glanced at the TV, then picked up the fly-fishing magazine. "It won't be a problem."

"How can you be sure?"

"I've already taken care of it. The process was in motion before Rose ever got here. I anticipated this possibility before we ever started this thing."

"But —"

"I deal with capable people, Adam, people who carry out my orders exactly as I want. I have absolute confidence that Michael Rose will not be fired from Trafalgar, the same way I have absolute confidence that neither Rose nor the Fairfax County police force will ever figure out who really killed Sheila Rose. They'll think they will, but they won't." He smiled. "Unless I want them to be right." His smile grew wider. "Or wrong."

"What does that mean?"

"Don't worry about it."

Pierce searched LeClair's expression. He'd known LeClair long enough now to recognize the tone. "Do you know who did kill her?"

LeClair nodded, eyes gleaming. "Yes, I do."

"How?"

"I gave the order."

"Oh my God," Pierce whispered, in a split second so much more impressed with this man. This was the kind of high-stakes, high-wire game he'd always wanted to be a part of because, at his heart, he was a serial thrill-seeker. The Energy Department job was just cover for his family. He went to Vegas and Atlantic City at least once a month and bet huge on the craps tables. He drove the Ferrari at night on back roads as fast as he dared — a few months ago he'd outrun a cop who was chasing him and it had been the biggest single thrill of his life. And he loved affairs with married women, loved doing it with them in their homes, sometimes — if they had big houses — while their husbands were there. It wasn't about money for him, he had enough. For him it was the thrill of the chase. In this case, bagging a president. "Why did you do it? Why'd you kill her?"

"She got suspicious that something was going on with Rose. And I don't care how she found out or what she suspected, I just care that she did. Now *she* could have blown everything for us."

"How do you know she suspected something?"

"I have someone on the inside. A week ago, Sheila Rose mentioned to my friend that she thought something was wrong."

Pierce looked at LeClair like the old man was crazy. "The au pair?" he asked, his voice barely audible.

LeClair's eyes danced. "Yes. The au pair."

Pierce put his head back and laughed loudly. "I love it."

Somehow Peter Beck had figured out what

had happened. That Wes Barry had been approached. Which was a problem. A *huge* problem.

Klein eased into the desk chair in the den of the bunker, into Beck's old chair, and gazed at the picture of the president. He'd been scared out of his mind to meet with Barry, to lay everything out for him, but it had been the right move. Beck's reign as ED of The Fourth Order was officially over and now they were hunting him down. It wouldn't take long.

Barry had told him that the other two members of the Directorate had harbored doubts about Beck for quite some time as well. Harbored suspicions that Beck had indeed gone soft, that they needed to do something about it. It was an unprecedented situation, but there was no choice except to oust him. They were glad that Klein had approached them and they could think of no one better to succeed Beck than Klein. Now it was just a matter of finding Beck and putting an end to him. Which ought to be terrifying, Klein thought. That the Directorate could turn so fast on a man who'd sacrificed his life for the cause, for them. Except that Barry knew he'd never go weak for the Order. So there shouldn't be anything to worry about.

Shouldn't be.

Freese pulled the big Mercedes into the long driveway leading to his stone farmhouse. He loved living out here in the countryside because it reminded him of the estate he'd grown up on in England when he was a child. He was forty-five miles west of downtown Washington — quite a hike in the mornings, especially with northern Virginia traffic. But the beautiful thing about being CEO was that he could come into work anytime he damn well pleased, so he got in late in the mornings — after traffic had mostly died down, and left early — before the stop-and-go heated up again. Plus, he had his own space right by the elevators, so parking wasn't a problem. Besides, he traveled two to three weeks a month so it wasn't that big a deal. And his farm was very convenient to Dulles.

He gritted his teeth. The only one who'd ever given him any crap about his schedule was Michael Rose. Rose had actually dared to question him about his work ethic a few times, and the only reason he hadn't tried to drum up anything on Michael before this was — well, he was right. Freese chuckled to himself. Michael was the blocking and tackling dummy. So let him say something every once in a while. Freese's happy expression faded. He just hoped the next guy was half as good as Michael. Grant Boyd had assured him this afternoon that what they had on Rose was airtight. Manufactured, but airtight. Michael wouldn't be the CFO after the board meeting.

Freese raced up the driveway, mounds of snow two feet high on either side. The Trafalgar shareholders had taken a bit of a hit on plowing this winter because northern Virginia had gotten more storms than usual. Thankfully this one had passed by. A couple of days ago, they'd been predicting a foot and a half, but it was going off to the north. At least he wouldn't have to present another thousand-dollar-bill to the controller.

He screeched to a halt in front of the garage, a converted barn, home earlier than anticipated. He'd been expecting a hot night, but the young woman he'd taken to dinner had refused, claiming it wasn't a good time of the month. He'd told her angrily to make sure she said something next time beforehand, which she hadn't appreciated, but it irritated him when they didn't understand the quid pro quo. He'd tried a few other numbers but gotten only answering machine greetings. Sometimes Caller-ID was your friend, sometimes it was

467

your enemy.

Freese pushed open the car door and glanced up at the house. It was dark. His wife was back in England for two weeks visiting her dying mother. He laughed as he headed for the house. The old bat had been dying for five years now.

As he slipped the key into the lock, an odd feeling hit Freese. Someone was close.

He whipped around. The dark figure was barely visible on the path he'd just traversed, but it was there.

"What do you —"

That was all Freese got out. The first bullet hit him in the stomach. He slammed back against the door, then keeled over, clutching his belly, groaning loudly.

The figure moved close, aimed carefully and fired twice. Both shots into the back of the head.

Colin Freese was dead.

Kat glanced at her watch as she came through the front door of the town house. It was almost two in the morning. Amazing, time with Michael Rose really did seem to fly.

She locked the door, then set the alarm. It cost three hundred dollars a year for the alarm, but it was so worth it. It and that

Smith and Wesson .32 caliber pistol she had hidden upstairs in the dropped ceiling had gotten her through more than a few nights. She'd always thought they'd find her, but they hadn't. Always thought when she'd heard that strange noise downstairs, it was them. But it wasn't. Now the alarm and the gun didn't matter anymore. Not as much anyway.

Odd, she thought as she turned away from the door to head down the dark hall. Joey had never bitched about the cost of the alarm. Usually, he was so cheap about everything, especially things like that. She'd always wondered about that.

"Hi."

She shrieked, almost running into him. She hadn't seen him standing there when she came in. "What are you doing scaring me like that?" she demanded angrily. She grabbed her cell phone from her purse and held it up so he could see it. "I swear to God, I'll call those friends of mine if you lay a hand on me."

Joey shook his head. "I'm not going to touch you, Kat. Even though I know where you've been," he said calmly, "and I know who you've been with, I'm not going to touch you. I just want to ask you one question."

469

"Were you following me?"

"Maybe. Or maybe Margie told me."

"She'd never do that."

He shrugged. "It doesn't matter." He shook his head. "I never thought you'd go for the older, corporate type. Not that he's that old. It's just that I figured if you cheated on me, you'd do it with a rock star or one of the Redskins or something."

"Oh, shut up."

"The corporate family guy thing didn't make any sense to me, even if he is loaded. That doesn't necessarily excite you."

"Joey, I'm tired and I'm going to bed. I'm not going to talk about this anymore."

"Then I figured it out."

Kat had been about to push her way past him, but she stopped in her tracks. "Figured what out?"

"Why you're throwing yourself at him." He reached over and flipped on the hall light. "It all started making sense when I thought about how you lied to me up front."

There was no way he could have figured all of that out. "You're out of your mind."

Joey grinned. "I agree. For getting involved with you in the first place," he said, his tone growing strong. "You were from Norfolk, but you and your family hated one another. That was why we never met any of them, why you just wanted a quickie wedding at the justice of the peace. You remember telling me that?"

Kat felt her breath growing short. "I told you that because it's the truth."

"Liar," he retorted quietly. "Liar."

His voice had been barely audible, which unnerved her. Joey had always been a shouter. Up until the other night, he'd never done anything physical to her, either. It was weird. "I'm not going to debate my family situation with you at two in the morning. I'm going to —"

"Someone's doing you a big favor, and, in return, you're throwing yourself at Michael Rose."

Kat swallowed hard.

"You're not from Norfolk," Joey continued, "like you've been telling everyone. And your name isn't Katherine. You were born Angela Beacon in Detroit, Michigan, and you're wanted in connection with the murder of a bank security guard during a robbery six years ago." He leaned close to her. "See, I have friends, too."

52

Rose stood in front of his desk at Trafalgar. It was exactly seven o'clock in the morning as he dropped the *Wall Street Journal* he'd picked up in the lobby down on the desktop. He leafed through it until he found the half-page Offer to Purchase. He should have been tired — he hadn't gone to bed until three o'clock, just a few hours ago — but he wasn't, he was invigorated. He stared at the notice for several moments, feeling the adrenaline course through his body. CIS was now in play. So was the president of the United States, if LeClair was right.

"Mike."

Rose glanced up. Cortez was standing in the doorway. "Come in, pal." Cortez didn't usually get in this early. Usually he didn't make it in until at least eight.

"Did you hear?" Cortez asked, moving into the office.

Rose studied Cortez's expression. It was

strange, like he was sad and happy at the same time. "Hear what?"

"You're not going to believe this, man," Cortez said breathlessly.

"What?"

"Colin Freese is dead," Cortez blurted out. "Somebody shot him late last night out at his house in Middleburg. Execution style. Three bullets, two to the head, one to the stomach. I guess he fooled around with one too many married women. Or his wife finally decided she didn't like their arrangement."

Rose sank slowly into his chair. "Oh my God," he whispered. Cortez was way off. It had nothing to do with married women or spousal arrangements. Sherman LeClair had struck. There could be no doubt.

"You have to call an emergency board meeting, Mike. I checked the bylaws as soon as I got in this morning. Colin was CEO, chairman and officially our secretary, though, of course, he never actually took any minutes. Always had Tammy's assistant do it. Anyway, the bylaws are very clear on this. The chain of command runs straight to you. You are now the top officer, and it's up to you to call a meeting," Cortez explained. "The board must be convened in person or telephonically to name an interim CEO within twenty-four hours of the CEO's death. That interim CEO will have all powers of a permanent CEO for at least sixty days."

"How did you hear?" Rose asked, barely able to focus on what Cortez was saying.

"It's all over the television, Mike. Local news, CNN, everywhere. I was in the damn shower at six this morning when I heard it on the radio. I couldn't believe it. I tried to call you on your cell phone right away, but it went straight to voice mail. I didn't want to call the house because I didn't want to wake up the kids."

Rose pulled his cell phone out of his pocket and looked at it. Sure enough, it was off. Christ, now he remembered. He'd turned it off last night and forgotten to turn it back on again this morning. He'd listened to music on the way in.

"You've got to call the board meeting, Mike," Cortez urged. "Right now."

"We're dead in the water."

"What do you mean?" Klein asked.

Barry tossed a copy of the *Wall Street Journal* down in front of Klein, opened to the page announcing Trafalgar's takeover of CIS. "We don't have anyone who can step up and top this bid. I've checked the network." He moved to the window of the hotel room and pulled the drapes back slightly. It was a crystal clear, bitterly cold morning in Chicago. One of those mornings that froze the inside of your nose while you walked along Michigan Avenue, bent over at a forty-five-degree angle into the wind. "Bill Granger will reject this first offer," Barry continued, turning away from the window. "Rose will counter with a few more dollars a share, and CIS will be forced to fold up the tents and give in. I checked with the investment bankers. What Rose is offering is very fair, a classic bear-hug move. When he comes up a few bucks, Granger will be forced to accept it. Otherwise, he'll be sued. We can't even get this thing into a proxy battle according to an attorney I talked to. The offer's too good. The president is going to be livid."

"Grant Boyd's got that fraud thing on Rose. That'll get him out of there when the board meets."

"I don't know," Barry grumbled. "I don't know if it's enough. The board loves this Rose."

"Then kill him," Klein said matter-of-factly, a thrill surging through him. "I've already got people checking on him. I can get to him whenever you want."

"No!" Barry barked. "President's orders. We've got to find out who he's working with. The president believes very strongly that there's someone in the background pulling the strings and he wants to smoke this person out."

Klein nodded. According to his people, Rose had disappeared after the burial ceremony yesterday. One moment he'd been there, the next gone. They hadn't picked him up again until later on in the evening. Rose must have slipped away to meet his handlers.

"I'm thinking about sending him to one of the bases," Barry spoke up. "Probably Seventy-seven."

Klein shook his head as it dawned on him. "No, I have a better idea."

"What is it?"

"How about Beck?" Klein asked, stalling. Barry had taken on the task of tracking Beck down personally. He didn't want to use agents of the Order, worried that they might be loyal to Beck and give him a chance to get away for good. So he was using "others" as he had described them, with no more details than that. "Any sign of him?"

"No. He's disappeared into thin air."

Klein grimaced and stood up. "I've got to

go." He had to call the dogs off Michael Rose, and he didn't want to do that in front of Barry. He had to check on the status of this afternoon's operation, too.

"What about your plan?" Barry demanded.

"I'll be back in thirty minutes. I'll tell you everything then."

"I want to know —"

"Thirty minutes," Klein snapped, surprising both of them with his brashness. But it felt good, and suddenly he realized he'd been born for this job. He watched Barry sink into a chair by the window, resigned to waiting. "Thirty minutes."

"I call the meeting to order," Rose said firmly. He and Cortez were sitting in a conference room along with Tammy Sable. They were using a call-in. "Tammy Sable is going to act as secretary today. She will call the roll."

Moments later, she was finished. Everyone was on the line except for Grant Boyd. Cortez had conveniently forgotten to call him, but it didn't matter. According to the bylaws, all they needed for a quorum was nine. They had ten without Boyd and Freese.

"We have a quorum, Mr. Rose," Tammy

said in a formal tone, her voice shaking slightly.

He nodded to her reassuringly, aware that she was very nervous. "Thank you, Madam Secretary." He glanced at Cortez, his jaw set. "You all know why we're on the line. Colin Freese was killed last night at his house in Middleburg. The bylaws say that I must call a meeting within twenty-four hours to elect an interim CEO as I am the most senior officer of the corporation right now. I open the floor to discussion."

Seven minutes later, Rose was the interim CEO of Trafalgar Industries. No one had even brought up the fraud allegations.

Klein hurried down the hallway toward the hotel room after making a burst of telephone calls, including the one to his man in northern Virginia to tell him *not* to go after Michael Rose again. But they hadn't connected, which was very worrisome. If they didn't talk in time, it was going to be a problem. He might even have to follow Peter Beck into the shadows. Problem was, he wasn't nearly as good at going underground as Beck had proven to be. Klein knew that about himself. He was good behind the desk, but not in the field.

Wes Barry was sitting in front of the television when Klein came through the door, staring at it hard.

"I've got a lot to do," Klein blurted out. "If you want to hear my plan, let's get to it."

Barry put a finger to his lips without looking up, then pointed at the screen.

Klein moved slowly beside the chair Barry was sitting in, and glanced at the CNN announcer. Then his eyes flashed down to the bottom of the screen and the blurb rolling to the left across it: Colin Freese, CEO of Trafalgar Industries, murdered at his home in Middleburg, Virginia. "My God," Klein whispered.

Barry nodded. "Yeah, I definitely want to hear your plan now. I think our opportunity to frame Michael Rose just died on that farm in Middleburg."

53

Frank Davis wobbled through the moving train. He was weak, felt as if he'd been wrung like a wet towel. He could barely keep himself upright and moving forward.

They'd threatened him over and over with the snake, until he'd broken down in tears. Then they'd beaten him, and shown him a tape of what they'd done to Ellen at Base 19. Shown him how they'd hung her upside down and nearly drowned her time after time. He'd cringed when they'd lifted her head up out of the tub at the last second over and over, and she'd been sobbing and crying like a baby. At the end of the tape they had her sit on a stool, hair dripping wet, and beg for her life. Which she had, pitifully. Pleading over and over for him to do whatever they demanded. Crying to him that she was sorry for telling them about his awful fear of snakes. That she felt horrible after watching them almost put him in the room with the thing. Then the tape had gone black and they told him they'd kill her if he didn't do exactly what they ordered him to do. That they'd slowly torture her to death and make him watch.

The New Jersey Transit train lurched to the left and Davis almost fell into a young woman's lap. "Sorry," he muttered. The local to Trenton had pulled out of Newark a few minutes ago on its way south. Newark was the first stop after leaving Penn Station in New York City. He wanted to whisper in her ear, quickly tell her about his awful situation and beg her to get help. But it wouldn't do any good. They'd probably just detain her, too. "Please forgive me."

He stumbled ahead, grabbing onto seat backs as he moved through the car. Fortunately, the train wasn't full — it was three forty-five and rush hour hadn't started yet. He finally reached the head of the car and pushed open the door into the vestibule connecting this car to the next. The clattering of wheels was deafening out here. It was freezing, too.

Suddenly the engineer hit the brakes. Davis was hurled against the cold metal door of the next car and the smell of burning pads hit his nostrils almost immediately. He threw open the door and moved inside just as the engineer accelerated again, and he almost ran into a blue-suited conductor.

"You shouldn't be out there," the conductor warned. "We're the only ones allowed out there. Read the signs."

"Yes, sir."

Davis waited until the conductor was gone, then moved ahead again, counting seat rows. Feeling a rush of adrenaline hit him as he closed in on his contact. This was the fifth car, and Jamil was supposed to be in the fourth row on the right. Which he was, just as he'd promised in the coded text messages they'd exchanged this morning. Davis recognized Jamil's wavy silver-flecked hair immediately, even from behind.

The train had two seats on the left and three on the right — bench seats not separated by arm rests. Jamil was on the right side of the train, in a three-seater, next to the window. Gazing out blankly at the urban world zipping past. No one else was sitting in the row and Davis eased into the seat by the aisle.

For several minutes they didn't acknowledge each other, then Jamil finally spoke.

"We were worried about you." It was loud inside the car. There was no chance of anyone overhearing the conversation as long as the train was moving. "Very worried when we couldn't reach you."

"I wanted to be careful after New Zealand. I thought maybe someone was watching, but I was wrong. Everything's fine. You told me to be careful. Especially as we got close," Davis reminded Jamil, his voice rising, glancing past him out the window. "Right?"

"Yes." Jamil paused. "And we are close. Very close."

Davis swallowed hard. "When will it happen?"

"Probably the day after tomorrow. The weather forecast is good. Clear skies in the flight paths. There will be three planes, all taking off from Philadelphia. Two will strike Chicago, the other Washington. The men won't take over until the last few minutes so there will be no chance of being shot down before they reach their targets. Your brother-in-law and his team will hide the weapons as agreed. I will message you the flight numbers tomorrow. Do you understand?"

"Yes."

"Good. Now get up and go outside," Jamil ordered, his voice turning steely.

"What?"

"Between the cars. Go. I have one more thing to tell you."

"I don't understand."

"Just *go.*"

Davis rose from his seat and headed back the way he'd come, into the vestibule. As the din and cold hit him, Jamil grabbed him by the shoulder, spun him around and slammed him against one of the sliding outer doors. *"What are you doing?"* he shouted as Jamil ripped open his coat, then his shirt.

Jamil smiled when he saw Davis's chest, white and hairless. "Good," he said. "No wire. I can't be too careful at this point, my friend."

Davis watched Jamil head back into the car. His chest heaved as he let his head fall back against the door.

Rose glanced up as Willis and Harrison moved into his office at Trafalgar. "What are you doing here?" he demanded, rising out of his chair. "No one told me you two were here."

"We told them not to," Willis said. "We need to talk to you, Mr. Rose. We didn't want you running."

"*Running?* That's ridiculous. Why would I run? Listen, you have no right busting in here like this."

"Oh, yes we do," Willis said, sitting down. He motioned to Harrison, who was hanging back by the door. "Please close that, Detective Harrison."

"Yes, sir."

"Look, I'm not going to stand here and let you two —"

"We had a long talk with a man named Johnny Sykes this morning, Mr. Rose," Willis interrupted. "Apparently, the other night you and he had a bit of a run-in outside a bar in Georgetown where he works. That's what he claims, anyway." Willis glanced over his shoulder at the young, black detective who was still standing by the door. "What's the name of the place, Detective Harrison?"

"The Hog's Breath, Detective Willis."

"Right, the Hog's Breath. Sykes said you came to see him," Willis said, turning back around. "Said you threatened him, then decked him outside the place when he came after you asking you what the hell you wanted. Said he had no idea you were Sheila's husband." Willis hesitated. "He was the man having an affair with your wife, wasn't he?"

Rose's eyes narrowed, and he sank back down into his chair. "I suppose."

"Well, he had lots to say."

Rose knew what was coming. "I'm sure he did." Rose berated himself silently. He'd let passion get the better of him, and he hated it when he succumbed to emotion like that. It had been so stupid to go down there. "All lies. You can't believe anything he says."

"Sykes claims you told Sheila you'd kill her if she ever filed for divorce," Willis said, undeterred. "Claims you told her you hadn't worked your ass off for twenty years just to let her steal half of it. Now your CEO is dead. And that press release Trafalgar put out this afternoon says you're the new CEO. That right?"

Rose nodded defiantly. "Yeah, so?"

"Pretty amazing coincidence, huh? Your wife *and* your CEO dead within a few days of each other? Both of them murdered."

"Pretty amazing you think I had anything to do with it, too," Rose shot back. "That would be damn stupid of me. Don't you think, Detective Willis?"

"Perfect cover actually."

Rose clenched his jaw. "You want to arrest me?"

Willis rubbed his chin for a moment. "I talked to one of your board members a little while ago."

Rose's fingers curled around the arms of the chair involuntarily. "What?"

"A man named Grant Boyd," Willis continued. "He was furious. Said you froze him out of an emergency meeting you called first thing this morning to get yourself elected as the new CEO. Said you put the meeting on the rocket docket, but you didn't have to."

"He wasn't frozen out, he wasn't available. And the corporate bylaws require me to call a board meeting immediately. I'm happy to make them available so you can see."

"Boyd said he had some damn incriminating evidence about you committing fraud at the company."

"Grant Boyd is a walking case of fraud."

"So everyone else is lying but you, huh?"

"Yup."

Willis stared at Rose for several moments. "There's a lot of strange stuff going on around you, Mr. Rose." He pointed at Rose as he stood up. "We're closing in on you, pal," he said, then turned and headed for the door. "Let's go, Detective Harrison."

As they walked out, the phone rang. Rose didn't wait for his EA to pick up. He recognized the number. "Hello?"

"You know who this is?"

It was Adam Pierce. "Of course I do."

"You okay? You sound a little raw."

"I'm fine. What is it?"

"Our mutual friend wanted me to pass on a message. Wanted me to congratulate you on being elected CEO of Trafalgar Industries today," Pierce said calmly. "He saw the news. It happened just like he promised it would."

Rose bristled. No one had ever said anything about killing Colin Freese to make it happen. If LeClair had said anything about that possibility, Rose never would have gotten involved. He hated Freese, but not enough to see him dead. "Uh huh."

"He also wanted to make sure you didn't get any ideas about switching teams now that you are CEO. He told me to remind you that he knows who killed Sheila Rose and Colin Freese. How he knows that you're responsible for both of their deaths. How he has evidence to that effect."

"What the hell are you talking about?" Rose shouted, banging the desk and shooting up out of his chair again. Christ, Willis might already have this line bugged. Worse, someone who was a lot more powerful than Willis might be listening in. "I didn't do anything to anyone," he hissed. "There's no evidence to incriminate me and you know it."

"Don't worry," said Pierce, "no one's listening to the call, we've already checked. Hey, as long as you play ball just like we talked about, it'll all turn out fine." He paused. "One more thing. As far as evidence

488

goes, check that lockbox in your bedroom closet when you get home tonight. The black one on the third shelf beside your sweaters. It's empty." He laughed. "Our friend has all the evidence he needs because Colin Freese was shot with what was in that lockbox. I'm sure Detective Willis would be most interested in getting his hands on it so he could run a few tests to confirm that it is the murder weapon. Which, I can tell you, it is. Then you'd *really* have some explaining to do."

Rose swallowed hard. God, he'd never seen this coming. He shut his eyes tightly. Corporate politics was bush league compared to this. This was for keeps.

"What's the deal, Frankie?"

Davis was back at the Vineyard, back at Base 12 in his cell. There were three other men crowded into the cramped space, including the leader. The guy who had shoved the pistol in his mouth the first night and threatened him with the cobra. "It's going down in the next few days," he said, his voice low. "All three flights will come out of Philly. Two of them will strike targets in Chicago and one will attack Washington. I guess they're planning to take over planes heading in those directions because my contact says they won't rush the cockpit until the last minute. So you guys won't have a chance to scramble F-16s and shoot 'em down."

The leader turned to one of the other men. "Start running down flights out of Philly leaving anytime between six and ten in the morning. Now!"

"Yes, sir."

"What else, Frankie?" the leader demanded as his lieutenant jogged away.

Davis hated the way they called him Frankie. A couple of bullies had called him that in fourth grade all year, and he'd hated it ever since. "My brother-in-law puts the weapons on board with the food like I told you. They're going to text-message with specifics, with the flights they want. Probably tomorrow morning." They'd taken his phone away as soon as he was back in custody. He assumed they were keeping it somewhere aboveground so it had reception. "It'll be coded, just like before."

"You better not be lying about anything," the leader hissed, "or you'll be sleeping with that snake every night."

"Let my wife go," Davis pleaded. "I want to know she's safe before I tell you anything."

The leader chuckled. "She rolled over on

you and you still want to save her?"

Davis looked down. "Yeah, I do."

Rose wheeled the Buick into Great Falls's one shopping center — a small strip mall with a grocery store, a dry cleaner, a bank, a bar, and a few other knickknack shops. He found a parking space just as Kat called on his cell. He answered as he swung the car in headfirst. "Hi," he said, rising from the driver's seat.

"Hi. I had a great time last night, Michael."

"Me, too." And he had. It had been amazing. Such a wonderful time that once again he'd failed to be tough, failed to ask the question that *had* to be asked. "Sorry I haven't called today. I've been busy."

"So I understand."

He'd been about to close the car door but held up. "You do?"

"Yeah, Margie called." Kat laughed. "She's started the Michael Rose fan club, for crying out loud. I'd introduce you two, but I think she'd start stalking you once she saw how good looking you are in person."

Rose put his hand up, about to say something, embarrassed at how she was always doing that. But she kept going before he could cut her off.

491

"Anyway, she was checking the Trafalgar news at her apartment this afternoon on the Internet and she saw that you were named chief executive officer at some board meeting or something. God, I never thought I'd be dating the CEO of one of the biggest companies in America."

Dating? That sounded strange. He hadn't dated anyone since he was twenty-one. "Did she tell you why I was named CEO?" He closed the car door and started heading through the darkness toward the store. He was going to pick up a bottle of wine, maybe two. Today hadn't been the easiest day of his life and he needed something to take the edge off. "The circumstances?" He shivered, partly because it was still very cold, partly because he was thinking about Freese being shot.

There was a short pause. "Yeah, she told me. The guy who was CEO was killed at his farmhouse out in Middleburg. That's creepy. Should you be worried, too?"

"Huh?"

"Did the guy get killed because of something that's going on at Trafalgar?"

Rose hesitated. There was a man loitering near the automatic doors of the grocery store. A man dressed in jeans and a sweatshirt, hood pulled up. He seemed to have been looking his way, then glanced away quickly when they made eye contact. "Ah, what?" It had to be his imagination, brought on by all the crap swirling around him. "No, no," he said quickly, remembering her question. "It didn't have anything to do with Trafalgar." Of course, how could he be sure of the negative? He might know that the murder *did* have something to do with Trafalgar, but he wouldn't necessarily know that it *didn't.* "As far as I know anyway."

His eyes skipped back to the guy at the door.

Controlling a hundred Type-A personalities. It was like herding lions, Beck had always said. All but impossible.

Klein had been in contact with nine of them today, all the team leaders — except one. The one in northern Virginia and the one he most needed to talk to. But, of course, he hadn't heard back from that one. The guy probably realized the call was going to be an abort message — no killing Michael Rose — so he wasn't answering. Just like the leader of the team that had killed the Anduhar family hadn't called back in time. Maybe these guys really were turning into bloodthirsty crazies, as Beck had warned. Maybe Beck had known more about the job than Klein had given him credit for.

Klein grimaced and shook his head hard. No way. Wes Barry and the other two men of the Directorate wouldn't have had doubts. Klein took a deep breath and tried the guy's number again.

Rose moved deliberately toward the doors of the grocery store, aware that his breath was rising up in front of him in the cold night air. It was almost as if everything was in slow motion: The mist in front of his face. A bag boy pushing a cart full of groceries through the out-door. An elderly woman behind the bag boy, purse slung over her shoulder, scarf to her face against the blast of frigid air sucking through the doorway. An SUV to the left of Rose in the pickup lane, emergency lights blinking amber, exhaust rolling out of the tailpipe. A couple trotting toward the doors from the parking lot, heads down, holding their hands to their faces. The guy loitering near the doors, leaning against the brick wall of the store, eyes visible at the back of the cave formed by the hood of his sweatshirt, obviously gazing straight this way now, eyes not straying anymore.

Then the guy near the doors reached

beneath his shirt.

Rose saw the gun sticking out of the guy's belt instantly and bolted for the SUV. But it was like a dream: He couldn't seem to make his legs go fast enough. The guy had the pistol out and aimed in a flash, both hands wrapped around the butt of the gun, while Rose was still several strides from the SUV. Rose saw the first spit of flame burst from the gun barrel, heard the first deafening report of the gun a nanosecond later, cringed as he dove for cover at the back of the SUV, sure he'd been hit. Aware as he tumbled to the asphalt that the bag boy had pushed the cart off the yellow curb into the parking lot and hit the pavement in front of the doors with his arms over his head; that the elderly woman was standing in the middle of everything, hands to her mouth, paralyzed; that the couple had turned around and were racing the other way; that spent shell casings were caroming off the pavement.

Then everything sped up to real speed. Three more gunshots and someone was on him, lying next to him, shouting in his ear.

"Get out of here!" the man yelled. "Get to your car and get home. Our people will follow you!"

Rose stared at the guy; he seemed vaguely

familiar. It was one of the men who had been at the small house in Maryland where he'd met Sherman LeClair last night. Rose glanced around the SUV toward the doors. The guy with the gun was still moving forward. Rose grabbed the man lying next to him by the shoulder and pointed. "He's still coming."

"He's one of us."

Then Rose spied a body lying on the sidewalk in front of the store, behind where he'd been walking just before the guy by the door had pulled the pistol. The body was facedown and there was a gun at the end of one outstretched hand, just beyond his twitching fingertips.

"Come on, go!" the man lying beside him shouted. *"Get out of here!"*

"We got two men down," the agent shouted into the phone. "Including the captain."

Klein felt the receiver shaking in his hand. "Shit, shit, shit!" Keep your cool, he told himself, but it was impossible. "What happened, what happened?"

"We went for Rose, just like you told us to."

"I tried to call the captain, called him ten times. I tried to tell you guys to abort."

"We never got the message."

"What happened?"

"Rose has coverage. We were on him, we were about to take him out, and we got ambushed. There were at least eight of them. Captain's down and another guy, too. We had to get out."

Klein closed his eyes tightly and ground his teeth. Now how the hell was he going to get to Michael Rose?

Rose skidded to a stop in his driveway, jumped out of the Buick and raced for the back door, not wanting to wait for the garage door to go up. He took the steps to the deck three at a time and burst into the kitchen. Glenn and Trudy were sitting at the kitchen counter, eating a pizza.

"Dad, we've been trying to —"

Rose didn't wait to hear the rest of Glenn's sentence. He bolted past them for the stairs and raced to the bedroom, to the big walk-in closet and the shelves of sweaters. He reached beneath a stack of three for the key, then realized he didn't have to. The lockbox sitting beside the stack of sweaters had been jimmied, he could see. The door was hanging slightly open. He pulled it all the way open and peered inside. The gun was gone. Both clips, too.

"Dad."

Rose whirled around. Glenn stood in closet doorway. "What is it, son?"

"Dad, Jamie's gone."

For several seconds, Glenn's words didn't register. It was as if Rose's mind had suddenly shut down, suddenly been overloaded with data. "What?" he whispered.

"She's gone."

He shook his head incredulously. "What do you mean, 'gone'? You mean . . ." He couldn't finish.

"No, Dad, not dead. She left this afternoon. She sent me a text message to tell me she's going to a friend's house. Said she's not coming back for a while."

"Why? Why is she going to a friend's house?"

Glenn looked down and kicked at a spot on the carpet. "I don't know," he said quietly.

Rose moved to where Glenn was standing and knelt down. "Tell me, son."

"I don't want to, Dad. Please."

"Tell me," Rose repeated, this time forcefully. "I mean it."

"She said she doesn't want to live in the same house with you anymore." Glenn choked up and a tear rolled down his cheek. "I'm sorry, Dad."

Rose pulled the boy close and hugged him

hard. "It's all right, son, just tell me where she went. I'm gonna go get her right now."

Glenn sniffled and leaned back. "I don't think so, Dad."

"What do you mean?" He searched the boy's expression. "Don't hold back on me. Tell me where she is, Glenn. It's very important that you tell me where she is *right* now."

"I don't know."

"Glenn!"

"I don't, Dad. All I know is that she got on a train this afternoon for Philadelphia."

Rose hesitated. "Philadelphia?"

"Some girl she met at camp last summer lives up there with her mother. That's all she said in the message. Just that she was going to Philadelphia."

"What happened?"

"It was a cluster fuck, sir. Klein doesn't know what the hell he's doing. He sent us into a fucking ambush. We got two cold, including the captain. If I didn't know better, I'd say they wanted it to happen that way."

"Two cold? Jesus."

"Yeah. Now he wants the rest of us in Philadelphia, but he won't say why. This secrecy thing is bullshit. You were always

499

honest with us. We're the ones out here taking all the fucking risks, he's sitting back in the den, nice and safe. If I hadn't taken the oath, sir, I'd be out of here."

Beck could only imagine what had really happened. Klein had probably tried to get in touch with the team over and over, but they'd ignored his calls because they knew what he was doing — calling off the hunt. And they didn't want the hunt to be called off. They liked killing, loved the license they had. They'd grown accustomed to the taste of blood and it could only be satisfied with more — and only for a short time. "I hear you," he said sympathetically. "The guy's a prick, he doesn't get it." Beck had to keep the line of communication open. It was his only chance. At the same time, it was what could do him in. "Look, I gotta go, but call me again tomorrow."

"Yeah, all right."

Beck grabbed his bag and headed for the motel room door. He couldn't stay in this place another second. For all he knew the guy he'd just talked to wasn't really as loyal to the old regime as he claimed. Beck shook his head and took one more look around, making sure he hadn't left anything that could give them any clue as to where he was headed. This was how life was going to be for a while. A long while.

"Dad."

Rose looked up from the desk chair of his home office. He was trying to review several European marketing reports ahead of a noon conference call he had scheduled for tomorrow — his duties at Trafalgar had suddenly expanded, though it was still hard to fathom the fact that he was CEO. But it was next to impossible to concentrate on anything other than Jamie at this point. His ability to focus had suddenly failed him, for the first time since he could remember. He knew he was careening toward his limit, recognized that he was almost at the breaking point. He kept staring at the pages in front of him, but his mind kept trying to figure out a way to find her, just to get in touch with her. But he kept coming up empty. He'd have to go to the authorities in the morning. That was his only shot.

"Yes, son?"

"Can I talk to you for a minute?" Glenn asked.

"Of course." Rose pointed at the couch, dropping the reports down on the desk, and was smacked by a memory of trying to put his arm around Jamie in a futile effort to comfort her only a few nights back. He wondered if that was how this talk was going to end, too. "Have you heard anything more from Jamie? Any more text messages?"

Glenn shook his head.

"Damn. Well, what do you want to talk about, son?"

"What are all those guys doing outside the house?"

"Protecting us," he answered directly.

"Why? What's going on?"

Rose hadn't answered this question earlier, he'd been too concerned with trying to track down Jamie as fast as possible. He inhaled deeply. "The man who was president of the company I work for was killed last night at his house," he explained, using "president" not "CEO," figuring that would be easier for Glenn to understand. "The police are worried that the man who killed him might come after me, too." Glenn looked lost. "I know it's scary, but it'll be okay. I promise."

"It's not that," Glenn answered dejectedly.

Like someone had let him down, Rose realized. "What is it? What's wrong?"

"I'm not a hundred percent sure, Dad, but I don't think the police carry the kind of weapons those guys outside are carrying. At least, not the normal police guys. I looked it up on the Internet." Glenn sat down on the couch. "What's really going on?"

Incredible that a twelve-year-old would know something like that, but Rose couldn't explain things any further at this point. It would just scare the hell out of Glenn. "It's just to protect us, son. You've got to believe me. That's really what it is." Not a lie, either. The truth, just not all of it. Not by a long shot. "Okay?"

Glenn nodded. "Okay."

Kids were so different, Rose thought. Even in the middle of all of this, he recognized that. Jamie would have pushed and pushed until she got an answer she was satisfied with, but Glenn just let it go. And it wasn't because of their age difference. They'd both always been like that. "You all right, son? I know this has been an awful few days."

"Yeah, I'm all right." He looked up. "Dad, I . . ."

"What is it?"

"I don't know how to . . ."

"It's okay, Glenn, just —" Rose was interrupted by the front doorbell. "What now?" he muttered angrily, standing up and motioning to Glenn. "Sorry. Let me see who this is. I'll be right back."

Waiting at the front door was Detective

Harrison. Beside him was one of the men LeClair had detailed to Rose's house.

"Mr. Rose, this is Detective Harrison. He's with the —"

"I know," Rose said. "It's all right." He glanced past Harrison, looking for Willis. But the older detective was nowhere in sight. "Please come in." He nodded to the man on the front stoop, then closed the door once Harrison was inside.

Harrison glanced around the spacious foyer, apparently impressed all over again. "Is there somewhere private we can talk?"

"Are you here to arrest me?" Rose asked. But that couldn't be it, he reasoned. LeClair wouldn't have his men at the house if he had turned the gun from upstairs over to the cops. And the detectives might have heard Sykes tell them some ridiculous lie Sykes and Sheila had concocted about murder threats if she tried to get a divorce, but that wasn't enough to arrest someone for murder. At least, he didn't think it was. "What's this all about?"

"I don't want to talk out here."

Rose muttered to himself as he led Harrison to the study. It was one thing after the next. "I'm sorry, son." Glenn was still sitting on the couch. "I need a few minutes alone with this gentleman."

"Sure." He got up and headed out of the room quickly.

Harrison closed the door when Glenn was gone.

Rose pointed at the couch Glenn had just vacated. "Have a seat."

The detective shook his head. "This won't take long."

Rose had been about to sit down in the desk chair, but stopped. He'd heard something strange in Harrison's tone. "What's this about, Detective?"

"It's what you thought it was about."

"Huh?"

"I'm here to arrest you for the murder of your wife."

Rose's eyes flashed to Harrison's. "You've got to be joking."

"I'm very serious, Mr. Rose," Harrison said, reaching for the handcuffs on his belt loop. "Now turn around and put your hands behind your back."

54

Rose glanced around. He was chained to a wooden chair in the basement of a warehouse somewhere in downtown Washington, hands still cuffed behind his back. The room was large, dimly lit, and reeked of mildew. He watched as a short, chubby man wearing a suit and tie entered the room from a doorway off to the left and walked deliberately to a chair facing his, hard soles clicking on the puddled, cement floor.

"Who the hell are you?" Rose demanded.

"The one who can tell you how to find your daughter," the man answered evenly, sitting down, crossing his legs at the knees.

Rose's eyes widened. "Jamie?"

After cuffing and leading him out of the house in front of a stunned Trudy and a sobbing Glenn, Harrison had taken Rose to his unmarked car. Then forced him into the back behind the metal grate and belted him in tightly. LeClair's men had tried to stop the arrest, but Harrison had drawn his weapon and told them if they didn't stand down, he'd call in reinforcements. They'd backed off, though not without a lot of shouting and cursing. Oddly, Harrison had never asked who the men at the house were or what they were doing there. He hadn't read Rose his Miranda Rights, either.

So somehow it hadn't surprised Rose when Harrison hadn't gone directly to the Fairfax County Police barracks. Harrison had done some pretty nifty driving on the way down here, too. Rose assumed the detective had executed the maneuvers to get away from one or several of LeClair's men.

"Yes, Jamie," Tom Klein answered, pulling out a pack of Salem cigarettes. He'd never smoked before, but Wes Barry had recommended that he start at their last meeting; different brand every time, of course.

"Where is she?"

"In Philadelphia, with her friend from camp."

"I know that." Rose strained against the ropes binding his ankles and his cuffed wrists to the chair. "*Where* in Philadelphia?"

Klein smiled, lighting up and taking a drag. "Now why would I fly all the way to Washington, get Detective Harrison to bring you down here, tie you to this chair, then just answer all your questions right away?" He tossed the smoking match into a puddle beside the chair. It sizzled for a second, then died. "You're an intelligent man, Mr. Rose. You must know that there will be a quid pro quo. You must have anticipated that this wasn't really about the murder of your wife. That maybe it had something to do with Trafalgar attacking CIS," he said, his tone strengthening.

"Did you kill my wife?"

"Of course not."

He knew he wouldn't get a straight answer, but he wanted to watch the man's face when he asked the question. But the guy was a damn good poker player. He hadn't been able to detect a sliver of emotion either way. "Who are you?"

"The other side, Mr. Rose. The side that doesn't want you poking around CIS. I'm the sheriff of the white hats, the good guys, the ones that keep this country safe at night. Unfortunately, and I'm assuming without your knowledge, you've become a pawn of the black hats. I'm assuming you didn't really start going after CIS all on your own. Right?"

Rose shifted uncomfortably in the chair. If he gave away Sherman LeClair's name,

the Fairfax County cops would undoubtedly be handed a piece of evidence they
could use. The gun that had killed Colin
Freese. Rose's gun. Then they really would
make an arrest, maybe one that would stick.
If Rose didn't give away LeClair's name, he
wouldn't find out where Jamie was, at least
not tonight. Somehow he knew this unim-
pressive looking little man sitting across
from him was the real deal.

"I don't know what you're talking about."

Klein switched the cigarette to his left
hand, then held the palm of his right hand
up in front of his face for a moment. Next
week, surgeons at Walter Reed would im-
plant the suicide fuse. "I had hoped this
wouldn't be so difficult," he said, dropping
the hand back into his lap.

"How can I be sure you really know where
Jamie is?"

Klein reached into his jacket, pulled out a
photograph and held it up so Rose could
see. "This is your daughter walking through
the Philadelphia train station late this afternoon."

Rose felt tears building in his eyes as he
gazed at the photograph. God, she was so
beautiful. So vulnerable, too.

"A beautiful young woman, Mr. Rose. An
excellent student as well. Yes, we've done

our background work. You should be very proud of her."

"I am," Rose said, his voice raspy.

"I'm sure you don't want to see her harmed in any way."

Rose gritted his teeth. "You do anything to her and I kill you, pal. I swear on my father's ashes."

Klein chuckled, nodding at the ties binding Rose. "Oh, I'm real scared."

"I don't care what you —"

"Shut up, Mr. Rose. I'm not going to kill your daughter. It's not me you should worry about when it comes to that." Klein took another long puff off the cigarette, then his expression turned dead serious. "But I think she may be stepping into the middle of a terrorist attack. I have this strange feeling she's going to be on a plane that'll be hijacked." He paused. "Unless, of course, you come up with the name of the person you're working with."

Rose gazed at the man, data coursing through his brain.

Klein leaned forward. "We're the good guys, Mr. Rose, and we can help you. Work with us. Work with me. I can do so much more for you than whoever you're working with now. I promise you."

■ ■ ■ ■

Frank Davis's eyes flew open when he felt them poking his shoulder.

"Get up, Frankie, get up."

"What is it?" Davis asked, rubbing his eyes. "Jesus, what time is it?"

"It's four in the morning and you've got some decoding to do."

They shackled him and led him down the hallway to the elevator, which rose quickly to the first floor. Then they dragged him into a small room near the barn's entrance. On the table in the middle of the room was Davis's cell phone.

"A text message came in five minutes ago, Frankie," the leader explained gruffly, nodding at the phone. "Looks like a garbled bunch of crap, but I bet it actually says quite a bit. I think it's from your buddy Jamil," he said pulling out a chair and forcing Davis into it. "Tell me what it says," he demanded.

Davis gazed at the small screen. It was definitely from Jamil. The date of the attack, flight numbers, everything was there. "It's going down tomorrow morning," he explained, his voice low. "These are the flight numbers. Give me a pen and paper and I'll write them out for you."

511

"Good," the leader said, gesturing for one of the other men to go and get the pen and paper. "What are you supposed to do now?"

Davis gazed at the leader for a few moments. "Call my brother-in-law. Give him this information."

The leader nodded at the other two men who started unshackling Davis. "Then do it, Frankie. Decode the flight numbers and call your brother-in-law. Don't waste another second."

"What the hell happened?" Adam Pierce demanded from the other end of the line. "Our people told us a Fairfax County detective showed up at your door and arrested you last night."

"That's right," Rose said quietly. "For the murder of my wife. I posted bail."

"You were supposed to tell us if they were turning up the heat on you."

"I had no idea it was coming."

"The detective didn't take you to the barracks," Pierce said suspiciously. "At least not without a lot of moves Jeff Gordon would have been proud of."

"He wanted to know what the hell all those people were doing at my house. That's why he was driving like a maniac. They were following us."

"What did you tell him?"

"That I'd hired a private crew of body-guards. That I was worried the same person who had killed Colin Freese might be after me. That it might be a Trafalgar thing."

Pierce was quiet for a few moments. "You better be telling the truth, Michael. And nothing but the truth, so help you God."

Rose hung up the phone and let his head drop into his hands. Then was jolted by a knock on the study door. "Yes?"

"Dad?"

"Come in, son," Rose said quietly. "I'm sorry about last night," he whispered, taking the boy and hoisting him up onto his lap. "I didn't kill your mother. You have to believe me."

Glenn nodded. "I do." He hesitated. "I got a text message from Jamie."

"What?" Rose snapped.

"Yeah, she's leaving Philadelphia."

"What? Where's she going?"

"She didn't say."

"Why's she leaving?"

Glenn shrugged. "She said her friend's mom won some big prize out of the blue, an all-expense-paid vacation somewhere way cool. Some free trip to see a new development somewhere. Jamie's friend asked her to go, too. I guess they had to go right away because there was some kind of screwup and the availability was running out. The mom actually won the trip a few months ago, but the announcement didn't get to her. So they had to take it right away or lose it."

Out of the blue, out of the blue. The words echoed in Rose's head. Then it hit him. "Text-message her back, Glenn," Rose ordered. "Tell her she *has* to call me." He hesitated, knowing how this would sound. "Tell her it's life and death."

Glenn nodded.

As if he wasn't surprised, Rose realized.

"Dad, there's something else I need to tell you."

"What?"

"It's bad."

Rose's eyes narrowed. "Tell me, son."

"It's about Trudy."

55

"Come on, boy, come on. Good boy."

The security officer whistled and led the German shepherd down the aisle of the U.S. Airways 737, stopping to look out the window at row 12. It was a gorgeous, crystal clear morning and the sun was just coming up to the southeast of Philadelphia International Airport. The food service people had finished stocking the galley at the back of the aircraft a few minutes ago, and now he and the dog were making sure everything was as it should be.

After a few moments he continued down the aisle, stopping at the restrooms. He gave the dog the command to sit, then moved inside the bathroom to the right. He knelt down, removed a small panel behind the toilet and checked the small space. Four pistols, exactly as he'd been told there would be.

When he'd replaced the panel, he headed

back up the aisle toward the cockpit, shepherd in tow. He had to get over to the other concourse and the two United flights — one heading directly to Chicago, the other going to San Francisco first, then on to Hawaii. He had to make sure the guns were on those planes, too. But first he had to disengage the electronic cockpit lock on this plane.

Rose sat in his downtown Philadelphia hotel room. In the hotel where he'd been specifically ordered to stay by the man he'd met with in the warehouse. He was watching the phone. The man had claimed he'd call two hours ago, before dawn, but now the sun was up. It was nearly eight o'clock in the east. "Ring," he muttered. "Ring, damn it."

Yesterday, he'd been forced to slip away from LeClair's men, to sneak out the back and walk through the woods to Great Falls where he'd caught a cab to Union Station, then a train here to Philadelphia. He hadn't given away Sherman LeClair's name yet because the man he'd met at the warehouse hadn't given him any specific information about Jamie's whereabouts.

On the way back from the warehouse, he'd tried to get Harrison to tell him how they'd gotten to him. They must have had something on the young detective to have gotten him to make the false arrest. But Harrison wouldn't say a word, wouldn't even engage in conversation.

"God damn it!" he shouted, dialing home again on his cell phone. He was going nuts sitting here by himself, unable to do anything but wait.

"Hello."

"Glenn?"

"Yeah, Dad."

"You okay?"

"Fine."

"Is Mrs. Cortez still asleep?" Rose asked.

"No, she's up. I heard the shower running."

David's wife had come over yesterday to stay after Glenn had explained what he'd found out about Trudy. That Trudy knew who had killed Sheila. That she was in touch with someone whom she had talked to when she went to the store the other day. Glenn had put a simple listening device in the car Trudy took to the store after becoming suspicious of her being on the computer. A device he'd made in his electronics workshop at school.

Rose had fired her just before he snuck out. Hadn't given her a reason, just told her never to come back. He shook his head. He'd actually been thinking about working

517

with the guy at the warehouse, taking his chances with the legal system and LeClair turning the gun that had killed Colin Freese — Rose's gun — over to the authorities. Then he'd found out about Trudy's treachery. She had to be working with these people.

"No problems with Trudy, right?" he asked. "She hasn't called or shown up?"

"No."

"How about the men outside?"

"They're gone. They came in looking for you and when they couldn't find you, they took off. They were pissed."

"But they didn't do anything to you? You're okay, right?"

"Yeah, I'm all right."

"Have you gotten anything back from Jamie? Any messages?"

"Yeah."

"*Yeah?* Great," Rose said excitedly. "What did she say? Why didn't you tell me?"

"I didn't want to," Glenn said quietly.

"Why? What's wrong?"

"She said she knew you were just making it seem like there was some big life and death situation so she'd call you. She said she knew it was a fake, and that you shouldn't try fooling her again."

"Can't you talk to her? Can't you call her

and get her to come home?"

"I've tried calling her, but she won't answer. Her phone goes right to voice mail now. I don't think she's checking her text messages at all. She won't believe anything we say."

"Well, how about —"

"Wait, Dad."

"What, what is it?"

"My cell phone's beeping. I got a new message. Hold on."

Rose's heart was suddenly pumping hard. "Son! *Son!*"

"Yeah, Dad," Glenn said breathlessly.

"Is it from Jamie?"

"Yeah, yeah."

"What does it say?"

"It says she's going to Hawaii with that family. It says that she's at the airport right now and that the plane is taking off in an hour. Dad? *Dad?*"

Rose was already racing down the hallway toward the elevators. He had sixty minutes to get to her.

"He's what?"

"Rose is on the move. He just ran out of the hotel and jumped in a cab."

"Follow him!" Klein shouted. "Don't let him out of your sight." He slammed the phone down. Then picked the receiver right back up again and dialed.

"How much is it to the airport?" Rose asked, leaning over the front seat, then glancing back over his shoulder several times. He was sure someone was following them.

The cabbie shrugged. "Hard to say."

"What is it usually, come on. *About* what is it?"

"Seventy bucks."

Probably way over, but it didn't matter at this point. He had fifty-five minutes. "How long will it take?"

The cabbie pushed out his lower lip. "Forty minutes, maybe a little less if traffic's not too bad."

"I'll give you two hundred dollars if you get me there in twenty-five minutes."

The cabbie glanced over at Rose. "Show me the cash."

Rose pulled his wallet out and threw the bills down on the front seat. "Now, go," he ordered. "And do you see the guy behind us in the blue Taurus?" He moved to one side so the cabbie could look out his rearview mirror. "See him?"

"Yeah."

"Lose him. Lose him now." Rose pulled

his cell phone out of his pocket as it began to ring and answered the call without bothering to look at the number, assuming it was Glenn or Adam Pierce. Pierce had been calling constantly. "Hello."

"Michael, this is Grant Boyd."

Rose's first instinct was to hang up, but then he stopped. Maybe he could pick up some valuable 411. "Yeah?"

"What are you doing?"

"Reading a book in front of my fireplace. What are you doing?"

"I'm serious," Boyd barked. "We know you aren't in Virginia, we know you're in Philadelphia."

Confirmation that Boyd was working with the other side. He'd assumed that was the case all along, but he'd just heard proof. He was about to say something when the cabbie took a hard left, throwing him against the door.

"Rose!"

"I'm going to the train station, Grant. My daughter just sent a message to my son that she's headed to New York. I'm trying to get to her before she gets on the train." The silence at the other end of the phone was deafening. He figured Boyd had no idea what to say. Figured he knew Jamie was at the airport, but didn't want to say the wrong thing.

"Why don't you work with us, Michael? We're trying to protect the country."

"You're torturing innocent people." Rose took a quick look behind them as the cabbie raced down the block. The Taurus was way behind them. "It's gotten out of hand. It can't go on."

"You're daughter's about to become a victim of the war."

"What does that mean, Grant?" Rose shouted. "Tell me where she is."

"Tell us who you're working with."

The cab squealed left, then right, then raced down an on-ramp. Rose saw an airport sign. "Come on," he urged.

"Tell us who you're working with, Michael. We can still save your daughter. There's still time."

"You tell me where she is, Grant, then I'll tell you who I'm working with." He hung up abruptly and called Cortez. "Come on, David, pick up. *Pick up.*"

"Hello."

"David, it's me."

"Mike, where are you?"

"Don't worry about it, just do me a favor. Get me the number for that travel agency we use."

"What?"

"Just do it!"

"Okay, okay." Cortez reached into his desk and flipped through the pages of the Trafalgar corporate directory, then recited the number when he found it. "What else can I do?"

"Just be my friend, David. Like you always have been."

Cortez looked up as he put the phone down. Tammy Sable was standing in his office doorway.

"Was that Mike?" she asked.

Cortez gazed at her, uncertain of what to say. "No, it wasn't."

Her expression soured and she moved off quickly.

Thank God he hadn't said anything to her.

There were two flights leaving out of Philadelphia in the next forty-five minutes for Hawaii. One going to Los Angeles that connected with another flight coming in from New York. The second flight had a ninety-minute layover in San Francisco, then continued on to Hawaii. They were both United flights and they both left from Philadelphia at almost exactly the same time. He'd tried calling United twice to see if they'd tell him which flight she was on, but they wouldn't release the information.

"Which airline?" the cabbie shouted as they raced toward the terminal.

"United."

It had taken thirty-five minutes to get to the airport, but Rose couldn't blame the driver. He'd taken a few extra turns to make sure they lost the Taurus, and they'd run into some terrible traffic. Rose only had twenty minutes now, but he was still going to give the guy the money.

He tried one more time to get Jamie on her cell phone, but still no answer. Boyd's words kept ringing in his head. She was about to become a victim of the war. And the guy at the warehouse the other night had said she was going to be on a plane that was hijacked. But if they knew the planes were going to be hijacked, why wouldn't they do something?

Suddenly he realized what was happening, realized what they were going to do — or not do. But why? Because the American people had become complacent? Because the public thought it couldn't happen again? To shock people into giving an administration a mandate to be more aggressive with outlaw nations again.

The driver screeched to a halt in front of

the United Airlines ticket counter and Rose jumped out, leaving the money on the front seat. He bolted past several skycaps to a set of departure screens and scanned the information quickly. Concourse C, gate 3 for the LA flight, gate 14 for the San Francisco flight. Now he needed a ticket so he could get through security.

He glanced at the counter, but the line was doubled back all the way out of the ropes. First class. Only two people there. He raced to it, getting to it just ahead of another guy, banging his leg with his fist as he watched the man behind the counter taking his time. It was maddening.

"Come on!" Rose yelled.

The ticket agent gave him a nasty look and seemed to go even slower.

He should have known better than that. His cell phone rang and he yanked it from his pocket. Kat. "Hello."

"Michael?"

"Yeah, listen, I can't talk now. It's a bad time."

"I'm sorry. Call me back when you can."

Just then an announcement blared over the PA system announcing that the security level had recently been raised at the Philadelphia airport. He paused, furious with himself. He should never have answered the phone. Now she knew exactly where he was. "I will, Kat."

"Michael, I miss you."

"Me, too."

He rushed to the counter as the woman in front of him finished up. "One way to San Francisco," he said, pulling out his driver's license and credit card. He glanced at his watch. Seventeen minutes.

The agent took his license and began inputting. After a few moments, he looked up. "Sir, your name is on the no-fly list. It's going to be a few minutes."

"What?" It was the first time this had ever happened to him. Some of his friends were on it, so he knew exactly what it was. "You've gotta be kidding."

"I've got to call it in. I'll be right back."

As he watched the agent disappear through a doorway he realized it was no coincidence that he was on the list. He was beginning to believe there was no such thing as a coincidence.

"This is amazing isn't it?"

Jamie was sitting in an aisle seat, her friend was in the middle, and her friend's mother had the window. She'd been watching the man across the aisle. He seemed fidgety, almost upset, and he was looking around a lot. Especially at another man who was three rows up on the aisle. It was probably just her imagination. "What did you say, Diana?"

"This whole thing is like, incredibly amazing. I mean, who ever heard of a credit card company paying for a trip to Hawaii?"

Jamie shrugged. "You said your mom uses it a lot."

Diana rolled her eyes. "For everything. I don't think she even has a limit anymore."

Jamie leaned in front of Diana. "Mrs. Redmond."

"Yes, honey?"

"Thanks so much for letting me come. You've been so nice. It's been nice to be able to get away from everything after what happened."

"I understand."

"Thanks for not calling my dad, too. Thanks for letting me make my own decision to come."

A worried expression crossed the woman's face. "I really think I should have called him, but you talked to him, right?"

Jamie nodded. "Yes."

"And the last thing I want to do is get in the middle of a family problem. I just hope you work things out with him."

"I will," she promised, "as soon as I get

home." She glanced at the man across the aisle. He was perspiring.

Rose dashed out of security. It had taken forever to get through the long line, and now he was out of time. Maybe the plane had been delayed. That was the last desperate hope. He sprinted ahead crazily, following signs for Concourse C, then gate 14. Christ, it was almost all the way out at the end. As he finally raced up to the gate, he saw that the plane was just beginning to push back from the Jetway.

"Hey! *Hey!*"

The agent had been about to walk away from the desk in front of the gate. She looked up. "Yes, sir?"

"I'm on that plane. That's my flight. You've got to get it back here."

"Sorry, sir, but I can't do that."

"You have to."

She gave him an obscenely compassionate smile. "There's another flight to San Francisco leaving at eleven. If you give me your boarding pass, I'll see if I can get you on the flight."

Rose stared at the plane as the tow truck slowly pushed it out onto the tarmac. He didn't even know if Jamie was on there, but he didn't have any choice now. He couldn't let it take off. The whole story about a plane being hijacked and Jamie becoming a victim of the war could be bullshit, but at this point he couldn't take the chance. "That's all right," he said politely. "But thanks."

"Certainly."

He moved to a restroom nearby, and, when he came back out, returned to the gate, hoping the agent had left. She had and he moved quickly to the desk in front of the Jetway, where passengers handed the agent their boarding passes. On it was a stack of boarding passes. He rifled through it, and almost shouted when he found Jamie's. He hurried to a pay phone, called information, got the main United Airlines number, and dialed. He moved quickly through the automated greeting system until he finally got a reservation agent.

"Good morning, this is United Airlines. My name's Janet. How can I help you?"

Rose took a deep breath. No choice. "You've got a bomb on board your San Francisco flight out of Philadelphia."

"Excuse me?"

"There's a *bomb* on flight 1271 out of Philadelphia. It's pressure sensitive and it'll go off at ten thousand feet. The plane is going to the runway right now. You've got to stop it."

"I need you to stay on the line for a moment, sir."

"Just make sure that flight doesn't get off the ground." He hung up, praying that what he'd just said was a lie.

"What a pain."

Jamie nodded. "Sucks." The plane had been number three for takeoff when the captain had come on the PA system and announced there was a mechanical problem and that they had to pull off into a waiting area. That a bus would pick them up and take them back to the gate and that an agent there would give people further instructions. That the airline was already sending another plane to the gate.

As Jamie followed Diana and her mother off the bus that had pulled up beside the Jetway, a young man in a parka tapped her on the shoulder. "Miss."

She shivered, pulling her sweater up around her neck. It was freezing out here. "Yes."

"Are you Jamie Rose?"

She glanced at Diana and her mother who were heading up the stairs. "Yes."

"Could you come with me, please?"

Rose sat in the waiting area across from gate

530

14, watching the steady stream of passengers come out of the Jetway. He couldn't wait to see her. He'd give her a hug. Everything would be all right in a few moments.

After a few minutes the steady stream turned to a trickle, then an agent closed the door to the Jetway. Rose watched as a girl and what looked like her mother approached the agent and pointed to the door. Instantly he knew what had happened.

Fifty miles south of Pittsburgh two F-16 fighters settled in behind the United Airlines 757 headed to Los Angeles. The pilots had been told only that there was a possibility the planes were going to be hijacked. That they were in the air only as a precaution. They were two miles behind the airliner, but they could bring it down in no more than thirty seconds if necessary.

56

Rose sat at the counter of a busy coffee shop at Philadelphia's 30th Street train station. He had another twenty minutes until he could catch the next train back to Washington. He didn't know what else to do. He had no idea how to even start looking for Jamie. The police wouldn't be able to help, they wouldn't believe him. He'd never been so emotionally beaten up in his life. He'd let everyone down. Most important, Jamie.

"Mr. Rose."

Rose's gaze snapped left, toward the voice. Sitting next to him was an overweight, middle-aged man. He hadn't been aware of the man sitting down. The stool had been empty a minute ago. "How do you know my name?"

The man shook his head. "Don't worry about it," he said in a soft voice. "Just listen to me carefully." He took a sip of water. "As we speak, your daughter is being transported by van to a secret base in Idaho, to one of those places whoever you're working with probably told you he thinks exists. Well, he's right. They do exist, and there are three of them in this country. The one in Idaho where your daughter is headed, one in Tennessee, and one on Long Island. Five more offshore. People are being tortured in the name of counterterrorism at these bases, Mr. Rose, but it's gone too far. It's going beyond that. It's becoming a tool for personal revenge, for advancing agendas. Not just for protecting the country. I can't do anything about shutting these bases down anymore, but I can at least help you get your daughter back. I have one more favor I can call in. I really am your only chance, Mr. Rose, and I should know. If you don't believe me, keep watching that television screen after I'm gone. In about ten minutes, every station on the planet will be covering the same story. Our military planes will have shot down two commercial airliners that were taken over by terrorists. One was heading for Chicago, the other for Los Angeles." He patted Rose on the back. "There were going to be three planes, but you stopped one of them. At least, I'm assuming you were the one who called in the bomb threat."

Rose nodded, his mouth falling slowly open. "Who are you?"

"My name is Peter Beck," he said. "Until a few days ago I ran what you've been looking for. The Gray Ops program whoever put you up to buying CIS told you existed." He shook his head. "I don't run it anymore. Thank God. I couldn't take killing innocent people any longer, so they turned on me. Now I want to see the whole thing come down. I want to see you get CIS because if you do, you'll find everything you're looking for. And more." He pointed at the screen. "Our people knew the planes were being targeted, but they didn't act. In fact, they made sure the terrorists were able to take the planes over. They cleared the way."

Rose stared at the man in disbelief. "But why?"

"They want to jolt the public, they want their mandate back. They're furious that people have gotten complacent, that people don't think we should occupy nations in the Middle East anymore. And, there's an election coming up. They want votes, they see this as a perfect opportunity to get them. To get people back on their reservation."

Rose gazed at the man. Who knew why, but he had no doubt that this guy was legitimate. "So they're willing to let people die?"

Beck shrugged. "Sure. Why not? What's a few hundred people? Hell, I used to be that way, too. But not anymore," he said, his voice almost inaudible.

It was all as LeClair had laid out for him, exactly as he had assumed. Everything was true. "Who turned on you, Beck? Who are you talking about?"

Beck took another sip of water. "No, Mr. Rose, I'm not going that far. I'm not giving away all the secrets. If someone's going to blow this thing to bits, it's going to have to be you." His expression turned grave. "Now let's talk about your daughter, how you might be able to rescue her. It's going to be very dangerous, Mr. Rose, even with my help. But I'm warning you, if you don't get her this time, you'll never see her again. Never."

"Bobcat 1, Bobcat 1, this is Thunderbolt. You are ordered to acquire the target and bring it down. Immediately."

The pilot heard what he'd hoped he wouldn't. He'd never imagined that all the hours of training would be for this purpose. To bring down a domestic airliner, to kill

U.S. citizens. "Say again, Thunderbolt, say again?"

"Acquire the target, Bobcat 1. Bring it down. *Immediately.*"

The pilot took a deep breath and boosted the engines. "I copy, Thunderbolt. Here we go."

A few moments later the flight to Los Angeles exploded when the air-to-air missiles raced up the back of the starboard engine. Bodies and pieces of the plane rained down on central Indiana.

Rose watched the television screen in horror.

The first few reports were coming in now. An airliner downed in Indiana, another in western Maryland. Audiotapes of the final moments. Proof that the planes had been taken over by terrorists, proof that the military had been forced to take the ultimate step. That there had been no alternative.

"This is unbelievable," the guy sitting on the stool beside Rose said, voice hushed. "Don't you think?"

But Rose was already gone, sprinting for the rental car desks. Everything was going to be shut down for the next few days — planes and trains — and he had to get a car fast before they were gone. Somehow he had to get back to Virginia, then get to Wyoming, and it certainly wasn't going to be on a commercial airliner. There was only one person who could help him now.

57

"You've got to help me. I've got to save my daughter. I lose her, and I really don't care what you do to me. You can give the cops the gun, and frame me all you want to. At that point it doesn't matter."

Sherman LeClair scratched his head. He glanced at Pierce, then back at Rose.

"God damn it, you help me," Rose said angrily.

"I can't have my people involved," LeClair answered. "I can't have them involved in any kind of attack, can't have them involved in anything that could lead directly back to me."

"You son of a —"

"But I will do everything short of that," LeClair interrupted. "I'll get you there, I'll call the local authorities, and I'll give you cover on the way back and while you're here. Until everything is worked out."

Rose allowed himself to breathe. "All

right, but we've got to get moving."

"You will finish the acquisition of CIS once you're safe. You will get CIS for me. You understand?"

Rose nodded.

"The man you spoke to in Philadelphia, he said that we'll be able to find everything if we get CIS, right?"

"That's what he said, Sherman. He said you were exactly right. He said you were right on target."

LeClair nodded. "Good."

Rose stood up and took several steps, then turned back around. "I've got one more question."

"What now?"

"Did my au pair work for you?" As Rose asked, he saw LeClair and Pierce look down.

"No," the older man said firmly. "I don't know how you could have gotten that idea."

But Rose had his answer. LeClair was a liar. He just hoped LeClair wasn't lying about what he'd just promised to do.

Peter Beck relaxed in the chair of the hotel room and took the last sip of his third scotch in the last twenty minutes. Then he put the glass down. It was over. He'd done all he could. He glanced down at his hand, then pressed his little finger down against

his palm, for ten seconds. And the cyanide
was released.

58

The van crested a hill in southern Wyoming in the middle of nowhere, on a lonely stretch of road that saw only a few hundred vehicles a day, and almost none at night. They were thirty miles from the nearest town, which was more of an outpost than anything. Not even a stoplight at the one main intersection.

It was two thirty in the morning when the headlights appeared.

"That's them," the sheriff said quietly to Rose, motioning toward the two specks. "That's the van, according to our boys back in town. This better not be a God damn wild goose chase."

Sherman LeClair had made good on his promise. He'd gotten Rose to Wyoming on a private jet, obtaining a special clearance for it to fly despite the fact that the nation's airways had been shut down again; he'd contacted the local authorities out here and convinced them to take action, to listen to Rose; and some of his men were standing by to get Rose and Jamie back to Virginia once this showdown was over. To protect them in case someone decided to exact revenge — which was a damn good bet.

"It's not a wild goose chase," Rose assured the sheriff, glancing around. God, it was barren out here. A dusty, desolate landscape with a few scraggly bushes and trees beneath the starry sky. "Believe me."

"I don't know who you know," the sheriff muttered, "but it must be somebody important."

There were fifteen state cruisers and at least thirty men waiting in the darkness of the moonless night, all heavily armed. They'd been told only that men had kidnapped Jamie because Rose was wealthy, and that they were looking for a lot of money. That was all.

"Here we go, guys," the sheriff said quietly into his intercom. "This is it. Be careful. Like we talked about, these people are armed and considered very dangerous." He turned to Rose. "You stay here. Let my men handle it, don't get involved."

"Right."

"Promise me that."

"I promise."

As the van closed in on their position, four of the cruisers flipped on emergency lights and sirens and darted into the middle of the road, blocking its path. As the van skidded to a screeching halt, four more cruisers rolled onto the road behind it, hemming it completely in.

As Rose watched in the glow of the emergency lights, people began spilling out of the van onto the roadway like ants from a nest. He counted four men, then what looked like a young woman being dragged by one of the men. Suddenly there were several bursts of gunfire, and he lost track of the man pulling the young woman as they disappeared into the brush on the side of the road. He bolted out from behind the sheriff's cruiser and headed toward the spot where they'd disappeared. It had to be Jamie.

"Rose!"

But he ignored the sheriff and sprinted past the van, leaping over one of the men who'd been hit as he ran from the van. Then Rose was into the brush, racing into the darkness after the sound of Jamie screaming — he recognized her voice. Another burst of gunfire and Rose tripped over something lying on the ground. He went flying face-first into the dust. He made it back up to his hands and knees quickly, and looked back. He'd tripped over a body.

"Oh, Jesus," he murmured, crawling over to it, praying to God it wasn't Jamie. It wasn't. It was a trooper. Rose closed his eyes, said a quick prayer, then grabbed the pistol lying at the end of the man's outstretched fingers, jumped to his feet and kept going.

He heard someone moan to his left, very close, and dropped to one knee. He could barely make out a large rock outcropping through the gloom. He crawled forward, pistol in his right hand.

Suddenly they were directly in front of him and he stood up slowly. The man was holding Jamie from behind, his left forearm choking her neck as he held his gun out at Rose.

"Daddy," she whimpered, "help me."

"Don't come any closer," the man warned. "I'll kill you, then I'll kill her."

"Just give me my daughter," Rose pleaded. "Give her to me. I'll tell them I shot you. I'll tell them you're dead out here. You can escape."

"Daddy," Jamie sobbed.

"Shut up!" the man shouted, pressing the gun to her head.

Rose rushed forward, slamming the man's

head with the butt end of the pistol, and the three of them tumbled to the ground in a heap.

The man and Rose each got off two shots. Then everything fell silent.

59

Rose sat in the living room of his house in Great Falls, watching a college basketball game. Glenn was downstairs on the computer, and Jamie was at Georgetown Medical Center in a coma, a bullet lodged near her spine. Rose had killed the man who was holding her hostage out in the brush, but not before the guy had nailed Jamie. Rose and Glenn had visited Jamie for several hours this morning, though, of course, she had no idea they had been there. It had been a week since the showdown in Wyoming, but the doctors still had no idea when she would wake up, *if* she would wake up. No idea if she'd walk if she woke up. They'd flown her back from Casper two days ago on a specially outfitted medical plane.

The Wyoming authorities were still trying to figure out who had kidnapped Jamie. All four of the men in the van had been killed in the shoot-out, but the sheriff wanted answers — and revenge, Rose assumed. Six of his men had been killed in the gun battle, too. The sheriff had become suspicious because of the weapons the killers were carrying. It was high-tech military hardware, he'd said, and the men appeared to be a trained unit, not some band of hoodlums looking for a quick payday. A lot of things didn't fit, he kept saying. For starters, why would the kidnappers be all the way out in Wyoming, he'd asked, if she'd been taken somewhere out east as he'd been told? And how had Rose been able to fly to Wyoming if the skies were shut down? Good questions, Rose and LeClair had agreed, but, of course, he wasn't going to get to the bottom of anything.

LeClair was giving Rose — and Jamie — round-the-clock protection because there were still three weeks until the CIS acquisition became final. LeClair was worried that if "the other side" as he kept calling it, could get to Rose, could kill him, the acquisition wouldn't go through. That whoever inherited Trafalgar's leadership after Rose would shut down everything after losing two CEOs to murder in only a few weeks. He was probably right, Rose realized. He'd given Rose strict orders not to leave the house unless he absolutely had to, and, in that case, only with bodyguards. Once Trafalgar had acquired CIS, the threat to Rose's life would be gone, they both reasoned, because then anyone could send in the accounting storm troopers. Until then it was still very dangerous.

Rose shut his eyes and eased back into the sofa. Cortez had fired Tammy Sable yesterday on Rose's orders. They'd had another conversation with Cortez's private eye friend and found out something else. Sheila and Tammy had been lovers for a short time. And Cortez had confided in Rose that he was suspicious of Tammy, that she'd been going through files she shouldn't have been.

Rose groaned. There were enemies everywhere. He really didn't trust Sherman Le-Clair, still believed down deep that LeClair was responsible for Sheila's death, but he couldn't prove it. And, at this point, he honestly felt a sense of higher responsibility to the country. After his conversation with Peter Beck he was certain his government had known in advance about the terrorist plot to take over the three planes. He was also now certain that there were domestic bases at which the government was carrying out a torture campaign. That was where Jamie had been headed. Incredible.

Rose's cell phone rang. He recognized the number immediately. "Hello."

"Michael, I need your help."

He sat straight up on the couch, her voice racing through him like a shock wave. She sounded desperate. "What's wrong, Kat?" They hadn't seen each other since before he'd gone to Philadelphia. He missed her, he had to admit.

"It's Joey," she sobbed into the phone. "He's gone nuts. He figured out that I was seeing you. I guess he followed us that night we met out in Reston. He's drunk. He said he was going to kill me. Please help me, Michael."

Rose stood up and grabbed his keys off the kitchen counter. "Where are you?"

Kat couldn't be working with them, he kept telling himself as he drove to meet her. She couldn't be that great an actress, couldn't make him feel so special but be lying. Could she?

She asked to meet him at the Dulles Town Center, a sprawling two-story mall a few miles from the Dulles airport. He spotted her right away standing in front of a Radio Shack on the second level, and ambled toward her as she stood against the wall beside the front of the store. God, she looked so good. Beautiful blond hair, incredible blue eyes. He'd still never seen anything like her.

"Hi," he said as he reached her.

She looked at him like he was crazy. They'd done a hell of a job, he thought.

"Do I know you?" she asked.

Rose hesitated a moment, stroking the beard they'd put on him before leaving the house. "Kat, Joey's been in custody for two days. He told us about your problems back in Michigan, how you're wanted as an accessory to murder, how you might actually be charged as the one who pulled the trigger, how you'd probably do anything to avoid jail." He saw that she recognized him now despite the beard and mustache, the hat pulled low over his eyes, the lifts in his shoes.

She swallowed hard and her eyes misted over. "Michael, I'm sorry. I didn't mean to hurt you." She glanced down. "I care about you so much. I didn't think I would, but I couldn't help it."

He gazed at her for a few seconds. Even now, even though he knew for certain she'd been working against him the whole time, he still couldn't turn his back on her. He still had to come today — despite LeClair's objections — still had to see her one more time. "If you care, you'll answer one question for me."

She nodded.

"Point like you're giving me directions," he said.

She did, giving him a nice smile, too.

"Are they trying to kill me?"

Her arm fell back to her side. "Yes. They're trying to do any thing they can to keep your company from getting CIS."

"Okay —"

Rose glanced up.

She was pointing, this time in the other direction. "They figured it out!"

Two men had burst from an entrance three stores down. As they sprinted they pulled guns from beneath their coats and aimed. Then she was on him, dragging him into the store, keeping him from running.

EPILOGUE

"Katherine Hanson saved your life, you know?"

"I know," Rose said quietly.

It had been almost two years since he'd seen Adam Pierce. Since the day after Trafalgar had officially acquired CIS and the accounting storm troopers had descended on all of CIS's subsidiaries. Then Pierce and LeClair had faded into the background.

"If she hadn't pulled you down into that store," Pierce continued, "our guys wouldn't have had a clear shot at the guys coming at you."

"I know."

"You think she was trying to help you? Or was it . . ."

"I hope she was trying to help me. I'll always think of it that way."

"Of course." Pierce hung his head for a moment. "Too bad she bought it during the whole thing."

"Yeah," Rose agreed quietly. "Too bad."

"It was a damn good thing you had that vest on."

Rose nodded. In the melee he'd taken two shots to the chest, but the thick Kevlar had saved him. He'd had the wind knocked out of him, and there were two terrible bruises on his stomach when they got him back to the van. Other than some pain, though, he was fine. But Kat had been killed. One shot to the head. No chance to save her.

"Sorry about, Sherman," Rose said quietly, watching the palm trees sway.

He'd brought Jamie and Glenn to a very private retreat in Antigua for a week. He and Pierce were sitting out on a veranda perched atop a cliff overlooking a beautiful, undeveloped bay. It had probably looked this way for thousands of years. The color of the water was incredible, just like Kat's eyes. He felt that familiar lump building in his throat. He still thought about her all the time.

"He lived a good life," Pierce said. "He got his wish, got his revenge. He brought down the Order."

It had taken two years, but the investigation had finally run its course. Everything had been uncovered. The domestic and international bases, the atrocities that had been committed, Spyder, everything. Tom Klein and Wes Barry were in jail, but the former president was still hiding behind executive immunity. However, it didn't seem like that defense was going to last for long. The cries for justice were growing too loud from every corner of the world.

"Sherman wanted me to tell you personally how much he admired you," Pierce continued. "I was with him when he died." He hesitated. "He wanted me to apologize to you for threatening you with that thing that happened to Colin Freese. He wanted me to tell you that he would never really have framed you."

Rose raised one eyebrow. "I didn't know it at the time."

Pierce pursed his lips. "It was crazy. There was so much going on. He helped you out with the Fairfax detectives. He made sure they never came after you, made sure they understood that you had absolutely no involvement in your wife's death."

"Yeah." Rose knew he'd never get the real story behind all that, especially now that LeClair was dead. His expression brightened, and he stood up. David Cortez was coming out onto the veranda with Jamie. "Hello, honey, how are you?"

"Fine, Daddy." She hesitated. "Will you

do me a favor?"

"Sure," he agreed, smiling down at her. "Anything."

"Will you start calling me Munchkin again?"

ABOUT THE AUTHOR

Stephen Frey is a managing director at a private equity firm. He previously worked in mergers and acquisitions at JPMorgan and as a vice president of corporate finance at an international bank in Manhattan. Frey is the bestselling author of *The Successor, The Power Broker, The Protégé, The Chairman, Shadow Account, Silent Partner, The Day Trader, Trust Fund, The Insider, The Legacy, The Inner Sanctum, The Vulture Fund,* and *The Takeover.* He lives in Florida.